MISS
TAKE

MISS
TAKE

RÉJEAN DUCHARME

TRANSLATED BY WILL BROWNING

TALONBOOKS

Copyright © 1967 Réjean Ducharme
Translation copyright © 2011 Will Browning

Talonbooks
P.O. Box 2076, Vancouver, British Columbia, Canada v6b 3s3
www.talonbooks.com

Edited by Martha Sharpe.

Typeset in Scala and printed and bound in Canada.
Printed on 100% post-consumer recycled paper.

First Printing: 2011

The publisher gratefully acknowledges the financial support of the
Canada Council for the Arts; the Government of Canada through the
Book Publishing Industry Development Program; and the Province of
British Columbia through the British Columbia Arts Council for our
publishing activities.

Le nez qui voque by Réjean Ducharme was first published in French in
1967 by Éditions Gallimard. We acknowledge the financial support of
the Government of Canada through the National Translation Program
for Book Publishing, for our publishing activities.

LIBRARY AND ARCHIVES CANADA CATALOGUING IN PUBLICATION
Ducharme, Réjean, 1941–
[Nez qui voque. English]
     Miss Take / Réjean Ducharme ; translated by Will Browning.

Translation of: Le nez qui voque.
ISBN 978-0-88922-669-2

     I. Browning, Will II. Title. III. Title: Nez qui voque. English.
PS8507.U4N3I3 2011   c843'.54   C2011-902482-9

TRANSLATOR'S NOTE

Miles Miles, not Miles Kilometres, is an unreliable narrator *par excellence*. Everything he writes in his journal in this novel by Réjean Ducharme is viewed through the playful prism, or prison, of his sixteen-year-old perspective. This includes historical dates, so-called "facts," and even the characters' own actions.

Réjean Ducharme was writing on the cusp of the Quiet Revolution in Québécois culture that would ultimately lead to a significant degree of autonomy for French-speaking Quebec within English-speaking Canada. The reader of *Miss Take*, make no mistake, will join Miles Miles on a roller-coaster ride through the then still-traditional French-Catholic Montreal of the 1960s.

Bon voyage.

Will Browning

GLEANED AT RANDOM FROM THEIR WORKS
FOR THE EDIFICATION (ERECTION)
OF THE RACES (OF ERASMUS)

"Oh, how the snow is rife,
My heart consumed by rhyme.
What's the spasm of life
Compared to my hard time?" (Émile Nelligan, from memory)

"Ah!" (Colette)

"I ... myself." (Barrès)

"Oh!" (Kierkegaard)

"Ah!" (Plato)

"On the ..." (Mauriac)

"*Ich* ..." (Hitler)

"They ... not ... the ... your ... your ... their ..." (Musset)

"Ah!" (George Sand)

"He makes ..." (Gide)

"The Gentlemen so assembled ..." (Iberville)

"A scatterbrain full of English presumptuousness ..." (Iberville)

"We encountered an American whaler who was whaling."
    (Léandre Ducharme)

"The author begs indulgence for the quality of this production."
    (Léandre Ducharme)

"Beauty is not necessarily hard to achieve. Beauty is not
    necessary. Beauty is not. Beauty's snot!" (Imaginary author)

PREFACE

Which of these two contractions is better: *aren't* or *ain't*? If it's *ain't* then it's not *aren't* and if it's *aren't* then it's not *ain't*.

A can of pee looked at a canopy and said to it, "I am not a can of pee. I am a canopy."

A canopy, which did not want to be taken for a can of pee by the other canopies, looked at the other canopies and said to them, "I am a canopy. I am not a can of pee."

I am not a man of letters. I am a man.

The evening of the surrender of Breda, Roger de la Tour de Babel, a lawyer at the Châtelet, took up his cane and went on his way. In 1954, in Tracy, Maurice Duplessis, a lawyer at the Châtelet, died, celebrated and celibate, of a cerebral hemorrhage. I'm sixteen years old, and I'm a child of eight. It's difficult to understand. It's not easy to understand. No one understands except me. Not being understood doesn't bother me. I don't care. I don't give a hoot. I'm staying where I am. I don't want to go any farther, so I'm staying put. I don't want to keep going because I don't want to end up at the end. I'm staying as I am. I'm letting it all go—becoming vile, infected, parched. I'm letting them all grow old, far ahead of me. I'm staying behind, with me, with me-the-child, far behind, alone, intact, incorruptible, as fresh and bitter as a green apple, as hard and sturdy as a rock. What I'm saying here is goddamned important. It means everything to me. There's got to be someone with me-the-child, someone who looks after him, who protects him from the tragedy of the world, which is ridiculous and which makes things ridiculous. I can't leave me-the-child alone in the past, the only one present in all the absence, at the mercy of oblivion. I watch over him, back there. I keep watch, my belly covered in ashes, with cadavers that calm me, with everything that is a cadaver, alone with the me-child, alone with an image whose tinfoil is wearing thin under my fingers. I don't want to change. In secret, I'm still running with my dogs, wearing my shorts, fishing for tadpoles with Ivugivic. I'm not crazy. I know what I'm doing and I know where I am. It's seven o'clock in the evening. It's September 9, 1965. But men need men, even those who are dead. I need men. I'm composing this chronicle for men the way they write letters to their fiancées. I'm writing to them because I can't talk to them, because I'm afraid to go up and talk to them. Near them, I suffocate; I sense the dizziness of the abyss. The reason I'm afraid to address them directly is not because I'm shy, but because I don't want to get bogged down in their quicksand, in their swampy depths. I write badly, and I'm rather vulgar. I'm thrilled about that. My unfortunate and offensive sentences will go forth from this table, where imaginary people are gathered to hear, lovers of flowers of rhetoric.

2

They're in the middle of redoing the dome of the Bonsecours Market. They're in the middle of restoring the skylights of the Papineau House. They have historic tasks. They have historic tusks. Tsk tsk. That's a mistake. Am is take. A Miss Take. My Miss Take. My dear name is Miles Miles. I think that's better than Miles Kilometres. I've never complained about my name. Besides, I've always had a hard time with my capital *k*'s. Yesterday, I left my village on the St. Lawrence River. Yesterday, I left my parents and the island they live on in the middle of the St. Lawrence River. I'm quite discouraged. There isn't even any toilet paper to wipe yourself with when you go to the bathroom. There isn't even any hot water to take a bath in. I walked as far as Berthier; I crossed the three white bridges with black legs on foot. At Berthier, I took the bus. I got off at the East Terminal in the middle of the night. I wandered around among the sleeping until daybreak. The streets were black and glistening because of the rain that fell on and off in the cold. Whatever was open, I entered. I bought five postcards to furnish the room I was going to rent—five identical ones, five of Marilyn Monroe in a bikini, laughing like a lunatic. Around six o'clock, I went back to the East Terminal, and I waited until around nine o'clock. Then I went room-hunting. I rented this one. I'm at 417 Rue Bonsecours. I live under the roof of a house that is almost as tricentennial as the Notre-Dame-de-Bon-Secours Chapel, which is on the other side of the street and fills up my whole window like a poster of itself. My room's house is funny; it's as though the houses that were built next to it had attached themselves to it by anastomosis, and then were pried loose: you can see stairway marks on the walls. My room's house remains standing, made of stone like in the olden days, with its two broad chimneys protruding from each side of the black roof like two ears. It remains standing alone between a parking lot and a parking lot. The Notre-Dame-de-Bon-Secours Chapel houses a Marguerite Bourgeoys museum; next to the door hangs an inscription in neon and in English: SAILORS' CHURCH 1654. They're doing publicity, kiss-assism, to make the English-speaking tourists' mouths water. Go home! The Virgin Mary, who stands on the roof of the chapel and holds out her arms to the sailors and the longshoremen, turns her back on me. On the other side, behind the grain elevators, behind the houses stuck together like Siamese twins, all time-worn, there's the water, there's the river that has accompanied me since the beginning of the misunderstanding; the one that they fight over for the privilege of dirtying, the way you fight over getting to see a movie star; the surest of my childhood friends, the St. Lawrence. Sometimes you can hear a ship cry out. I removed one hundred dollars from the family fortune. Just before leaving, I took it from the money box where Maman hoards the fifty-cent pieces. A little while ago I bought a second-hand bike. I got it for ten dollars. I'd rather say *dollar* than *buck*, because of Dollard Saint-Laurent ... I mean Dollard des Ormeaux. Many a slip 'twixt pen and lip. In New Quebec, where Ivugivic is from, there's a cape called Dollard-des-Ormeaux. The word *Canada* could be born of the Spanish words *acá* and *nada*, which mean nothing there. I don't know where to put the bike. I tried to park it in one of the parking lots. The man came over and said no with a tyrannical voice and a tyrannical face. Everything on earth is for automobiles now. The streets, the police, the iron, the rubber, the petroleum—everything falls within their sphere of influence. Everything. Instead of saying *automobilist*, we should say *automobile*, and instead of saying *automobile*, we should say *manilist*. Man in the automobile is the superior man that Nietzsche was calling for. Alas, that superior man is more of a supermachine than a superman. How many automobiles can fit inside an average manilist? Six. I'll come back to that. Poor Miles Miles! All bewilderinged, all disorientaled, all disillusionismed! All alone! Labrador by right belongs to Quebec. I don't want to see any English with the Eskimos. It's genocide. It's like the massacre of Genoa by the Huns and other Wons. I claim the islands of Belcher, because there's iron there, and iron is made to make things of iron, like irons and irony. Hold your Norses! Belcher is an English name. What is the Ministry of Toponymy up to in this—French—province? Does the minister pass his time buying (procuring) knickers with the money of the toiling rabble? To arms, citizens! Down with the Ministry of Toponymy! Down with the draft! Down with the Two Hundred of Toronto! I read, in that work on New Quebec, that Port Burwell, where Ivugivic was born, has been translated into French by the Ministry of Toponymy. Ivugivic was no longer born in Port Burwell. I can't wait to see her face when I inform her that she was born in Havre-Turquetil. Brilliantly translated, Ministry of Toponymy, brilliantly translated! Tonight, Miles Miles may go to the movies, to the System, where it's not too expensive. Miles Miles to go before he sleeps. Miles Miles to go to the System, by bike, to see Marlon Brando in *The Young Lions*. On the program, there are two other films in English as well. Sugluc, in the North, at the tip of the French continent of America. Sugluc. Sugluc. It's like some kind of thick oil that you swallow—oil of whale liver. How can this continent be French if, in order to be French, you must speak French, and a continent doesn't speak, doesn't have a mouth? This continent has a mouth, a muzzle, the soft muzzle of an old, drunken wolf—the St. Lawrence. And that muzzle speaks French. Goddamn comedian! The goddamn comedian is now going to roll himself a cigarette and smoke. "Smoke, smoke, smoke ..." It's a song by the Eccentrics—kinda like the Beatles with a pink automobile, pink hair, pink clothes, and no pink eye. It's five o'clock in the evening. It's October 10. It's September 10. It's not October 10 at all. Poor Miles Miles! All mixed up in his dates!

3

Miles Miles is not long for this world. He's burnt out. He's done for. He's just finished reading a sexual book and he feels more done for, more burnt out than ever. He wouldn't like to commit suicide, but that's the obvious solution. The most ferocious bus-waiter doesn't wait for the same bus for more than two years. I'm sixteen years old; I've been waiting for sixteen years. Soon, Miles Miles will be sick and tired of waiting, and he'll hasten his end. He'll die an unavoidable death. Some people make themselves throw up. Others throw up because they can't help it, because it's unavoidable. Miles Miles is all dirty. He stinks. He's exhausted. There's no juice left in his orange, no rain left in his cloud. He'd really like to go crazy, but he can't. He'd like to, but at the last second, he gets scared. As soon as the madness enlaces him, he rebels, he stiffens, he defends himself. He despises himself. Justifiable contempt for oneself is a disease from which no one recovers. Last night, as though ejected, he left by bike to go to the System. At the corner of Saint-Denis and Dorchester, he changed his mind. He changed his route. He gave up on the route to the System and took the one to Mexico. But at the first bridge, he had to turn around. A police officer with a red light on his roof and a siren in his mouth apprehended him.

"What's your name?"

"Miles Miles. Before, my name was Million Miles Miles. But when there are two first names, there's always one too many. I had to drop the first one. Then again, who'd ever think of calling one of his children Urine Trouble?"

"You've got a glib tongue. You'll go far. Where are you off to now?"

"Mexico."

"Alas! It is my duty to require you to turn around. The bridges and the shoulders belong to the automobiles. If you're not an automobile, you can't cross this bridge or any other. He (God ... the Pope ... the prime minister ...) has said that it's prohibited. Besides, that's what's written there in English, there, on that small sign: 'Pedestrians and cyclists prohibited on this structure—violators will be fined.'"

"I'll fined myself."

"Don't push it. Turn around."

Miles Miles, not even having saved face, having lost face, did what he was told to do, and did not do what he was prohibited from doing. Then he came back to the room, went to bed, and didn't sleep. This morning, just for kicks, he went by bike to the Employment Agency, on Rue Notre-Dame. They kept him waiting. Then a woman behind a desk started to ask him questions. She had a form to fill out. You can't just fill out whatever you want.

"What's your name?"

"Miles Miles."

"How old are you?"

"Sixteen."

"Where were you born?"

"In a white boat, on the Saguenay."

"I meant, where were you baptized?"

"The next day."

"Where?" With pokes of her pen, she was driving her *wheres* into his eyes. "The word *where*," she said, "is an adverb of location. Where?"

"In Bagot. Bagot, the word *Bagot*, looks like *Bigot*, the word *Bigot*. Ah, Lieutenant Bigot! Oh, Quartermaster Bigot! Many a slip 'twixt tongue and lip."

"That's quite enough! Sex?"

"I haven't checked."

"Sex?"

"I don't care ... It's not important. I'm goddamned desperate."

"What are you saying? I'm going to lose my temper. I'm going to make you swallow my pencil if I lose my temper."

"Soup's on—that's all I'm saying."

"What's that?"

"It's an expression. It's like *holy mackerel.*"

"What do you know how to do, my dear Miles Miles?"

"Nothing, my dear. I don't mean that I know how to do nothing. I mean that there's nothing that I know how to do. It's not very economical, financial, or pecuniary, not knowing how to do anything. And so on and so forth."

Then Miles Miles heaved a huge sigh, as if he were truly tired, very weary, and he left the Employment Agency forever. He did nothing for the rest of the day. He bought the sexual book. Too bad! The book didn't last until he fell asleep. The book finished, he was still awake. At the store (the plumbing store) where he got his book, he heard something that only he found funny.

"Quick!" cried the man. "Some chewing gum! I ate garlic and they won't have anything to do with me."

Sexual book. I came up with the expression at the Villeray Cinema. Indeed, on the marquee in red capital letters, here's what's displayed: *"Because of Eve.* Eighth week. Sexual film." The French Canadians who run movie theatres are ignoramuses; they are responsible for the bad reputation of French Canadians among the French French, who ought to spend their whole lives in France. And because of the numerous homosexuals on Rue Saint-Laurent, I mean Boulevard Saint-Laurent, all American homosexuals think that all French Canadians are homosexuals. My cousin, who hitchhiked in the United States, told me that all the homosexuals who picked him up assumed he was on their team as soon as he told them he was French Canadian.

"Montreal!" they would cry, my cousin confided to me. And they would unbuckle their seatbelts.

Poor Miles Miles!—who, in addition to being all dirty, is French Canadian. But he's proud of the fleas, the feet, the miles, the ounces, the pounds, the hundredweights, and the whole system! It is, it was, September 11. One more day less. One less day more. All the French Canadians who try to talk like the

French French and who wear dark glasses in all kinds of weather—I hate them. They are not like Sacajawea of the Shoshones. People who don't know about Sacajawea don't know anything. For several weeks, she was the squaw of a certain Charbonneau, who contributed to the success of the Lewis and Clark Expedition. She was proud to be Shoshone, to be a female savage.

"I want to go back to my people," she said to Jefferson.

Jefferson gave her some money, and she went back to her tribe. I'm so exhausted, so discouraged. Last night, instead of spitting on the ground, I spat on myself. My strength failed me; I couldn't spit any farther.

4

The fourth, my brother Chateaugué, ensign of the Lord of Sérigny, whilst guarding the fort of the enemy (Nelson) *in order to stop them from coming out, was slain by a musket ball.* Iberville's the one who wrote that. I have a sister. She's not a blood relative. You might say that she's a sister by air, the air of winters and of summers, the air of snow and of rain—an all-weather sister. She's like me. She's fourteen years old, but she's a child of six. I spend a great deal of my time at the Saint-Sulpice Library. My bike is called a road bike, and, at present, it has a flat tire. My sister, whose name is really Ivugivic (she is of Eskimo origin and learned French with the oblates)—I've been calling her Chateaugué since this morning. Chateaugué! My sister Chateaugué! *The fourth, my sister Chateaugué* ... I sent her a post-card to inform her of the matter.

"From now on, your name is Chateaugué."

In German, so that no one could understand, I added an sos.

"Come here. I need you. Come quick if you don't want me to die."*

It's a beautiful postcard with autumnized trees. I'm sure she'll think it's beautiful. Come quick, my sister Chateaugué! Now that the furnace is running, you'll have hot water for washing yourself. Come quick, we have all the books we could ever want at the Saint-Sulpice Library. Bring your bike; I'm going to get mine repaired. We climb to the top of the mountain; we get there all sweaty. We hold on to the handlebars and we let ourselves tear down the crooked and bumpy paths of the cemetery.

---

* Translated by a great translator. (Editor's note.)

It's even better than throwing ourselves off a cloud. We go down at a million miles an hour, we almost fall, we're scared; the wind we make wipes away the sweat. Chateaugué, my all-weather sister. It's nine o'clock in the evening. It's the 12th. While riding my bike, I stopped at some gas stations to ask for road maps. I got three of them, and I put them up on the partition, in front of my table. I have one of Quebec, one of Ontario, and one of Montreal. They didn't want to give me one of the Maritimes. The name *Maritimes* came about because they live side by side on the Atlantic coast. We are the Fluvials, Chateaugué and I. We are friends who live side by side on the banks of a river. My dear Chateaugué, we are the Fluvials, I love you, and we'll share the tobacco and the paper.

5

Today, in 1696, with Iberville, I laid waste to the entire Avalon Peninsula, at the Saint-Sulpice Library, while thinking of Chateaugué my sister. I got my bike repaired, and tonight I had to bring it up to my room, in the third-floor attic, for fear it would be stolen. I had been leaving it outside and securing the chain with a padlock, but I lost the key to the padlock. Just what does Canada look like, with the tip of Maine penetrating Saint-Éleuthère, penetrating the heart, penetrating the water of the St. Lawrence Valley, like a wedge in a log! It couldn't get any worse. Who sold Louisiana, the whole valley of this Mississippi that Cavelier de La Salle went down by canoe? Row, Cavelier, row! Whenever I read Benjamin Sulte at the Saint-Sulpice Library, my head spins. Row, Cavelier, row! In this country I come from the race of the lords, the lords alone in snowshoes deep in Minnesota, the lords rowing alone between the banks of the Ohio, the lords sailing alone on the Atlantic, the lords in spades alone on a continent. Then came the blacksmiths and the automobilists. Here, *automobilists* means manufacturers of manilists. The governors told Perrot to go to Michilimackinac. He went there, in lordly fashion. He left at the beginning of spring and arrived at the end of spring. That fills up a season. Walk, Perrot, walk! There's a Perrot where my parents live. He works for Marine Industries, as a degenerate, for $1.75 an hour. Poor Benjamin Sulte! They want Miles Miles to work by the hour, like the degenerate Perrot. They're wrong. Miles Miles comes from the race of the lords. He won't do any kiss-assism before automobilism. This Maine, on the map before my eyes! How awful! This Labrador, in green, lying like a rapist on Quebec

12

all in white! How ugly and constipating this green is! As soon as I have the time, I'll set off to reconquer Maine and Labrador. In Labrador, all I'll have to do is take Goose Bay. In Maine, all I'll have to do is set fire to Millinocket and Bangor. Come, Chateaugué my sister! Come help me set fire to Millinocket. Bring your bike; mine has been repaired, mine has been mended. We'll erect a wall of China around the lakes where our river will drink, in order to stop their factories of a feather from flocking together to drink there, with their blasted steelworks. In Goose Bay, we'll kill everybody with blows of a bike. But yesterday, before falling asleep, I had some serious thoughts about ideas, or (take your pick) some serious ideas about thoughts. Here they are. An idea is not as immobile, powerless, and docile as you think; it acts, engenders, and arranges; it shapes and comprises its own dynamism; it runs, and runs all by itself. Furthermore, at the moment of its conception, the idea splits in two; that is, as soon as it is born, it works toward its own materialization and toward the materialization of the opposite idea. It tends simultaneously toward both poles, and, if we do not judge it, do not stop it, it carries us along in both directions. But in the case of most civilized beings, there operates automatically, upon their awareness of the idea, a choice, a violent revolt against one or the other of these two impulses that it gives rise to: they think it's crazy to devote yourself simultaneously to the north and the south, to the right and the left, to slowness and swiftness. In others, of a younger, purer, less sclerotic intellect, the possibility of a double action in opposite directions is perfectly clear, perceptible, logical, and understood. Why, in addition to moving and being moved in its own direction, is the idea moving and being moved in the opposite direction? Because it is the nature of the soul, an avidly creative will, to represent spontaneously for itself in the form of ideas all the possibilities that an object offers to its action, and to want to accomplish all of them by this very fact. The soul cannot not want what it imagines: there is no such thing as unwill. When you don't want to, all you're doing is not doing what you want to do. This explanation doesn't elucidate anything. For example, I simultaneously feel both the need to see

Chateaugué and the need to tell her to go hang herself somewhere else. But those are things that are too subtle for civilized
beings. You'll understand, perhaps, if I say that you feel, under
the influence of two simultaneous impulses born of the very
same idea, both the need to do good and the need to do evil. My
thoughts are so serious and subtle! He's so afraid of not being
understood and appreciated! Enough! It's September 14.

6

Hierarchical. Gide wrote somewhere that it's a horrible, awful word. For Gide to have written that, he must not have looked closely at his words and his letters. Any word is as beautiful as any other. Is a *u* prettier than an *i*, an *i* less well turned than an *e?* A word, for me, is like a flower—it's made up of petals; it's like a tree—it's made of branches. *Hierarchical* is a mountain with twelve fantastic sides, and these twelve sides are like the twelve apostles. The twelve apostles were named *H, I, E, R, A, R, C, H, I, C, A,* and *L. Pi* is a village with two houses and these houses are joined at the hip, like Chateaugué and me. Chateaugué is here, setting on the bedding (*setting* rhymes with *bedding,* but *sitting* most definitely does not), right behind me, like a pea in a pod. Indeed, if we're like two peas in a pod, each of us is like a pea in a pod, and Chateaugué is like a pea in a pod. I went to get her, by bike. I had to cover fifty miles going and fifty miles coming back. I made the trip there in four hours. On the way back, she slowed me down. She was astride her own mount, a girl's bike, but she constantly got cramps and constantly ended up in the ditch, for it was dark, it was pouring, we couldn't see a damned thing, and big trucks were passing and spraying and blinding us non-stop. At the slightest slope, at the slightest incline, she put her foot down and walked; I had to wait for her. Against the wind, against the slope, and against the rain (against the current, I should say), Chateaugué leaves much to be desired. She just couldn't get it up. Anyway! Upon our arrival, after an aeneid (an odyssey, I should say) of ten hours, she fell into bed like a stone. She just just woke up. *To just wake up.* What a funny expression. I wonder where I dug that up.

Where have you been, Elphège? I just woke up, Brunhilde. I can't see her, since she's behind me, but my back sees her, as well as my neck. It's as though her presence were making the skin on my back and my neck bristle. If there were no one behind me, my back wouldn't see anything and wouldn't have goosebumps. We've set the date for our suicide. It's a vague and upcoming date like that of any death. Before that date, we're going to raise hell. Now that we only have a few days to live, now that we're sure we're going to die, we're free, we no longer exist, we know the voluptuousness of being. It's as if all of life, all the energy of the living world, were concentrated in each of our hearts. The pale grey of the ceiling has turned into bright red, beet red, carrot yellow. The water tastes of fire and acid. The meat in our mouths is crunchy like glass. We are emancipated from anguish, from the humiliation of aging, of rotting, of having to become uglier and more banal year after year, hour after hour. We have crossed the limits of death; we have passed its limits, passed the houses of men, and we have kept our honour, our panache. We have survived the test of death without losing ourselves; we are intact—lively and young as before, and for as long as death lasts.

"What is stronger than anything?" I asked Chateaugué.

"The strongest thing of all is an ocean."

"An ocean cannot destroy itself. We can destroy ourselves. We are stronger than an ocean. But, an ocean does stay an ocean. It can build up its mountainous and majestic waves free from all anxiety; it doesn't have to dread winding up one fine morning as a lake, a tidal pool, a swamp, a puddle, or even dry. Its dignity is guaranteed."

Chateaugué said yes, seemed to understand, appeared to agree strongly. Her enthusiasm, feigned or genuine, was something to see. Her bike is leaning against the partition. My bike is leaning against hers. Our bikes are mingled together like rosaries. They look like garbage. There was a strike yesterday, the strike of the garbagemen, of those who collect (who glean) others' trash. Ashes to ashes ... What exalts the little Protestant chapel of Berthier, empty and dilapidated, is the memory of Cuthbert's wife. Cuthbert, a Scottish officer who was a friend of

General Wolfe, bought the seigneury of Berthier in 1765. In the summer, cows stand in the shade inside the chapel, one at a time, no more than two at a time. Beneath lie the white bones of Cuthbert's wife. The skeleton is not in the chapel; it's six feet underground, like the others, to avoid scaring the crows. Chateaugué blows on my hair with all her heart, and says that my hair flies away just as poplar leaves do when it's windy. She adds that, in the fall, the maples seem full of Malarian butterflies. *Malaria*, in her language, means *Malaysia*. She settles on one arm of my armchair and puts her arm around my neck.

"It's fun to have ridden fifty miles by bike when you know you're going to scuttle your ship in a few days," she says to me with a serious air, her eyes filled with wonder. "I feel a big emptiness in my belly, and I'm short of breath. What are we going to do now?"

"We're going to go to the Saint-Sulpice Library by bike," I reply in a neutral voice. "We're going to go sit across from each other in a restaurant, drink some coffee, eat some toast, and pay. The toast and coffee cost twenty cents a person."

"Now? Right away?"

"Not right away. The library isn't open at night, during the night, while night is nigh."

The skin of my neck bristles under the warm hand of my sister Chateaugué. What makes hands warm? Life.

"Where's the bafwoom?" she cries in the voice of a child of six.

"The bathroom is on the right, across the hall."

"The bafwoom! The bafwoom!"

She starts to laugh and clap her hands. And the horse started to laugh and clap its hands. She raised herself all alone, like a tree. Mr. and Mrs. Brasseur never took care of her. She comes back from the bathroom with soot all over her hands. Where did she get that soot? With one fingertip, she puts some of it on my lips, as if it were lipstick. She tells me that we've got to make a good showing, that we're going to kill ourselves, that we've got to keep our lips painted black until the hour of our death.

"Of our death, amen ..."

And she bursts out laughing. What does death mean to her soul? Nothing. A feather. Tripping the light fantastic. Given that death is too big for her, it will be funny to kiss it. Chateaugué is happy and delighted to die, the way a little girl would be happy to take a mountain into her arms. Playing in the snow bare-handed. Our hands used to turn red and burn like fire.

"It's lipsoot."

She wants me to put some lipsoot on her, like she put some on me. She frisks about a bit before I begin the operation, like a little girl of six. I take a little soot from the hollow of her hand, as you take holy water from a font—by the fingertips—and I begin. Is she doing it on purpose, or is it true that she's still a little girl of six? Miles Miles, for one, does it on purpose. Miles Miles is cheating. Is Chateaugué cheating? You'd think that she wasn't cheating. Even the hair under her arms, blonde like her skin, seems childlike, cheerful, innocuous—smooth and inno-cent as a nascent lamb.

"Let's go to bed, Chateaugué."

"I'm going to roll you a cigarette, Chateaugué, and initiate you into the smokers' club."

"Hand me your cigarette, Chateaugué, so I can light your fire."

"We slept a little while ago, Miles Miles; we're not sleepy."

"We're going to keep watch, Chateaugué. Smoke. Do grains of tobacco get stuck on your tongue?"

In bed, we keep watch. I tell her to keep her eyes wide open and watch whatever goes by go by, to be attentive, to keep con-stant vigilance.

"What's going by, Miles Miles? It's as dark as hell. I can't see a thing. What's going by?"

"Night, of course! We're the jolly troubadours. Oh, come on, come in! If there's nothing going by, there's something going on. The proof? Look. My hand is trembling. On my forehead, beads of sweat are forming. Look under my pillow to see whether my sabre is really there and look under your pillow to see whether your revolver is really there."

When you crush the embers of your cigarette with your fingers, it burns, my dear Chateaugué, it roasts like chicken legs. You feel your skin simmering like eggs. I sing to her "Aybolé, Aybolé," the song of the Maniboulas, the singers who were so popular in the olden days. It's September 14. Cha. Cha. Cha. September 14 all day long. A boat exploded in the port yesterday, in the pork yesterday, in the pig. I'm just like Maurice Bourassa, I mean Maurice Duplessis. Do we know what the latter called his adversary Lawn, deputy from the county of Pontiac? He called him the "Ass of Pontiac." But the "Ass of Pontiac" will not know the glory of "Claude of France," for we are not French. You'll be beautiful, Miss, with a feather in your cap. Goddamn comedian.

7

Red sky at morning, sailors take warning. Red sky at night, sailors' delight. I like it when it rhymes. I like to commit crimes. I like to commit crhymes. Let's put Commodus, the poisoned and strangled emperor, in one of the drawers of the commode. Let's accommodate the unaccommodating. Let's monopolize Alaska. Alaska is part of Canada, the way a panda's foot is part of the panda. *Panda* rhymes with *Canada* and with *Alaska*. Who's the Judas who sold Alaska to the Disunited States? If I catch him, I'll put him in the drawer of the commode, with Commodus. The more I think about Labrador, the sleepier I get. For the more you think about Labrador, the later it gets. Outside, it has started to get cold. For the more time passes, the closer winter gets. The latter apothegm only applies when (whenever) it is not winter. In winter, the more time passes, the closer summer gets. Between 4:20 and 4:25, the big hand extends over the little hand, sleeps on the little hand. Between 5:25 and 5:30, the same thing occurs. Our bikes became avant-garde film stars. Here's how our bikes became avant-garde film stars. Before going into the restaurant for toast and coffee, we leaned our bikes one on top of the other against the restaurant. One on top of the other, our bikes made us think of two crosses fallen one on top of the other. After paying, we left the restaurant, walking. We'll go to Trois-Rivières by river, to Chicoutimi by bumble-bee, to Ottawa on a shoestring. There's a lovely trip! Someone who needed a shave was casting covetous looks at our bikes, some sort of convolvulus, someone who doesn't get his feet wct, someone who doesn't get his sheets wet, and, for greater precision, someone who was making an avant-garde film.

"Are these bikes yours?"

From the accent, we understood that he was Frenchie French.

"Oui. They're ours."

"Will you lend them to us for a single shot, a single scene?"

Oui, we said, oui, we will, oui.

"It'll just take us a second."

An hour later, we were still standing and waiting for our bikes, because our bikes were still in the middle of making an avant-garde film. Cuthbert, lord of Berthier by purchase, was an officer in the Black Guard before the purchase, before the sale; that's what I read. In order to wait longer and more comfortably, Chateaugué and I sat down on the sidewalk. I'm noting with precision everything that unfolds before my death and her death. Everything that happens, happens before death; for death is always after, and after, there is always death. In a word, after death, nothing happens. I'm not saying that to seem serious and subtle. I'm saying that because I feel like it. There are so many who speak of death to scare others, because they want to be taken seriously, because they want to take themselves seriously. If death is great and serious, those who have the capacity to die are great and respectable; that's how they reason. Some exaggerate the importance of death to exaggerate their own importance, to rise in their own esteem. If life is monotonous and boring, what is this death that is merely its termination? Death is the end of the monotony and the boredom, of the empty wait, of the platitudes, of the pluvitudes. Death is the end of nothing, of nothing at all, of less than nothing. There are others who exaggerate the importance of politics, others agriculture, others astrology, others astronomy, others astronautics, others love. They get excited by what they extol; they whortensturbate. They all want to be considered worthy and solemn. Solemnity! If the monkey had solemnity, if it didn't pee out in the open and blow its nose on its hands, the monkey would be a naturalized human, that is, Greek, French, German, Vanisapese, Bandilapine, Austro-Hungarian,

Irish, Scottish like Cuthbert, or even Luxembourger. What should we make of the solemnity of the owl? Is it ridiculous and vain like that of man? The solemnity of the owl is natural, founded on the fact that if it moved or laughed, its prey would know it was there and would keep its distance. Is that clear? Is that clear enough? The Frenchman finally gave us back our bikes.

"Thanks," he said to us.

"You're welcome," I replied in a faint voice.

If there were no Frenchie French here, there would be no cinema here. Let's acclaim the civilizer. Let's rejoice. He comes here to wise up the masses who are ninnies and who do not know how to say *fuck*. Let's read. Let's go to the movies. Let's buy dirty books. Let's buy books that are quick reads. Let's repel the invader. Let's engage in debauchery. Let's walk tight-assed and pigeon-toed. Let's wear tight pants and buy sexual automobiles. Let's go do an internship at the Sorbonne. Let's attend the French disuniversities and let's be ashamed that we have only attended the disuniversity of Montreal. Let's hide if we have only attended a technical school. Let's let our beards grow and let's not shave them. For they will believe that we are disintellectuals when we go by on the sidewalk like female peripatetics. Let's repel the Italian, a vulgar profiteer who thinks only of his family and who spends his time laughing and dancing with them. Let's use the word *cunt*. Let's speak French. Do not tolerate any substitute for the word *cunt*. Let's put them all in the same place as Commodus, in the drawer of the commode. What does a dandelion that's making itself out to be a dahlia look like? That dandelion looks like a French Canadian who's making himself out to be a hero in avant-garde films made in France. Let's stay behind, with Crémazie, with Marie-Victorin, with Mary of the Incarnation, with Félix Leclerc, with Jacques Cartier, with Iberville and his heroic brothers. Let's stay behind. Let's stay where we are. Let's not advance by a single step. Let's keep the faith. Let's remember. Time passes; let's stay. Let's lie down on our sacred holy ruins and let's laugh in the face of death while awaiting death. Nothing is serious. Nothing is serious. Nothing is serious.

Everything is laughable. Everything is ridiculous. There is nothing solemn. What little there is of earthly organization is founded on the hypothesis that life is precious. Miles Miles is in favour of a disorganization that would be founded on the truth. And here is the truth: life is monotonous and everyone is bored. To tell the truth, death is all there is. It's the only interesting thing in life. The rare moments in life when you're not bored are when you narrowly escape death and when you die. There is love. But there is no happy love. I know love really well. It's all we ever talked about at home. Either love is hopelessly unhappy, or love is deadly boring—you need toothpicks to keep your eyes open. Until ten o'clock, we read together from the same book at the Saint-Sulpice Library. On the same bench, leg to leg, arm to arm, we read. The bell rings at ten minutes to ten. At ten minutes to ten, you have to return your books to the clerks of the Saint-Sulpice Library. We kept reading as if nothing had happened, until ten o'clock. Only at ten o'clock did we turn in our book; we stole ten minutes from them. *The Patriots* by Aegidius Parent—that's what we read. There's a copper profile of Aegidius Parent hanging on one of the pilasters at the entrance, where you can catch sight of the bookshelves. Is that clear? Is that clear enough? That's why we read *The Patriots*. Two for one book. Two vultures for one zebra carcass. We read for a long time. But the time passed quickly. Every word under our eyes was bathed in the sulphuric light of life after death. By the light of the funeral torches, lying side by side in our coffin, we were reading. When you're dead and embalmed, open a book and read— you'll feel what we felt this afternoon. You'll see what I mean. For we are going to commit suicide soon. I'm writing these lines, so dear to my heart, on my knees. Before me, her legs dangling, Chateaugué is sitting on the table. In our room, there's this green table, a green commode, two little green chairs, a green armchair, and an iron bed with cylindrical posts, hollow and brown. The green I'm talking about is the same green as the green of nascent apples. A coffin for two: the hollowed-out trunk of a tree, an eviscerated column, a shaft, hollow like the bedposts, where they'll put us in the oven, one at the foot of the other, the head of one between the feet of the other. It is difficult to haul yourself up to the third floor of a house by way of a corkscrew staircase with a bike around your neck serving as a noose or a necklace, especially when you have to open the door of each floor with a key. For Chateaugué and me, it's nothing—it's routine. Chateaugué weighs ninety-two pounds; her bike weighs ninety-three. For our efforts, all we get are cuts and bumps. Hoists and pulleys are all we dream of. This is the era of machines; it's not the era of arms. We're going to have to change eras. For this is the era of machines, and here we are stagnating and getting cuts and bumps like in the era of arms. Arms. Embraced. There are women right now who have just been embraced—they are the embraced ones of the world. Let's think, with our eyes closed, of the embraced women of the world, of the slapped women of the world, of the betrayed women of the world, of the sleeping women of the world, of the unjustly ugly and forgotten women of the world, of the seven wonders of the world. We bought cigars after eating hotdogs on Rue Saint-Laurent, I mean Boulevard Saint-Laurent. Right now, we're smoking those cigars while glaring at each other. Chateaugué has beautiful eyes. Does she have beautiful eyes because she has a beautiful face, or does she have a beautiful face because she has beautiful eyes? She has neither a beautiful face nor beautiful eyes. Some even say she's unsightly. Unsightly or beautiful, her eyes and her face go straight to my heart. What is Chateaugué doing? What is she doing? She's making smoke. Is that enough? Is that what she must do? What am I supposed to do with her? Why is she here? What good is she? What do you do with your sister Chateaugué? Do you tell her to go hang herself somewhere else? She is good for something. She keeps me from whortensturbating, and I simply loathe whortensturbating. She makes me feel uncomfortable in a good way, in that sense. We're always together; we're together twenty-four hours a day. I'm not the daring kind; I couldn't whortensturbate in front of Chateaugué without getting hysterical. I'm the kind that is thin-skinned about shame. When I'm alone, I can't fall asleep without whortensturbating. But Chateaugué doesn't just get tangled up between my legs in that sense— she reassures me. With her in the bed, I'm not afraid, and I fall asleep right away. It's September 15, and we have sixty dollars left.

8

The reason we've decided to commit suicide is not because of the money; we admit it, to our enduring shame. It's because of men that I'm committing suicide, because of the rapport between human beings and me. Every human being affects me; that's affection—friendship, love, hatred, ambition. I've come down with a bad case of affection. Affection has sickened my soul. My soul is constipated with affection. The older I get, the worse it is. I left the Islands because everybody affected me so much that I'd have killed everybody. The more your mother cries, the more your sisters and brothers turn bitter, the more your father loses it, the worse you do at school, the more you whortensturbate, the more you're affected. The more you're affected, the more your mother cries, the more your father drinks, the more your brothers and sisters turn bitter, the worse you do at school, the more you whortensturbate. Affection never works. Affection sickens me. It leads to sobs of hatred, to the despair of impotence, to cruel hopes, and to sexual moans. I'm killing myself because the only way I could ever live would be completely alone and because no one can live completely alone. My fellow men affect me to such a degree that I'm as frightened as I am of a rattlesnake to address the least of them. It's not because of the money that we're committing suicide. We're not communists. We don't believe in those things. We couldn't care less about the loan sharks, several of whom claim to be scandalized, and we shall continue not to care less about them until the end of time if they stay in their cages, if they don't come sniffing around our room, from now until the end of time. The earth could be full of rich crooks and we wouldn't even pay attention. In the eyes of the children that we are, adults are mere child's play. I could meet a millionaire on the sidewalk, and I'd take him for a duster of door handles and doorbells on strike for 444 days. I don't like automobiles, but that has nothing to do with it. Besides, you don't meet up with any automobiles on the sidewalk. Except for those that are very aggressive. But my impotence, my powerlessness to overcome affection and sexuality—that's what I can't bear. When I was younger, I had only to bear my powerlessness to overcome affection, had only that kind of poetic impotence to bear. I could deal, especially since I had high hopes. Now that sexuality has gotten mixed up in it, I can't deal anymore. Filth. Ever since sexuality has become part of me, I've felt sickened, I've felt repugnant toward myself and for myself. I'm no longer pure— that's why I'm killing myself, that's why I can't bear my soul's pain, that's why I think I'm no longer worth the trouble of feeling the pain. I can't cope anymore, but it's not for want of courage: it's because sexuality makes people repugnant, it's because I'm no longer worth the trouble. Is that clear? Is that clear enough? I know. I know. It's not Voltaire. But only three things were missing for *Volta* to be *Voltaire*: an *i*, an *r*, and an *e*. No matter how much I repeat that I'm still a child of eight, that doesn't change anything: it's not true. It's not only the sexuality inside me that has sickened me, but also that which at first glance I detect in everybody and everything. Check out the ads, the posters, the cinema façades, the newspapers, the pregnant women, the dresses, the calendars! Ever since my thirteenth year, everything has been sexual, from the ankle boots of those sisters who take a vow not to copulate, right up to the flowers that men offer women to make them inclined to copulate— from the shoes right up to the dandelions. Is that clear? Is that clear enough? When I look at Chateaugué, I tell myself that I don't want to touch her, to profane her. Are those the thoughts of a child? Is that sexual? Isn't that sexual enough? Everything is sexual, even purity incarnate, even my sister Chateaugué, even the only true sister in the entire world. I'm committing suicide because I've lost the purity of my body and the purity of my intentions. My sexual desires are fatal, insurmountable hindrances to my ideals of liberty, dignity, and beauty. You're not healthy when you've got tuberculosis. You can't lay claim to greatness when you're mixed up in sexuality, voluntarily or involuntarily. It's worse to be mixed up in it involuntarily than to be mixed up in it voluntarily. You're caught between ridiculous dignity and proud indignity. It's the 15th, I believe, Chateaugué my sister. If it's Monday, it's the 15th, but if it's Tuesday, it's the 16th ... Chateaugué, my sister. The trick is to know whether it's Monday, Tuesday, or Wednesday, Chateaugué, my sister. So much for calendars.

9

It's not the 16th, since it's Friday. Is it Friday of last week, this week, or next week? There are four rows of numbers on the calendar, four or five. The trick is to know in which row of numbers today's Friday falls. As for the use of the word *goddamn*, I'll come back to it. At the library, we read so much that we left disgusted. We went back to the room in silence. We were supersaturated with reading, in every respect sickened by the library. It was nice to remain silent, to not read anymore, to smoke. But our heads were disgusted from having read too much and we were unhappy. What's more, there were fifty people typing upstairs. It was the most symphonic sound. There are so many people who want to become famous writers that we couldn't hear ourselves think in the room, we couldn't hear ourselves being silent. They're in such a hurry to become famous writers that they can't even allow themselves to take the time to mend a pen, to dip a pen, to stain the inside of their fingers. For those who can't wait to become famous writers, the electric typewriter is indispensable. Those who want to become famous writers quickly need only go see the sales rep for "Quikquikquik" electric typewriters. That sales rep is Finnish. He wrote the UnFinnished Symphony. I know him well.

"Let's go for a walk!" I said to Chateaugué, disgusted, sickened, and depressed.

Rue Saint-Paul was empty and black, and Chateaugué had put on her beautiful dress. The street was black because of the rain that squirts from the steamrollers that spray the streets every evening. Well, we left very unhappy. At the outset, I didn't even notice that Chateaugué was wearing another dress. And, well, we came back very happy. There wasn't a single soul on Rue Saint-Paul. We walked down it while listening to ourselves remain silent, while watching ourselves watch nothing, and our smiles came back. Plus, I've put so many miles on these legs, we've walked so much, the fact that I'm not walking anymore may account for the jubilation with which I'm writing these lines. Life is complicated. We were walking more and more serenely in our solitudes—my solitude, whortensturbated to the point of bleeding, and her solitude, immaculate. Words began to fall from our mouths, heavy and spaced out like the first drops of rain in a storm. Chateaugué was beautiful like a young girl taking her first communion. Tonight in the dark, she was so clear and so luminous in her little pink dress that was unembroidered, unpleated, and unaltered. Because her dress had not grown and Chateaugué had, I could see and feel that under Chateaugué's dress there was nothing but Chateaugué's legs. We covered a short distance by streetcar. In the streetcar there was a man whose hands were so white, so pale, so colour-less, that you might have said there was no blood left inside.

"Look," whispered Chateaugué in my ear. "He already has the hands of a dead man."

After getting off the streetcar, we started to sing. For an hour, at the top of our lungs, to the same tune, we sang the same four lines, lines that had come to me all of a sudden:

> I feel such a longing
> To expel you from my life
> That I won't resist the longing
> To expel you from my life

After that, for an hour, at the top of our lungs, continuing to wander up and down the streets, we sang four other lines, which had come to me all of a sudden:

> Adventure is so beautiful
> In her unembroidered pink dress
> Adventure is so beautiful
> Let's let her come in.

He walks goddamn fast. She pedals goddamn fast. It's a goddamn beautiful play. You have a goddamn good sense of humour. Leave me alone, you goddamn idiot. Girls run goddamn fast. Now my goddamn gun has jammed! So much for the use of the word *goddamn*, which can be used both adjectivally and adverbially. I end with this alexandrine, which is not mine:

Where the golden insect on the olden trunk roams.

Lots of people from this country laughed at this alexandrine produced by one of our own. Miles Miles finds it to his taste. *Olden* is the opposite of *golden*, in a certain way. In any case, one is contained within the other. Anyway ... Those who are intelligent understand and will appreciate it. Besides, for a fly, a trunk is extremely old. I'm not writing for imbecility but for posterity. They took my husband to the cleaners. I know him well, the rep for "Quikquikquik" typewriters. We went to the original sinema together.

10

If I were to ask the Virgin Chateaugué to tell me what periods were, she'd reply along the lines of portions and punctuation.

"They're round. They separate sentences. They're used to divide time and end conversations."

She is white from one end to the other. For her, her sex organs consist of nothing but a urinary opening, and for her a urinary opening is funny. Never, in her body or in her mind, has she been mixed up in sexuality, in ghastliness. She is all white, white as a dove coming out of the breast of the Creator. Despite her fourteen years, her beautiful and pretty ovaries have remained mute and silent. Do not use the word *ain't*; it's a vulgar contraction. Long live the word *aren't*! Let them laugh; use *aren't*. He who laughs last laughs best. As for Chateaugué's periods and her virginitude, I don't have a clue. I watched, I guessed, I concluded. Maybe I'm inventing, too. When you only have a few days to live, you can take the liberty of dreaming, of claiming that you're going to enter death dazzled by the sun of purity. Right? Ovaries. Period. Urethra. Why did I go into all these execrable details? How ugly I am! How dirty I am! How I hate myself! How black I am!

My soul is the dungeon of black mortal sins.

That's Nelligan. It's neither genial nor general nor marshal. But it's clear. Nelligan was a victim of the blackness, of the squalor of the soul, of impuritude. It's still Friday, the 16th. No! It's the 17th. What was I thinking? Chateaugué is sleeping, all white, all huddled up, and all cocooned in the white sheets. Hold every-thing! Hold everything! Hold everything! I am too. Aren't I? I ain't. You ain't. *Beatitude* rhymes with *virginitude*, but not with *virginity*. Virginitude is a state, a kind of beatitude.

II

I won't even mention the temperature. It has rained. It will rain. We're thus between a rock and a hard place. As for my soul, it's between a cock and a hard place. We just got back from a long bike ride around the island city. We followed the water as closely as we could. There was the water from the sky, which was falling on our heads, and the water of the river, which we were following. Coming back into the room, we almost died of asphyxiation, it smelled so badly of stale smoke, stale ashes, cigar ashes, and smoke. We smoke tons of cigars. We never stop smoking cigars. We always have a cigar between our teeth. We swallow the smoke; we inhale it all the way into our bellies. Sometimes Chateaugué loses consciousness. How beautiful to see her, stretched out on the bed, unconscious, even whiter than usual, with her lips black, in keeping with our pact. We blacken our lips with anything at all. We've bought black ink, black paint, and black chalk. What's important is that we have black lips. It hardly matters if, through clumsiness, while blackening our lips, we also blacken all around our mouths and the whole tongue. We're not afraid of dying of poison—we're going to die anyway. The passerby whose steps I can hear right now is going to die, too. Everyone's dying here. But in this corrupt century, in this scummy society, you can't go around with your mouth black without getting noticed. We couldn't care less if they point at us; we're going to die. Just now, Chateaugué reports that a little girl has stuck her head out of the window in the house across the street and is watching her papa walk away while waving to him. I run up. I like to watch children wave.

"Far far far far far far?" the child asks her papa in a voice full of distress, with no fear of repeating herself. "Far far far far far far?" the worried child asks her papa, who seems to be going off to work.

My God! It was sooooo far, how far far was when I was eight years old. They'll teach that little girl, as they've taught her to wave, that the farther things are, the more they remain the same. Chateaugué is talking about slashing her face with a razor blade.

"What difference does it make, since we're going to die?"

I forbid her to. I tell her no.

"Stay beautiful," I say to her. "Let's die beautiful. Tomorrow, we'll go buy you the most beautiful dress in the world, the most beautiful hat in the world, the most beautiful pair of shoes in the world, and the most beautiful pair of gloves in the world. Before dying, we'll wash ourselves and we'll comb our hair. I'll comb yours and you'll comb mine."

She jumps up and down; she is jubilant and applauds.

"Yes, yes. Yes. That's a very good idea. I'll put perfume on you and you'll put it on me. We'll make the bed. We'll sweep up."

"That's right. We'll sweep up."

"But why buy the most beautiful dress in the world?"

We'll steal it. It's September 18. We've got fifty dollars left. Dying old or dying ugly and sick is like dying killed. It's ridiculous. It just isn't done. It's not polite for the person it happens to. The idea that it could happen to me keeps me from falling asleep. It's unbearably humiliating. My death would be paler if Chateaugué didn't enhance it with the pink glow of her whitetude. The *ude* quickly becomes an attitude. Spare the *ude*, spoil the child. Raise the wall. Rewall. To rewall. Rewalled. I rewall you. You rewall me. We rewall each other. You all rewall. They roam and rewall. Watch out for walls. An accident can happen so quickly.

12

Marinella,
Your feet sweat,
You smell of tobacco ...

That's how my uncle used to sing the song by Tino Rossi, who was so popular in the olden days. Vincent Scotto's the one who composed it, that song by Tino Rossi. Vincent Scotto or Vincent Scooter. Here I am in front of myself once again. Under my eye, I've got a crease, and if I let myself go, it would deepen, widen, and multiply. There's only one remedy for the deepening of creases. Death. We've drunk a lot of beer. Thirteen big bottles. There are little ones and there are big ones. It's acrid. I've got a headache. My belly is as hard as a rock. Chateaugué is vomiting out the window. The little slut. She has blonde hair that shines pink and shimmers. She doesn't know who I am, and she gets undressed in front of me; at night, when we sleep, she puts her feet on me. I wake up with her face on my face, and I'm becoming sort of blinded by it. She doesn't know who I am. She doesn't know that I'm obsessed with sexuality. The poor goose! If she only knew! If she saw what I see in her when I whortensturbate in secret, when I look at her. She has little breasts, white like white birds, little breasts that bleed. There's a drop of blood on the head of each one, congealed, ready to break free and run. If she only knew who I am! She'd be so discouraged! All she gets for being so virtuous is a friend obsessed with sexuality. If she only knew! She'd throw herself into the water. She'd be driven to drink. She'd do something stupid. There's no justice on earth. All that a good and innocent being attracts is disgust and, consequently, despair. All she attracts are attempts at corruption and rape. Theories that cause a stir are beautiful theories. My theory of the tree will cause a terrific stir, for it's a very pretty theory. It's not a very clear theory, but the prettiest theories, like the most beautiful houses, are the most obscure. The tree senses that it's beautiful, which means that it delights in it. All trees are beautiful. The tree grows imbued with the assurance that it's beautiful and dies as it lived— in harmony with the world and with itself. The tree is beautiful, it knows it, and that's good enough for it. It doesn't caress its trunk with its branches, it doesn't speak, it doesn't walk. It doesn't need to do all that—being beautiful is good enough for it. It doesn't walk because it's fine where it is. It doesn't move because it's fine in its present state, so fine that it doesn't even think of trading places, so fine that it has quite forgotten to think. It remains where it is. It makes no gestures at all. It seeks not and wants not, because it lacks not. If it knew how to talk, it wouldn't talk, because it has nothing to request. The tree is an unqualified success, a gem. It is beyond satisfaction. Satisfaction is born of dissatisfaction, and the tree is devoid of dissatisfaction—of need, of aspiration. It is impossible to satisfy beings who have no needs whatsoever, those who by their nature are themselves all they need. The tree needs nothing other than what it is, and it's a never-ending need. The tree is alone and is sufficient unto itself. Snow or rain, it doesn't suffer. It doesn't need heat. Let's all be trees—like Chateaugué, who needs nothing, who finds within herself all that she needs. Chateaugué doesn't need lips on her neck, arms around her neck, the warmth of another body on her body. A tree doesn't even know what it is to kiss, to embrace, to love. Let's all be like Chateaugué! Man is incomplete, a flawed creature, a creature that lacks everything, a parasite. Perfect things can be easily recognized: they are mute and don't move; they don't talk to you and don't run after you in order to hate you; and you leave them impassive and indifferent. Go look at an ocean, a mountain, a stone. They will keep still and will leave you in peace; they won't even look at you. They won't even look at a nude femme fatale; their eyes and ears are turned toward their inner selves. For in their inner

37

selves, it's beautiful. Everything that walks, cries, laughs, and talks requires satisfaction. Walking, crying, laughing, and talking are going down on your knees in order to get something. Everything that can't get satisfaction clamours for satisfaction. Everything that can't get perfection clamours for perfection. Everything that is satisfied and perfect is silent ... If there is a God, he has nothing in common with men or with elephants; he is not made in the likeness of men or of elephants. If there is a God, he did not create us, because God, perfect as he is, needs nothing—didn't need us, didn't need to create. We created ourselves, or an imperfect and dissatisfied being created us— some Martian. For God is in the category of the trees. So much for the theory of the tree. I hope that you—yes, you—are completely baffled. God did not create us as a good deed, because He is infinitely good and infinitely kind. God is not a scout. God is not a Child of Mary. God didn't create us at all. So much for the theory of the tree. That's all for today. Ha! Ha! Ha! Ha!

13

The left-wing caterpillars and the right-wing caterpillars went on their way. The ants of the Orient and the ants of the Occident went on their way. All the caterpillars and all the ants left. There were no caterpillars and no ants left on earth. In Halifax, during the strike of the pilots of the Isthmus of Chignecto, a little woman and a little man kissed each other. I have no more life left in my body. I have no more of anything left in my body. I am tortured. My soul, totally empty, is suffocating. My breath sets my mouth on fire. My thoughts strangle my brain. Last night I didn't sleep, and tonight I can't sleep. I've eaten like an elephant. I've drunk like a dormouse. I've given up everything—even life. I have neither hunger, nor thirst, nor hope to lose, nor dangers to await. Why can't I sleep? Why, like a slap in the face, does each beat of my heart keep me in a state of vigilance, in a state of battle, in a state of confrontation with myself? Why must these lashes of a whip, these burns, these cries course through me while everything for miles around is sleeping? All the others are sleeping. As for me, I'm battling against the void, against the very thing that I avoided so as to no longer have to battle for naught. The devourer, the devouring dissatisfaction, keeps plaguing me in the dark and in the void. I want nothing; why can't I have peace of mind? I've repudiated everything, and still, an abyss in me inhales painfully. The red-hot abyss keeps me awake. It's midnight, but the sun has stayed with me—it's in my eyes, blinding me; it's in my belly, burning. You try sleeping with the sun in your eyes! With rays of sunshine across your body ... Dying. That's what it takes. But I don't want to die right away. I don't want to go away right now. Before going away, I want to understand, and, above all, to vanquish. I don't want to die in such a state. I don't want to die at the end of my rope, exhausted. I want to die joyful, laughing out loud, vigorous, triumphant. Chateaugué, who sleeps with her mouth open, like a baby, immutable, sated, invulnerable, recharging her appetite ... I, who am exhausted, and who must keep struggling so as not to lose face, lose ground, lose my mind. I know what will happen if I turn tail. I'll run through the streets crying for help, pounding the air with my fists, pounding on the houses with my fists. Then I'll have lost, lost everything. I don't tell myself it would be too unfair for me to lose everything. For I know that there are some people who lose everything and that no justice whatsoever, whether human or immanent, will ever attend to them. There are some people who cry all the time, and no one wants to console them. There are some people who have more friends than they have tears. There are some people who are good at everything. There are some people who make a mess of everything. There are some people who ask for everything and receive everything. There are some people who ask merely to maintain a certain dignity and lose it. There are all kinds. There are billions. There are lots of Chinese. The Chinese are the most numerous. The word *cunning* doesn't come from the word *cunt*, but from the word *ken*. A sea. A sassin. Is a sassin in a sea? Where has the sea gone? Is the sea off to see a sassin? Let's try to kill the sea with a knife. Let's shut the hell up. Let's lie down in order not to sleep. Let's stretch out on the mattress in order to suffer. Let's stretch out on the altar, near Chateaugué, who has cold legs and dry feet even though it's hot and humid. Let's write anything at all. Let's write until we are overcome with sleep. Sleep will have to come over us with asbestos gloves, for we are red-hot like molten iron, like iron in fusion. We did nothing today. We killed time. It really sickened me. It really pleased Chateaugué; she appeared to be having fun. She laughed all day long, if I remember correctly. Let's go drink some water. Children say *wawa* instead of *water*. Children are pure. When children are sad, their mothers say to them, "You don't know what you want anymore." Wanting something that you're big enough to catch. If you're big enough, you catch it, and afterward, you don't know what you want anymore. Wanting something that you're not big enough to catch. You jump, you jump, you jump! Or you don't jump—for you know that it's perched too high, that it's no use jumping. I'm in the middle of writing a masterpiece of French literature. In 101 years, schoolchildren will learn whole pages of it by heart. But I don't want any glory. Some people want glory and—alas!— will never write a masterpiece of French literature. Glory is like a dictionary. A dictionary is like a door: it opens and closes. A desert is like a match, but it's much bigger than a match. But there are many more matches than deserts. It's like the Chinese. There are many more Chinese than violins. If the Chinese each had a violin, there would be more violins than Chinese. You could easily see it by adding up the Chinese violins and the French-Canadian violins. There are some women who smoke a pipe. There always have been. A woman is like a horse; all she's good for is swapping for sheep. A woman is like a squirrel; she's beautiful. A woman is bigger than a match. I could go on like this for 200 pages. Having a beautiful wife is like having a beautiful horse. Men who get down on their knees at women's feet are men who get down on their knees before their own penis—they're sex maniacs, they're sexually obsessed. A woman can be lent, swapped, sold, lost, and given, like a horse. The more beautiful the woman, the more expensive she is. Putting women on an equal footing with men is like putting squirrels on an equal footing with men. Women often win against men, but only when the man agrees to play the woman's game. Men would always lose against horses and squirrels if they agreed to play the games of squirrels and horses. Men aren't very clever when it comes to climbing trees. A horse runs quite a bit faster than a man. I know of horses who would make a man run for a long time if the only legal means of catching a horse were to run after it. Women have become insolent. They are glorified by the police, the magistracy, and the legislative council. The most insolent woman is the one who has the most beautiful behind. The more beautiful her behind, the more serious and untouchable she is. A woman measures her importance by the beauty of her behind;

that's why she deserved her bondage. The woman who doesn't have a beautiful behind despises herself and is humble. A beautiful behind is equal to a beautiful face. The beauty of the face has no other merit than to incite lust for the behind. Chivalry is fundamentally sexual, since it can only be practised by a member of the masculine sex. Chivalry must thus be judged as we judge the rest of sexuality, including pornographic magazines. To say that women are magnificent and that sexuality is horrible is to say two contradictory things about the same thing. There you have it, ma'am. Chateaugué doesn't take herself for a woman and doesn't want to be taken for a woman. Chateaugué is exceptional. Chateaugué is not one of those girls and boys who parade their sex right under your nose. It is often a question in literary language of the "favours" of a woman, of "her favours." We say, for example, that a woman granted "her favours" to a gentleman. What favours? A woman has nothing to grant. All the woman has to do is shut up and come to enjoy—or suffer, depending on the individual case—the favours of the man. A woman is like a homosexual; she's a type of effeminate being, exhibitionistic and ridiculous, who can think only of men. A lesbian is not like a man; she's an exhibitionist. I've had enough. Bang! Bang! Bang! Actors are like women—sexhibiting themselves. Bang! Bang! Bang!

14

I don't like reading anymore. I was upset by the first book I ever read. Inside that book, a woman was unbuttoning her blouse. With her blouse unbuttoned, Chateaugué is reading. Chateaugué is in the middle of reading, with her blouse unbuttoned. Her unbuttoned blouse reminds me of the unbuttoned blouse that was in the first book I ever read. Most of those who read are between nine and sixteen years old. The others, those who read and who are between twenty and sixty years old, read because they haven't been able to cross the wall of maturity; they're sitting in the shade of the wall of maturity with a book on their knees, and they're reading. In books, children seek the secrets of adults. Girls cross the threshold of maturity sooner than boys; that's why they stop reading before boys, and become disinterested in disintellectual problems before boys. Most intellectuals are men. Women writers of importance remain the exception. The adult reader is a whortensturbator, a bachelor, a revoltedbymyself. I don't know whether what I'm writing here is true. But, in any case, these lines are true since they faithfully convey what I'm truly thinking just now. Do you think so, truly? Yes. Then you're telling the truth. How's that for a definition of human truth. Now try saying I'm not intelligent. I don't give a hoot about scientific truth. I'm not talking about those who read to shine in high society like the star Vastalacuitalpa. I'm thinking of those who read because they find it to their liking. Books of genius interest no one. Hegel interests no one; he interests only those who make money off of him, only those who earn their living through theses and essays. It's quite an accomplishment to have read Hegel, Kierkegaard, or

Racine. There are no women undressing in Hegel or in Racine. So why bother? Why should those who aren't yet married and who haven't seen any nude women even bother? I don't know what I'm driving at, but I'm sure I'll get there. Some people read because, for them, it's a duty, one of those assignments like the ones that schoolchildren do. Those people, if they didn't read, would be afraid, one of those fears like the ones school-children have when they haven't done their assignments. We have so often associated literature with beauty, beauty with greatness, and greatness with duty ... When they want to sing the praises of Racine, they speak of his Phèdre by saying that she was passionate, that she was almost as passionate as the passionate women of contemporary pornographic literature. They go so far as to invoke possibilities of incest, of insect. The Americans come straight to the point: *sex*. They don't have a sense of empty subtleties. On the cover of all the novels originating in the South, there's the word *sex*, there's a woman who is more or less undressed, there's a woman who's more or less having an orgasm. That way, the least well-informed, the least educated whortensturbators know where they stand right away. It jumps out at you: it's a good novel; there isn't even any way to wonder whether it is or isn't a good novel. The disintellectuals go to the Élysée Cinema. They know that, at the Élysée, they won't blow it. They know that in every film that this art house presents there's a bit of breast and some bedroom scenes pro-scribed by the Catholic censor. Our fathers and our bourgeois are quite right to beware of disintellectuals and goatherds, I mean goatees. Another slip 'twixt pen and lip. Bergman is bril-liant, but fewer people would realize it if, in addition to being obsessed with the problem of God, he were not also obsessed with sexual problems. Try telling the Clerics of Saint-Viateur and the Franciscans not to tell their pupils to love literature and films. There is abuse; that's why I abuse here. Books and films are made, first of all, to sell, so that you'll buy them. How much does a camera cost? Bear in mind that the printers are still on strike. The printers are hungry. They've got to eat a little. For them to eat, the books have got to sell. Gide wanted to teach me fervour. By reading him, I learned suspicion. My deer, I'll show you suspicion. My deer, don't listen to what those who earn their living through art and literature say about art and literature. I have nothing against abstract art, but what will the unrest that it awakens lead to? May clarity flourish! May confusion perish! What's the salary of Burt Lancaster? What's the salary of Brigitte Bardot? Who pays the salary of Brigitte Bardot? You do. I sound like Caouette, a politician I know. It's hot. It must be an Indian summer. However, I don't see any Indians. I only see Chateaugué, who's reading, her feet up in the air, fresh as a rose. Buy not. The Temple is full of salesmen. The salesmen know their customers, the whortensturbators. Buy nothing. Let them die of hunger, the publishers and the producers. "Joseph E. Levine presents ..." Let him die of hunger. On the street, he wouldn't even look at you; you've made him so rich that he'd believe himself obliged to despise you. He'd even wear dark glasses. But I love Marilyn Monroe. She didn't know what she was doing. The disintellectuals told her that showing her bare behind was beautiful, and she believed them. They told her that she was a work of art, like the *Venus de Milo*, and that, therefore, she shouldn't be afraid to show her bare behind. She believed them. She wasn't wary of them. They're wily. They're sly foxes. She thought that they wished her well, that they loved her. She wanted to be loved. She really didn't give a hoot about the money. She died stark naked, like Job. She wasn't as intelligent as they were. It took her a while to understand. Before dying, she must have wondered how they could have been so heartless as to betray her ... to betray her for money. She must have wondered, a few minutes before committing suicide, "What do you do with money?" As for Mary of the Incarnation, she didn't let herself be fooled. She stayed beautiful, white, pure, and serene, till her dying day. "Purity! Purity!" Rimbaud's the one who shouted like that. I don't like prostitutes. It's not my fault. It's not very intelligent. It's not in vogue. I don't like disintellectually legalized, financed, and organized prostitution. I don't like low-necked clothing, transparent blouses, the panty line through the skirt, lipstick, knees in the air. I don't like that. It makes me sick. I'd rather have war and rivers of blood. I'm quite serious. In books and films, they spend their time taking

45

off their clothes. You'd think it was a conspiracy, the undressing conspiracy. I'd rather have beer, cigars, and death. Goddamn comedians. Goddamn sickos. Do you know the one about the rotten apples in the basket of good apples? The rotten apples ended up rottenizing all the good apples. Only illnesses are contagious. The good apples never purificated the rottenized apples. Soon you will all be rotten to the core. Try telling the architects to build fewer centres for the arts and more hospitals for rotting minds. Sexuality, like communism, is the easiest solution. It's easy to be convinced by those who preach ease with ease. Poor peasants! Don't sow your fields; the exploiters are sowing theirs. The exploiters reap what they have sown. If you reap nothing because you have sown nothing, don't be alarmed. For it is undeniable that all men are created equal and that each has a right to as much wheat as any other. It's just as much mine as yours, for I am your equal; for I, like you, have a body and soul, even though I'm lazy, even though I have no self-esteem, even though I don't have any qualms about eating another's wheat. Let them do as they like. The important thing is to be happy, to attain maximal serenity, like Mary of the Incarnation and the others. Not to be Catholic. To be true to the aspirations of your soul. To be courageous enough and proud enough to listen to the voices that rise up from the soul and obey the most beautiful one. To be courageous enough to carve out your happiness, to follow the way that leads to the heights. It's easy to know which way is the right one. It's the most difficult of all. It ascends ... It's as abrupt as a cliff. I'm talking like a vicar. I no longer know what I'm saying. You can either be celibate or slutty. Why must we be celibate? Who doesn't regret not being celibate? Who would not want to be pure? You can be strong or cowardly. Why be strong rather than cowardly? Who doesn't hope to be strong? The gymnasiums, the gymnasts, the gymnauseums, and Mr. America are only four of the billions of facts and examples that argue in favour of my theory. Even if there were no God, who would want to be cowardly, feeble, dirty, and vicious? You don't want to be cowardly. If you're cowardly, it's because you've forgotten, because you don't even bother remarking that you'd really rather be strong. You don't think about it. You don't have time to think of choosing. You don't dare think about it; you don't think about it. You follow the crowd. You let yourself slide right in behind the others, your head empty, grinning from ear to ear. Repression. Don't listen to Freud, my deer. There's always something that we've got to repress, for there's always an alternative. Concerning sexuality, for example, there are always two desires: the desire to do it and the desire not to do it. If you don't do it, the desire to do it is repressed. If you do it, the desire not to do it is repressed. Miles Miles is of the opinion that you've got a greater chance of going crazy if you repress the desire to be celibate than if you repress the other desire. In psychoanalysis, Miles Miles is like the beer "Labatt"—he's "labattomized." But what I dislike more than anything else is the automobile. When we go for a bike ride, Chateaugué and I, they honk at us as if we were pariahs, undesirables. We don't like it when automobiles have the impertinence to reproach *us*, to reproach us—two human beings—for our conduct. Who rules the road? The automobile. Nothing can be done to stop it. How can you go up against an automobile that has more than four hundred horse-power? There is the tank. We're considering it. A tank, well armoured, zooming down the wrong side of Rue Sainte-Catherine at a hundred miles an hour during rush hour ... It would be like a gunshot in a sack of feathers. The streets of Montreal would fill up with automobile blood. You can be an automobile or a walker. Who wants to be an automobile? Think of Peter Snell or Michel Jazy. Raising a regiment of snipers and posting them in the church towers at rush hour ... The snipers could kill lots of them. To be cowardly before God is not the worst thing. To be cowardly before men is not the worst thing. To be cowardly before yourself, to be cowardly alone in your room—that's the worst thing. Now Chateaugué's blowing her nose on the curtain of the skylight window. Who wants to die (to live) bald, impotent, tubercular, rickety, and ridiculous? Who wouldn't like to die young, at the height of vigour and purity? Who likes to live any other way but young, at the height of vigour and purity? Chateaugué replies that it's better than blowing her nose on her skirt; that besides, it's an old curtain that's all dirty; and that,

47

besides, the curtains only serve to stop the light and the darkness from coming in. Then, sniffling in order to see whether she's blown her nose properly, she talks to me about how the surf of the darkness is driven off by the big birds' wings.

"It's like the surf of the waves that the boats make."

Chateaugué comes over to me, after leaving her book on the bed, after tearing down the curtain, after making a nun's veil for herself with the curtain, and after turning off the light. She sits down on one arm of my armchair and puts her arm around my neck.

"Shhhhhhh!" she says, a finger to her lips.

"Wait," she commands me, with a mysterious air. "Wait. Listen. Don't say anything. A boat's about to cry out."

She presses one of her ears on one of mine. Our two ears form a kind of oyster. We wait. We listen. Visitor ... Visitor ... Visitor ... One of my arms hurts, and she has clasped her hands around that arm, just where I'm getting shooting pains. Suddenly we hear a great hoarse cry, a great deep cry, like a universal bellow. We give a start, and that makes Chateaugué laugh till she cries.

"I told you that a boat was going to cry out."

Me, I don't laugh. I never feel like laughing. How can you laugh when loads and heaps of automobiles move freely in the streets of Ville-Marie? No one understands my hatred of automobiles. Chateaugué, despite her benevolence on the subject, doesn't understand it either. She sympathizes. She sympathizes. My deepest sympathy. My dearest brethren. Women understand nothing. Chateaugué laughs, her head thrown back, her thighs in the air; her belly jiggles, her nostrils flare. She trusts me. You don't laugh with someone you don't trust, a complete and unreserved trust. Often, I feel uncomfortable about sleeping with her.

"Sleep in the bed. I'm going to sleep on the floor."

"What's gotten into you? Why did you come get me if you don't even want to sleep with me?"

For her, I'm like a sister. Not once has she said, "You're like my little sister. I trust you. I'm not afraid of your taking advantage of the situation. Buddy-buddy. I never think about the fact that you're the opposite sex." She's not a theoretician. What she

48

doesn't think about, she doesn't talk about. She's an ace. She's the companion of your dreams for a suicide. Doesn't she feel my eyes, as big as ostriches, swoop down on her thighs, revealed by a laugh too trustworthy, too open, too brutal? Doesn't she feel the narrow white columns of her main gate, the size of an insect, rivet my thoughts like a magnet? She doesn't even know, the idiot, that she has one of them—a main gate. Sometimes, I think that Chateaugué is cheating, that she's as false as a plaster pear. The truth is, she doesn't know that she's a cathedral of evil. I could write hundreds of pages about plaster pears. They're empty inside. We had one of those plaster pears for a long time, Chateaugué and I. It was broken into three pieces. It was ours, but I was the one who kept it. After using it, I'd put it back in its place on the commode, in the centre. It was in the centre of the commode, as well, where, after using it, I would replace the glow-in-the-dark crucifix that Chateaugué had lent me and that I have never returned to her. It had been given to her by a schoolteacher, as an end-of-the-year award. In the light, in bright sunlight, you can see everything; you can see the heavens and the earth; you can see all the grass and all the clouds. Under my blankets, in the dark, there was nothing but the crucifix full of white light. The light of the crucifix didn't shine; it filled the crucifix the way water fills a pitcher. Under the covers, there was nothing but the depths of darkness and the luminous crucifix of Chateaugué. As for the plaster pear, it was yellow, red, and green, and we should have brought it here. For us, it was alive, more alive than a real pear, alive like a bird. As soon as the three shards were fitted together, a kind of invisible blood started to circulate from one to the other; networks of pulp were woven within and became saturated with sap. It was like the motor of an automobile—we could undo it and redo it, take it apart and put it back together. In the middle of the commode, near the crucifix, it looked like a brand new plaster pear, an unbroken plaster pear, not made up of spare parts. Chateaugué rips the curtain in four, lengthwise, and ties a tie for me in Nelligan's style with one of the strips thus obtained.

"You blew your nose on that. It's full of snot!"

"Snot's not nasty. You never swallow your snot?"

"Yuck! Yuck!"

I could write pages and pages about Nelligan. When we were seven years old, we'd disappear into the woods and, sitting at the foot of some pine trees, we'd read and reread his poems. A few of his lines, like, "When we would read *Werther* deep in the woods ..." seemed to speak about us. At the library, in an edition of his complete works, we discovered a picture of him. We tore out the image and kept it. We were seeing our friend the poet for the first time; we might never see him again. We didn't hesitate; we brought him back here by force and fastened him to the partition with nails. Chateaugué finds him handsome, says that he has hair on fire, the nose of a lion, and eyes as sweet as butterfly wings. The picture that we stole shows him with a loose necktie around his neck. The picture could have portrayed him with a loose necktie around his forehead. Then he would have looked like an Arab. Fiery hair, the eyes of a woman, the nose of an animal, soft lips, a hard mouth; he is just as we imagined him—that's what struck us the most when we met him between the lines. I mustn't forget the calendars. This is perhaps the last entry in this journal, and it would be disagreeable for me to end it without speaking of the calendars. There were two calendars on the partitions when I arrived. Out of respect for the memory of the previous occupants, I didn't touch those calendars. One of them shows the month of October of last year; it's illustrated with the bust of a woman with ruby lips who's laughing and has a white fur around her shoulders and a row of pearls around her neck. The other was left over from the month of June of this year; on it, a little girl with brown eyes and brown hair forcibly kisses a brown dog as big as she is. The ripped portrait of Nelligan is in front of me but above me; it's above the map of Ontario. To see it, as to see the sky, as to see an eagle, I must lift up my head. For greater precision, it's to the left of the calendar that left off in the month of June. A little Frankenstein face is stuck on the door frame, up by the girl. Chateaugué's the one who stuck that green, scarred face there. On my table stands a dancing dame, as tall as a top and all dirty. She's made of plaster, and her creator botched her—her fat fingers are fused together like teeth, and the roses

on her dress are nothing but dried-up drops of red. The osten-
tatious yellow dress with wavy pleats that encompasses her hind
limbs is about to disappear under the thin brown layer of dust
that's settling on it. She carries a spray of roses in one arm, a spray
of red spots, of red ink blots. Her head is as big and shiny as an
eye. Yet she has a thick face, an ugly mug that Chateaugué, with
a fingertip, has smeared with black ink. Diagonally, from one
corner of the ceiling to the other, a hemp clothesline is stretched
for hanging out the wish, I mean the wash, for drying the wish,
I mean the wash. Still wishy-washy ... after all these years! ...
Chateaugué has washed my underwear and hung it out to dry
on the clothesline. Chateaugué wants me to move over, to make
some room for her on my armchair, to pass her the pen, to let
her write a few words in my notebook. She straddles one of my
legs. She tries to grab the pen out of my hands. We struggle.
The armchair, a rocking chair, ends up falling over backward.

"Are we together or not? Let me read what you're writing."

Sometimes something comes over me, and I see in her
nothing but a soul, a way of being. Other times, desire chases
all the blood to my head, and then I tremble for us, for her, for
me. Make me the same as you, dear heart. But you don't ask
such a thing of a Chateaugué. What would I look like if I told
her, "Make me just like you, dear heart!" Dear heart! She'd think
I was off my rocker. You mustn't ask anything of Chateaugué;
you could destroy everything by letting your true colours come
shining through. Dear heart! You mustn't say anything with
her. With her, everything you say must mean nothing. You've
got to let her be. You've got to watch her be while preserving
your anonymity, while letting yourself get some fresh air
through the breath of the cathedral that she encompasses,
through the air that comes out of her mouth, through the air
that her blood has purified. In a rough voice, I tell Chateaugué
to go to bed and leave me alone. That's how you've got to talk
to women. Man! Man! Get up. Leagues have been formed that
are dedicated to the defence of women's rights. It's high time
some leagues were formed to come to the rescue of men's rights.
And that has nothing to do with Robespierre, the Incorruptible.
Chateaugué, are you incorruptible? Can you swear it to me? Be

incorruptible. Teach me to be like you, if you are what you appear to be. Are you some kind of lesbian? Who are you? I'm so scared. If you were to unmask yourself at the last minute, it would be appalling; I would have nothing left but to wish I had never set foot here in this valley.

The Edinburgh Series
(Be Syria's, Edinburgh)

Leave or don't leave. Do what
You want to, my dear chickadee.
I really don't give a hoot because
I have a well-forged sword lodged in my belly.

Leave or don't leave on your trip.
Go or don't go to Syria.
As you like it, fickle dove;
I have a golden blade caught in my belly.

My blood lies like a rug.
Blood? Gall? How should I know, woman?
But the more it lies like a rug,
The rarer the gall in my soul.

Between Scotland and Syria,
Your heart wavers, your heart wavers.
Let it waver—for frankly, my dear,
After all these years, I don't give a damn.

15

They've finally delivered our case of beer. We've been waiting two hours for this case of beer. We haven't done a thing all day. For two weeks, we've been together constantly. Sometimes we're right next to each other. Sometimes we're on top of each other. Sometimes we're behind each other. We're never far from one another. Sometimes, but it's quite rare, we're separated by about fifteen feet, the length of the largest dimension of this room, which only has three dimensions. We did not choose death. We had no choice. Such proximity grates on your nerves. After two months of this life—the only one possible—we would detest each other. After two months of this regime, boredom and monotony—those abrasives that eat away at a man down to the nub of his hatred, that set men to fire and sword, that scour the skin of the soul to the bone, that scrape the heart until it bursts, until the cries that swell within come out, spurt out— after two months of this life, I say, boredom and monotony would have disfigured, dumbfounded, and bewildered us both. After two months, that first touch, so gentle, would be turned into the insufferable friction of two bodies torn limb from limb, of two perished souls. I went to get Chateaugué on the Islands because I could no longer stand living alone and didn't want to die right away. Life as one, life when you're alone, can't last more than a week. Now I realize, little by little, that life as two can hardly last longer. Two months and one week make nine weeks. So the longest life lasts nine weeks. You live one week of solitude. You live two months of friendship. After sixty-seven or sixty-eight days of life, you've got to kill yourself or be content merely to survive. Two friends may cheat. They can live together for two hours, leave one another, wait a week, meet up again, live together for another couple of hours, separate once more ... and so forth, until the number of couple of hours totals two months. But waiting is not living. You've got to be duped and not love the intensity and the absolute. I can tell that our friendship is burning, that it's wasting away, that in a short while our friendship will be burned up. I can't cry; it's beyond me. I'm scared. My hands aren't trembling, my eyes are dry, but I'm scared. But when I close my eyes, it seems to me that I can hear myself crying, that someone is crying his heart out, that I'm sitting in my belly and I'm crying. Right now I'm writing. But if I didn't write, I'd do nothing. Armless and legless, I'm sitting. I can't do anything. I suffer from being armless and legless; I suffer so much that my sole desire is to cry. But I can't cry. Writing is the only thing I can do to distract my pain, and I don't like to write. My state is difficult to describe. Everything within me is empty and shattered. My house of dreams, empty, has shattered. My house of friendship, empty, has shattered. My house of lust, empty, has shattered. My house of courage, rotten, will soon shatter. My house of thirst, hunger, and fervour, empty, has shattered. I don't want anything anymore. You can't want the impossible. You can place your hopes in the impossible, so long as you're an imbecile. I have no desire for what is, for what can be. Everything that reaches out toward my hands, whether walls or skies—I don't want any part of them, I don't want to grasp them, I wouldn't know what to do with them. Arms take their orders from the brain, which takes its orders from the soul. My arms would remain immobile if I didn't write, because my brain says nothing to them, because my soul has lost its voice. I'm in an acute state of death. I'm a dead man who takes part whole-bloodedly in his state of death. My story is very gay, very eventful, and hardly cemetery. These lines that I'm writing, I'm writing them against my will. A cadaver has got to strain in order to write. It's not living that I find revolting, it's that my soul asks nothing of me, it's that my hand is constrained. This beer that I'm drinking sickens me; I must force myself to drink it. I am ... against my will. My soul stays steadfastly silent; it wants nothing. I'm forgetting about Chateaugué. I don't want (to want nothing) Chateaugué, for I have her. Do I have her? Have I exhausted her as I've exhausted myself? Do I have doubts about her, and are those doubts keeping me from sinking into the abyss of madness? Is it the sickening desire, the unavowable desire, invisible, inaudible, too well repressed, and neatly tied up in its sack, the desire to play Mr. and Mrs. with her? The vulva of Chateaugué. The war of the Gauls. Chateaugué of the Gauls. The vulva of war. The Gauls of Chateaugué. So many possible combinations … One thing's for sure: Chateaugué has a vulva. She has a vulva the way she has a nose—a villous vulva. I know it, I've seen it. I resemble a pornographer of my acquaintance, Henry Miller. If justice existed, gentle friend, you wouldn't have a libertine traitor for a friend, an adolescent whose face is hypocrisy, whose words are idle talk, and whose underwear is speckled with dried sperm. Chateaugué is sitting on a little green chair next to me and has the sullen and set expression of a pupil given detention. She has a cigar in one hand and a bottle of beer in the other. Come to think of it, she has more the expression of James Bond than the sullen and set expression of a pupil given detention. But she has two expressions. Today we didn't go to the library. We don't like to go to the library as much as we used to. Youse two. Youse two. Youse two. Today, we only used our bikes to go to the restaurant. We don't like to pedal as much as we used to. We're deteriorating. Teriorating. Riorating. In a little while, as usual, Chateaugué will dash toward the skylight, open the window, and vomit wholeheartedly on the nocturnal passerby, if a nocturnal passerby passes by. And she'll come back to sit down while laughing like a lunatic, leaning every which way at once.

"Vomiting is unpleasant," she'll say, "when you're afraid of death. When you're no longer afraid of death, it's pleasant, it's funny. Before, when I vomited, I had the impression that my heart was going to come out through my mouth, and I was afraid of dying. Now who's afraid of dying?"

I have only one presentable pair of pants left. The other is all ripped up. I'm wearing nothing but underwear at the moment. Because, at the moment, my only presentable pair of pants is drying on the clothesline. Yesterday it was my boxers she was washing. Today it's my pants' turn. She was so drunk, she couldn't stand up. She washed them anyway. She went at it tooth and nail. When she's been drinking, she gets on a washing jag. The floor, the door, the calendars, the walls, the ceiling—none of them escaped. A little while ago, perched on the commode, her rag in hand, she was washing the ceiling. All of a sudden, she fell, and the commode fell on top of her. That didn't discourage her. She got back up again, righted the commode, picked up her rag, climbed back up on top of the commode, stood on tiptoe again, and, as though nothing had happened, without changing expression, with no change in her absorbed expression, she kept cleaning the ceiling. That's nothing. Next, she filled up the tub and gave the little green chairs a bath. When I stopped her, she was about to plunge the mattress into the tub, after the commode drawers, the empty beer bottles, and the grandfather clock. I stopped her just in time—she was about to soap down the mattress.

"Take off your pants," she said. "They're all dirty. I'm going to wash them. You'll look clean."

"No!" I cried, full of virile prudery. "Plus, I like wearing dirty pants. Plus, it's none of your business. No! No! That's the last straw!"

She rushed me from the rear, grabbed me by the waist like a wrestler, and pressed her little belly up against my big behind.

"Say yes. Say yes," she said in a languorous voice, her breath reeking of beer. "You'll look clean. We've got to be spotless."

Since I remained immobile and voiceless for one reason or another, she made the most of it. As quick as lightning, she had unbuckled my belt and was unbuttoning me. I barely had time to react. If I hadn't reacted, I'd have been caught with my pants down without even having—in order to console myself—the thought that I put up a fight. I quickly did an about-face, and I tried hard to get away from her, to get the fanatical cleaner that she had turned into under the influence of the beer to let go. We fell to the floor, one on top of the other. We fought. But she was laughing like a lunatic. When they laugh, it's hopeless. I ended up giving in. I relinquished the pants to her. But I insisted on finishing the disrobing all by myself. She washed them with the soap she uses to wash her face. Cats wash their faces with their feet. What do I look like with this long hair on my legs? My legs have become so ugly these last few years! It used to be they didn't sicken me. Where are my legs of yesteryear? I'm repugnant. When I was a child, I ran rapturously with my legs. Today I look at my legs the way you look at the legs of a woman. When you start looking at your legs and find them ugly, there's no point in clinging to the smokestack for dear life—your ship is lost. Chateaugué has beautiful legs; they're polished, silky, and full, like fruit. The skin of her legs is like the skin of an apple—it's so fine and so nude that it shines. My legs are all crooked. Hers, in the evening before going to bed, when she stands at attention to salute O.L.J.C., fit together perfectly; they're so straight that you couldn't slip a piece of paper between them when she joins them to give O.L.J.C. a martial salute. My knees are all scratchy, chapped, and calloused, with dog-eared skin. My knees stand erect on the front of my legs like a rocky mountain on the surface of an island. I have awful knees because I knelt too often when I was a child. Chateaugué knelt as often as I did, since we went to the same church. But a woman doesn't disfigure her knees by kneeling. Chateaugué's knees are beautiful; you can only tell they're there when she bends her legs. This beer, yellow as pee, acrid as uric acid. For Chateaugué, beer is a kind of melted wheat, it's liquid oats, it's yellow as barley. We're not made for dying together. Before, I used to think of Alaska and Labrador, before she was here. Since she's been here, all I can think of is her geography. Two mountains of flesh, teeny-weeny. Her nose is a cape. Her lips are a cavern. In a nightmare that I had recently, I managed to fit my whole head inside her mouth. With my head in her mouth lined with warm velvet, I was like a little bird in its nest, like a little bird in its egg; I was sleeping happily, sleeping softly and safely. I simply loathe women. I have supreme contempt for women. Women are sordid, and everything in me that draws me toward them disgusts me. Women are like dolls. Men who spend their time with women are just like little girls—they spend their time with dolls.

"My doll's prettier than yours."

"No way! Mine's prettier than yours."

Here's another excerpt from the dialogues exchanged in a glance by men as they stroll along the sidewalk with a woman on their arm.

"I bet you don't even have one."

"Mine is cleaner than yours."

"Mine has a prettier wristwatch than yours."

Something very seductive in me commands me not to take any interest in women. Something else, equally strong, pushes me to idolize them, to go down and adore them underground, where they cluster together, where everything's mouldy. Believe it or not, the trash is full of cigars. We bought as many cigars as it took to fill up the trash, just for fun. We have two *Gigis*—one in French and the other in Spanish. She reads a sentence in French and I read it again from the Spanish version. It's just another way to learn Spanish. Why are we learning Spanish? Why did we buy a French-Spanish dictionary? At first, we had the intention of filling up the trash can with French-Spanish dictionaries. "Death is Spanish." That's a line from one of Jacques Brel's songs. We're learning Spanish in order to die properly. If Death is Spanish, the most intelligent way to die is in full possession of Spanish and of one's faculties. Why else would we learn Spanish? Death is Spanish; I'm learning Spanish in order to be in a position to reply to her when I meet her. If Death is Spanish, she doesn't know the first thing about French. We want to die properly, prepared, ready, in top form, all set. We don't want to die lying down or sitting still. We shall receive Death standing up, a dagger in our fists and a dagger in our hearts. "*What is the majesty of that which ends, next to the staggering departures, the disorders of the dawn?*" We read that in *Gigi*, while learning Spanish. Here's how we reply to Colette: "What are departures while staggering, next to departures while running?" I don't want to leave staggering and hesitating, but rather in an alert way, with gusto. We aren't thirsty, Chateaugué and I, and we're drinking bottles of beer by the dozen. Chateaugué taps her belly, her little belly full of beer, and her little belly full of beer makes the sound of an empty barrel, of the bottom of a barrel where there's no more maple sap. The sap house was in the middle of the woods; we used to go there, sinking up to our bellies in the melting snow. Behind us, the big holes from our steps would fill up with black water, the black water of the snowmelt. Now she has hair under her arms and I have hair all over my legs. Where are our legs of yesteryear? They've gone the way of the snows they sank into. Where are the legs we'd walk on to get to the sap house? Where are they, for me to kiss, for me to adore? *Sugar* in Spanish? *Azucar. "Azucar! Azucar!"* That's what we'd shout at Death. Death knows what that means, *azucar.* Yesterday we went to see a film in Spanish with English subtitles. *The Exterminating Angel,* or *T.E.A.,* as the Americans say. In the film, they were all speaking Spanish. The only thing we understood was *azucar.* They said it two or three times, *azucar.*

"Sugar!" Chateaugué would cry out each time that one of them would say *azucar.* "Sugar!" she would cry in my ear, while elbowing me in the ribs.

There's not much beauty in that film. Chateaugué liked the bear that walks through the empty house, down the corridors of the beautiful house. Also, she was impressed by the scene where the woman who has feathers and hen feet in her purse opens her purse to take out her handkerchief in order to blow her nose. It's not a very sexual film. I wonder what accounts for its renown. It probably comes on the rebound, since the other films by the same director were not recommended. No use adding that I don't know anything about movies. I didn't understand a thing in *T.E.A.* There were some in the theatre who understood. They were easy to spot—every time they understood something, they raised their hands, like intelligent and zealous pupils.

"The door opened; there was no danger; why were they afraid to go out? Why did they suddenly all go out, as if they had never been afraid to go out?"

"Come on! Come on, you blockheads! Can't you see, it's because of the virgin. The exterminating angel spares virgins. And in the end, the virgin from the beginning was no longer a virgin. It's like Noah in his ark with his frogs. He came across Mount Ararat by chance. The boat was merrily rowing gently down the stream with a dreamy fly on its mast. That's why flies rush out where angels fear to tread."

When we've left childhood behind, there's no way to go anywhere without sickening yourself. Licentiousness lying feigning pretending intending misunderstanding prefer me over the others. Convinced that her chair has caught her intoxication and her loss of balance, that her chair's wobbling and that it's going to give way, Chateaugué gets off her chair and sits on the floor. On the floor, she drinks beer and burps. Do you know the one about the man who, each time he burped, would say, "I'm burping"? He was a writer; he wrote plays. He thought he was in the theatre. He'd say, "I'm burping," each time he burped so that everyone would understand that he was burping, even those who were at the back of the auditorium. When he was alone, that didn't stop him—he'd say, "I'm burping," anyway. French-Canadian snobs don't say *theatre*, but *theatuh*. They're such goddamn comedians. There's a "theatuh" on the street corner, over where the asphalt is worn down and lets the bricks peek through, an avant-garde "theatuh." Since all human beings are fleeing, those who are in the avant-garde are the ones who are fleeing the fastest. But that truth is not a verified truth; it is therefore an unverifiable truth. That truth is therefore nothing more than something that I couldn't stop myself from saying, nothing more than a human truth. Now Chateaugué, after each burp, cries, "*Alrededor!*" She acts as if she were already facing Death, or she's practising to be ready to face up to her. *Alrededor* is a beautiful Spanish word that just means around, round about, or in the vicinity of. Such a beautiful, sonorous word to signify so little!

"They committed suicide after learning Spanish, because we found a French-Spanish dictionary and some Spanish novels in their arms."

They won't be witty enough to write that in their newspapers. They don't have a real sense of humour. They'll assume a solemn air and will take advantage of it to cast a stone in the direction of our dear deputies. The democratic regime is not good, they'll write, since all the adolescents commit suicide mercilessly. Such goddamn comedians. And they'll be deeply moved, thinking that we made the most of our isolation to spend our time copulating. I'm a sex maniac. But I do have the good sense to commit suicide. There's a gypsy tune entitled "What News?" in French that Chateaugué is just now slobbering a very personal version of.

"What nudes? Any nudes? What nudes? Any nudes? What nudes? Any nudes? What nudes? Any nudes? What nudes? Any nudes? What nudes? Any nudes? ..."

She sings sadly while slobbering. Might she be sad, all of a sudden? She feels me looking at her: her face lights up again. A joyful laugh makes her teeth and eyes sparkle. I don't know what she thinks, what she's thinking about, what she thinks about me and this whole production. She says nothing. She keeps her still waters running deep within her, if she has any. She has some. She speaks only to say nothing, when she does speak. A strange fact that I was going to forget to relate: last night, while coming back from the bathroom, I saw, in the dark, trickles of tears glistening on her cheeks. She was dead to the world, she was snoring, and a trickle of tears was glistening on the side of her nose. She's strong—she says nothing.

"Okey-dokey!" she said when I asked her whether she wanted to commit suicide with me.

Okey-dokey is in Eskimo language. Maybe she doesn't want to commit suicide. Maybe she's never wanted to commit suicide. Maybe we're not committing suicide swiftly enough for her. Who knows? What does this easily amused sphinx think? She seems to understand everything, to take part. Maybe she doesn't understand anything. By human truth, I mean a truth that is truth only for the one who speaks it. I'm doing my little Camus act. I'm sick and tired of the word *suicide* and its derivatives. Henceforth, I'll use another word. I give the dictionary to Chateaugué. I tell her to open the dictionary at random and to read me the first word from the left-hand column of the left-hand page. She starts clowning around. She claims not to know which left is in question. She looks up the word *left* in the dictionary.

"The left part of a painting," she reads, "corresponds to the left of a spectator located across from it. The left part of a building," she continues, "corresponds to the left of a spectator turning his back to the façade."

She pretends to start thinking this over.

"This dictionary isn't a building," she reasons. "Therefore, it's a painting. This dictionary isn't a painting; therefore, it's a building. Therefore, where is the left-hand column of the left-hand page?"

After reasoning like this for several years, she finally gives me the word that I asked her for.

"Hurly-burly."

Therefore, we won't commit suicide, we'll hurly-burly ourselves. Which word will I use if I ever need the word *hurly-burly* in the sense of hurly-burly? For my purpose here is to enlighten, not to confuse. I must therefore make sure not to let any ambiguity slip in. I'll think about all that tomorrow, *mañana*. My left eye hurts. There's something stuck in the mucous membrane of my eyelid, some kind of tiny speck, pointed, rough, and obstinate. It's like a little sliver of broken glass, but it's not a little sliver of broken glass. If it were a sliver of broken glass, my eye would have been scratched ages ago, and my eye isn't scratched at all. Glass scratches eyes, the way diamonds scratch glass.

"Poor you!" she cries. "Yikes! Your eye is all red already all red-eye."

She's alarmed. She wants to come to my rescue and lavish care on me. She stands up. She can't come to my rescue as fast as she'd like to. She can't even stay on her feet. She collapses. She drags herself along. She crawls in order to bring me help. She drags herself to the bathroom and comes back, supporting herself on the partitions that are located along the way. Now she's falling again. She fell flat on her face this time. In the bathroom, she moistened the bottom of her dress with cold water. She applies that to my irritated, inflamed eye. It's good. All of the stinging pain dissolves in the sensation of cold; I feel metallic twinges and taut threads melting in my head, becoming absorbed, draining away. Never have I loved my sister Chateaugué so much.

"I'm so hot!" she cries, all of a sudden.

Now she's hot. She's too hot. She takes off her nylons, her shoes, her dress, and her bra. She sits back down on the floor and starts drinking again. Our bottles of beer are no longer as cold as when we got them, but they're still cold. Chateaugué thinks about that, and, while falling and getting back up again, she comes over to press the bottom of her bottle on my poor eye, which has begun to burn again. I close my eyes in order to fully feel the voluptuousness of my eye no longer hurting. But Chateaugué holds the half-full bottle upside down, and all the beer flows onto her, spills all over her and spreads out on the floor. She doesn't mind. She lets it flow without a care in the world. Flow, beer. Suddenly, she takes an interest in the phenomenon, and, with the riveted gaze that is the exclusive domain of the drunkard, forgetting my eye, she dedicates herself to it, devotes herself to it. She opens all the remaining bottles of beer and empties them, one by one, onto the floor. I let her do as she likes. The more your eye hurts, the more indifferent you are to everything. The drunker you are, the funnier everything seems. Her labour complete—one of the seven labours of Chateaugué— she sits down in it. She sits down in the beer, stretching her legs all the way out in the puddle of beer. She's so tired that her eyes close all by themselves. I take her in my arms, I carry her, I put her on the bed. She sleeps. Exceedingly beautiful, she sleeps. And she smells like beer. Broad rivers of beer with big round heads advance slowly down the corridor, down the hall, bound for the stairs—broad, flat rivers. I'm not sorry about it. Having all that beer left to drink was putting me in a bad mood. Chateaugué is talking in her sleep. I lean over, the better to see her speak.

"Fourteen plus sixteen is thirty. Since you're sixteen years old and I'm fourteen years old, we're thirty years old. We're thirty years old, you and I. I'm not fourteen years old, and you're not sixteen years old; I'm thirty years old, and you're thirty years old. We're one and the same thing, one and the same person. We have the same age and the same name, the same hair, and a single head on a single neck. We have the same name. Why two names for the same thing? We are Tate. Tate. Tate. Call me Tate. I'll call you Tate. Come, Tate. Yes, Tate. Let's be on our way,

Tate. Yes, Tate, let's be on our way. Tate's on its way, hand in hand. Tate sleeps together, smokes together, drinks together. Come sit here, Tate, next to me. Stop writing this bullshit, Tate. He who has a Tate's not lost."

Has a Tate ... He's a Tate ... Hesitate. The more she speaks, the more quickly she speaks, and the more she garbles her words. She speaks too quickly; I no longer understand a word of what she's saying. Chateaugué, Eskimo blonde and pink, Eskimo slender and small, my dear sister through rain and snow, blonde as a dawn, as the one that's breaking ... The date? I don't know.

16

In the valley of the green fish,
In the navy blue of the harvests,
A young woman and a dog
Walk hand in hand.

An avalanche swallows them
Along the path of the horse.
They are encoffined in arborvitae,
Just like Penelope and Phaedra.

Go by there tomorrow morning,
Young girl. And if you come back,
Under your beautiful long hair of iron,
You shall have been in hell.

All the children for miles around
Decide to take a trip
Along the path of the horse,
Which leads to the land of evil.

It's that age; it's death in the soul,
Death in the man and in the woman.
It's that age; it's true sadness,
The one where tenderness flickers out
And with it, the flame of the drama.

I was quite right to be leery of automobiles. A little while ago,
coming back in the rain from the System, we were almost killed
at the hands of an automobile. To hurly-burly oneself—okay.
But to be killed, to die against one's will—never! Oh! How

awful! How decadent! My bike only has brakes on the rear wheel. What's more, they're bad brakes. Even applied all the way, they do nothing but lick the rim. When it rains, these brakes have no effect; the bike keeps merrily rolling along, as though nothing had happened. Chateaugué's bike was equipped with excellent brakes, with good year-round brakes, with those archaic brakes that you apply by reversing the direction of the pedals. The late, great bike of Chateaugué was equipped with responsive, quick, efficient, superb brakes, ready to act all the time, on the qui vive day and night, good under every imaginable atmospheric condition. So, we had just seen three great films at the System. It was cold, it was raining, and our teeth were chattering. Pedalling hard, we had gone down Sainte-Catherine until we hit Saint-Denis, and at Saint-Denis we had turned right. Everything up until then had unfolded without incident. Everything was fine. As usual, we had been reviled by all the automobiles going down Sainte-Catherine along with us.

"Get outta the street!"

"Go to bed!"

"You've got a screw loose."

"Go find your mother and see if she's looking for you."

"Carburetor trouble?"

The foul language of automobiles is well known; I won't take a stand. Our frozen handlebars were freezing our naked hands. Our hair was full of cold rain running down our faces. Our teeth were chattering and we were pedalling. Everything was fine. We were eager to find ourselves once more in the warm softness of the room, and the room was getting closer and closer. About a block away from Dorchester, the traffic lights of the boulevard as broad as a river twinkled their good-to-go wink at us. We had just enough time to make it through. We stood up on our pedals and poured it on. Safe and sound, we reached the other side. Everything was fine. Everything was as usual, except that it was raining and we were frozen. True-blue and silent, Chateaugué was following me. Her eyes in a state of contemplation, her face still quite puffy and set from the movies, Chateaugué, behind me, was clenching her jaws so that her teeth would chatter less. We always come up on Craig gently. It's another of those rivers and it's the worst—green light or red light, the automobiles launch an attack all at the same time on the thirty cardinal points. But at that moment, we were frozen, we were in a hurry, and we were in no mood to take the time to be careful. The signal had been green for a long time, but it wouldn't change; it seemed determined only to change when I'd made up my mind to run the risk of crossing. I was saturated with frozen water—I had no time for playing around. At about twenty feet from the intersection, I closed my eyes and gave four enormous pedal pushes to my mount. When I reopened my eyes, it was almost too late—on the poles of all four corners, the lights were blazing their brightest red; on all sides, restive automobiles, pawing the ground, whinnying, and massed face-to-face like two enemy legions, were about to leap up, were already leaping up. Panic-stricken, I slammed on my brakes. Nothing. Air. I quickly looked back, saw Chateaugué stopped, regained·my composure, and resumed speed. My heart was thumping, the automobiles were stampeding, and I heard Chateaugué shrieking, shrieking. I was caught between the lips of a gaping maw, on the brink of an abyss lined with teeth that were going to snap shut, that were triggered, that were going to bite, to tear me to shreds and crush me to death. But all of a sudden, as if by a miracle, I was coming out of it, I had left it behind. Thinking only of myself, of my own salvation, and of my miraculous luck, I was going to collapse or gloat, when suddenly, upon turning my head, the memory of Chateaugué tragically came back to me. A red automobile, a frisky little European, even more jealous than the others of its right of passage, was skidding off to the side at top speed, screeching victory from every tire, and swooping down on Chateaugué. Due to the force of the shock, Chateaugué, the only living thing in the midst of this motorized football game, was taking wing. She was gambolling through the air. She was moonlanding, lying in a pool of blood at the edge of the sidewalk, huddled up, enormous, immense with gravity, and larger than a mountain. At once, I let my bike drop beneath me, abandoned the vehicle then and there, flew over, flung myself on

Chateaugué, who was already groaning, grabbed hold of her by the shoulders, and shook her the way you shake a carpet. What had come over her? All this? So quickly? All this blood? Mother Nature had made a mistake; she had let something impossible happen; she had been violated; she was unhinged and out of her mind. I shook my sister with all my strength so that the state that had left her, through some blunder, might come back, to make her come back to her true state, her true air, her inoffensive sweetness, her sweet innocuousness, her astonished airs, and her cheerful young animal ways. That's when everything took a tragic turn, a serious turn, as if on stage. That's when Montreal herself put on cothurni. That's when I myself began to declaim. Leaning over her, I looked at her fixedly, implored her with all the strength my eyes could muster, beseeched her to think better of it. I gathered her together. I loaded her into my arms. Leaving my bike in the middle of the street, not even feeling her weight, I started to run. The busybodies were multiplying like mushrooms and pursuing me. Police officers arrived on the scene, intercepting me. I shouted at them to leave us alone, that this was none of their business. I didn't know which end was up. I lost awareness and got it back. I found myself here, there, and everywhere, without remembering that I'd moved. I had Chateaugué in my arms; she was bleeding like a stuck pig. I was on the stairs, I had Chateaugué in my arms; people were following me. I was before the door of the room, I had run faster than Horatius Cocles, I was bathed in sweat, she was bathed in blood, blood was dripping from her hair; they were still following me. I had laid Chateaugué on the bed, and the room was teeming with people, full of strangers. I had managed to chase them away by showering them with kicks, for I found myself once again alone with her, as before, as it ought to be. She opened her eyes; my hands were full of blood.

"You're bleeding, Miles Miles?"

"No, Chateaugué; it's you who's bleeding."

"It's me who's bleeding. I don't care if it's me who's bleeding."

She closed her eyes again. I thought of my bike and of hers—of mine, alone in the night, alone on the asphalt, lying on its side and abandoned, and of hers, twisted and dead. I had to go get my bike. I couldn't let her spend the night alone in the middle of the road. I thought of the intense emotions that she had experienced. I thought of the dangers that had just stalked her—the murderous hatred of the automobiles, the irreplaceable loss of the sweet sister Chateaugué. I just about cried. I went back to get my trusty and gentle bike and came back to the room with her. The police and the doctor were there once more. They were bending over the bed; they were auscultating Chateaugué. I leapt up, made a beeline for them, and flung myself on them. I yelled, trembling all over; I enjoined them to leave us alone, to leave her alone. I yelled at them that we wanted nothing from them, that she wanted nothing. I felt infinitely ridiculous all of a sudden. Why was I mixed up in all this, in all these theatrics? The doctor and the police officers were pestering me with questions, and I was replying seriously, stammering with solemnity. How ridiculous it all was. We had fallen into a booby trap. They were in our room like whores in a cathedral, like maggots in a tabernacle. I had lost all desire to laugh. At last, they left. But they haven't left all the way. They've discovered the nest. They've climbed up, they've taken the eggs in their hands, they've explored these sacred eggs like the fuckers they are; the eggs will be forever sullied. Men's eyes have drawn near to our little green chairs, to our partitions, to Nelligan; their eyes have explored; their simoniacal eyes have annihilated the magic. They've left, but we don't feel as hidden as before anymore. Now that they know where we're hiding, it's as though all the doors were open, as though the snow were coming in through all the windows, as though our souls were naked and the wind were blowing on them—we're cold, soul cold. They'll be back. They know the way. They're on to us. The door is open now, and the wind cuts right to the sick heart of our friendship. For so many months, we were walking alone in the desert; we thought we were sheltered, walled in, locked up tight, and very far away. All at once, they swooped down on us. Suddenly the desert is invaded and occupied. I'm dramatizing. All those strangers in our room!

"She's my sister. We go to grad school."

Grad school! Sweet Jesus! How ridiculous I felt! But we were tracked down. Everything had fallen through. To them we were nothing but two suspicious children, two nameless children not living with their parents. I had to invent, clear my throat, be shy, charm, speak, and gesticulate. I had to defend us, like it or not; I had to have us acquitted, for lack of evidence, of what, in secret, we were so proud of; I had to take part in society; I had to play their game by their rules, the degrading game, their god-damn game. We were tracked down, caught *in flagrante delicto* of living in holy solitude.

"No, she doesn't live here. She's staying with friends on Rue Saint-Hubert, not far from here. I'll take her back there in a little while, when she's better. You can leave now. She's not badly hurt. I'll take care of everything."

"Parents' name telephone number how many brothers and sisters how long have you been in town what is the number of her house on Rue Saint-Hubert your date of birth are you Catholic or Protestant are you Negro or white were you born in Canada where were you baptized the maiden name of your grandmother you're sure that she's your sister and that your parents know that you live in a room in town do you have any scars where are your student notebooks students go to school without books and without pencils now everything's changing science insurance progress communism ..."

I write. How ridiculous! Why don't I toss this pen in the trash? This ink, why don't I drink it? Order has been restored to the room, and soon it will be daybreak. We won't leave this room. We won't give up. It's in this room that we'll hurly-burly ourselves, nowhere else. We'll hurly-burly ourselves? ... It may be too late, now that they've found us, now that they've come to play in our coffin, now that they know. They know ... Well, then, let 'em know! Let 'em come back! Let 'em put their balls and chains on our feet! Let 'em come with their big wooden shoes! Let 'em fuel their own suspicions! After all, we really don't give a hoot about them, we really don't give two hoots about them, and we certainly won't give three hoots about them once we get our strength back. I've torn off all the adhesive tape that the doctor of doctoring wrapped around her head. I made her other bandages with rags that I found in a cupboard in the bathroom. The bastards! The scumbags! Chateaugué is sitting on the edge of her butt on the side of the bed. She's whiter than ever.

"What are we going to do, Miles Miles? Are we going to go away from here?"

"We're staying here."

"What if they come back ... Why don't we kill ourselves right away, before they come back? Let's rent another room if you don't want us to kill ourselves right away."

"We're staying here. Let 'em come back!"

Then, with great animation, we start talking about the accident, our tongues wagging like gossips.

"What got into you? I look back; you're stopped, you're waiting. I think everything's okay, I pour it on, I manage to make it through. I look back again; you're getting hit. You braked when the light changed; why did you start up again?"

"Poor Miles Miles ... I don't know, I have no idea. I couldn't help it. It was the only thing to do. I was sure that you were going to get yourself killed. I wasn't about to stand there stock-still, watching you get killed, watching them kill you. I said to myself, I'll get myself killed, too, and the bike started up all by itself. I was shrieking, shrieking. What would I have done, all alone, with you dead? I didn't mull it over for long. I closed my eyes and let myself go. Then I went head over heels. Ow, my back hurts! I was so scared. I'm so glad. Your hands are full of blood. Give me your hands."

Chateaugué's hair is full of blood. She pets my hand the way you pet a cat. Her hands are bathed in sweat—she who always has dry hands. She pours out her heart while stroking one of my hands. Her eyes are brimming with tears.

"Miles Miles. Miles Miles. Miles Miles Miles Miles Miles Miles Miles Miles. I thought I was dead. As I woke up, I heard your voice. You said, 'She's my sister,' it's true. I've never heard anything more ... more ... beautiful ... It pleased me so, I felt like crying. It relieved me so, I felt like laughing. It reassured me so, I sort of deflated—whoosh ... like when all the air comes out of a balloon. You said, 'She's my little sister.' You were stammering."

"Wouldn't you like to be my little sister?"

She starts laughing and blushing. I've peed in my pants. It's true. I just just noticed it. It must have happened in the heat of the moment. I must stink. I must smell like carp. I have a headache; I just just noticed it. Chateaugué gets up and tries her legs. She totters. She's a little weak in the knees, as they say. She no longer has a bike. It was no longer there when I went to get mine. Skiing. Skiing. Why am I thinking of skiing, all of a sudden? On the Islands, in the springtime, when the floodwaters had receded, there were more carp in the stream than there was water. When the water went down, the stream was cut off from the river, and all the carp in the world got caught in it. We could fish heaping shovelfuls of them. We could catch them with our hands. The adults said that they weren't any good, that they weren't edible. But they were beautiful and golden. It was intoxicating, thousands of fish, big fish, in a rivulet. The snow would melt, the water would rise, and the vale would fill up and overflow onto the road. There'd be water in the basement; it was as if we were on a boat. There'd be water under the floor; the water would visit us. We'd go to school in the water; we'd walk on water. There'd be a foot of water on the road. We'd sail our boats along the risen riverside, boats that we dangled from the ends of our arms when we were tired of making them float. We'd construct a raft for ourselves every year. It was a real boat. We could have drowned. There were some who had drowned while navigating by raft. The higher the water, the happier we were. When we got up, we'd run to the window to see how far the water had come. When the water started to subside, it was horrible. Goddamnit! Now all that is bad literature, reminiscence, nonsense, the past, the overpast, the trespast—downgraded, downsized, honey for flies, rhubarb for pigs. It's all over now. Can't go back for seconds. What is the present? Here is the present: I'm sitting down, sitting tight, and all that I have is done for. If I weren't sitting down, I'd be standing up, standing tall, standing comfortably, like Alexander, Xerxes, Joan of Arc, or Saint Lucy of Alexandria. If I weren't standing up, I'd be lying down, lying low, lying low-down, like Brigitte Bardot, like anybody. The present is only beautiful once it has passed, and once it's past it is no longer.

The present is only conjugated with us in the past; the only time it's not boring is when it's in the past. The present, when it's in the present, never finds us doing anything except sitting down doing nothing, standing up doing nothing, or lying down biting our nails. Standing, sitting, or lying down, the only interesting thing you can do is think about the past. When the present is the past, you can regret it bitterly. Bitterness—it's the only thing of any interest, the only thing that's worth the trouble, the only thing strong enough to test your mettle. You can do nothing but bitterly regret the past. Even what was gay is bitter now and will stay bitter. The sweetest memories are the bitterest. Bitterness is the only way to play tricks on boredom. Boredom isn't even bitter. When the present passes, you can do nothing but watch it pass; even if you were to fling yourself in front of it, it wouldn't stop. But when the present is past, you can regret it, you can suffer softly, softly, softly. That's very profound, but it doesn't mean anything. It just came out of my pen, that's all. I'm doing my little Jean Racine act, my little La Rochefoucauld act, my little La Fontaine act, my goddamn little comedian act. It's not true. Nothing is true. Everything's done for, nothing exists anymore, everything has passed—passed or coming to pass. There's no future in the future, only what comes to pass. Everything is past, but everything is present; it's the softly or unbearably suffocating presence of the past. I'm not present; it's the past that is present—it's the presence before me of the absent, of my absent ones. I am nothing. I'm not even true. All I'm doing is The True Being, with the capital letters representing "the past." That's quite profound, The True Being. It's pretty goddamn abstract. This is nothing—I could go on like this for hundreds of pages. If I wanted to go on like this for hundreds of pages, I'd make myself right at home, I'd ask nobody's permission. The others make themselves right at home. It's making sentences. Sentences—they're nothing. Words— they're hardly even visible. In some dictionaries, they're so small that you've got to arm yourself with a telescope. Here comes Chateaugué back from her little walk in the hall. Chateaugué—now there's something. Something ... is what? It's like fire on the water that is me, it's water on the fire that I am; it's an action on me. Chateaugué is not a word but an action. Is that clear? Is that clear enough? Something! Chit-chat! Shit-shat! *Chit-chat* comes from chatting and *shit-shat* comes from shitting. The more subtle it is, the more profound it is, the more in-depth it is; the farther it is from the surface of the earth, the further it is from the truth. This last sentence is false. There is a kind of true depth; there are presences that affect a man in depth. We shall call the penetrating presences Esso presences. The Esso presences are like the Esso soap, the detergent that works deep into the dirt. Who hasn't heard of Esso soap? Some people have heard of Esso soap and have never heard of Brigitte Bardot, a human being. I invented the Esso presences. Give me the patent! Give it here! Chateaugué is a living illustration of my Esso presences—presences whose origin and destination are the past. Sentences are a vivid illustration of no presence whatsoever. Chateaugué ... Chateaugué is watching me write, watching me trace the letters of her name. She seems quite discouraged to see me write her name. I have her before me, why do I need to write her name? Between the strips of repugnant trimmings with which I've mummified her head, whatever humanity is left in her is quite discouraged and quite astonished. Her forehead has been wrapped with rags under my care, there, there. Life: to see clearly, to feel calm. For the philosophers, everything is clear, everything is correct, everything is understood, everything is tidy. To understand everything. That must take a lot of blindness, a lot of deafness, a lot of missing clairvoyance. Life: to see within it clearly. Everything in our room is clear, calm, and correct. Everything in our room rests, sleeps, and lets itself be grasped and understood. I won't leave this room. We mustn't leave our room. Outside, everything shrieks, everything swarms, everything mingles and astounds us. I love our room. Everything is so clear and calm in our room. The dimensions of our room contain the maximum amount of space and objects that I can understand at once, that I can consider without terrifying, exhausting, or leading my eyes and reason into despair. My ideas about what my room does not contain—about the rest—are obscure and obscuring, agitated and agitating, entangled and entangling, short-circuited and electrifying, unbearable and unborne. The bigger it is, the livelier it is, the more people there are—the less I understand. For me to understand perfectly, it's got to be really small and it can't move. *Understand* is not what I mean. I'd have to use another word, a word more directly associated with ideas of clarity, prehension, serenity, unity of action, and hospitality. Hundreds of these words must exist; I know none of them. In our room, I'm at home. Outside, I'm in the void. And the void takes, seizes, and inhales. In the eyes of Chateaugué, it's worse than outdoors. The sparkle of her eyes, their modest sparkle, does not shed light, it blinds. Their luminous warmth is black; it radiates from the shocks of the nights that mingle with it, press together in it, squeeze in with it. Her eyes are not so pale or so slightly grey as they seem to be. The essences of nothingness and darkness are concentrated there, and it's from there that they rise and are propagated. And it's there, in her gaze, that the sun grows dim and asphyxiates. I look into Chateaugué's eyes, and I have a taste for taking, embracing, conquering, and subjugating. The void forces its way in, forces my hand; the force of the void incites me to violence, to revolt. I look at Chateaugué and one word seizes my throat: kiss. I imagine that I'm kissing Chateaugué, and a taste of wine swells my lips—the taste of her mouth. *Kiss.* I won't let myself be talked into that word. I don't really feel like kissing her. If the word *kiss* didn't exist, I wouldn't even feel like kissing her. I have one word in my head. One word keeps going round and round in my head. There's a fly zooming and buzzing around in my head: the word *kiss.* You can't do anything about a word; it's a fly that you may shoo away, and that may leave, but it always comes back and never dies. If I obey the word *kiss,* if I kiss Chateaugué, then I must bear the yoke of the flies. What? Let the flies lay down the law? What? A word, an academic parasite, comes to me out of nowhere, and I'd obey it—I'd follow it the way fire on the tail of a cat follows the cat, the way the cart attached to the horse follows the horse? You've got to think it over before obeying a word. After thinking it over, I realize that I would regret having kissed Chateaugué. Because our friendship must remain chaste and vegetal, mineral and puerile. Because that's how I want it, how everything wants it; because the face that I want to present to heaven and earth requires it. Why? Why? Why? Life isn't ready-made; I have to be ready to make it; I'm ready-making it; I'm ready-making it mine. I have in my head the image of my life the way the carpenter has in his head the image of his table. When my life is made, that's how it will be, that's the face it will have. The carpenter works according to a plan; he doesn't surrender himself to chance. The proud carpenter is proud of saying that he knows what he's doing, that what he's doing will be the way he wants it to be. You've got to live the way you'd like to live, according to laws and measures, according to the laws and measures of the one you want to become. You don't surrender yourself to chance. You don't surrender yourself—you struggle. You're born surrendered to chance, and it's by creating yourself that you render yourself free, by creating your life. The sculptor who brings out the bust that he wants from the incomprehensible thing, from the black thing that is a bed of marble, is the perfect image of the man who brings out the soul that he wants from the running void (think of running water), from the mighty night that is life. Shit-shat! Chit-chat! Miss Inference! Sir Cumference! Vicious circle! Vitiating circle! Everything that is me is safe, saved from the nothingness. Everything that is mine, I snatched from the fog where the other men are evolving. Everything that I have, I took; I'm not going through it anymore; I snatched it, and everything that we snatch snatches us from the unknown. There's a bottle of ink on my table. Before, it was nothing but a bottle of ink among the billions of bottles of ink that wait in the darkness and freeze when you brush past them. Now it's my bottle of ink, it's the one I dip my pen in, the one I sometimes feel like drinking, the one that has a face whose image and taste I have in my head. It's a bottle of ink that I bought at Lozeau's. It was given to me dead. I brought it back to life. Hello, My Miss Bottle of Ink! How are you? This ashtray is Our Mr. Ashtray. He was here when we arrived; if we hadn't come to live here, we never would have met him. He acts as a coffin for the skeletons of the cigars and cigarettes that we smoke together; he's the only one who acts as a coffin for the cadavers of our matches. Do you know

Our Mr. Ashtray? Surely. This notebook? Yes, I am familiar with it; I'm the one who wrote every word in it. This room, these partitions? Yes, I know; I understand; I'm familiar with them; we're the ones who live in them. This table? Yes, I know; my fingers have scoured this table's every joint; for my fingers, this table is like a canvas to a painter; there are billions of tables on earth, and this table is the only one that I happen to be resting my elbows on right now. The world? No, *désolé, très désolé*; go ask someone else; I'm not familiar with it; consult your dictionary; ask one of those citizens of the world; I'm just a citizen of our room. Physics? No, I'm not the one who made it; I don't have a clue; I'm completely baffled by it. Chemistry? I've never set foot there. Arizona? Is that in Chinese? Me? Who am I? I don't know; I happened to be there when I arrived; I'm still here. Life? I don't know; I found it there when I was born; but I have every intention of making my life out of it; but when I've finished, it will be my life; when I found it, it was chance. Victor Hugo? Who's he? A miserable writer. (Play on words with *Les Misérables*. Those who know Victor Hugo reply: *Les Misérables*.) Is Pagnol a dog? (Play on words with *spaniel*.) Chateaugué? I'm not really sure; she's my friend; she'll be my friend if I do a good job on her; before, when I didn't know her face, it was water in the unknown ocean, tenebrae in the unknown world. Who's saying all this stupid stuff? Me.

17

We're smoking Cuban cigars while eating chips. At each drag, vertiginously, our courage fails us. Smoking a cigar while masticating substances saturated with salt beats all the vertigos and bewilders all the senses. Inhaling a deep drag of acrid smoke while your mouth is full of salted nourishment seizes, seizes the soul with cold gloves, reaches the ethereal within you with the shock of an ice cube. Each inhalation of acrid smoke is an abortive blackout, an abortive blackout of the world, an abortion of the blacking out of this world. It's as if, all of a sudden, we had nothing left under our feet, nothing left under our skin, nothing left in our arteries, nothing left in our bodies. Chateaugué pipes up, sitting on one arm of my armchair.

"How about if we call each other Tate and add up our ages?"

"Have you seen the *ow* in h*ow*? Have you seen the *ad* in *add*? Have you seen the *sage* in *ages*?"

"You're looking at what I'm saying. You're not even listening to what I'm saying."

"I heard. You'd like us to call each other Tate ... Didn't you mention that the other night, in your dream?"

"I wasn't dreaming. Was I sleeping? I thought I wasn't dreaming. I thought I was living as usual and that we were talking together as usual."

I tell her that her wish is my command, and that from now on, we'll be called Tate.

"Do you know why animals live, Chateaugué?"

"No."

"Because they can't do anything else. The robot who might like to stop himself wouldn't be able to."

"You wake up in the morning, and you find yourself alive. I've never been able to get used to that. What makes me alive, there in my bed every morning? What puts me at my service every morning, I who have nothing to do? I'm like a clock— I'm wound up. All I have to do is mark time. Who wants to know what time it is?"

"There's an engine in Tate. There's an engine in the elm. There's a heart in the automobiles. We're all windup toys, like automatons."

"Except the stones."

"The elm, even if it wanted to, wouldn't be able to break its engine. It has to wait for its engine to break all by itself."

"But Tate can take an axe to its engine, if it wants to."

"Tate is a brilliant subject."

"Tate is not one, but two, two brilliant subjects. We are two within a single thing."

"Which thing, Chateaugué?"

"Tate. Tate is something like our room, something that gathers us together and locks us up tight, that binds us together, all alone under heaven. Don't call me Chateaugué anymore; call me Tate."

"Tate, you're doing your little Juliet."

"Tate, I'll do whatever you want, anything you want."

Chateaugué stops laughing, lowers her head, and hides her eyes with her eyelids. Suddenly, with a flick of her eyelids and a flick of her head, she seizes me with her eyes, she grabs hold of me with her gaze, she asks me for something with the colour of her eyes in a language that I'm not familiar with. She has never looked at me that way. She has caught me with her gaze and has got me where she wants me, holding tight as if she were afraid I might escape. What does she want? What is she not saying out loud? She stops staring at me, hides her face by turning her head, and laughs like a child who feels uncomfortable laughing, like a child who knows that she shouldn't laugh but who can't help laughing. She's sitting on one arm of my armchair; she's so embarrassed about what she has done, about the way she just looked at me, that she nearly falls flat on her back. She catches hold of my neck to keep from falling. She says she's crazy. She presses one of her cheeks against one of mine. She does that often. When she does that, I'm scared stiff that I'll blush. I pray the good Lord to grant me the grace not to blush when she presses her head covered with hair against my head of close-cropped hair. When my ears sting, I know that my ears are turning red, and I'm mad at myself. Women make me melt when they play at being women. I am not a man, a real man, a gorilla of a man; I'm unworthy of the beard that I'm growing.

"Why Tate?" I say, seeking to create a diversion. "Why not another name?"

Once more, on her initiative, our cheeks are joined. Of the two cheeks, mine is the one that's burning. Hers is as cold as ice.

"Why Tate? ... Well ... I don't know. When I was quite little, in New Quebec, in Port Burwell, the Eskimo language was the one I spoke, like all the little Eskimo boys and girls. Now I've forgotten. All that remains is a single word in Eskimo language, and I think of it often. The word is *tateka*, *tate*. *Tate* is the same thing as *tateka*. In French, *horse* is the same thing as *horses*. I don't know what *tateka* means anymore. I mean, I can't translate *tateka* into French. But I know that it means something beautiful, very beautiful and very, very happy. When I'm sad, I think of tateka the way I think of something I've lost—I call for tateka. When I'm happy, I think of tateka the way I think of something I've gained. Maybe it means *sun*, maybe *fire*, maybe *whale*, maybe *maman*."

"Maman! Good grief! Whale ... Were your parents whale hunters?"

"I don't know. I think so. Because when I see a whale, it's as if I hadn't seen it for a long time, as if I were meeting up with it again."

"When you see a whale ... When do you see whales? I've never seen any whales, and we're always together."

"I see whales when I dream. I also see them in the newspapers, in books, at the movies."

"You're not a real Eskimo. You're blonde, your face is narrow, and you don't have almond-shaped eyes."

"You're trying to hurt my feelings; I don't care. Plus, you know, Tate plus Tate equals Tates, our own united Tates, our combined estates."

"Who will inherit Tate's Estates?"

"Let me meditate ... Why, the late, great Tate! Because what's yours is ours, because your room is our room."

We've never talked so much at one time. She lets herself slide down to the cushion of the armchair, between the arm of the armchair and me.

"The closer I am to you, the more we're Tate," she says.

We talked a lot this afternoon, too, while walking, while switching from sidewalk to sidewalk. Since she no longer had a bike, we decided to go throw mine off the end of a dock. Afterward, we went for a walk. We crossed through the intersections and looked at the city, at what makes the earth bristle wherever it's city, at what has been built up: houses, stores, factories, apartment buildings, skyscrapers.

"Do you know why they built all that?" I asked her.

"No."

"For nothing. For going to bed, for working, for waking up, for earning money, for eating, for digesting, for counting money, for buying themselves clothes. Why do they buy themselves clothes?"

"So they won't be cold?"

"No. To avoid being cold, all you have to do is kill yourself. If they were dead, they wouldn't be cold. They buy themselves clothes to avoid dying of cold. They buy themselves clothes in order to keep living. Why do they live? In order to buy themselves clothes."

"I share your view."

"You're quite right. They build these houses, these factories, these apartment buildings, and these skyscrapers because it's useful or necessary for life. I think that's ridiculous, all this trouble, all these works, this feverish and tragic activity, all that just to live, just to be bored, basically. They're right—all that, it's useful for living, or necessary. But they've never asked themselves whether living is necessary or useful. They believe themselves obliged to live. They think that's all there is to do—

81

to live. They could have avoided all this, all these proud and painful projects. All they had to do was realize that life isn't worth the trouble of living. This city, these houses ... just to live! It's insane! All these nails hammered in boredom. All these bricks shoved in by bricklayers who were bored, who were thinking of other things, whom the master builder had fun humiliating. The city is men who seek to take root forever. Man wastes away, dies, lies in his coffin and is reduced to dust; his roots of brick are left standing, are left there, flouting his grave, immortal, superbly indifferent and impassive. There's nothing funny about it, actually. It's merely ridiculous."

"You're right, Miles Miles. Yes, it's ridiculous. I quite agree with you. Everything you've said makes me tremble, it's so true. Men spend their lives living, spend their lives working to maintain and prolong a life that is worthless. I just don't like living."

Talking pessimistically is pleasant. The reason we were talking pessimistically is not because we were convinced of what we were saying; it's because black ideas, like black tulips, are the most beautiful. As we kept walking on the sidewalks and conversing sombrely, something occurred that will not be without consequences, and those consequences will take place before we hurly-burly ourselves. We were going past a designer shop window, and Chateaugué remembered the promise I had made to buy her the most beautiful dress in the world. She stopped in front of the luxuriant display; she planted herself there, took up residence there, and wouldn't budge.

"That's the one!" she cried. "It's so beautiful! That's the one I want."

Her hands glued to the shop window like suction cups, her face all flattened against the glass partition, she was experiencing appalling waves of happiness, alarming waves of desire. She was telling me to come.

"Come. Come near. Come see. Come over here. Look, that one, there! That's the one—the one I'm pointing at—that I want to die in."

The dress in question was white and studded with stars, a moonlit dress that went curving outward from the waist down, a dress for a real woman, a dress for a woman who has her feet under her dress, for a woman who walks underneath her dress, undercover.

"You're absolutely crazy. It's a wedding dress."

"It's a wedding dress, but I don't care, I love it anyway. If you want to buy me one, buy me that one. I never asked you for anything."

The vast shop window curves inward under the pressure of Chateaugué's covetousness.

"You'll have it. We'll come steal it."

"When?"

"Tonight."

We played detective. We went around the block. We went over the walls of the five-storey apartment building with a fine-tooth comb to see whether there was a way to break in, nocturnally. In the back, along a macabre cul-de-sac, we found what we were looking for: a small basement window whose grating was fastened with nothing but screws. The grating is fastened with nothing but screws; the theft is for tonight, for a little while from now. So it is tonight, this very night, that the consequences of what happened this afternoon will take place. We await the middle of the night to go there. We, Tate, are cold right now; it's cold in our room. Chateaugué is so cold that she has to massage her legs to avoid freezing.

"Skin is so ugly," she says while massaging her legs. "It's like flawed, undercooked porcelain. It's like it's dead. It's limp. It doesn't do anything; it's like paper. We look at it, and it doesn't appeal to us in the least."

I look at that skin that doesn't appeal to her in the least, that skin that my ears hear playing the violin. I summon all my courage; I've had a question to ask Chateaugué ever since we came out of the restaurant. At all costs! I've got to ask her. In the restaurant, we, Tate, were inadvertently seated within range of a quartet of school-age adolescents in heat. They were talking dirty, and Chateaugué could hear everything they were saying. She was even listening, pricking up her ears, and laughing. Besides, I believe it was for her benefit that they were talking dirty.

"Do you know what the Indians call a bra? A tit-rack!"

"I know one who's got 'em so big, she's gotta wear a hammock."

"That doesn't top the one who's gotta buy two parachutes for herself each time, since she couldn't find what she needs in one piece."

Chateaugué was listening, guffawing, barely blushing, and leaning over to hear better. I've mustered all the courage I need.

"Tate, for the first time in our life, I want to ask you an embarrassing question. Can I?"

"I don't care. I don't believe you."

She's clearly intrigued. At the same time, she's getting ready to have a trick played on her. She sits up straight, she's ready for anything, even the impossible—a revelation.

"Tate, Chateaugué, do you realize ... that ... you have breasts?"

"I have what?" she replies with a start.

She doesn't understand, not at all. She's lost her bearings. She has the impression, given the supposedly embarrassing nature of the question, that I'm speaking of pustules. Lowering her eyes, she tries to look at her face.

"Where?"

"You don't know what they are? ... I mean those ... right there ..."

Gesturing as I speak, I point to her hidden little mammaries with the tip of my finger. Suddenly, her face calms down, and lights up again.

"Those! Well, of course! What an idea! I have some, you have some, everybody has some. Why wouldn't I realize it?"

She seems relieved that it's about nothing but that; she was a bit scared.

"Me? I have some? I'm not like you. I'm not a woman!"

I said that in an indignant voice, cynically, confident of the prerogatives of my flat chest. Chateaugué bristles, "What do you mean? You have some, too ... They're not the same as mine, but you have some. Mine are bloated, like a pig's. Yours are teeny-weeny, like a cat's. But it's the same thing. It's in the same place; it's the same thing. Right?"

"Forget about it."

She comes back to it. She insists. Her curiosity has been aroused. She digs to see what's in the back of my mind. She can sense that I'm hiding something from her, that something is happening behind her back. The silly discussion excites me so much I can't see straight, like a beast. How I long to kiss her! She seeks, waits, wants to, then offers herself—she holds out her hand for me to help her go down to hell. All I'd have to do is catch her, holding out my hand, for her to fall into the depths of the abyss from which I gaze up at her. I so long to kiss her little mammaries that my ears are ringing, that it seems to me that my lips have made contact with the red cotton of the blouse that masks her little mammaries. Discouraged suddenly by the violence of my sensuality, I let my big head droop forward and hang on my chest. Chateaugué keeps talking, but I'm no longer listening to her. Let her talk! Let her keep talking! To hell with her and her simplicities! Let her keep spouting them, her simplicities that so readily change into atrocities and then into filth! She has grabbed hold of a tuft of my hair and is shaking my head, tenderly, hesitantly, and clumsily.

"Miles Miles. Miles Miles? You're all red. Are you sick? Are you sick, Miles Miles? Is your stomach upset? Do you feel like throwing up? Answer me ... Answer me? ..."

"Ivugivic!"

She's standing in front of me. I feel her face hanging over me, suspended above me, like a danger. There before me, close by, I have her skirt, that part of her skirt that covers her belly, behind which her belly lives, behind which her belly is hot. Not giving a hoot about anything all of a sudden, I let my heavy head go onto that belly, enter into the warmth of that belly, and let it stay there and rest. To the hand already on my head, Chateaugué adds another. Now both her hands are moving on my head, scarcely moving on my head.

"What's wrong, Miles Miles? Are you in pain? What's wrong? Tell Chateaugué."

She speaks with a sob caught in her throat. She's afraid of me. Women are afraid of men when they lose their composure. They're afraid of men when men get scared. I grab hold of

Chateaugué by the wrists and squeeze, in order to hurt her, so that she'll suffer.

"I'll tell you what's wrong! You sicken me! You're not pure; you're merely ignorant. You're not chaste, you're silly. You're nuthin' but a goddamn woman! You can't wait to find out how a woman works, huh? A pressing need, huh? Distressing being a woman, having all the lousy equipment and not knowing how to use it, huh? You never wanted to be pure, right? You didn't do it on purpose, if you are pure, right? You're completely innocent, right? Grinning from ear to ear, whatever happens, right? You're ready for anything; just show you the lay of the land, huh? The first man who comes along—that's what awaits you! You'll think it's good. You'll think it's funny, like all the other girls. You'll laugh, grinning from ear to ear. You're nuthin' but a goddamn woman, Chateaugué; that's what's wrong! That's what's so sickening."

The idea of evil has never occurred to her. She's a goddamn fool! Suddenly, I hear someone speaking. Suddenly, her voice is sombre and solemn.

"You better not say everything, Tate. You better not say everything. Keep your secrets, Tate. Take care. Don't force anything. Don't hurt anyone."

I feel a malaise all over my body. I know what I've fallen victim to. In the beginning, in the very beginning, when I conceived of the idea of Chateaugué's purity, at the same time, I conceived of the idea of Chateaugué's impurity. The more I love her purity, the more I love her impurity. I chose the purity—the purity of Chateaugué, the purity of our friendship. But the idea of the impurity of Chateaugué keeps coming up, keeps seeking to be fulfilled. The stronger an idea is, the stronger the opposite idea is. Words! Words! Air! Water! Chateaugué. I am a monster, an inveterate whortensturbator, a holier-than-thou sex maniac. If I were to let myself go, I'd never stop caressing Chateaugué. By now, we'd be dead of debauchery. We'd be dead and buried, both of us. All of Tate, all of us, would be of the chthonic realm. For that's all she's waiting for, the little slut. I can't wait to die. If I don't go right away, it'll be too late, and I'll have to go wreathed in ridicule. I still have a little dignity left; if I wait any longer, I'll have none. Why this delay before the hurly-burly? For whom? I know why, in my conscience. I'm waiting for our friendship to have triumphed; for it to have emerged, luminous, from the muck where we stuck it; for it to tower, luminous, on the summit of the white mountain, whiter than the snow of that summit. I'm waiting for our friendship to have lost, for it to lie defeated in the muddy and stagnant water, for the greenflies from the muck to have finished eating its rotten flesh. It's the law of opposites. Our friendship is all I have, and I'm waiting to have done the mundane deed that will ruin it. I want to die, and I want to live. I want to live! I've never wanted to live as much as I have since I've had to hurly-burly myself. The desire I have to embrace this world that sickens me is as strong as the desire I have to embrace Chateaugué. My desire to triumph over everything is as irresistible as my desire to lose everything. He's a Tate! Hesitate! O Almighty One, do me a favour, make me more than mere putrefaction and putridity! O Almighty One, make me like the dead cat's body floating atop the stagnant water! O Almighty One, make me queasy when I see myself in the face of Chateaugué! O Almighty One, change my skin to bronze, fill my chest with light, turn my warmth into ice, make me worthy of myself. Goddamn filth! If we must call a spade a spade, the verb *to love* must yield to the verb *to wanttodofilthythingswithyou*. Let's conjugate it, the verb *to wanttodofilthythingswithyou*. I want-todofilthythingswithyou. Youwantmetoplaytheslutwithyou. We-wanttodosickeningthingstogether. I love Chateaugué. If I love Chateaugué, I wanttodofilthythingswithyou. I don't even have to force myself to find myself sickening. I am naturally sickening. I have to force myself not to find myself sickening. I love you. You love me. We love one another. We sleep together, and we don't do anything bad, but I have to force myself. Sometimes, before falling asleep, we talk together, while smoking, face to face, as though we had nothing but faces, one blowing smoke in the face of the other, as though it were our wings that were clashing under the covers, as though we were angels; but I have to force myself. To remain pure, you've got to find the strength, you've got to force yourself; you've got to be brave, you've got to get your courage up. The most tempting thing about chastity is the courage necessary to keep it up. If I'm chaste, it's because I've been strong; if I'm strong, I'm worthy of myself, and I have the right to be proud of myself, to climb up onto the pedestals that I see.

"Are we going?"

"Where to?"

"To get my dress. It's two o'clock. It's dark enough—it's dark dark. No one will see us stealing at this hour. With all these shadows, no one sees the swallows stealing away."

"The dress? ... Oh, yeah. That's right. I forgot. Up 'n' Adam."

We're not about to cross Montreal and get our feet wet with a stolen wedding dress in our arms. We hail a cruising taxi, just like in the thrillers. We ask the taxi driver if he has a screwdriver. There's one in the glove compartment. We ask him if he's willing to lend it to us. He lends it to us. We ask him to park at the entrance of the cul-de-sac to cover us and to wait for us. He says yes. We disappear into the thick shadows of the cul-de-sac, which resembles a mountain pass. We disappear with the screwdriver, while thinking of Napoleon and the crossing of the Mont Cenis Pass. The black buildings that tower from the sides of the alley soar up to the surface of the night's firmament; it's as though we were in the depths of an abyss in the depths of those constructions that tower almost side by side, and that bathe in the night's black and volatile liquid. The four screws that screw on the grating that fortifies the small basement window are unscrewed in a trice. With a kick, Chateaugué blasts the small basement window to smithereens. I embark, feet first, into the gaping maw lined with teeth of glass, and I jump. I land low; I was expecting to land a lot higher than that. I fall on a surface bristling with broken furniture and smash my face in. I get back up and call Chateaugué. I'm covered in blood and all broken up, but that doesn't bother me. A sliver of glass has gotten caught in my cheek; I pull it out sharply, shuddering. Without seeing me, Chateaugué follows me, and I precede her without seeing where I'm going. To get to the shop window, we've got to move forward in the direction that we're moving forward. I move forward. I break down the doors that loom up before us. I like that, breaking down doors; it soothes my soul. If I had no doors to break down, my heart would burst like a bomb. Chateaugué follows me in silence, overturning everything along the way, touching me to assure herself that I'm still in front of her—and she's the cause of the rage that makes my heart bleed. The shop window is lit up *a giorno*. Tate, in silence, hidden behind a muslin screen, watches together the lone automobiles pass by and the last passersby pass by. Tate holds hands before crossing the Rubicon. Tate looks into each other's eyes and knows full well that, after the perpetration of such a burglary, there will no longer be any place for us in society. All of a sudden, we're scared; we're on the verge of stealing. If we change our minds, our wild friendship was nothing but a game. If we steal, it wasn't a game—either we'll have to hurly-burly ourselves or go to jail. Will our courage fail us? Will we give up at our first real test? Will we turn back terrorized and empty-handed? We won't let Tate be betrayed.

"Tate, why aren't you a girl, like me? Why don't you wear a dress like me?"

Now Chateaugué is starting to have ideas. This theft is useless; the roots of our friendship are all gnawed away by ideas. After a survey of the situation, a plan is developed. We won't just make off with the dress; we'll make off with the mannequin, too. We're not about to start undressing the mannequin before the eyes of the lone automobiles and the last passersby. Time's wasting. The taxi's waiting. The ten or eleven mannequins are standing on a kind of common pedestal. Quite out of sight behind the platform, we crawl until we get within reach of the mannequin that we want to attack and abduct. Having grabbed hold of it by one foot, having tipped it over, having received it in our arms so that it wouldn't be too smashed up, we make our escape with it, we flee on all fours, laughing from fear. The object of our desire, with its arms open wide, doesn't fit through the opening of the small basement window. We try, to no avail, to think of a way of getting it outside without dismembering it. Suddenly, in the small basement window, a haggard head appears, the head of the taxi driver. It inspires in me a resolute spirit.

"There's a big tip for you if you don't talk. Take this mannequin by the head and pull. Either make it or break it. Hey! Take it easy! It's not flour, it's brocade, it's damask. Hey! Don't sweep up the alley with it! Lift it! Lift it up! Carry her in your arms; she won't eat you."

I could keep shrieking insults at the taxi driver all night, I'm so angry. A girl! Me, in a dress! She'd like me to be a girl, like her! The taxi driver holds the mannequin by the head, and Chateaugué holds it by the feet. I open the door of the taxi for them; they lay it on the back seat with care, as if it were a baby. The taxi driver is a jolly fellow. He drives us back home, singing. He sings "My Torn Trousers" to the tune of the wedding march by Rocky Mendelssohn. I give him a ten-dollar tip. He changes his tune. He looks at my poor ten-dollar bill, all crumpled up, as if he wanted to vomit on it. He thinks that's not enough, and he gives it to us straight. I who was bleeding myself dry to gratify him! He nearly runs over us, starting up again. He takes off like a shot, spinning his rear wheels as fast as he can, peppering us with pieces of gravel from his rear wheels. Let him go denounce us. Let him go, the horrible spoilsport! The bride's forehead is torn off, her nose is broken; she's missing an arm on one side and three fingers on the other. That's all, folks—that's all she broke. We don't know where to put her. We put her at the head of our bed so that she can watch us sleep. We put her in place of the orange crate that served as our wall-to-wall library. Her head touches the ceiling, a ceiling that slopes to wed the exact shape of the roof. We contemplate this tranquil intruder. We turn our backs on her, then suddenly we turn our heads to surprise her; but she's the one who surprises us. We're really not used to seeing a mannequin in our room, a stolen mannequin in our room. To tame her, Chateaugué baptizes her. She smears ink on her face, the way she's done to the ugly little statue, but being quite careful not to stain her dress. The dress is not as dirty as it could be. But it's not as white as it was. It has its tears, too.

"We have two sculptures now, Tate—Bride and Ugly. This is Bride, who is dead in a living dress; and this is Ugly, who is dead in a dead dress."

"You mean false in a true dress, and false in a false dress."

"No."

The theft is over. She has her dress. I can breathe again. Our friendship, after millions of words, has finally done the deed and is finally beginning to take shape. The day is over, too, since we're sleepy, and we'll have to wait until we've slept to live a little longer. Tuckered out, Tate lies down, side by side. We fall fast asleep. Leg in leg, our eyes closed, gazing at each other through our eyelids, we sleep. We look like two angels. Our feathers are ruffled under the covers; my feathers ruffle hers. Tomorrow, in the sun, like flowers, our ruffled feathers will be smoothed. All of a sudden, life is so sweet. All of a sudden, life is so sour.

18

Pasteur, in 1495, invented the protostostate of pentacleine. In 1497, someone found him in his coffin; there he was, pale and famous. The embalmers bleed the cadavers; that's why they're pale. Who hasn't heard of Pasteur, the malefactor of humanity? Men live longer and die older, thanks to Pasteur. Thanks to Pasteur, there are more miserable little old men and more miserable little old women on earth than there otherwise would be. In the good old days, men died young, handsome, splendid, and dramatically, stabbed right in the face by bacteria. Pasteur didn't manage to restore the dying little old men and the dying little old women to health; he merely managed, thanks to his method of in vitro isolation, to increase their number. It's like Velázquez. Where, oh, where would so many prosperous museums be today without Velázquez? Isn't it a disgrace? What? Museums? When there are homeless hares, lions without cages, whales that wander homeless in the depths of the deceptive ocean, so many pythons that haven't a roof over their heads, so many lizards that sleep under the stars, so many homeless giraffes, innumerable rhinoceroses that are reduced to sleeping stark naked in the water? Museums? Oh! Oh! It's unthinkable! The municipality of Montreal puts trees in cages. In summer, the municipality of Montreal lines them up along the sidewalks and hangs begging bowls on their branches. In winter, it puts them in a shed so they won't catch cold. It's the emasculation of the trees! Why does it put adolescent trees in sandboxes and place them along the sidewalks? Is it so that they make shade for the skyscrapers, or is it so that they look crazy in their faded and spattered king's robes? Apparently women like that; it must console them to see that they aren't the only ones who look like hookers. When trees don't have their feet in the grass, they're pitiful, they're hideous with vileness; they look like sardines in oil, like those cod that become parched before your eyes in the fishmongers' stalls. Trees are made to be tall and immovable, to hug the roofs of dwellings with their branches, so that the zinc roofs might make their emerald bracelets and opal necklaces resound; so that, at night, the stars might get caught in their branches; so that, in winter, snow snakes might sleep along their branches. Maybe the municipality of Montreal thinks that unnatural trees are quite in harmony with unnatural men. Everything I'm saying is insane, insignificant, and badly said—a hateful message to the automobiles. Automobiles, I do not like you. The assassins return to the scene of the crime. Today, we returned to see the shop window that we assassinated in a most cowardly way. It was beautiful to see us going hand in hand. It was raining. The freezing rain rose up into our woollen socks via capillarity. It spurted out of our shoes in bouquets, with each step. She had me by the hand, and she was glad. She tried to trip me up (with underhanded manoeuvres), and she was proud and laughing. There was next to nothing under her coat, next to no breasts; there was nothing but a slope—gentle, light, and low. She didn't look like a milk cow, like a cow; I was glad. She was glad to have me by the hand, and I was glad that she didn't look like a milk cow. We were both glad. She likes to take me by the hand, and she likes to be taken by the hand. Taken by the hands, we went among the crowd, and we delighted in our great spiritual solitude. For we were robbers, nearly barons; for we weren't with the crowd, but against it. In a low voice, so that they couldn't hear it, Chateaugué would talk to the passersby that we crossed or passed by while running. She didn't even hesitate to point them out.

"I don't need you," she'd say to the anonymous figure. "All that you could give me, I want none of it. I have all that I want. You can keep being a tightwad about all that you have; I have no use for it. Don't look at me; I don't care. Keep your eyes to yourself; I don't care. Don't smile at me; that doesn't bother me. Keep your rictuses to yourself."

Sometimes, I suffer from not wanting anything. Sometimes, I'm so proud of it, I chuckle, I run, I fly. That's why we were running, why we were dodging while running between the inhabitants of the sidewalks. The presence of the bride in our room is like a sun. She's so bizarre that she compels and rivets our gaze. When we turn our backs on her, we feel the rays of her white dress shooting into our backs. When we look at her, her bright light dazzles us. At night, her face is sombre and the dress is phosphorescent. At night, she shines. Chateaugué could spend hours looking at her. She says it's too bad that she's not a Virgin Mary. The dress is way too big for Chateaugué; you could fit two of her inside it. But Chateaugué doesn't take offence. She says that she'll put it on anyway when the time comes for her to wear it. To take offence—I have no idea whether that means what I mean. But who cares?

"It's an absolutely beautiful dress," exclaims Chateaugué. "I don't have the right to reproach it for being too big. It's not its fault that I'm small."

At the start of our living together, we used to spend our time outside, riding our bikes or reading; we were never back before midnight. It's eight o'clock, the sun hasn't even set, and we're already ready to sleep, and we're done for now with living outside—with living, period. We went to see the shop window, and we came back; we had nothing more to do outside—or to do, period. It wasn't six o'clock yet when we came home. Mothers have fat butts, even thin mothers. I said so to Chateaugué a little while ago, on the way to the shop window. I didn't mince words. We were strolling behind a woman who was still young but whose butt was already enormous.

"Look at her butt. That's what'll happen to you if we don't hurly-burly ourselves. You'll have one just like that in ten years if we don't hurly-burly ourselves. You'll be half broad, half butt in ten years if we don't hurly-burly ourselves. You'll be sickening to look at. You'll be less than shit."

"But ... we're going to hurly-burly ourselves, Miles Miles. You're just talking. In ten years, they won't even be able to tell if the grey dust that'll be in our coffin is from one or two cadavers. In ten years ... oh! Why are you talking like that? We're going to hurly-burly ourselves, aren't we? It's true, isn't it?"

I repeat myself. I pass my time repeating myself. When you're sixteen years old, what you say, you've already said at least a billion times. There are two or three thousand words; to avoid repeating yourself, you can't say very many of them per hour. I repeat myself in my soul; sometimes, eager for brand-new words, I open the closets of the past. The closets of the past are made to remain closed. I've opened the closets of the past so many times that the tablets are empty, that a strong musty smell seeps into my soul when I reopen them. Chateaugué has tears in her eyes when we speak of the past. Me, I feel queasy, the smell of an icebox without ice is so strong. I repeat myself in this notebook. But there's plenty of space in my notebook, and I'm not stingy with my time. There's plenty of space in my notebook, and I'm not stingy with my time. There's plenty of space in my notebook, and I'm not stingy with my time. There's plenty of space in my notebook, and I'm not stingy with my time. I'm not stingy with my money, and notebooks aren't expensive. Notebooks aren't all that exxpensive. I put an exxtra *x* in my second *expensive*. I'm not stingy with my *exx*'s. Exxone. Exxtwo. Exxthree. Exxfour. Exxfive. Exxsix. Exxseven. Two thousand three hundred thirty-four *x*'s! Have you seen what I've done to this lake? I've filled it with capital *x*'s. Come see this lake that I've filled with golden capital *x*'s. Take my hand to avoid falling; come, come! Look deep into the water. All those golden *x*'s. You'd think they were crosses. Pillow of an immaculate whiteness, you wed the form of a head whose face is of an immaculate whiteness. Chateaugué's mouth is like a drawer; it opens. I have nothing to say. I have nothing to say to you, races. Talking to you is futile. The reason I talk to you is not because I have something to say to you; it's because I feel like talking. What I love most in the world is a book sculpted in vellum and adorned with a title, with a title adorned with blue acanthus leaves, with cantharides of leather, and with Doric columns. It's so beautiful, a beautiful book. It looks so grand. Who ever said you've got to read the books you buy? A book is made to be looked at. Do you read the painter's paintings that you buy? No! It would take much too long; you're content merely to look at them; it's much less tiring. A book costs less than a painting, is as beautiful as a painting, and is more prestigious than a painting. A book by Lope de Vega has much more prestige in intellectual circles than a painting by Velázquez. It's easy to understand—books are jam-packed with words, and paintings don't have a single one. Those who speak have much more prestige than those who shut their traps. You never hear of those you never hear. Those you don't hear die without prestige. For example, who has ever heard of Rembrandt? Go for a walk with a book under your arm—the little girls in leather jackets, leather boots, and dark glasses will take you for Pablo Picasso. They'll be moved in a moving way and will make moves on you. Writing renders one worthy of love, as Barrès says. Do you know why Barrès writes? It's because he couldn't shake off the influence of his teachers, because he remained a schoolchild. All teachers are future or would-be writers. Nothing pleases a teacher more than to convince one of his pupils that there's nothing more beautiful than literature. Nothing pleases a farmer more than to convince someone that nothing is more beautiful than a plow that's all dirty. Mr. Barrès, are you dead? If you aren't dead, and if you are outraged by my using your name in a pejorative sense, all you had to do was not let your name be bandied about in the street. I didn't use your first name in a pejorative sense. Alas, I no longer remember it. I do not have the honour of knowing you, Mr. Barrès. In my head, there is nothing but your surname. Your name is like all the other names that you can read in the dictionaries and that you learn at school. Paul Morand is equal to Francis Carco who is equal to Elvis Presley who is equal to Pius XII who is equal to Pancho Villa who is equal to Ignatius of Loyola who is equal to Arnolf Hitler. When I quit school, I was full of names the way one is full of scarlet fever. I'm having a hard time getting over it, standing on my own two unknown feet. If I hadn't quit school, I'd have died of scarlet fever. Who put it (put tit!) into the head of the municipality of Montreal to plant trees on the sidewalks, under the frozen eyes of the skyscrapers? Who ever said that trees on a sidewalk were beautiful? Who swore that they didn't look so much like female peripatetics that you couldn't tell them apart? To think that among those wretched trees there may be some of the masculine gender! Save the males, at least, naughty municipality of Montreal! Which Valery Larbaud, which Shakespeare, said that trees on a sidewalk were beautiful? Soon they'll put seamless nylons on them, whether males or females, so they won't catch cold. They'll put gloves of sweetened pigskin on them—one on the end of each branch. Soon, tomorrow, tomorrow at dawn, they'll plant artificial trees all over; artificial forests will go up on the stock market. You have to be consistent, you have to apply, in every instance, the line of least resistance. Why not spare the poor trees the worry of growing, the trouble of eating up all the sun that shines and drinking in all the rain that falls, the sorrow of having to remake their leaves every year? Trees work too much! Trees have no free time! It isn't fair! Let's call on communism and bring on science! My dearest brethren, I am a tree just like you; that is why I am in a position to understand you and to sympathize in an intelligent and constructive way! My dearest brethren, if you elect me, if you elect my party, you will all be replaced by artificial trees as soon as the first two-year plan is over! Miles Miles passes his time saying silly things, but he doesn't regret it. Why would he regret what he can be proud of and take delight in without overexerting himself? I am the king of stupidity. Long live the king of stupidity. If I were the king of the nitwits, I would say, long live the king of the nitwits. Why get all upset over nothing? I am the king of stupidity, and I'm proud of it, because stupidity is quite widespread. The king of the Disunited States is a lot prouder of being king than the king of the Eskimos is proud of being king; the Americans are a lot more widespread than the Eskimos. Enough for today! *Basta*, fool!

19

Something fishy has been going on between Chateaugué and me since yesterday. I emerge from Chateaugué's arms the way you emerge from a geological era. Last night, the weather was sad. The moon was nothing but a faded grey stain at the heart of a sky drowned in dust. Last night, we had nothing to do. We have nothing left to do, since the man in the moon left the moon, since dragons no longer exist and no longer want to eat us. I'd say to myself, "Get on with it, we have that to do!" Now it's all over. We have nothing left to do. What needs us now that we no longer need ourselves? Nothing. Maybe we would still need ourselves if we still were what we were. Last night, we had nothing to do, and we had had nothing to do all day. We didn't want to do anything. We didn't even want to learn Spanish. We didn't want to read, or walk, or eat, or wash ourselves, or talk, or breathe. I was sitting in my armchair, and she was sitting near me on one of the little green chairs. We had our feet on the table, and we had taken off our shoes.

"Is it time?" Chateaugué asked me in a voice as sweet as it was exasperated.

"Time for what?"

"Time for the hurly-burly ..."

"No. Shut up, if you have nothing to say."

I wasn't thinking of anything. She didn't seem to be thinking of much. We spent hours being motionless and doing nothing but that, falling prey to idleness, the deadly idleness, not the one that is sloth but the one that is impotence and despair, that takes hold of the person who is exhausted and exhausts him more and more, until the mere beating of his heart hurts him, burns him. Suddenly, propelled by the wild idea that something about her had changed, I swivelled my head—which was heavier than a truck differential—in order to look at Chateaugué one more time. I looked at her with all the disgust that was choking my throat. She bowed her head; she shut her eyes tight. From each of her eyes, like an egg, a big tear came out, fell, slid in a single surge to the bottom of her face, and stayed suspended under her chin, as if above an abyss. I was so sickened that it only sickened me more. I even felt like slapping her. I swivelled my head back as though nothing had happened. I could hear that it had started to rain again. I wiggled my toes; the dormant stench of my feet woke up and floated up to my nose. I made every effort to listen to the rain fall on the other side of the roof. Everything about me was sickening; focusing my attention on something other than myself was the best thing to do. One more time again, I glanced at Chateaugué. There were as many tears on her cheeks as there was rain on the windowpanes. These tears swelled in silence, fell in silence, trickled in silence, jostled each other in silence, and dried in silence. Her eyes were so full of water that you could no longer see the colour of her eyes. I didn't care. I tried to talk to her in a tender voice. But I spoke to her in such a cynical voice that it scared me and shook me out of my torpor.

"Someone's sad. Someone has hurt feelings. Someone has a heavy heart."

I stopped myself just in time. I ran my hand through her hair.

"You're sad, Chateaugué. You have a heavy heart, old girl. Was I mean? Was I mean to you?"

As though she'd been whipped or stung, she threw herself into my arms while uttering cries, moans, and groans.

"No, Miles Miles! No! No! No! You're not mean! You're not mean! I'm so hurt! I'm so scared! I'm scared! Am scared ... Am scared ... Scared ... Scared ... Scared ..."

She cried her eyes out. She was sniffling, she was pressing and writhing her face on my ribs, and there was no end to it. Through my shirt, I felt the fragility of the bone of her nose, the mobility of her jaw, the hardness of her cheekbones, the burning sensation of her inflamed mouth, the humidity of her tears and of her nasal mucus ... She asked me to take pity on her and blow her nose.

"Console me, Miles Miles. Take pity on me. Blow my nose. Blow my nose. Blow my nose, please. I'm only a little child. When you don't take care of me, I'm scared. Say something."

Once again, I ran my hand through her hair. That didn't console her much. She started to bawl again even louder. I was feeling infinitely unhappy, but not in the hideous, mean, nauseating, and bitter way that is mine. It was her sorrow that I was experiencing, an irresistible and unjust sorrow, but sweet and good, albeit unjust. What do you say when you console? I don't know. Everything I said to her seemed to make her even sadder. How do you feel pity for a being whose tears warm you up and do you good? I didn't have a handkerchief. What should I blow her nose on and dry her eyes with?

I told her to wait, that I was going to stand up and go get her a handkerchief.

"No! No! Stay! Stay! Don't go away! Don't move!"

I gently pushed her away in order to stand up and go get a clean rag from the bathroom cupboard. She ran and flung herself onto the bed and started to sob louder than ever, in an even more heart-rending voice. I lost patience. I hurled the rag onto her head and told her to blow her nose all by herself, and go back to the Islands if she was scared. I sat down again in my armchair. I put my feet back up on the table. I went back to thinking of nothing, looking at nothing, and listening to nothing. I was cozy, sitting down. I was no longer disgusted; instead, I was sad. Chateaugué loved me, needed me. She loved me; I must not be so bad after all; maybe I didn't have a beautiful face, but I had beautiful eyes. I let myself be sad. Sadness is a sort of sleep—it absorbs, and it coats; it embraces, like water, gently, without rushing things, without impact. I rolled myself three or four cigarettes, and I smoked them. I was more and more aware of delighting in Chateaugué's helplessness, and I was less and less ashamed of it. A gentle indifference crept over me at the expense of her helplessness. All the while hearing her sob, I looked on, as a sort of softening of my acts of violence and severity occurred within me. I'm the one she's crying for. When a cry or a sob would break through, they seemed to come from farther away than the others; they did nothing but thicken the gentle air of boredom that was enveloping me, did nothing but add to its depth. Almost unconsciously, I was extolling my strength, my harshness, my incorruptibility, and my cruelty. I was the cruellest there was; I was invulnerable. What did I care about a woman's vehement sobs, the irresistible caress of woman, about the absolute necessity of woman? I was cozy, sitting down. It felt good to be strong. The time passed quickly. My cigarette tasted of honey. I was lost in the depths of the comfort of being virile. Women were nothing but powder puffs, and Chateaugué was nothing but a poorly powdered puff.

"You're so ugly from behind!" I suddenly heard.

"From behind, you're unbearable!"

At this other assault, I gave another start. She was sitting on the edge of the bed, bolt upright, her arms crossed low, with the bearing of a woman who isn't scared of blows, who's ready and eager. Her face red, her lips puffy, her hair rumpled, she was staring at me with all the roundness and all the size of her eyes, which were paler than ash.

"You've dropped me, Tate. Have I ever dropped you? Have I once in the course of our whole life lacked tenderness, loyalty, or friendship? You despise me! I get on your nerves! I aggravate you! I do all I can for us to be on good terms, and you do all you can to hate me. All you had to do was not come to get me in the first place."

"I am a man; I don't understand a thing about women's tears."

"That's not true. You're not a man; I'm not a woman. Plus, I don't understand a thing about my tears, either. When I cry, I'm not really hurt, I'm not suffering; I'm just scared. When I cry, I don't want to be alone, that's all. Crying only really hurts when you have no one, or when the ones you have let you cry all alone. You've got to lean on someone you love to cry well. A little while ago, leaning on you, I took so much pleasure in crying, each tear soothed me so, pacified me so, that I wished it would last, that it would last, all night, all my life. Why did you push me away? Why were you tense as though you'd been angry? Why didn't you hold me close in your arms? You have no heart! Heartless beast! Heartless beast! Meanie!"

I did not reply. She waited for me to reply for a long time, but I did not reply. She collapsed once more. Face down, her head in her arms, she indulged in another little crisis of frustration.

"Turn off the light. Come to bed. It's pretty late."

She had slipped under the covers; only her head was showing.

"Are you done yet? Or are you going to start up again in five minutes? You've been going off every fifteen minutes for a while now."

"I'm done. Turn off the light. Come to bed. It's cold. We're cozy. I only took off my nylons. We're going to bed with all our clothes on; it's too cold."

I pulled the covers over my head, and I turned my back on her. I hadn't turned out the light. She stood up on the bed, caught hold of the short chain, and pulled on it; the bulb, attached to a long black wire, went out. She started to walk on the mattress. The mattress rolled and pitched. She calls that "making the mattress make waves." She adores making the mattress make waves. It's one of her favourite pastimes. It's her way of puttering around. It's how she kills time. It's her Ingres guitar. I was her Red Sea. To avoid getting wet, she had to jump over me. She straddled me, then continued her promenade on the mattress. Sometimes, she'd cross over me without getting her feet wet, like the Hebrews. That's when it was funny, when she'd laugh the most.

"Your big bottom!" she'd chortle, perched on my higher hip.

Finally, she calmed down, she quieted down, she'd had enough of it, she lay back down. She stretched her legs out on top of mine. It's another of her favourite pastimes. She is a woman, no matter what she says. There's nothing more vile, more hypocritical, more of a nuisance, more of a viper than a woman. She'd sniffle. And the silence would be restored. She'd sniffle. And the silence would be re-established. She'd sniffle. And the silence would be reinstated.

"If it were light, if you were looking at me, you'd see that I'm still crying. Do you know what that means? I'm giving you an opportunity to be forgiven. Help me. Never ever let me cry all alone again."

"Shut up and sleep. If you're not happy with your lot, take the bus. You're a baby! Go get someone else to rock you back and forth. You're ridiculous; you ought to be ashamed, at your age, to want someone to take you in his arms. Go get someone on the Islands to kiss you. Take the bus and go back there. They're waiting for you. They're hoping to see you. They love that, all that kissing, and you love it, all that kissing. Run and find them again. I don't give a hoot."

She stopped sniffling. She pressed up against me, taking my neck from behind.

"For the love of Christ, Chateaugué, get off my back! You sure are clingy when you get going—you're worse than flypaper!"

"I'm getting to know you. You don't really believe what you say. You're playing the man. I'm as frigid as an ice cube, and you're as hot as a cat in heat. Leave me alone. Let me warm myself up. Don't play the man with me anymore."

I let her do as she liked. Actually, she didn't even bother me. She was such a baby. I was cozy. I might have even purred. I was the pasha who's sick of women. And if she went away ...? Let her go! When I'm dead, who will remember what happened? She started wiggling; she snuck her fingers under my sweater.

"Cut it out! Do you have ants in your pants?"

My sweater—too big for me and found in the trash—is amply ample. After getting into it up to her shoulders, Chateaugué wrapped her arms around my waist and stopped wiggling.

"In an igloo, everybody sleeps in the same bed. When I was in Port Burwell, I had to sleep in the same bed as my father, my mother, my brothers, my sisters, my grandfather, and my grandmother. At my parents' house, the Brasseurs, there was no one in my bed and no one in my room."

She was pressing her chin between my shoulder blades, her bony chin, her hardest and pointiest chin. Her teeth started chattering, and I felt the chattering reverberate throughout my chest. I feigned sleep. I fell asleep.

"We ought to have the bride sleep with us. But her dress would get wrinkled. She'd get up with an accordion dress."

After that, I didn't hear anything else. When I woke up this morning, she had her hands profoundly penetrating my pants. I was so angry and so ashamed, I almost fainted.

"Chateaugué! For the love of Christ! What are you doing down there?"

She didn't understand a thing. My cries didn't even wake her up. She was sleeping, curled up under my sweater, all limp and drenched in sweat. I took her clammy hands out of their refuge, gently, so that she wouldn't notice. That was taking the need to warm oneself up—the naïveté of the Eskimos—a bit too far. But actually, I was sure that she'd put her hands in my pants without malice aforethought. I was playing the deeply humiliated one, the deeply offended one, but without much conviction. Actually, I was touched. Chateaugué could make me find anything touching, even my sex organs.

"What? What? What?"

Every time she wakes up, it's the same thing. She sits up, quickly rubbing her eyes, utterly surprised: "What? What? What?" Drawn up on her knees, she lets herself fall seated onto her legs, ponders with all her might, and succeeds in situating herself in space and time. It's her way of starting the day. She felt the bloody scabs concealed beneath her hair and the ones that adorn her forehead.

"Do I seem to be getting better? Brrrrrrr! It's so cold! I feel like fighting. Let's fight! And the hurly-burly? You don't talk about it anymore ... Is it still on? I need to go to the bathroom. Look at the floor, you'd think it was made of ice. I'm in no hurry to put my feet on that. Do I still have gunk in my eyes? Look! Look at me! Do I still have gunk in my eyes? I've got to go to the bathroom. Get up, lazybones! Real men get up! Let's stay in bed today. Let's keep sleeping until the end of the world. Let's die warm. Look! It's still raining. I don't feel like doing anything when it rains. Why bother going out? It looks like freezing rain. Brrrrrr! I wonder whether I have a white tongue. Look! Look at my tongue! Do I have a white tongue? Take a whiff! Do I have bad breath? Go ahead, take a whiff!"

She continued to pull the wool over my eyes. It's the same every morning. When I reproach her for telling me her life story in six volumes every time she wakes up, she replies that, in the morning, the birds sing.

"In the morning, my friend, the birds sing. The birds are crazy in the morning. They sing and sing until they fall from the tree, dead drunk."

She came back from the bathroom running. She ran as if the floor were on fire. Speed kills. She flung herself sideways onto the bed and onto me. She tidied up the covers, the pillows, and the sheets. She stretched out alongside me, snuggled up to me, chilled me to the bone.

"I'm so cozy! The floor is freezing! We're nice and cozy together, aren't we? Aren't we, Tate? We're all alone. The mightiest can't say a word to us. The meanest can't do a thing to us. We won't be caught with our hands in the cookie jar. We can ransack all the closets. No one can see us. No one can hurt us. Our home is our castle. Won't you put your arms around me? I put my arms around you a lot. You never put your arms around me. I'm quite a bit smaller than you. You don't need me to take you in my arms like your maman. Take me in your arms as if you were my maman, like I was a little girl. Say yes. Be nice. Coochy-coochy-coo? Why don't you want to play with me? I'd be so cozy in your arms. You'd be like my maman, and I'd be like your little girl."

I remained impassive and poker faced. I was curious—how far would she go? To cheer me up, she would stop at nothing. She started to tickle me; she was once again grinning from ear to ear, and I recognized her. Beaming! Beaming ignobly! Leaving behind the soles of my feet, she flung herself at my armpits. I fell victim to both rage and laughter at the same time. The laughter stopped me from getting mad, and I couldn't stop myself from laughing. I was perfectly cheered up! I was beaming like her. Like her, I had a grin from ear to ear. She could be proud of how she pulled it off. I was laughing—hee-haw, hee-haw, hee-haw. How can you pursue hateful or impure intentions when you're laughing? A Homeric struggle ensued. Kicks and punches flew. Laughter disarms and paralyzes.

Despite the disturbance to my nervous and muscular systems, I managed to grab hold of her hilarious hands, to muzzle and disarm them. I wanted to shower insults on her, but I couldn't; her eyes were sparkling too much, there was too much glee and vivaciousness from her head down to her toes. I gave up the fight. With infinite care, so they wouldn't escape and fly away, I stretched out her arms alongside her body and fastened them there while embracing all of her. She was no longer moving, no longer struggling. She relaxed. All along my arms, I felt her nerves vibrate like guitars. Then I felt them relax. Under my hand, a string was loosening. In my palm, five nerves were slackening. Under my chest, an entire network was weakening and melting. She closed her eyes. I closed my eyes. We let ourselves go. We let everything go. We pretended to sleep. We weren't sleeping.

"My eyes are closed, but I'm not sleeping, you know. Are you sleeping?"

I didn't answer, but I opened my eyes again. She looked at my eyes the way a housewife looks at a pot that she's just scoured.

"You've got gunk in your eyes. Let me get it; I'm going to get rid of it for you."

"Leave the gunk alone."

She tried to free her arms in order to get the gunk out of my eyes. But I was holding her tight; I was stronger; I didn't let her get it. She liked that, being entwined; she was, indeed; she would stay that way. Whole hours went by. Hour by hour, she'd say something and try to free herself. I'd tell her to shut up, and I'd squeeze a bit harder. I had to crush her a bit in order to stifle her vague impulses. Apart from what happened hour by hour, nothing happened. Since we kept on pretending to sleep, we must have slept a bit. After each period of shorter or longer unconsciousness, I found myself once again with arms that were a bit number, a bit deader, and more tingly.

"I'm not hungry. Are you hungry?"

"Shut the hell up!"

She must have been numb, too. Sometimes I'd catch her grimacing. We didn't do anything. We listened to the hours pass by. The hours passed by at a horse's gallop. Our hearts were straddling and galloping one against the other. Two horses were galloping, one on top of the other—they were the hours. When I made an effort to listen, I could hear our hearts beating. They were making noises like rats caught between partitions.

"It must be late. I think it's afternoon, Lady Sand Gentlemen. You haven't eaten a thing. You're not hungry, hungry hungry hungry hungry, Lady Sand Gentlemen? Doesn't your stomach growl sometimes? I heard your stomach growl a little while ago, you know. But you didn't hear a thing. You were sleeping. If you had heard, you would have laughed. I did. If you're hungry ... you only have to say so."

"Shut up, macabre discovery."

"I'm not hungry either, Lady Sand Gentlemen. To be hungry, you've got to want to be hungry, to want nourishment, to want to prolong your life. I myself want to dieyeyeyeyeye, to leave. If we don't die right away, we're going to have to start from scratch again, walking, walking, walking on pins and needles, walking on our hearts, until it comes round again— this, this *resounding silence*, being happy, being dazed in your arms, being scared in your arms. I'm crazy, Lady Sand Gentlemen. To die. Today. To die today. Two die. Two die today. Tie-dyed. Tie-died today. Today two died to die tie-dyed."

"Shut up, you insured piece of shit."

All automobiles must be insured. Most human beings have turned into automobiles. Therefore, since human beings are insured, Chateaugué is an insured piece of shit. Continuing to hold Chateaugué captive without realizing it, I thought of that, and I burst out laughing inside my soul. What was going on in that brain that I had, right there under my nose? Was a hideous drama playing out inside that head that I had right under my nose? The fact that human beings, those insured people, sleep together in order to copulate—does she know it or not? Does she know that we could do filthy things if we wanted to? Copulating. Does she want to, she who seems to know nothing about it? Is she ignorant or hypocritical? You think about things like that when you've got a powder puff in your arms. Chateaugué, I recant. I know perfectly well that you have no secrets, you who have always been an open book to me. You wouldn't be so blunt and so gauche if you knew how to have afterthoughts, aftermaths, afterbirths, afterlifes, and aftertastes.

"Look outside! The light is waning. It's evening. You haven't eaten a thing for twenty-four hours, Lady Sand Gentlemen. You must be hungry. Your lips are all dry. You are a man, after all. A man's gotta eat. I like a man when he's eating. That's what Maman Brasseur used to say."

We eventually pulled ourselves apart at the seams and got up. My arms had left their mark on her slender arms. The blood had coagulated in our arms; we couldn't move them anymore. We had just been through not so much a test of friendship as a test of sportsmanship. We went out. We went into the night of a day that had waited for us for naught, that we hadn't even been in. We went to eat. On the sidewalk, she took my hand and assured me that she wasn't scared anymore.

"I'm not scared anymore. I was so scared in your arms that my old fears don't bother me anymore. I'll never be scared again. I'll never cry again, never ever. Now I don't give a hoot about anything."

We went into a restaurant that we weren't familiar with, a restaurant that we had never seen before in our lives. In this restaurant, everyone was eating. We ate like pigs. Chateaugué started to declaim a poem by Nelligan that she had learned on the sly in order to surprise me. While reciting the poem, with an eloquent gesture, she knocked over her coffee cup, and everyone started to whisper about us. Everyone was staring at us. Glances rained down on us. For fear of death by glances, we quickly paid and left.

"I didn't know you knew the 'Ballad of Wine' by heart. Do you know any others by heart?"

"The *Funeral Oration of Henrietta of England* by Jacques-Bénigne Bossuet."

"The *Funeral Oration of Henrietta of England?* By heart?"

I was playing the little non-believer. I was sure we weren't talking about the same *Funeral Oration of Henrietta of England*. Then, in a voice strong and deep, punctuating her delivery with formal gestures similar to the one that had caused the loss of her coffee cup, without hesitation and without effort, she addressed to the impassible faces and façades that we were passing the impossible *Funeral Oration of Henrietta of England* by Jacques-Bénigne Bossuet. Having begun to exclaim at the corner of Guy and Sainte-Catherine, she only finished exclaiming at the doorstep of the house belonging to our room. I was so out of breath and so full of wonder that I had to sit down on the doorstep before undertaking the scaling of the stairs.

"You didn't believe me, huh?"

I humbly confessed that she had astonished me. She told me the whole story.

"I learned that when I was at the convent. I don't understand a word of it. I don't even know what half the words mean. It's been a long time. I was eleven. The steward of the convent was putting on a play. I went to see her, and I told her that I wanted to play the role of the orphan princess. She pinched my cheek, and she told me that it would take a good memory to learn the role of the orphan princess and that I was too little to have one. I lost my temper, and I decided to get revenge. I spent the whole winter learning nothing but the *Funeral Oration of Henrietta of England* by Jacques-Bénigne Bossuet. I'd spend my days and nights at it. The next day I'd forgotten what I'd learned the day before. But I'm hard to discourage. I'm stubborn, you know. When I've got something stuck in my head, I won't walk away from it. After a couple of months, I was finally able to recite it all one night to myself by heart, from one end to the other, from the first to the last line, without skipping a word. I was glad. But when I woke up the next day, it had all left my head. I wept like Mary Magdalene, and I started all over again. When I went to see the steward at the end of the year, I was sure that I could pull it off. I knew when the paragraphs began and when they ended. I knew where there were exclamation points and question marks. I could even recite page thirty-four, skip ten pages and recite page forty-four. After the awards ceremony, I went to see the steward again. I went into her office, I told her that I knew the *Funeral Oration of Henrietta of England* by heart and that that proved it wasn't true that I didn't have a good memory. And I slammed the door on my way out, with tears in my eyes."

I stood up again, and we went up the stairs. I asked her whether she had given the steward the proof so courageously established of what she was asserting.

"No. Why? It wasn't necessary. I knew it was true."

"You might have gone in, told her that you had a good memory, and then left again without even memorizing the *Funeral Oration of Henrietta of England* by the Genius of Meaux."

"That wouldn't have been true. Telling a lie would have been of no use to me."

"You don't have to learn the *Funeral Oration of Henrietta of England* by heart in order to tell a convent steward that it's not true that you don't have a good enough memory. Chateaugué, you're losing me."

I've said enough for today. I think that I'm happy, that life is beautiful. It goes without saying that I'm only happy if *happy* means what I think *happy* means. If *happy* means something other than what I think *happy* means, then I'm not happy, obviously.

20

Hook, Line, and Sink Her

On a lofty peak,
A man made a scene.
For he's just just arrived
In the land where Bodale reigns.

Bodale is no demon.
Bodale is a blue woman
Who eats both by hook and by crook.
From her mouth, flames shoot forth.

And one morning, in front of the church,
She had put up a throne,
One of mahogany and grey silk,
On which the other thrones burned.

After that, she proclaimed,
After sitting down on it,
Keeping her llama on a leash,
That her right to rule came from Adam.

After proclaiming that,
She stood up, drew herself up.
Only then did they see that her bot-
Tom was full of cinderellas.

Last days here above. Six feet under, or in hell, is lower than
here. Days, you pass by, wide open. Days, don't pass by here
anymore; go somewhere else. Days, stop passing; keep out of
sight, keep still, leave eternity alone. Let's talk a little about

Canada, an immaculate concept. Let's talk a little about money, a pure concept. If I were a tightwad and nothing but a tightwad, I would be glad, for I wouldn't be vicious, I would be innocent. Unfortunately, money doesn't interest me. Love alone interests me, filth alone. The assassin is pure; he doesn't act with his sex organs, those disgusting things; he acts with his revolver, a gold-plated gem. Assassination is not sexual; it does not disgust, it is not shameful; it exalts, it subverts. I forgive everything except impurity. I consider myself inferior to every man who is chaste. Let's talk a bit about Canada. Let's spread some gloom and doom. Bucking the trend, let's rush toward the white regions of human activity. Let's look toward religion, the arts, work, racism, and paytriotism. O Canada, my homeland, my forebears, your forehead, your breasts, your glorious florets! Canada is a vast, empty country, a land without houses and without men, except in the south, except along the border of the Disunited States, except in the places where the Americans have overflowed. There are no cities in Canada, only lakes. There are no men in Canada, only otters and martens that poke their heads out along the lakeshore, and the Americans who have or have not jumped over the border. Those who have not jumped over, who were already on this side, they are the Canadians who come from the Americans, they are the bribed ones, that's what the Americans who jumped over have come to buy. Americans of a feather flock together, flock to American swamps, sheltered by the border; they don't dare venture onto the steppes where the lakes loom up; they're scared of otters; they've never seen otters before. Canada, immense palace of cold, O Canada, empty castle of sun, O You who sleep in your forests as the bear sleeps in its coat, did you only rouse when they told you that you were vanquished, when you fell under English domination? Do you only realize it when they run across you, sitting in their chromed automobiles, when they drop in on you from up high in their exploded airplanes? Sleep, Canada, sleep; I sleep with you. Let's keep sleeping, Canada, until a sun rises that's worth the trouble. When the thunder shakes the sky, we don't even turn around; do they think that a few exchanges of musket fire in the silence of the woods during the course of the Seven Years' War bother us? Who do these lice and bedbugs think they are? Canada is. Is Canada, or isn't it? In Canada, the minks and the Eskimos are the only ones who don't speak, sing, dance, eat, and dress American-style. As I write, zealous Protestant missionaries are teaching American English to the Eskimos and selling them American books and LPS. In Canada, even the Eskimos live American-style. In Canada, nowadays, the ambassador from the planet Mars is the only one who's not American. On earth nowadays—by automobile so that it happens faster—everybody's rapaciously buying and selling everybody else. They say there are twenty million Canadians. Where do they live? Where have all the Canadians gone? Where are they? There isn't a single Canadian in Canada. Where are the twenty million Canadians? Where are we? Who in Canada is not of the race of hotdogs, hamburgers, barbecue, chips, toast, buildings, stop signs, *Reader's Digest*, *Life*, Metro-Goldwyn-Mayer, rock-'n'-roll, and woolly-bully? Who among us, my brothers, is not an apostle of Popeye, Woody Woodpecker, *Naked City* (Metropolis Unveiled), *Father Knows Best* (Papa's Always Right), Simon Templar, Dodge, Plymouth, Chrysler, elevated tracks, wheezy carburetors, the watusi, the cha-cha-cha, Coca-Cola, 7UP, Jerry Lewis, and Tcharles Boyer? Who here has the courage to go punch out the singers that get paid by Pepsi, singers who have the gall to sing that we are the Pepsi Generation? For those who may not be up to date, who don't pick up the stations of CBC Radio, I specify that Pepsi is a liquid from the Disunited States, a kind of Coca-Cola. Texaco comes from the word *Texas*. Texaco gasoline is a Canadian gasoline. Does that hold water? Anyone who might like to become a Canadian couldn't become one. Some people try really hard to become Canadians (tough guys to Americanize); they smoke Gitanes, read *L'Express*, drive Citroëns, go applaud for Luis Mariano, drink Château-Thierry, and use the word *cunt*. I hate those guys. How I hate those would-be French, those damned pyromaniacs who are ashamed of being born on these banks, who would rather have landed on them, who regret not running aground instead. Those who listen to me find that I have a rough tongue, that I speak French badly. Am I French?

Was I born in Paris? I am not French. Furthermore, I don't want to be French; it's too tiring, you've got to be too smart, you've got to be too polite and too much of a connoisseur of wine vintages, you've got to talk too much for no reason, you've got to deem yourself too much better than the others. I've never set foot in France; I am not French. *La Dolce Francia?* Ugh! Harsh Canada! I don't speak any language fluently. I understand French poorly and American English poorly. At the beginning of the colonization—the French one—there was some talk in France of Canada's being exchanged, quid pro quo, for one of the Virgin Islands, or one of the islands in the Caribbean Sea, in any case. It didn't take much for the French to steal from the king of France. The winters were much too cold. In the West Indies, the French didn't get such cold feet while colonizing. They didn't want to come populate Canada; it was much too cold. They froze the silk of their doublets. Now that central heating has been installed, they make themselves more at home; the French are coming, to colonize us, to wise us up. You can see them coming back from a long way off in their little velvet slippers. *Canada* is a proper noun designating a dominion that does not exist, for lack of Canadians. Are the English who colonized India Hindus? No. Are their sons and their grandsons Hindus? No! Why not? Because there are other Hindus than the English and because the real Hindus are the only Hindus imaginable. The English have managed to kill all the Indians and herd the others into reservations. But the English haven't managed to kill all the Hindus. There were way too many of them! The English had to give up the idea of being Hindu. For the English, it was much easier to succeed at being American. I'm getting bogged down, and I'm straying from the point. That doesn't bother me. What was I talking about? What was I driving at? There would be French Canadians, and they would be French Canadians because their fathers were in the fur trade. We're talking about the past when we talk about the fur trade. French Canadians (such is the very name) claim to enjoy a privilege that other Canadians (such is the very name) do not hold. This privilege is that of having discovered Canada and having first plied it with a plow, of having made it bleed wheat (bleed white) for the first time. I myself, Miles Miles, when I was in the belly of my great-great-grandmother, I was the first habitants. Can you have been in the belly of your great-great-grandfather? No, sir. You can only have been in the belly of your great-great-grandmother, the belly of a woman. If you concede that there are French Canadians, you must also concede that French Canadians have shed much more blood over France than the French have shed over Canada. On the Plains of Abraham, there weren't that many Frenchmen—two or three hundred. In '14 and '40, the French Canadians were all there on the Armorican beaches. You mustn't take me seriously. All I'm doing is repeating what I've heard. I don't believe a single word of what I'm saying. I only believe in Tate. I believe in nothing. Plus, Tate makes me laugh. That's more than enough. My tub runneth over. In a nutshell, I don't give a hoot.

21

I have a light. Do you have a light?

"Do you have a light?" Chateaugué asks me, handing me an enormous cigar with her discriminating face.

We all have a light. It's the century of light-holders. Those without a light are few and far between. Stop a passerby and ask him for a light. He'll give you one. Isn't it enough to sicken you? A light isn't worth anything anymore, since everybody has one. What would money be worth if we all had pocketfuls of it? They all have pocketfuls of gold and oranges. What are gold and oranges worth? If we had ... Have you seen the *ha* in *had*? You never see anything! Are you mute? What are you doing there with your mouth closed, over the sink? Vomit, dammit! Let it spurt out! Let it roll like an avalanche! Nothing will be left in your body. You'll be ... You'll be ... empty. Are you deaf? Are you deaf, Isabelle Rimbaud? Everybody has a light. Isn't it enough to make you vomit? Have you really vomited, Isabelle Rimbaud? Here's a toothpick, Virginia Woolf. Take it and pick your teeth and pick the ewe lamb out of your gums. I see a vulture. It's there before my eyes. It's on the page of the dictionary. You can find anything in a well-illustrated dictionary. It's a printed vulture. Come see the vulture, Chateaugué. Come! Come! Come! Come! Don't stay there, waiting, waiting for nothing. Vultures don't wait; come on! Come! Open my chest and come on in. Close my chest when you go out. Come reinhabit my chest, which is as empty as a drum. What's in a drum? Nothing. If there were something in a drum, what might there be? I find a cat in the first drum, a nose in the second, a door in the sixth, a globe in the sixteenth, a thousand keys in the fourth, a seal in the fortieth, Vauvenargues in the twentieth, and communicating vessels in all the others. Come, Chateaugué! Come! Come! Come! Kommm! Kommm! Kommm! Kommm! I'm not making up these shouts. I'm not straining to shout. I'm not forging these calls; I'm full of them. Where is Vauban? In the seventeenth century! I repeat: Vauban is in the seventeenth century! I'm losing my marbles! I'm not losing them, I'm leaving them of my own accord because they're not getting me anywhere. Let's sink into debauchery, Chateaugué. Give me your hand, Isabelle Rimbaud. Why do you give me your hand, if it's not for sinking into a stupor? Let me bite into your flesh, your flesh where no one has bitten, your flesh that until now has been as useless as the bronze of a statue. If I bite your ears with voluptuousness, it will stop you from hearing. Your ears taste of honey; I know—the guys told me so. In my mouth I already have the taste of honey so particular to your ears. Your whole skin is sugary, Virginia Woolf. I know—the guys told me so. My mouth is already full of sugar. Let me draw up the warm milk, the milk as white as your skin, the milk your mouth is full of. Your lips are swollen with pink blood, with blood ready to burst, with pale, unhealthy blood. I could go on like this for two hundred blood-red pages. Isn't it enough to make you vomit, burp, and feel sick to your stomach? Isn't it enough to lean over a sink and empty yourself, enough to hate Virginia Woolf and Isabelle Rimbaud, enough to get angry about match-holders? Chateaugué, that idiot, is the one among all females whom I desire the least. I desire a female. A muzzled crocodile would do the trick. I need a vulva. A still-warm cadaver would do the trick. My passion for women is hatred, contempt, disgust, neurosis, and one failure after another. You don't excite my passion, Chateaugué, you hinder it, you ridicule me. Watch out, Chateaugué. If ever my passion loses its way, my mirror will fall and shatter, and I won't be able to see how much you render me ridiculous and repugnant. As a woman, you will never be anything to me but a stopgap, a lesser evil. I suggest you take back your sex organs; with me, they won't contribute to your happiness. The women

I need most are the ones I most loathe: those of the species that we got to study a little while ago, while getting a breath of fresh air on the sidewalk—the ones you find beautiful and I call ugly. I'd rather not see them; I blow my stack whenever I see one. Oh! If only you knew ... cockroaches, bunches of cockroaches, nibble at my sides and my innards. My chest is a buzzing hive, a hive of cockroaches. Worms run through my blood. Loads of stinking toads will jump into the face of the woman who will open me up to see my soul, of the embalmer who will slit me open to embalm me. Big fat greenflies, a cloud of greenflies will sew itself to their faces, will attach itself to their faces as if with a needle and thread. I'm sick of carrying my insects inside, of hiding myself. I am ugly. I am dirty, very dirty. I stink. I whortensturbate. I am spineless and hypocritical. I love no one. I hate you all as much as I hate myself. I wish you all ill; I want you all oozing with evil. I slither where you slither. I loiter where you loiter. I stink like you stink. I hate you all. There is also the elite of humanity. There is not only you, the mire. There is you, the chaste, the gentle, the truly high and mighty. I do not fly where you fly. I do not sing where you sing. I hear your voices, and they fill me with despair: I hate you all. Chateaugué is from another dimension. That's why she doesn't see me, why my odour doesn't reach her nostrils. I am nothing whatsoever. I am, at the very most, a spineless and long-winded victim of whortensturbism. Go spread the word. I really don't give a hoot. Go quickly and tell the match-holders, the match-professors, the match-managers, the match-builders, the match-makers, the match-engineers, the match-producers, the match-directors, the match-doctors, the match-stylists, the match-smokers, the match-firefighters, the match-skiers, the match-holders who ski, the match-holders who ski themselves—whomever you like. I really don't give a hoot. Go shout it from the rooftops if you like! You've got to have matches. Let's keep our city clean; let's kill all those who soil. Matches are part of life. Matches are useful to consumers of matches. Matches are useful to pyromaniacs. Matches are useless and inadequate.

The Reign

You can't do anything about the reign.
You can watch it fall.
Or, whether it's one o'clock or midnight,
Get soaked joylessly.

You can say, "Life is dull."
You can lie down in the middle of the road.
If you are struck by lightning,
You've got to die, at all costs.

You can walk on the sidewalk
Whether it's raining or not.
With that water, fill up a drawer
That you'll open on dry days.

Children cry out. Boats cry out.
Just now, it's sunny.
It's sunny and he's writing
While emptying another bottle.

22

It's cold. I won't mention the temperature. I'm not a weather-
woman. It's so cold that at night you can hear nails popping.
Thanks to this dreadful cold, the landlord has turned the
furnace back on. It's a motorized furnace; you can hear it
rumbling from here. We've opened the transom window to let
the heat come in. Let the little children come unto me, through
the transom window. I am not responsible for my free associa-
tion of ideas. I am not a meteorological Germanic wasp; the
temperature doesn't interest me. You've got to strain to make
the link between the first and second clause of that last
sentence. A little while ago, while coming back from the bathroom, I sat down in this armchair, and, since that time, I've
been sitting. Orolo! Mete orolo gical. I only leave to go to the
bathroom. To break the monotony of the days and the hours,
Chateaugué took advantage of one of my rare absences to hide
under the bed. She was playing hide-and-seek. I didn't even
bother looking for her. Finding her didn't interest me. No one
wanted to look for her. No one wanted to find her. She was
obliged to find herself all by herself. She came sadly out of her
modest hiding place. She seemed disappointed. In any case, I
would have found her right away, on the spot. Life is monotonous. Onoto! M onoto nous. What is monotonous? Is it life or
is it me? In order to practise whortensturbism without Chateaugué's noticing, you've got to hide. You retire to the bathroom
and have a quickie. You come out of there the way a Polish
cucumber comes out of the brine: you're bitter through and
through, saturated; you taste of brine from head to toe. What if
Chateaugué saw me doing it—she who looks at me as if I were

the golden calf, she who washes my underwear the way one polishes a crown, she who hangs on to my arm as if it had moved mountains, she who takes my hand as if it were a flower. If she saw me doing it, she would be appalled, she would become ugly out of desperation and treason. I am a madman, a psychopath. Freud would have been interested in me if he had known me. Why do you do that? I don't know. Is it for the pleasure? You don't feel any. Is it for the disgust? It must be for the disgust, for the wave of disgust that floors us when we get there, when we reach the summit of pleasure. I don't know. I don't understand myself. I don't understand anything. Chateau-gué took me for a friend and is afraid of losing me. She thinks I'm strong, loyal, and handsome, big enough to protect her, big enough to vanquish for her the cruelty of the world, the insidiousness of the world, and the ugliness of the world. Chateaugué is fearful. Her world is a world in peril; a thousand dangers continually make her earth quake. She knows that the mean, the treacherous, and the vile are lying in wait for her, will fling themselves onto her, will empoison her, and are just waiting for her to be alone. If she suddenly saw my true face, which is the very face of her nightmares, she would start to shriek and run like a lunatic. Women give themselves because they are weak and scared, because they see so many scorpions, snakes, and tigers that they don't know where to go anymore. They give themselves to those who seem to know what to do; to know, or seem to know, how to escape from all the rats, the crocodiles, and the wolves out there; women are only too pleased. They're all looking for a master, for a master traveller; they don't know where to go. Women who are alone are scared. Most of the time women are with someone, a man onto whom they have off-loaded their fear, a man to whom they give their bodies by way of thanks. When, suddenly, a woman realizes that the man with whom she has signed a peace treaty is as weak as she is, she's scared again, she takes her fate into her own hands, she hardens and becomes ugly. Women today know what they want ... Is that true? No, that's what they make themselves out to be. They're more scared than before; there are fewer men than before. A woman is always searching for something stronger than herself, stronger than her little face. I talk. I talk. I pull the wool over your eyes. Ink is cheap. Saliva costs nothing. Women run after imaginary generals. Each and every one of them wants her little imaginary marshal. Chateaugué, my sister, I am not a general. I don't even claim to be a general. Don't give yourself to me; don't be a burden to me. Be content to be my sister, to belong *with* me; don't seek to belong *to* me. They say, "This is my wife," the way a cowherd says, "This is my cow." This is my sister, this is my companion, this is she who walks by my side. Get off my back; walk by my side, in your own steps. Don't give anything, numbskull. I don't accept anything, besides. But I don't want you to leave me; you'd be much too unhappy all alone. Who'd want anything to do with you? Those who want just anybody, the whortensturbators who are tired of whortensturbating all alone? Stay with me; I'm not better than they are, but I try. When a man says to a woman, "I am weak, my love," he has just lost her. Women don't forgive that kind of sincere admission. They don't pity a weak man; they heap scorn on weak men; they only know how to pity themselves, little birds, and little things. Little birds and little things need nothing. Women aren't afraid to pity little birds and little things; they know that little birds and little things ask for nothing and require nothing in return for pity. Women don't know how to give; they only know how to take. They give their bodies. That ain't much. They scorn their bodies, believing that they have no value. Their values are abstract: dreams, pride, warmth, gentleness, security. Prostitutes don't prostitute themselves, in their eyes. What they exchange for money—for lack of being able to exchange it for something better—this love, it irritates them, it bores them, it makes them find those who wallow in it, as though in a paradise, ridiculous. Nevertheless, if the woman doesn't think much of love and still scorns what has become of her love—a thing so vile, so seldom satisfied—she is not prepared to accept just anybody in exchange for her love. If the man she obtains in exchange for her love reveals himself to be weak and cowardly, she is humiliated, she weeps. She's made a bad bargain, she's been had; she cries tears of blood. Hide it if you are weak and cowardly; don't tell her; you'll insult her, you'll hurt her feelings; she'll take revenge, she'll no longer give you her love. Women are mercilessly susceptible to fortified towns, to fortresses, to impregnable fortifications. I'm speaking here of women in general, of the most widespread type of woman. There are exceptions ... that's the rule. There are more ordinary women than exceptional women ... that's also the rule. Cucumber. Yesterday, we met an exceptional woman. Cucumber.

"Did you see her?" cried Chateaugué. "Look! She's wearing a men's panty and a men's watch!"

For Chateaugué, a pair of panties is a panty. It's because you only wear one panty at a time, I think. The use of *trousers* is also quite widespread. Almost all men wear pants. However, they don't all wear the same pair. I love the truth and love to state it. I don't like ambiguity. Are you looking for the truth? Let your fingers do the walking through the Yellow Pages. I do not possess the truth, but I do possess around ten of them. Here's one of them: Baffin Island, in the Arctic Ocean, measures 178,700 square miles. Here's another one: there are a lot of Chinese. Here's a third one: the Quebec Biology Centre has a collection of 240 species of fish. I entrust you with one more: Joan of Arc has been dead since 1448; when you die, it's for a long time. Do you see the inanity in Joan? Crocodile. Tate hasn't done anything today worth recounting. Tate lived through the whole day, lived poorly through the whole day. Here, summarized in a couple of words, is everything that happened today: Chateaugué hid under the bed in order to play a trick on me. Are two black crocodiles and two black cucumbers as beautiful as two black tulips and two black swans? Ink is not expensive. The End. Do you want ink? Let your fingers do the walking through the Yellow Pages. Water is for sailors. Ink is for writers. The sailors and the writers exchanged kicks in the face and went on their way. Do you want salt water? Salt the water from the faucet, your running water, your water that runs. Do you want to drink pepper water? Put some pepper in your running water. Do you like Brahms? Yes? You like Brahms? Well, then, kiss him! Go ahead. Don't be shy. He won't eat you; he's not a carnival, he's not an anthropologist, he's not a numismatist. It's my notebook, and I'll write whatever I like in it. You want spelling errors? Make some! Make them yourself! *Conduisez-vous!* What difference is there between *summit* and *peak*? *Peak* does not dot its ice. There are many Chinese on the hearth, I mean on the earth. Excuse me, many a slip 'twixt tongue and lip. Our door, our chairs, our table, and our commode are green. One horse. Two horses. One idea. Two ideaz. *Idea* makes me think of Caesar. Caesar was assassinated on the ides of March, and there are *ides* in *idea*. What kind of literature am I doing, Elphège? Is it surrealistic, surrectional, or surrenal? Don't adjust your set. Smash its face in. Let it do as it likes, and be on your way. Chateaugué hid under the bed, and I didn't even look for her. I would have found her right away, in any case. I'm off to bed. I'm sickened by myself. Why wait for someone else to sicken me? It will all come out in the Washington! Jefferson! Lincoln! Buick! De Soto! Chevrolet! Plymouth! Full steam ahead, Fred!

23

Other people work for other people. Other people work in order to live. We just live; we spend our time doing nothing. We come straight to the point—we just live. We spend our time sleeping, doing nothing, and growing up. We drink, we eat, we smoke; the rest of the time, we just live. O life, O present so sweet! We do like the trees—we just live. Work? Why? To earn a living? Come on now, life is free! Look, we're just living. We're alive, Chateaugué and I. It's very visible. Well-lubricated, our hands would function like brand new ones. They'll function like brand new ones if we ever need hands to live. Life, the real one, is inside, all inside. There is nothing but the soul that lives continuously, that lives when you sleep and when you don't sleep, lives when you work and when you don't work. The soul, an industrious and indefatigable bee, a rambling and boring bee, continually repeats to man that he is present, continually puts his conceited presence in the world right before his nose. We, every time we hear what the soul repeats indefatigably, we feel a great discomfort, we feel a great fear; we are electrified; everything within us contracts violently, as though we were about to drown; everything within us rushes forward and rears up; everything within us, in an excruciating cry, seeks a way out of ourselves. Every time we hear what the soul repeats indefatigably, everything within us masses, clenches, leans, and seeks feverishly, furiously, wildly, and desperately, to catapult itself out of our bodies like submarines full of water. Something within us is captive and stifling. Only the hurly-burly can set free this thing attached within us that suffers like an eagle fastened by its foot to the cement of a sidewalk. It's true, what

I'm saying there. But that doesn't interest my fellow citizens. There's an eagle caught in my belly, and it's fluttering its wings with all its strength to break loose, to get out, to get back to *aira firma*. Who put that eagle there? That eagle is like a yearning for purity that might be about to drown, that could no longer bear to hold its breath, that someone might have anchored in the depths of the world to punish it. Hey, that's beautiful. That's well put. And it's true. Believe it or I'll kill you all. I see you laughing. You're laughing, you sly guys! Why, instead of an eagle, didn't someone moor within us a radish, an onion, a carrot, as in all the others, as in almost all the others? Cabbages and carrots make roots out of any old rot, but not eagles. Eagles take root nowhere. They only take the firmament, and when they can't take it all at once, they struggle to completely pluck their wings. Where can an eagle, other than in the firmament, breathe perfumes so pure that they put him to sleep? We can't all be satisfied with what there is here, with what is found between the skin of the belly and the skin of the back. There are eagles who need more air and more liberty than one chest can contain, than lungs can breathe. We're not all cabbages, worms, tapeworms, and piglets! I inhale and no air comes in; all that comes in is a bit of nitrogen. I beat my fins, but there's no water, only sand. We can't all find that funny—eating and drinking, sleeping and being awake, sitting down and standing up! We can't all find that funny and amusing—working to eat and drink. As for woman, I abhor her influence on my ideas, those yearnings that she caters to, those manufactured perfumes with which she tries to put my eagle to sleep. I endure woman the way a man dying of thirst endures the torture of a mirage. I deplore woman. Sometimes my eagle, tricked by her little face, falls asleep, quiets down, lets go. There's nothing here but eating and drinking, nothing but getting up again, going back to bed again and sitting down again! Eating and drinking wear me out. Woman—I would martyr her! I'd like to make her swallow her false oaths with some sulphuric acid on her little face! How I'd like not to drink, never to eat—to do something else. This is not our place, mine and that of Chateau-gué, who thinks like me, even if she doesn't shout it from the rooftops. Purity! Purity! Nelligan, dazed by his eagle, lost his way in the luxuriance of lunacy. Rimbaud winded and wore out his eagle. To let our eagles out, to let them escape from us, we'll open a big door in our bodies with a dagger; we'll hurly-burly ourselves. Let me swear a bit before being on my way. Love is not something, it's somewhere ... it's ... But no! I'll spare you the pornographic details. Today at Lozeau's, Chateaugué bought two things: some bone charcoal to blacken our mouths and a black notepad. She is writing in the black notepad next to me, following my example. What is she writing?

"I'm not secretive. I'll show you when I'm done. It won't take me long."

We never feel like going out anymore. When we do go out of the room, it's by necessity; it's to eat or go to the bathroom. When we do go out now, it's a big event, a big chore. Life is so monotonous, so onoto monotonous, so orolo meteorological, so boring. We are debilitated and disappointed to have nothing left to satisfy; we are dissatisfied. There are two malcontents in one room—that's us, that's Tate, that's friendship. I don't even know anymore how to grab life, or even death, by the horns. I don't understand at all anymore. The reason I don't grab life by the horns, the reason I leave it there, is because I don't know which horn to grab. But we like to smoke, and we don't deny ourselves. Apparently smoking kills. We don't care, not at all. *Oremus.* That means *let us pray.* Do you hear the *prey* in *pray*? The priest, in a gold-panelled chasuble, swivels before the golden altar, spreads his pastoral stumps majestically: *"Oremus!"* *Let us prey!* I love priests; they're chaste. All men are jealous of the chastity of priests. Chateaugué is writing while biting her fingernails. Chateaugué stops writing while biting her finger- nails and tosses her black notepad on my notebook.

"I'm done. You can read it."

"This is my last will and testament," she wrote. "I have noth- ing to give. I have nothing in the world. My clothes and Miles Miles, my friend, are all I have. My clothes are all worn out. I want to be buried in Port Burwell, New Quebec, where I was born, where my old father and mother died of hunger and cold, where perhaps I have uncles and aunts who still remember my name. I have lived without knowing my parents. I was too little when they died. I want to be buried by the Oblates of Mary, who baptized me. I thank my adoptive parents of the Islands of Sorel from the bottom of my heart for everything they did to make me happy. They had to bear great hardships in order to welcome me into their home. I hardly know anyone on earth anymore. Those I've known are in heaven or in the past. I want to say farewell to my school and convent friends: Marie-Paule, Claire, Louise, Estelle, Marcelle, and all the others. I have hated no one. I've always been afraid to hate. I've loved all those I've known, and they would have loved me as much as I loved them if I had been more generous toward them. I hope I don't cause anyone sorrow by dying with Miles Miles. Miles Miles is not to blame for what happened to me. I've always yearned to die. I've tried not to commit any sins. But I know that God does not forgive those who take their own lives. But he died on the cross for me, and I've tried to offend him as little as possible. I want the name of Miles Miles and the name that he gave me to be engraved on my tombstone. I'd like Miles Miles to be buried with me, but he is free to be buried wherever he likes. Signed, Chateaugué."

I have trouble swallowing my saliva. "For what happened to me ..." I have trouble holding back my tears. I avoid meeting Chateaugué's gaze. "The name that he gave me ..."

"What's gotten into you?" I say to her, looking straight in front of me.

She asks me if I want her to destroy the notepad.

"If you want me to tear it up, I'll tear it up."

"Did you get everything you wrote there out of your head?"

All we have left is fifteen dollars and thirty cents.

24

We stole two daggers at the drugstore. Sometimes, in order to die, two daggers come in handy. I have a past, and I think about it nonstop. I have the same past as Chateaugué, or just about. Our fellow citizens used to take offence at our playing together. At the age when you're rebellious, Chateaugué obeyed all my orders. At the age when you don't care about anyone, she pursued me, she dogged my footsteps. Whenever I preferred the company of boys to hers, she would become dejected and would wait silently for me to succumb to one or the other of the tender traps that she knew how to set for me. If not to her airs, it was to her laughter that I succumbed. If not to pity, it was to the candy. In those days, I had a real sweet tooth. On Saturdays, I would play in the woods with the boys. The woods were overrun with boys. Off searching for me since daybreak, having found me nowhere else, Chateaugué, at the risk of getting herself skinned alive, would go into the woods. The thorns of the hawthorns would rip her dress, she'd see woodchucks, she'd lose her way, her legs would bleed on the thorns of the blackberry bushes, she'd get hit by an arrow, she'd get her hair pulled. Finally, by chance, she'd happen upon where I was playing war. She'd plunk herself down under a tree and wait. One finger up her nose, one hand behind her back, her head to one side, with a hypocritical air, she'd lie in wait for my glances and catch them with broad smiles. She'd scratch her legs with her toes, she'd rub an eye stung by the sun with one arm and keep the other one behind her back. Plunked down there, she'd wait. I'd let her wait. I wouldn't let her wait too long. I knew her; I knew she hadn't come empty-handed. When, no longer keeping her pining, I'd finally come up to meet her, she'd burst out laughing and pretend to run away. I had to run after her. She wouldn't run fast; she did that on purpose. When I'd catch up to her, her eyes would be bursting with pleasure. She'd say, "Here!" and would relinquish a crumpled slice of bread and butter or a slice of bread with molasses or corn syrup. She'd say, "Here!" and would give me the apple that she'd hidden from me. She'd say, "Here!" and would open her dirty little gummy hand all the way, making coins glint in it. My happiness was provided for. The Brasseurs' restaurant was a cornucopia; to enjoy my friendship, she dipped into it angelically. We'd go fish for tadpoles with old curtains. We'd go eat cherries right off the cherry trees. We'd come back with black teeth. We'd go get surprised by the rain; we'd drink right out of the clouds. We'd go walk along the river. We'd take our shoes off and walk right in the river water. We'd go see the baseball game when it was Sunday. We'd go take raft rides. We'd go see the fires, whenever there was one. There were brush fires and shore fires. We'd go make roads under the porch with our trucks. We'd go see the schooner, whenever a schooner was loading at the dock. Actually, I liked to play with her more than with the boys. What I liked most about her was her astonishment. Everything I said astonished her. What wouldn't make the boys laugh would make her laugh till she cried. What the boys wouldn't believe, she'd believe; she'd listen while her eyes grew rounder and rounder. What I liked most was her funny air. She had the eyes of a woodchuck venturing out of its hole. With her, everything was terrific. With the boys, everything was boring. Her adoptive parents didn't take care of her. I myself took care of her. No one would have anything to do with her. No one has ever wanted anything to do with her. In winter, she'd come seduce me at the skating rink. The gummy fish that she brought to seduce me would get stuck to the wool of her mittens, and she'd laugh about it.

25

Today I don't have much to say. I'm happy without cause, and I've been happy all day for no reason. I'm afraid of suffering tomorrow. We suffer when something resists us, when someone leaves us, when we lose an illusion, when we're betrayed by a false hope. Now, I have nothing, I have no one, I possess no illusions, I have no hope at all. What will I lose tomorrow? What will I suffer from? What am I afraid of? Renounce everything, and you will never be afraid. Forsake yourself, and you will never suffer again. Forsake yourself as you would a hair shirt. When I suffer, it's because I haven't forsaken myself enough. But I just realized—purity? I'm not free to desert myself, for by deserting myself I renounce my duty to purity, for by forsaking myself I forsake every reason to hurly-burly myself ... because I'm hurly-burlying myself for me. Tomorrow I will suffer again. What do I care? My eagle's sleeping. I no longer feel the eagle driven into my flesh flapping its wings, raining down blows with its extractive axes, flapping its wings the way you pull with a clamp on a tooth that twinges. Flapping wings! Flappers' wings! My eagle's sleeping, but it's not sleeping from cowardice; it's sleeping because it's lost its nerve. It's trying to recover its strength. Tomorrow I'll feel it struggling again, fluttering at full sail, pulling on its talons caught in my senses. You can't get away from purity when it's within you and when it's an eagle. And woman? As for them? I want woman and impurity. I want impurity as savagely as I repel it. I want woman with all my blood. I want you, woman, to kill you! Go figure that out. Last night, once again, Chateaugué was crying in her sleep. I want woman, but not tonight. Tonight, I want nothing, I'm happy, I'm resting. Tonight, in me, everything serenely cancels itself out. What have I got to lose? I have the eagle to lose. A little while ago, I said that I had nothing to lose. In all good faith, I was lying. I love eagles; they elate me. Just what is my eagle? I say that it's an excruciating and thundering call to purity. Could it be that I'm only saying that out of pride? These harrowing cries and this fluttering of wings, could it be that they are nothing but the cries and torsions of my pride, heckled and tormented by woman? Tonight, my eagle is quiet because woman is leaving it alone. I've plunged into the obscure and the shameful with this pen. It's surer and surer that through the hurly-burly, I'll set my eagle free from the sexual trap, from a sordid and shameful trap. It's from the black magic of the shameful and the sordid—a magic in which I found myself without having steered my steps there, the galleys where I was sent without trial—that the hurly-burly will set me free. There's nothing but woman in this desert; how can I think of anything else? Woman is not the culprit, the cause, the devouring humiliation. The culprit is the desert where there's nothing but her—the world. My head isn't big enough to understand the world the way it understands itself. I understand it as I see it: they threw men into a desert with woman as sole combat and sole repose, with woman as sole shame and sole glory. They left spirits, angels, souls, and gods to groan in the desert, with nothing but women! Go forth and multiply! Just add woman, lukewarmness, spinelessness, and stupidity among men alone in a desert! Go forth and multiply! A fine slaughter! A fine orgy! A fine carnage! A festival of degeneracy and corruption! Here is an excerpt from what we read today at the library: "What the potato weevil was to the *Flowers of Evil*, were not the medium and Figuier the same to a veritable occultist work whose ideal might coincide with Rimbaud's (O) period and the achievement of Baudelaire?" "Rimbaud's (O) period"! When we read that, we laughed so hard that we choked. Someone deserves a swift kick in the pants. Some people make a cult of serious foolishness. Some people spend their lives seriously looking into the logistical problems raised by the reading of Rimbaud's cries and affectations. Some people seek to understand! Who cares if what you seek to understand has no importance? It's so sweet to understand something, to solve charades. Man is so flattered when he manages to understand something difficult to understand. Who cares if we don't understand why we live, why we spend our time suffering and being bored? What life means is nothing next to what *ithyphallic* and *rookie-esque* mean. What are you doing here in this arm-chair? I'm digesting. What are you doing there on that side-walk? I'm off to buy matches. There's no one but Miles Miles who's funny. Miles Miles can't live without worthwhile reasons. What do you think of those who do things without worthwhile reasons? You think they're crazy, really crazy. What do you think of those who keep living in the house where they suffer, where they know that nothing can come of it but pain? Do women know why they go teetering on artificial heels several inches, even several feet high? Is it so they'll look more like herons?

Pan Ick

In the completely empty house,
A man comes in wearing a green suit.
On his face, deep wrinkles
Speak volumes about his woes.

"Maman! Maman!" he finally cries,
Having waited without saying a word.
"Maman! Papa!" And he passes away.
But the people have already seen worse.

The house falls prey to flames.
The people watch, laughing.
A nun with an aching heart
Is there. Alas! She has no teeth.

"Alan, my father! Alan, my father!"
Cries the nun, sobbing,
Then she hails a taxi to hell,
After working herself to death.

26

It all started with Chateaugué's cough, a hoarse, powerful, grimacing cough, an insistent and inexhaustible cough that aggravated me more than she worried me. Her throat must have been burning and bloody from coughing like that. Her burning and bloody throat didn't matter much to me. Nonetheless, I was worried. What if it were pneumonia ... What if she died of it ... What would I look like with her cadaver on my hands? With what would I dig a hole in all this cement to bury her? We didn't have enough money to see a doctor or to buy medicine. With what money can you buy medicine now that men are on strike? What to do? Chateaugué said to let it be, that it would pass, that Eskimos don't die of pneumonia. She was coughing nonstop. After hearing her cough for two days and two nights, my nerves were all on edge. Every time I heard her cough, I said to myself, "She's doing it on purpose!" My brow was knitted, I was clenching my fists; I was taking her pain in stride. All of a sudden, I was fed up with it. All of a sudden, I put on my windbreaker and I stormed out. Taking advantage of her coughing fits to hurly-burly ourselves? The thought didn't even cross my mind. Nothing is clear enough in my head yet. Alone, I walked down the sidewalk that I had never walked down except with her. There was nothing next to me, and it was worse than if she had been there—there was an emptiness and a silence. Set free and yet still fettered, I strolled, going nowhere, following the sidewalk. At a certain point, full of apprehension, I turned around. It was cold enough to freeze your butt off. Chateaugué was there, trotting behind me, with nothing on but her dress and her panties. Naked arms, naked head, naked legs, she was trying to suppress a bout of coughing without losing her dazzling smile.

"Chateaugué! Go back to the room, or I will no longer be accountable for my actions! Go away! Do you understand? Go away. Get the hell out of here! Give me a break, I won't spend the night outside! I'll come back to you. I'm not the one who's an Eskimo!"

"Stop fooling around, Miles Miles. Don't leave me. Let me go with you. I can walk. It doesn't stop me from walking." I have no idea what I shouted at her, but I shouted up a storm. I chased her away by stamping my feet, the way you chase away a dog that's too faithful. I shouted, I gesticulated; I had lost control of myself. I would have stoned her. The passersby looked at me askance, but I really didn't give a hoot about the passersby. When you've got problems, you really don't give a hoot about the passersby. You take yourself seriously. I felt like getting drunk, but not on beer. I didn't feel like anything, actually. I felt like feeling like something, felt like going somewhere. I followed my footsteps, fiddling with a five-dollar bill at the bottom of my pocket—all that was left of our money. It was nighttime. It was Saturday. I had come to Boulevard Saint-Laurent, the Mafia boulevard. I burst into a seedy bar. I didn't sit at the counter; it was too densely populated there. I went to sit down at a table, in the darkest, least-inhabited corner. The waiter looked down his nose at me and asked me my age. He looked like he wouldn't hear another word. I have a heavy beard for my age, and it was long.

"A double gin, on fire!" I shouted to the waiter in a shrill voice, looking down my nose at him.

The manoeuvre didn't meet with the expected success. The heavy-set waiter looked down his nose at me one more time. In a fairly loud voice this time, in order to attract the attention of the whole (perverted) population of the bar, he asked me my age again. He didn't seem to have been intimidated by what I had said.

"A double gin, on fire! To drink, you don't have to be twenty; all you have to be is thirsty."

"Your age, slacker!"

I took a cynical pleasure in the little game. He started up again. I started up again. It was easy. It wasn't hard. And meanwhile, Chateaugué was alone and phthisicky in the cold room. And meanwhile, I had left her in tears in the middle of the street, I had called her a leech. She was dying of pneumonia, and I was defending the privilege that the provincial constitution did not grant me to drink our last five dollars away. We started up again, the heavy-set waiter and I, and I found it deliciously bitter.

"How old, slacker?"

"Forty-two, my friend. I'm forty-two years old. If I don't look it, that's because I'm an Eskimo. Eskimos look younger than they are. The Eskimo retains a youthful appearance his whole life long. The reason I don't have an Eskimo accent is that I lost it while crossing the Hudson Bay. The reason I don't have any identification papers is that I lost them while crossing the Bering Strait."

I sensed that I had gone too far, and that someone was going to hurt me. I stuck it out and waited. But the crowd of customers had heard and was laughing. But a middle-aged woman was coming over to me laughing uproariously; she was leaning on my table, and, to my great surprise, she was casually addressing me.

"Shimo! Old buddy! Old pal! It's been ages!"

With a natural and offhand insolence, she pushed the monumental waiter away and set herself down on the chair that the monumental waiter was threatening to throw at me. After seating herself comfortably, she turned toward the big waiter of tables (and chairs) and told him to go away, to leave me alone, that she knew me well.

"He's a real Eskimo. I know him well. If you don't leave him alone, he'll pop your fat beer belly with his big stone knife. Eskimos are quicker than lightning and faster than mercury— you'll have a knife in your belly and you won't even notice it. They don't look mean, but when they lose their tempers, they are."

She was on familiar terms with him. She seemed to know him. I let myself be protected. I talk, I talk. I elaborate, I draw out, I drag on; I don't spare you any detail. I wouldn't make a good writer, but I'd make a good rider. *Rider* is the feminine form of *writer*. *Archbishop* is the feminine form of *architect*. Prudence is the mother of Brigitte Bardot. I could go on for two hundred pages. The waiter of tables (and chairs) served me my gin and served her some wine. Do you see the *gin* in va*gina*? It's shocking! The gin in the vagina! It's indecent! She crossed her legs the way all adult women cross their legs, in a sickening way, making her nylons rustle, pulling on her skirt the way you bridle a mulish mare. I gulped down a lot of gin and asked her her beloved name.

"What is your beloved name?"

"No-Good! Fatty No-Good!"

"No-God? As in Nietzsche?"

"Not No-God. No-Good! Neither No-God nor No-Good! Questa. Questa! My name is Questa, just for you. Call me Questa. That means that thing there, that fat thing there. It's Italian. I'm Flemish. Do you know 'The Flemish Women' by Jacques Brassens?"

She proved to be a chatterbox. So I exercised every right; I took the liberty of being on familiar terms with her. Before my eyes was my first real woman, my Eve.

"You're not Flemish. You're as black as a crow, and Flemish women are blonde as ... as ... beets."

"No, I'm not Flemish. I'm ... solo. I wasn't born in Phlegmland, but in Sololand. I was born in Sololand, but I've been living in Bysses for ... for ... a long time. I'm solo tonight. Tonight, I want to stop living in a Byss. Hold out your hands, Eskimo; pull me out of a Byss. The rest of the time, I'm a mother of three, mothering up a swarm. I have three little ants, three little girl ants. They're sleeping. When they sleep, you can't even hear them breathing."

She looked drunk, and she looked married. She was wearing a bunch of diamonds on I have no idea which finger of I have no idea which hand. She talked volubly about her little girls for two and a half hours. She told me about the flowery pink wallpaper in their little room, about their little blue beds on casters that you see dotted around the room when you go in. I let her talk, let her be a chatterbox, let her come out of her shell all by herself. You can take every liberty with chatterboxes, both male and female. She never stopped talking. I promised myself to take some. Alas! Alas!

"They're as fat as your fist. They sleep all sprawled out like cows, as if nothing had happened, as if there were no danger, as if life—the bitch!—had spared them; as if life were going to keep, as it has so far, the sweet promise of their little faces. How ugly it is! I've only been a lush since I've known my little ants."

I ordered and gulped down another glass of gin. Under the effect of the alcohol, I thought of Chateaugué, of getting help for her.

"You've got kids? If you've got kids, you're married. Is your husband a doctor? That would work out well—I need a doctor."

"My husband? A doctor? As if I cared! He could be a Marshal of France for all I'd care. My husband believes himself obliged to maintain me. Maintaining flatters men. My little girls, my little pink cockroaches, he's going to corrupt them with his banks and his cheques, his clients, his bills, and his important business. If I were a real mother, I'd pull my little ones out of his house, that stone he is who numbs children's hearts. If I had a heart, Rodrigo, I'd take my little ones away to live where the heart doesn't harden while the rest blooms. Do I look like a degenerate? Yes, I look like a degenerate. What's your name? That's right, your name is Shimo."

It was her lipstick talking. Her lipstick was scintillating.

"My name is Scin Tillating."

"You haven't shaved. That means you don't like women."

"Women sicken me."

"Oh, my goodness! I really like that, a man who doesn't like women. I like to touch him. Let me touch you. Aha, you've got a big nose! That means you like women. That means you're sentimental. Will you take out your pen and write me a poem?"

With the tip of a long, well-painted fingernail, she caressed the bridge of my nose. She was taking me for a ride. Her fingernails were painted. Her hair was tinted. Her lips were buttered with lipstick. Her face was greasy. Her hair, as black as shoe polish, wasn't combed but rather starched, frozen into a block. This wasn't a woman, but a painted woman, a pained woman, a painter. Her jewellery jingled against her glass whenever she took a sip. She was a jaded, chattering, rich person. Luck was on my side. I staked everything on it. I slipped one hand under the table and tried to reach her knees, but my arm wasn't long enough. I would have had to lean forward, to penetrate under the table up to my shoulders. I had swallowed three glasses of gin, I had started on my fourth; I felt dizzy, and I didn't have a penny left. She noticed my ploy. Conspicuously, with two vigorous heaves of the chair, she drew closer to my curious hand.

"Go right ahead, little man. I've been married for ten years, been a prostitute for ten years. I understand these things. At sixteen, your age, I was getting married, I was entering Bysses. That's false, since I'm thirty-two years old. I was twelve when I got married."

I made as if to put my hand on her knees, but I didn't do anything. I had brought my last gin with me, under the table, and I poured it over her knees. When she felt the gin going down her legs, she made quite an expression. I got up and got out. I didn't get out very fast. I was tottering, and I was leaning on whatever I could get my hands on—chair backs, women's shoulders, chair shoulders, women's backs. I was proud of how I'd pulled it off, and I was laughing up my sleeve while making my way toward the exit. I was telling myself that that would teach her to play Mrs. Smart Aleck with Eskimos. I was so drunk I couldn't even see straight. I slipped on a stray French fry and fell flat on my face on a repugnant sidewalk. I realized that someone who reeked of perfume was helping me up. I realized that it was my painter woman, that she was still there. She was laughing like a lunatic, and the spilled gin was forming a big black stain on her red skirt.

"I've got a locomotive," she told me. "I'll bring you back to the fold in my locomotive."

She pushed me into her European sports car, and I gave her my address. I closed my eyes to let my head spin more comfortably, to let it spin without the flat stability of the world fighting its movement. When she woke me up, the air was strong and the sky empty and uninhabited. I understood that we were in the middle of the countryside and that she had played a trick on me. I went in behind her, into her house, and I kept following her. We went into the chapel of her three little girls, and we looked at their faces, one girl after another, in the glow of the flame of her cigarette lighter. The little ones were sleeping, their faces white and their mouths red, their hair silky and their skin soft.

"That one over there, she's the littlest one. She's a champ. She says I've got a big spider full of eyes at the back of my mouth and that it's nibbling. Open your mouth wide wide wide, Maman. She stares. Her eyes are strained and glassy; she sees the big spider full of eyes; she sees one of its big black feet full of thorns. She laughs at that. She scares herself and laughs. If she knew that one of them is growing inside her, at the back of her mouth—a big spider—she wouldn't think it's so funny. I can't do anything for her. I let her do as she likes."

She made me take some pills for dyspepsia, and we hit the road again. The radio was playing some saxophone or trumpet music.

"That's jazz," she said to me. "It's by Jean Racine. It's the Vauvenargues Quintet."

Farther along, on the road, on the highway, on the grey highway, flat, wide, and deep, she became silent, serious, and absorbed in her thoughts. Holding on to the edge of her seat, she was looking straight ahead. She was doing her little automobilist thing, her little automobile thing. Her skirt, in the green glow of the speedometer, was slipping up, inching up, uncovering. She asked me which direction Rue Saint-Denis was one-way. The question was too stupid. I didn't even go to the trouble of answering. I put one hand on her knees. I caressed her knees, and she didn't even notice. She was out of commission, like every automobile. I raised my hand above her and let it fall on her head, her shoulder, her chest, her legs. My hand was a stone that I was dropping on her, that I was picking up and dropping on her again. She didn't have time to tell me that what I was doing was stupid and ridiculous. The traffic was too heavy. She grunted, the way a cow grunts that isn't content but isn't mean. She was receiving communion, her hands grafted to the wheel; she belonged to the communion of the automobiles; she didn't have time to attend to me. I put my two hands on her face and let them tumble down along her body. I tried to be brutal, with the tokens of affection of a little girl for her mother. She was pricking up her ears, trying to hear what the other automobiles were saying. I fell back asleep.

"Last stop! Last stop! Last stop! Last stop! Everybody off!"

We had arrived. We were next to the house belonging to my room. She invited herself up. She thought perhaps that I lived alone; I did nothing to disabuse her of that notion.

"You have a house with two noses," she said, looking at the two skylights of the house belonging to my room.

I went up the stairs behind her. I looked under her skirt. I didn't see much; her skirt was too tight. She was going up the stairs the way all adult women go up stairs. Perched on her artificial heels, she was going up the stairs laboriously, stopping to catch her breath, leaning first on one butt cheek, then on the other. Before going into my room, I took her, caressingly, by the hair with both hands and pulled back until her neck was totally extended, totally stretched out. She had two furrows in her neck, like two wire marks. Her neck was laid out in tiers. She gave me a little gloved punch on my nose and asked me if I was crazy. I opened up. In the shadows, the white face of Chateaugué cast more light than the sheets. It was as though her head were set in them like a precious stone. That vision moved Questa and went straight to her heart. Shamelessly, she ran to the bedside of Chateaugué, sat down on the floor, to be face-to-face with her, and spoke to her the way a mother speaks to her little girl.

"Who's this? Who's this? Your nose is all red? Are you sick? Let me feel your forehead. Ooh! It's burning. Poor little munchkin! Do you have a cold? You're all alone in your big room, and you have a cold? What did you do to your mouth? Your mouth is all black."

"It's Chateaugué. I think she's caught a bad cold. I don't know what to do. I'm broke. We'd better bring her back home. It's not far, about fifty miles. It's in Berthier."

Questa took off her gloves to take Chateaugué's pulse. As Questa was digging about under the sheets to find her wrist, Chateaugué woke up, opened the round and burning eyes of an animal in danger, and started to cough without being able to stop. Questa picked her up, took her in her arms, slapped her on the back, and rubbed her vigorously. Chateaugué said nothing. Chateaugué wasn't saying anything. Mute with consternation, she looked hard at each of us in turn, she looked into the face of danger with her intent and incandescent eyes; she saw us coming a mile away. She had gone to bed completely dressed; all she needed to be ready to travel was her shoes. With a maternal hand, Questa put on her shoes. Chateaugué let her put on her shoes without a single word, coughed with all her might, and then fainted. The road was long. Dead tired, Questa kept blinking. She'd fall asleep, wake up, and then suddenly slam on the brakes. Every once in a while, I'd shake her. In the back, erect like a pious person on her posterior, her eyes enormous and shining, Chateaugué remained mute with consternation. When Chateaugué had regained consciousness, Questa had enveloped her in a blanket that she had found in her trunk, a blanket full of dead grass and dried mud. To get down the stairs, I had carried her in my arms. In my arms, she had pretended to be dead; she hadn't made the slightest gesture to help me carry her. When finally our procession pulled up to the Brasseurs' house, on the Islands, she found the use of her vocal cords again. She shouted "No!" three or four times. Afterward, holding herself in to keep from shouting and to stop coughing, she opened the door herself and got out of the car on her own. She was tottering with dignity without looking back. We followed her. She went around the house to go in by the service door. I took her arm, to help her go up the porch steps. She pushed me away weakly, with all the vigour that her state permitted. She was knocking on the door, knocking, knocking, without getting any answer. She wasn't knocking hard enough. The blows of her fist made no more noise than the flapping of a wing.

"Pound harder!" I shouted to her. "Pound harder!"

All this made me impatient and aggravated me. Finally, someone came to open up, and she disappeared. Questa wanted to go in, too, but I didn't let her. Coming back from the Islands, to thank Questa for her services, I reviled her. My insults didn't disturb her; at the very most, they kept her awake. She started it.

"Here I am the fairy in a fairy tale!" she exclaimed.

"You don't know the first thing about fairy tales, Mrs. Fatty No-Good. All you have to do is examine the thickness of your hips to realize that."

"I was a child once, too."

"No way! Never! You lie! Once a child, always a child. No one becomes a hooker through spontaneous generation, through mutation. You're born a hooker. People don't become what you are; they've always been that way. You're an adult, you're rotten; you belong to the race of spouses, of his and hers. You're an animal. You have no soul, no heart, no insides. Just look how you walk, how your behind swings when you walk. Watch the pendulum swing! Just look how you dress. You're so corseted, so adjusted, that it would only take one touch of a fingernail to make you crack."

"Don't play the lady-killer. This little piggy went to market. This little piggy stayed home. This little piggy had roast beef, and this little piggy had none. And this little piggy, this little piggy ran all the way home."

"Instead of a soul, you've got a thermometer. Nothing interests you but the temperature. Nothing can make you laugh or cry but changes in temperature. It's hot in your arms! Your heat makes my mercury dilate! We're so cozy, my love! You're hot or cold. You're never scared or ashamed. No one can humiliate you or make you proud. I hate adults so much that I'd say anything at all to you, provided it's in hatred, and provided you understand that it's in hatred. Either you're born a child, or you're born an adult."

"I was born an adulteress, my dear Scin Tillating."

After saying that, she burst out laughing.

"I'm seething with hatred. I don't even go to the trouble of choosing my words when I talk to adults. I shout anything at them."

Questa let herself be bawled out, blinking her eyes to stay awake. She'd slam on the brakes and jerk the wheel when she no longer knew whether she was asleep or awake. I called her every name that came into my head: thermometer, barometer, rotten tomato, rancid soup. I chewed her out for fifty miles. We pulled in safe and sound to one of the two parking lots to the left of the house belonging to my room. I slammed the door as I got out of her automobile, and I told her not to come poking her nose into my life anymore. She took her key out of her ignition switch. Her dashboard lights went out and her motor fell silent. She didn't seem to pay much attention to my farewells and my burning of bridges.

"I'm sleeping here. I'm too tired to go any farther."

On the stairs, I told her to leave me alone. She agreed but kept following me. She got undressed quickly and fell asleep immediately. When I saw her in harness and suspenders, in garters and straps, I looked away. Her strangled thighs, her thick and flaccid skin, her underarm stubble—everything, everything about her body was repulsive. I said nothing. She didn't seem self-conscious about her monstrous appearance. She unharnessed herself without paying me the slightest attention. I said nothing. I saw her coarse and brittle hair on Chateaugué's pillow, and I found that bitterly funny. She was sleeping. I woke her up to tell her to take off her diamonds. One of her fingers was bristling with brilliants. I was scared of getting my eyes gouged out. When you have bad dreams, you fling your hands all over the place.

"You must have nightmares a lot when you're an adult."

She dropped her rings on the floor without a word. She would have dropped anything at all on the floor, provided it made me shut my trap. She was tired. She wanted to be left alone, to be allowed to sleep. It was noon when she got up. She got up in a good mood. She got dressed in a flash and left immediately. She left declaiming.

"Wait for me, Scin Tillating, I'll be back. I'll be back, scintillating with cleanliness; wait for me, Scin Tillating. Rodrigo, do you have a heart?"

Here I am again, alone with my chimeras. I hope she comes back, dead or alive. I hope she comes, dead or alive—Chateaugué, Questa, Madame de Sévigné, Mary of the Incarnation, or anybody at all.

27

I'm dead drunk with Questa. She arrived drunk at one o'clock
in the morning. She was carrying a bouquet in her arms, a
bouquet of bottles. Her arms were full of those beautiful bottles
capped by a sphere of gargoyle silver that are reflected in the
mirrors of the bars. She came in and ran to empty out her arms
on the bed. She was so glad to have brought all those bottles to
safe harbour that she started to declaim.

"Art! Art! O art! Works of art! Boutiques of art! The rays of
art! The toes of art! O art, here are the flasks of art! Here are the
flasks full of golden flakes! Let's drink gold! Gold numbs the
chops, the tongue, the uvula, and the soul! Fire has broken out!
The bar fell prey to flames. From that deluge, I saved the best;
it's as good as gold. I'm a poetess; a bearded muse is sitting on
my headess. Oh, the leather that wakes up as a bugle! Oh, the
fir that wakes up as a violin! Oh, the pine that wakes up as a
coffin, pregnant with a dead cadaver! Oh, the bow-stroke thrust
and lost on the statue of flesh! O my legionnaire in the morning's red glare! When the firefighters arrived, there was nothing
left to save! Nothing but the chairs; the poetess with a muse on
her head had taken it all! Let's make rhymes, my adolescent
friend, rosy-cheeked like my sleeping daughters! O good apples!
O Zouave Yugoslav!"

She was wearing a big hat, a designer show hat; she took it
off and flung it toward the ceiling. With a kick, she flung to the
ceiling each of her shoes of gleaming skin. With greedy eyes, I
watched her fling herself onto the bed and embrace her bottles
of art. I was hungry. I had stayed locked in for three days, without a penny, without sleeping, without eating. Come or I die! If

no one had come, I would have let myself die of hunger, sleep, and claustrophobia. Questa asked me if there were any pyjamas, while versifying.

"Are there any pyjamas, bananas? I want to make myself at home. I've come here to put on pyjamas, bananas. Do you have some? I like being silly here. It's like Cilicia here."

I flung a dirty shirt at her head, and some dirty pants, unsewn and ripped. She unfurled them like flags and sang their beauty.

"Oh, the shirt of despair and resignation to fatality. Oh, the cloistered pants of the sequined brooches. Oh, the water! Oh, swimming so delinquent! Oh, holes in such quantity! *Fatality* rhymes with *quantity*, and *sequined* rhymes with *delinquent*."

Next, she said something interesting. She said that she had come to see me as a nursing mother, as a bearer of milk. She told me that her jalopy was outside and that it was full of soft bread and hard eggs. She was a sight for sore eyes, and it's with those eyes (do you see the *yes* in e*yes*?) that I went down the stairs. On the back seat of the automobile, I found enough to feed an army. Spices and meats, biscuits and cakes—there was an abundance of everything on the back seat of the automobile. Returning to the room, I found Questa dressed in pyjamas, asleep. With a few kicks, so that they wouldn't ruin my appetite, I pushed under the bed the corsets and harnesses that she had taken off before putting on the pyjamas; then I had a wonderful time. I got shit-faced, and I stuffed my face. Now I'm shit-faced, and I've got a stomach ache. I'm sitting, solitary and shit-faced, with Questa, who is shit-faced and asleep. I'm shit-faced, and I'm watching over her. Questa is shit-faced and sleeping, and I'm watching over her. Through the window, a faint light penetrates, a grey light enters. What is that light? Is it the grey light of evening? Is it the faint light of dawn? Is something ending? Is everything beginning again already? I'm all muddled! It's shouting at me! It's scared! It no longer knows whom to shout at or what to hit! My soul screams! This soul! This live target where the rays of the world converge, where all the spears of the air converge! All my blood shouts! All my blood wounds me! Everything in me swells and clenches; everything in me squeezes and strains. It hurts! O chaste alcohol, you who cast golden rays, warm the hand that holds you! What rhymes with *alcohol?* Wall! Paul! Saul! Loll! Hall! Sprawl! Glycol! Near the wall, Paul and Saul loll around the hall and sprawl, looking for glycol! What a scenariol! Paul and Saul didn't loll around the hall. Phenobarbital for all!

28

The Tower

The tower is tall. It's too tall.
Four ants climb up next.
On the summit, Lili, without fail,
Meets me when it's cool.

The tower is yellow, yellowy-orange
In the pitch-black night.
Lili, from the summit of the barn,
Fly after me, fly and follow me.

Fly after me, run after me,
Lili, Lili, Lili, Lili!
Together let's reach the roof
Of this tower that trembles and sags.

Jump, tower! Make the bitter sea dance!
Fling out your feet, toss ours about,
Let's fall and drown ourselves in the air
Like others drown in water.

My pain is not physical. My pain has its origins in a lack of light, a lack of understanding of the world; it has its origins in confusion and obscurity. My pain is mental—the pain that I'm suffering from at this very moment—a pain that spills out of my soul, that pours out its acid into my flesh. Sitting, I wait. I pretend to wait, but I'm waiting for nothing; I know that nothing will come. Sitting, I do not wait. My faculties have no effect on my pain; they merely record it. They don't help me;

they merely repeat, like parrots, that I'm in pain, that I don't know what to do, that it's quite dreadful, that it's quite pitiful. My pain is too vast, too deep; it drowns my faculties; it drowns my inner eyes. The immensity of my pain, like that of the world, precludes analysis. How do I understand and govern what surrounds me the way the sea surrounds the fish? You can't see what you're swimming in. Fish don't see the sea. Fish have their mouths full of sea, but they've never seen the sea. I have my mouth full of pain, and I've never seen the pain, and I don't know what it is. I see my pain in the shape of an eagle lodged in my insides; I see wrong. I am the eagle, and the insides are the world. I am the fish, and the sea is the world. I am the parasite. I am the far-fetched fish of pain, not of sin, but truly of pain, pain that I'm suffering from, pain when you say, "I'm in pain," not the pain that children speak of when, between two fits of laughter, they say, "Deliver us from evil." What is sin, next to pain? Love one another so that everything will go well ...! What stupidity! What indulgence and frivolity! The reason adults don't love one another is not because they have sentimental reasons for not loving one another, not because they don't believe in the sanctimonious prettiness of the thing, but because they're in too much pain to deal with such foolishness. To become an adult is to enter the kingdom of pain, to be caught up more and more in it. Why don't adults laugh like children? Do you laugh when you're in pain somewhere? Why doesn't the adult frolic, why doesn't he play? He doesn't have the heart to frolic; he has a heart burned by pain. His whole heart is steeped in the acids that gnaw away at it. Even when he's doing nothing, the adult tells you that he's busy. He's busy with pain, besieged by mental anguish. Leave him alone, he's busy, he's caught up in it; he's in pain; the pain activates all his muscles, the pain consumes all the energy that he expends. Nothing is more absorbing, more tiring, or more demanding than being in pain. Only his primordial instincts can distract the victim from it. Once you've made yourself into an adult, once you've been initiated into the intensity and the insurmountability of the pain, you have at the same time been banished from fecklessness and futility, you have at the same time seen the fecklessness and the futility of everything that cannot demolish the pain. I shall not seek to define the pain, which is the wretchedness of the adult and which finds expression on his face by a kind of fixedness called sadness, a soft or rigid fixedness according to whether the adult has adopted nostalgia or hatred to defend himself. I am content merely to name the pain. Some people claim to meddle with the causes of the pain and avert its effects, to unearth the roots of the pain and pick its fruits. They are imbecilic fish, fish that have seen the ocean, fish that have travelled a lot and have seen the world. One thing for sure: allowing for exceptions, all adults are caught up in the pain, and, allowing for exceptions, all children are nothing but victims of the time bomb of pain. All of the preceding, if you haven't guessed it, is nothing but a paradox, a bluff, an appetizer, and a farce. I often say ridiculous things without realizing it. I don't want to suffer anymore. If man understood himself, he would be able to act on himself the way the man who understands diesel engines can act on them. I'm speaking of competence, not of concepts. Who doesn't have concepts? Who is in possession of competence? Oh! Oh! Sometimes, the pain seems so far away to me, so improbable, so inoffensive, so ridiculous! ... Since I've come out of it, I tell myself that you only go into it in order to come out of it. The worst is to know that the pain is universal, that it's like an element of the air that all men breathe. The worst thing for someone who suffers is to understand that he's not the only one, that he's not the victim of an error or of a temporary difficulty in the world, but that all the others are suffering like him, that no one is spared.

"That's how it is," my mother used to say to my sister, when my sister was sick of being discouraged.

"That's how it is." My mother meant (I translate for those who only understand English when it's complicated): That's the way of being of all men. We can't get used to it, Maman. Gibberish! Let's talk about Questa. Questa woke up sick, but in an excellent mood. She opened the window, watched a few clouds go by, took in a few good mouthfuls right from the cold that accosted her, and said, "*Olé.*" I didn't sleep all night. I remained immobile in my armchair. I was sleepy, but I didn't want to sleep. When you're in pain, sleeping is the last thing you want to do, sleeping is not at all what you've got to do. What you've got to do is vanquish the pain, fight until it's over, and wait. Questa woke up sick.

"I'm as sick as a dog!" she exclaimed, laughing and sticking out a tongue as yellow as tobacco juice.

She left the skylight and came to sit on my knees. She blew a bit of her breath in my face to show me how her soul stunk.

"Look how I stink inside. Inside me, the aroma of alcohol turns into a stench."

I lent her our toothbrush and toothpaste. She didn't show any gratitude. Through the rips in her pants, I caught a glimpse of paradise. Poor Questa! Her eyes worn out like old coins ... The heavy and pasty flesh of her face ... She was laughing, and the creases of her laugh remained when she had finished laughing, and her laugh creases were added to the other creases, the other ruts. In henhouses, poets lay verses. They don't lay all their verses. In cemeteries, the verses they didn't lay gnaw away at them. In libraries, lovers of verse gnaw away at the verses they've laid. The way girls look infuriates and thrills me. At the library, where the girls in bloom proliferate, I experience as much joy and fury in not looking at them as I do in looking at them. I play at ignoring them. I stare at a trumeau on the ceiling, and I tell myself, "I'm not looking at them." The sight of the trumeau gets hold of my throat, gets hold of my head, delights me and distracts me. The girls in bloom don't go to the library to read, but to escape from solitude, to have company, to be together, to meet faces and miracles. Along the same lines, in order to make themselves out to be people who won't hear another word, they get rid of their homework and their lessons. They're not bad, the girls my age; they look great; I'm proud of them. They wear beet-red nylons and short skirts that are light and cucumber-green. They like bright colours; they have a sense of humour. They wear sweaters that are thicker and bigger than they are. When their mouths are closed, a mocking smile puffs out their lips. When they open their mouths, a mocking smile comes out of their lips. They make me lose my sense of reality, my sense of pain. When someone makes me lose possession of myself, makes me lose my fragile hold on the pain, I lose my temper, I get angry. The great look of girls in bloom, their lively and fresh air, makes me angry as much as it warms my blood. I don't look at them. I ignore them. I watch the blood running in my head on the ceiling. I watch myself be dazzled by the sunlight of the girls in bloom all along the stucco mouldings. The look of the girls in bloom at the library oxidizes the walls and the ceiling of the library. Here's what every young girl ought to know: tomorrow, you will no longer be; tomorrow, something cruel will have changed you into something else. Things are neither beautiful nor ugly; there is nothing beautiful, nothing ugly. We project our feelings onto things, and they reflect them back at us, like mirrors. How sad the trees are, when we are sad. When we are sad, the trees are neither beautiful nor ugly; they are sad. When we are sad and we find trees beautiful, it's because we find our sadness beautiful. When we are desperate, the houses we see are desperate. The reason we find the streets ugly when we are desperate is that we detest our despair, that we have a violent aversion to it, that we are suffering. The grey of the plaster on a wall is so arousing when we are aroused by young girls in bloom. But some people are lacking in feelings strong enough to be able to project them, to impose them on things. In order not to die of indifference, they foist upon themselves the feelings that the canons designate for them—not the artillery cannons, but the artistic canons. If art says it's beautiful, they start to cry, it's so beautiful. If art tells them it's ugly, they start to laugh, it's so ugly. Aren't the young girls in bloom beautiful? They are not beautiful. They turn some heads as they go by, and leave some giddy heads behind. They shower the air with laughter as they go by, and the air where they've laughed intoxicates us. They perfume the air where they go by, their skin is so brand new. No, beauty does not exist. Beauty exists neither in things, nor in dogs, nor in giraffes, nor in young girls in bloom. Beauty is merely an idea, an idea in the sense of Plato (or Aristotle). Young girls in bloom are not beautiful; they project what they are, that's all. Nothing is beautiful. *Beautiful* and *beauty* are words that have overstayed their welcome. I'm sure of it. The world is not ugly. To say that the world is ugly is to create a flower of rhetoric; it's merely a way of saying that the world hurts. O poetry! O novels! O swordplay! O wordplay! O spreaders of darkness! Kill the word, the fatal one, the sower of confusion! The word *tiger* is not a tiger. Who knows? No one. Questa is coming over to sit on my knees. Little by little, the soft and abundant flesh of her butt warms my knees. She's heavy. I support her like I should, like a man, like a male, without complaining, with pride. I feel myself blushing with virile pride. There is, in the overabundance of flesh on women's butts, something good, generous, nourishing, and helpful. Since the dawn of time, men have been moved and enticed by women's butts. Since the dawn of time, they've laughed about them and tried to hit them, touch them, and pinch them. Let's consider *Venus Callipygous*, and let's meditate. Butts are the most maternal thing about a woman, particularly when you see her from behind. Everything maternal about women disgusts me. Could I be unconsciously incestuous, and might I be unconsciously ashamed of it? Couldn't it be that what I find ugly about women is the passionate or exciting form (depending on the individual case) of my mother? I'm doing my little Freud act. I can't help thinking of my mother whenever I consider a woman who is the slightest bit mature. Only women who are no more than sixteen years old do not disgust me; only children are good for me. I believe in the theories of Freud; everything in them is possible and provable. Freud! Ascend your obelisk! Ascend the summit of marble that I erect for you! I urge the authorities of universal education to put the lucid work of Freud within students' reach. I have often seen, before my astonished eyes, the hypotheses of the most courageous man of these centuries of obscurity borne out.

"What're you thinkin' about?" Questa asks me, while twisting my nose back and forth.

"Nothing, Mother. Nothing at all."

How many husbands call their wives "Mother"! I hear the call of the psychoanalytic vocation, and I shudder.

"Roll up your sleeves!" Questa commands me, all of a sudden.

"What for?"

By what right does she order me around? Is she my boss? Like a coward, I obey her. Slavishly, I roll up my sleeves. She takes my naked arms in her arms; she kisses them at the crook of the elbow. She spreads them out on her lap and strokes them. She smiles as though she had something in the back of her mind.

" 'The Herculean nerves do writhe within your arms,' she tells me. "That's a line with a dodecasyllabic foot. Isn't it a beautiful line? It's a line from Gautier. In the beginning, I had difficulty introducing it into the conversation. With the passing years, that difficulty has worked itself out. Out of whom has the difficulty worked? It has worked out *itself*, meaning the self in question. An adverbial phrase set in galvanized and stainless steel. In order to tell a person that he has Herculean nerves, you've got to have his nerves before your eyes. If you've never seen the nerves of the person you're serving that line to, he'll believe that it's not serious, that you're talking through your hat. But with the emancipation of my inhibitions, my difficulties have fainted and lost consciousness. Now that I'm emancipated from my inhibitions, I can come straight to the point. Before introducing my line in the conversation, I ask the person to roll up his sleeves. Whenever the person doesn't want to roll up his sleeves, I roll them up myself. That's not the only line I know by heart. I'm well read! There's another line I know by heart. I'll tell it to you if you agree to pretend to walk. Move your feet! Pretend to walk! Are you having trouble? Don't you have a sense of humour? Do me a favour! Pretend to walk ..."

To prove to her that I have a sense of humour, I tell her a couple of lines of my own making.

"Whenever you pass in the street at the wheel of your cadaver, you get on my nerves, on my nerves, on my nerves, you palaver."

She won't hear another word. She wants me to pretend to walk. To get her to leave me alone, I drop one shoe to the floor. She tells me to drop the other shoe. Tired of obeying her, I tell her to wait for the other shoe to drop. Then, tired of making her wait for the other shoe to drop, I drop the other shoe.

"'Bronze, like gravel, becomes hollow under your steps.' It's an alexandrine. The other one was an alexandrine, too. I was sixteen years old when I wrote down those two alexandrines in the journal in which I wrote nothing else. Do you know the story of the cadaver gnawed away at by bad verse? Once upon a time there was a cadaver six feet under whose dodecasyllabic feet were gnawed away at by bad verse."

In memory of Chateaugué, I'm in the middle of rubbing some ink on my mouth. Questa asks me why I'm doing that.

"It's symbolic."

"Your mouth is like a newspaper now, all smeared with ink."

After saying that, she takes the inkwell in her hands and proposes that we each drink half of it. The deal done, we immediately apply ourselves to following through on it. Drinking two gulps of ink doesn't take much time, especially when it's done in silence. I lick my lips, cynically. She holds on to the back of the armchair to get through her retching and turns ironic.

"Our lungs and our guts are written now, Papa. I've got to go now, Papa. My girls are waiting for me, crying, and their father is waiting for me, not giving a hoot. When I come back, I'll bring wool blankets, dozens of thick thick thick blankets. It's freezing in here."

She left with nothing on but the shirt and the pants that I lent her, nothing on but my dirty shirt and my pants full of open doors and windows. She doesn't give a hoot. She left her apparel and her jewellery under the bed, where I pushed them. I like how she behaves. She's not afraid. She doesn't give a hoot. Everyone else is nervous. She's not nervous. Before the door shut, I gave her a resounding thwack on the butt. *Butt* rhymes with *shut*. I want you to see it when it rhymes. I am a poet; let everyone know it; let no one take me for a vulgar prose writer. Once again, I'm alone. I watch Chateaugué's absence walk around the room. I listen to the echoes of her words, her laughter, her coughing fits, her sniffling, her steps, her socks, her bare feet. I lend an ear to the echoes of the city. Over here, they're gentle, as though the city were breathing; over there, they're shrill, like the calls of cicadas. What am I? I'm alone,

I'm afraid; my executioners await me. It's nighttime again! It's nighttime already! What is it that renders everything slow and gentle? Dying. Yes! Dying! That's it. That's it. Already, everything's calming down, everything's going away. I'm cozy. Already, everything is simpler, easier. I was bitter because it was nighttime already. I am no longer bitter; I like dying, and I am dying. I am dying, gently, gently. The nights come too soon ... It doesn't matter that the nights come too soon, that days and nights rush by and run out of breath ... What does it matter to the one whom death, at his call, comes to take into her sweet inertia?

29

Far from You

You run, you run, you disappear;
You're taken in by the night.
Soon the world stops;
All the birds fall without a sound.

I am nothing, not even alone.
I have nothing left, not even my age.
I am alive in a shroud,
Veiled by a mirage ...

Fair one, come back before a month.
In a month, I'll be rotten.
Come trigger the great emotions
With a laugh or a random cry.

Come back here to wake everything up.
Come back. Everything sleeps, everything ceases.
Drums become pillows.
Everything seems to forget my address.

All of a sudden, I can't stand Chateaugué's absence anymore; I seem to be experiencing her solitude, her helplessness, her bitter powerlessness to overcome her ethereal executioners. All of a sudden, I couldn't care less about Chateaugué's absence; it's all the same to me. All of a sudden, I find her absence delicious. All of a sudden, I laugh cynically. All of a sudden, I have tears in my eyes. All of a sudden, what I was feeling guilty about as if it were cowardice, I feel proud of as if it were an escape; I laugh about it as if it were a good joke. All of a sudden, I am well rid of that woman. All of a sudden, I regret treating that sister as if she were nothing but a woman, as if she were nothing but sex organs. All of a sudden, a thousand faces and a thousand contradictory manners of Chateaugué buzz in my head, a thousand feelings and a thousand emotions about her collide in my heart. Might I be, by chance, nothing but a never-ending enumeration of visions that flicker off and on, of unexpected and ephemeral impressions? Chateaugué, however—she's not run-of-the-mill, she's not a negligible quantity. Chateaugué, however—she's my whole life, she's all my thoughts. After all, Chateaugué is friendship! A unique, ineffaceable, and powerful image of her should master and inhabit the place where these grotesque visions of her and of everything chase one another, should watch over me while these derisory sensations about her and about everything leave me as soon as they come over me ... But nothing masters the hodgepodge. Everything overlaps and mingles in a sleepy way. One idea replaces another. My soul is never inhabited. Everything goes out. My soul, more and more ravenous, lets everything leave. Nothing wants to stay within me. Chateaugué, I won't go get you. Keep your one-way ticket, if you're in the mood. Stop being gone, if you're in the mood. Everything appeals to me, and everything constipates me. Zero equals zero. Two and two don't add up for me. Questa, you fat, ineffable thing, come back, don't come back, leave me alone, come sicken me. I can do without absences as well as I do without presences. I have as much trouble getting used to my inconsistency as I do tolerating the inconsistency of others. Go make yourselves sick somewhere else, all of you. Come make yourselves sick at my house, all of you. Come in, come in, the room is big. Don't all come in at the same time, the door isn't wide enough. Purity tires me. I'm tired of hearing myself think about purity. Let's give filth a chance. Actually, I'd rather have *filth*. The word is less tiring, more modest. Vulvas, come. I'm tired of hating adults; I adore them, starting now. Childhood gets on your nerves eventually. It becomes worn and tarnished through use. I sit on it. I wipe my feet on my childhood. O innocence, you weary me; leave me alone; let me be.

Fresh meat! Fresh pork! I only hated adults when I thought of the word *adult*. I love all the adults that I know. I love my father, my grandfather, my mother, my grandmother, Jesus Christ, the concierge, Questa. I didn't know the adults that I hated. If I knew them all intimately, I'd be madly in love with them all. How decadent! After all, I'd rather have filth. Let's call it paucity of courage, inconsistency. I'd rather have fecklessness and inconsistency, after all. Let the fat adults, the she's and he's, come unto me. When will I stop quibbling and splitting hairs? Go look somewhere else if you don't like it. Try another address. The telephone directory is full of addresses. When will you go away, you drab face? Now. Do it now; manual labour is hard to find in the spring. "Buy Canadian!" The cigarette with the filtered tip, an aromatic aroma and a great taste—buy it, please—I promise you it's not a killer. Manuel who? Manual labour, you imbecile, you ignoramus! Already, already, I'm an adult! And that sickens me. It really was true. But it isn't true anymore, alas, except when I meet children in the street, except when I manage to slip back into my tight childhood skin. It's not the pain or the sadness that I'm mad at. It's the mediocrity that I'm mad at; more than anything, it's the mediocrity that has the expression of boredom and the face of an adult. The most difficult thing is not adoring the adults, but remembering that you adore them. I've only been adoring adults for five minutes, and I've already forgotten it four times. When I was a child, I used to muse about adulthood the way I'd muse about angels. I'm an adult. I've made it; on the square, men and women smoke, foaming at the mouth. Men, foaming at the mouth, show me their money. Women, foaming at the mouth, show me their behinds. "Approach! Approach! Step right up! Step right up!" No! I won't step right up! I've already stepped up; the foam is already rising to my lips; already, women look beautiful to me. Manuel who? Manual labour! *Your* labour, you imbecile, you ignoramus, you damned adult! Purity? Yes! Yes! Yes, even if the word tires me. Angels? Yes! Yes! Frogs, grasshoppers, races, laughter, plenitude? Yes! Yes! Yes! Is that fleeing? That's not fleeing; it's contempt, it's pity! If refusing to saddle yourself with the servant's little jacket—the vest of the valet happy with the woman and the money—is fleeing, then I'm fleeing. But I'm not fleeing as fast as I used to. Beautiful adult female sex organs wouldn't have to run after me very fast to catch up with me. Pigs! Pigs! Pigs! Servants of the woman and the money! Stepping right into a pigsty is agreeing to become domesticated pork. Maternity! Pigsterity! Stop quibbling and splitting hairs, quibbler and hairsplitter! The man is the servant. The woman and the dollar are the masters. At the factory, the man learns to obey and to submit to others' desires. At home, he trots out his lesson. If his wife says yes, he's happy, he drags himself around on his knees to demonstrate his gratitude to her. If his wife says she has a headache, all he can do is sulk, cry, and get drunk. "George, old boy, my wife doesn't love me anymore. Ahhhhh! Ohhhhh! George, old boy, my old buddy, give me your handkerchief. Ahhhhh! Ohhhhh!" When a man is not loved by a woman, he cries in his beer, like the devoted and faithful slave who is no longer loved by his master, like the zealous slave whose master treats him unjustly. Love! Love! Love! How decadent! A man is nothing more than a present from God to his wife. You can't rush her, George. You can't hurt her, George. You can't rape her, George. You've got to ask her permission, George. A woman's feelings are like her milk: if you shake them, they'll curdle. What a catastrophe, George, when she refuses me her love! Woe is me, George, when my beauty means nothing to her. What do I do, George, when it no longer tempts her, except wait for it to tempt her, while being unhappy? Beat her, George, throw her out, do without her? But that's crazy; how would I live without her tenderness, her motherly love, the candy she gives me when I leave for the factory? If I beat her, she'll call the police and get me thrown in jail, and I'll look ridiculous. Come on, George! The police are for women, George, not for us. The woman is idolized. What idolizes her, who grovels at her feet? The man. What considers it the supreme honour (a seat in the House of Commons is derisory in comparison) to please and be agreeable to the woman? The man. Pleasing! Pleasing! Her majesty's pleasure! Men offer up their beauty and their strength on a silver platter. Women choose. Who is the hero of all males? It's Casanova, the man that women find pretty. You have your doubts? Go to the movies if you don't believe me. Read the novels and poems that sell if you don't believe me. That's enough of that! *Basta con la luna!* Personally, I really don't give a hoot. Questa came. She was drunk. She brought two pitchers of molasses and two round loaves of bread, so that I'd eat. She was carrying a pile of multicoloured blankets on her head, so that I wouldn't freeze. She was proud of her blankets. She spread them out on the drab bed with volubility and consideration, so that I'd find them beautiful. Every time she unfolded a blanket, a curtain lifted on a fantastic zoo. We were at the circus; I was a jaded customer; she was a drunken bear leader, a drunken leader of red bears, green giraffes, yellow dogs, black moose, and blue beavers. Her blankets were not blankets, but tapestries. We were in Arabia; I was an indifferent customer; she was a seller of carpets. She went to bed under her blankets full of bears, giraffes, dogs, moose, and multicoloured beavers. She fell asleep. She woke up sick, laughing. She left again. She left barefoot so that I'd laugh. With a kick, I made the shoes, the nylons, and the hat that she left me disappear under the bed. She forgets a few pieces of her paraphernalia every time she comes and every time she leaves. I make everything disappear under the bed so that I won't lose my appetite. Under the bed, by now, there's enough rigging to harness all the wives of Henry VIII.

30

I opened the door; she just appeared out of nowhere. To her, I didn't look surprised enough that she had just appeared out of nowhere.

"You don't look surprised that I just appeared out of nowhere," she murmured, hunched over, her arms fallen by her sides, her head down, her hair full of wind, her eyes with dark circles around them, her nose snotty, and her mouth black.

After coming in, she let herself slide down the door to the floor, and she stayed sitting there, her eyes closed, her legs apart, without a word.

"How did you come?"

"On foot! Can't you tell? Some automobiles tried to pick me up, but I didn't let them. One of them stopped next to me, just to laugh at me. One of them just missed me, to scare me; it was doing 100 miles an hour. If it had hit me, I would have gone head over heels. I had to sneak out of the house. They never stopped watching me. I came back because I didn't understand anything anymore. You've been so stupid to me, so mean. I tried to understand; I couldn't. I couldn't even imagine how what happened could have happened. What happened that day kept replaying in my head, it went around and around in my head, it never stopped running through my head. It was like when you've got a headache. I was in pain nowhere, but I was ill; I couldn't sit still. I came back to see you. I can see you; I was crazy to get all upset over it, to fret about it. I was sure that by seeing you again, by coming into the room, everything would fall back into place, everything would calm down. You're standing there looking at me. I feel like laughing. Don't look at me like that; I feel like laughing when you look at me like that. You're just like before. The bad dream is over; it's not believable, it's not believable. Aren't you glad to see me? You're glad, but you won't say so. I know you."

I wasn't thinking of anything. She was sitting at my feet, and I was standing at her feet. One of her hands was between my feet. I was thinking of a hand like hers that someone confident like her had put in front of the wheel of a train just before its departure. I was watching her, and I was watching myself think. She felt like laughing; her eyes were burning, her cheeks were hot, what little ear was showing through her hair had turned crimson. Between my feet, her hand was limp and dozing, worthy of a wake-up call via a good thrust of my heel. Her joy was emitting waves that were filling up the room but that were reflected off me without reaching me. As a game, I let in the burning peace that was emanating; then, I felt as much friendship as she, I felt as pure and gay as she did. I held the door of my soul open for one second, then I shut it tight again with a spasmodic burst of anger; then I didn't let anything else in. I felt like crushing her abandoned hand the way you feel like crushing a yellowy-orange and black moth, the way you feel like making the frog that you catch suffer. She had to be hungry.

"I don't have any more money. I don't know what we're going to do. If you're hungry, there's some bread and molasses in the commode. That's all there is to eat."

"That's all you have to say to me. You're not very hospitable."

She saw Questa's rags under the bed. She looked at the animals on Questa's multicoloured blankets with the eyes of a hunted animal.

"Whose underwear is that? Who put those blankets on the bed?"

"It all belongs to Questa, the woman who brought you back to the Islands."

"That woman?"

"She's quite nice. She'd give all she has. She's married."

Questa had made the bed before leaving. She had made it diligently, in order to derive the most striking effect from her dazzling blankets. Chateaugué just couldn't take her hunted animal's gaze off that red, blue, and yellow bed, taut as a shirt front, looming up in place of the drab and rumpled pallet she had known.

"She makes beds well," she remarked.

"We would have ended up freezing. We needed blankets. She brought the most beautiful ones she had."

"I never complained. It was fun being cold."

She turned on me her gaze of the hunted woodchuck, of the punished faithful badger.

"What do you say to her? What do you do with her? Does she sleep here? Is she like your girlfriend, an old bag like her?"

She seemed scandalized. I was ashamed. I felt guilty, disloyal, treacherous, cowardly, and unworthy. As disappointed in me as she was debilitated by her trip, Chateaugué got up off the floor with difficulty and limped over to the bed while rubbing one hip. She put Questa's rags on hangers and put them away in the wardrobe. I watched her handle the corset and the bra as though she were afraid of getting poison ivy; we were cold and it was funny, and now it's over.

"Don't get all upset over nothing; she may not be back. You're not coughing anymore?"

She pretended not to hear. She stretched out on the exorcised bed. Dirty, pale, and dishevelled on the starchy and brilliant bed, she looked beautiful to me. She remained immobile, her gaze fixed on where her face was looking. She was alone under the oblique wall; lots of things must have been running through her mind. Her face expressed only an extreme weariness. It said, "Too bad," gently, gently, without venom, without lemon, with cinnamon, with sugar. I felt like telling her that she wasn't ugly when she wasn't grinning from ear to ear, but I changed my mind. I felt like telling her, "You're the one who's like my girlfriend." I said nothing. Words ascribe importance to themselves and give us orders when we have the misfortune to take them out of their own backyard. Words take on airs and make us take on airs. Often, in addition to being false, these airs are tragic. A single word can give the illusion that everything has suddenly changed and can take command of a transformed situation. And yet, nothing changes suddenly. What can a word change, even when it's a word of honour? Nothing. Words have no effect on things. Apply a word to the rain, and you'll see that it won't change colours. Often, when someone says, "I love you," or, "I hate you," everything seems to be transformed. But actually, nothing is changed. If you say, "I love you," it's because you loved already, or you're lying. When you say, "My friend," nothing is changed—if there already was friendship, there still is; if there wasn't, there isn't any more of it. When someone says something as a precaution, to be sure not to make a mistake, you should say to yourself, "What he says changes nothing; my situation remains the same." The word is not the thing. They can say all they want; it's not dangerous; don't quake in your boots over nothing. The word is taken for the thing these days. If you tell someone he's disgusting, you're likely to get your face smashed in. However, you haven't changed much by telling him he was disgusting; you haven't rendered him more or less disgusting than before. Verbs don't do the action. Inanimate objects themselves understand that. Indeed, if you tell a mountain, "You're nothing but a little hill," it won't even go to the trouble of replying to you; it will remain as it was and where it was. But if you tell a woman who has big ears, "My, what big rabbit ears you have, Madam," she'll come over to you, get all worked up, shower insults on you, and slap you silly. Anyway! Enough about that. In any case, Chateaugué plunged under the unpleasant covers. She forgot everything, curled herself up in the arms of a dream, and waited for it to take her away.

"You're not getting undressed?"

"No! I'm cold!"

"At least take off your shoes!"

"No! I'm cold! Leave me alone, you heartless beast."

She's been sleeping for an hour. For an hour, I've been watching her sleep, watching her be pretty, be my friend, be back, be slim, be despised by me. All children are beautiful. Everything we love is beautiful. Everything we love is nice to look at. There's nothing feminine about Chateaugué's beauty. It's as if she didn't know how to smile like a woman, to gaze like a woman, to walk like a woman, to hold her body and wear her dress as if she were afraid they might come undone. I laugh while musing about her extravagant way of moving—as irregular and uncoordinated as possible. Can a child take two steps without looking back, without slackening his pace, without kicking his leg or dragging his feet? The beauty of Chateaugué leaves the respectable seducer cold; it would render him ridiculous, he would feel repugnant. It is devoid of everything that adults call seriousness or solemnity. And yet, the respectable seducer knows that with a woman without seriousness, vice and voluptuousness are in no way compatible. You've got to be essentially serious to be able to indulge without self-consciousness, without tears, without cynicism, or without laughter, in the quiverings of the flesh. Seriousness is of sexual origin, is essentially sexual, and increases with desire or frustration. I'm tired of eating molasses. When Questa comes back, I'll ask her for some money, around twenty dollars, enough to live on until the upcoming hurly-burly. The reason she hasn't given me any money yet is not from lack of generosity, but because she's always too drunk to think of it. She knows perfectly well that I don't have a penny. Chateaugué is featherbrained and has the soul of a lightweight. Who knows? Does Chateaugué know, for example, that I am an inveterate whortensturbator? I feel much less alone, much less guilty, much less sickening with Questa than with her. With Questa I feel I could be myself without shock and without shame. I could tell her everything, do everything to her, and relieve myself of all my masks, without fear of hurting her or losing her. I feel like she knows me, like she's seen worse. It's as if she were saying to me, "Come, tell me; the admission of your shortcomings will facilitate for me the forgiveness of my faults." In advance, unconditionally, she welcomes me as I am into her strange tenderness. With Questa, I am free, at ease, relieved, and invited. Chateaugué's eyes, those eyes that see nothing but the soul, hinder me, paralyze me. The awkwardness is growing between Chateaugué and me, and enmity has come between body and soul. With awful people, there's no need to be embarrassed at all about being ugly. With beautiful people, it's awful to be ugly. Also, I often have the impression of leaving the real Chateaugué behind, of attaching myself intentionally to another Chateaugué, a Chateaugué that the real Chateaugué blows apart and shatters. Who wants anything to do with a passionate, perhaps even an exciting, Chateaugué? The more I think about it, the more I think it would have been better for her not to come back; the Chateaugué in my room doesn't measure up to the Chateaugué in my heart, in my head, and in my past. The immaculate Miles Miles of the immaculate Chateaugué is more and more dead, and it's more and more useless to kill him so that he won't go wrong. Only the consent of my will (it alone still struggles) is missing for all grace and dignity to be restored to adults and to me the adult, through the intercession of Questa. I am more and more adult, and I feel more and more keenly the need to protect and to defend this adult who is none other than me. This me is sad, pustular, arid, and sexual ...? So be it! What is an adjective? Who's afraid of adjectives? Plus ... Chateaugué will always be there to stand guard before those lily-white constructions of our childhood full of dandelions and tadpoles ... What decadence! Long live decadence! Why not? Long live decadence! It's only a question of words, after all. Decadence, independence, sufferance, intolerance, appearance, endurance, entrance, insignificance. Who's afraid of words ending in *ance* and *ence*? My soul opens and reaches out to welcome the mediocrity, the grotesque Americanism, the servitude, the dearth of heart and the insipidity of spirit, the submission and the surrender. Why persist in calling decadence that which my soul vociferously entreats for its own deliverance? Who knows best what *decadence* and *deliverance* mean? Is it those words themselves, or is it my soul? Who knows best the name of what my soul is calling? For my soul, decadence doesn't mean decadence but redemption. What my soul is calling, whatever it may be, my soul does not call decadence but resurrection. That by which the child soul demeans itself gives birth to the adult soul. Long live decadence! Since my soul, in advance, makes of it its joy, its strength, its health. Long live pain! Since my soul holds a ball in its honour. Isn't joy always the same, isn't it always, wherever it comes from, of the same odour and the same colour? If there's nothing disgusting about joy in the child, then what is disgusting about joy, the same joy, in the adult? What is disgusting about joy, the only strength, the ever victorious surge that sweeps us along in pursuit of joy? O joy! O dissatisfaction that urges us on! *Basta!* *Basta con la mar! Basta con il cha-cha-cha!* O joy! O victory that always makes me lose! O ocean that always saves you! O trees that always make you wait! O air that always waits for us! *Basta!* *Basta!* Whoa, horsey! Whoa, Nelly!

31

I had heard them from a distance raising Cain in the night. All four of them had come up the stairs pounding on the steps and on the walls and singing at the top of their lungs, "Mow, Mow, Mow Your Goat" to the tune of "Row, Row, Row Your Boat." They took turns, all four of them, drumming on our door.

"What? What? What?" exclaimed Chateaugué, waking up terrified, sitting up on her posterior, terrified and trembling with terror.

I opened the door, and she saw what it was. Questa, the trumpet, and her battery of girls rushed into the room. Questa did an astonished double take when she noticed Chateaugué. She rushed over and swooped down on her, showering her with affectionate nicknames.

"Pale little munchkin! Pale little ghost! Poor dear! Give me a peck. Hmmmm! So good to see you!"

Wrapped up in long black capes attached at the neck by an amethyst, and wearing black ballet slippers, the three little girls looked more white than blonde. Without waiting for instructions from anyone, they took off their capes, found the wardrobe, and threw them in the back. Dressed in their checkered leotards, you might have thought they were imps; they were running, jumping, and disappearing under the furniture. Questa called them to order and introduced them to us.

"You're seeing me in action. You're seeing me grapple with despair, despair, and despair: Anne, Anne, and Anne. Their baptismal names aren't Anne, Anne, and Anne. I didn't attend their baptisms; my husband took advantage of the occasion. He had them baptized Lucy, Lucianne, and Lucille. But these little girls are mine, and the only names that count are the ones I gave them. I'm married, and I'm a lush, but I've never let anyone take liberties with my children or my heart. You keep your heart! You mustn't give your heart to anyone! Anne, my dear, tell Chateaugué and Scin Tillating what you were telling Maman a little while ago."

The designated Anne didn't wait to be asked twice. She smiled and complied ...

"It's raining, and the little old man who's smoking has his hands behind his back. It's raining, and the little old man has a wet pipe and a wet coat. It's raining, and the little old man who's walking in the night is cold. It's raining, and the earth has black poles and glistening railroads."

"That's very beautiful, my dear. But I wonder where you came up with that. You too get to have your secrets, right? Scin Tillating, my dear, where is the bottle?"

I replied that all the bottles were empty, that I had drunk everything.

"Never mind! Anne, my dears, go in quest of the feast!"

The three little girls, with the same cry and the same surge, flung themselves against the door.

"Your capes, careless girls! Who do you think you are? Eskimos?"

At the stern call of their mother, they veered around and went to pick up their capes. They disappeared, pushing each other and forgetting to shut the door behind them.

"They obey me to a T, the poor little girls. I'm bringing them up right! They obey me to a T, like good little ninnies. They know how to live a lot better than I do, the poor dears. They're the ones who should give the orders, and I should obey them to a T. They're the ones who should tell me what to do, what to think, what to want, what to say, and where to go."

The little girls came back. Each one hadn't an ounce of strength left and was dangling a basket overflowing with fruit, wines, and packaged meats from the ends of her arms. Questa took the floor again. She seemed inspired.

"Children's happiness, and ours, ends when puberty begins. Children drink like us, eat, walk, laugh, cry, hear, and see like us. Children don't think about love like us. The secret to children's happiness is their chastity, and their ignorance of what we know that they don't know."

Questa communed with herself, mulled over what she had just said, and smiled to herself.

"That makes no sense. I renounce everything I just said. Scin Tillating, would you be so kind as to open six bottles, one for each of us. You won't be able to open more than five of them, for there are only five. These are bottles of a few of the most unsavoury wines I know. My Annes are the ones who chose them; they liked the designs on the labels."

Since I was occupied with a nail file in a ruthless struggle with the corks, Questa took the floor again. She seemed more and more inspired.

"What makes us all tick? Joy. What is so interesting about love, power, glory, and alcohol? Joy! What's the use of love, power, glory, and alcohol that don't end in joy? If glory and love tend toward the same goal, what is it about love that is so degrading and about glory that is so glorious? I renounce everything I just said. It makes no sense. What's important is not what it is (what it is socially), but the effect you expect from it, the effect it will have on me if it works. If it sickens me, it (whatever it may be) is sickening. I renounce everything I just said. It makes no sense."

Sitting in a circle on the floor, sitting in a circumference around the horns of plenty, we all ate and drank. Children eat and drink like adults; Questa was quite right. Two of the Annes were sitting on either side of their mother. The third one had comfortably stretched out between her mother's legs; a gallon of wine in one hand and a sausage in the other, she looked like a decadent Roman emperor.

"Anne! Come now! You eat savouries before sweets, not sweets before savouries. Put down that doughnut and pick up that sausage. But no! Eat your doughnut and don't worry about what I say. What do I know? Eat sweets before savouries if that tempts you, my precious. Maman wants nothing but your joy, and you know a lot better than I do where your joy lies. Where does Maman's joy lie? Tell Maman where her joy lies, my precious.

But you'll be sick if you eat sweets before savouries ... Well? So what? You feel so good when you're no longer sick, right, my precious?"

The Annes were caressing their mother and caressing themselves on their mother. Anne was hanging with both arms from her mother's arm. Anne was rubbing her nose on her mother's arm. Anne was rolling her head against her mother's belly. Anne was butting her head between her mother's breasts. Anne was walking her fingers up and down her mother's back. Anne was throwing her arms around her mother's neck and covering her face with kisses. They didn't like us watching them do it. When they caught us watching, they'd shoot scornful looks at us, insolent looks, haughty looks of lazy kings. Chateaugué, whom life has enjoyed depriving of affection, was observing the unfolding of this orgy of tenderness with eyes brimmed with tears. Poor Chateaugué! She reached the point of forgetting, now and then, to chew what she had in her mouth. But the Annes were tired; the wine had made them sleepy. At the end of this strange picnic, they couldn't even keep their eyes open. They fell like flies. They fell asleep on their mother. Now in the room, all the girls are sleeping, everything is sleeping. In the house, in the city, everything is sleeping, except me. I watch all of them sleep; I sit in my armchair. And I laugh to myself, cynically. No one's left to stand guard but me and a few automobiles. Even if I wanted to sleep, I couldn't—the bed is full. The bed isn't big. Nonetheless, with a bit of cunning, by snuggling up and cramming in, they all managed to fit. The two smaller Annes are end to end in the middle of the bed, in such a way that the head of one sticks out alone at the foot of the bed, while the other four heads, blonde, except for that of Questa, stick out together, hair entangled in hair, at the other end. The Annes all have the same way of sleeping. They sleep with their mouths open, their lips puffy, their heads thrown back. They seem to have been stunned or assassinated by surprise. I turn out the light. How horrible! It's already getting light. It's the beginning of a day, the unsavoury and pale renewal of what seemed finished, the vain renewal of the dull little game of the infinite, the resumption of all those things worn out by all those yesterdays. I'm thinking of those who get up at the same time every morning, of all those who are in the middle of drinking coffee from the same cup, at the same table, and at the same windows as on all the other mornings they've had. A morning is a worn-out cup, a worn-out table, worn-out windows, and a worn-out house. Smash everything. Nations of the world, we've got to break everything. Nations of the world, let us unite and, with great blows of an axe, let us fell the vicious circles. Nations of the world, leave me alone. Nations of the world, make me laugh. Villages and cities of the world, cottages and houses of the world, half-light and shadows of the world, go away, disappear, leave, leave, leave! No, don't leave! Wake up, the way a brass band wakes up the street. Wake up to me! Look at me! Look at me! Welcome me! Kiss me! O things, O beings, how inhospitable you are, how impolite you are, how haughty you are, how stingy you are with smiles! How do I love you? How do I not hate you, how do I not wish you gone, you who don't even see me? Don't forget that I came into this world that you've divided amongst yourselves the same way you came into it! Don't forget that I'm living in your life the way you're living in mine! Haughty hosts, haughty guests, how do I not get disgusted by you? What kind of world is this, where it's not enough to want to welcome and be welcomed in order to welcome and be welcomed?

32

I am a dishwasher. I wash dishes in the kitchen of a restaurant, like the hero of an opera. Chateaugué is a waitress; she distributes full plates and full cups to the customers in the restaurant, like the heroine of an operetta. To understand these last two metaphors, you have to accept that opera is the masculine of operetta and remind yourself that I am masculine and Chateaugué is feminine. Far away, in the room, the bride, alone and impassive, awaits us. Questa having sung our praises, they hired us without hesitation, they took us into their service right away. We've put our shoulders to the wheel with such enthusiasm that I'm a bit ashamed. While washing the dishes, I whistle, I sing, I dance, I am resplendent. Dishwasher! And I used to think that all dishwashers were machines. The squad of waitresses contains some pretty ones who are fun to tease and sneak sidelong glances at. They talk like street hawkers. They're still wet behind the ears, and they swear, even blaspheme. The head cook and his generals speak nothing but Greek and Latin. I'm happily awash in complete insignificance. A dishwasher happily awash! But the waitresses don't like the dishwashers— they have self-respect. The waitresses prefer the lawyers, the policemen, the judges, and the longshoremen. I was forgetting the firefighters. I was forgetting the doctors, the artists, the historians, the automobiles, the farmers, the officers, the soldiers, the generals, the actors, the scholars, the plumbers, the ranchers, the carpenters, the sailors, the travelling salesmen, the sales reps, the plumbers, the shoe salesmen, the plumbers, and the sailors. The ugly waitresses, as well as the old waitresses, already feel a maternal fondness for me. When

I say automobiles, I mean automobilists; the automobile and the automobilist are part of one and the same thing—the automobile. The heart of a man and the man are part of one and the same thing—the man. The heart of a man is in the man, the way the fish is in the sea, the way the bone is in the flesh, the way the sardine is in the can, the way the automobilist is in the automobile. Those are a few simple, clear, plain truths that are sure to please. Now we're useful to society, Chateaugué and I. All society has to do is be glad and take care of us. But members of the French Academy won't have anything to do with dishwashers, and with waitresses who won't have anything to do with dishwashers. Members of academies avoid dishwashers and waitresses, look down on them, don't associate with those common stockholders who lack society's diplomas. What do we care, Chateaugué and I? We're glad, at least for the moment, to serve society modestly, and that feeling of gladness that we experience favourably replaces all the love society would give us if it weren't so snobbish. We're proud of serving society modestly. However, putting our shoulders to the wheel did not take place without some upheavals of the soul for Chateaugué. Despite my abstention on this subject, Chateaugué courageously showed up for work with her charcoal mouth. Catching sight of her, the boss—a fat Greek—roared, flung a towel at her, and imperatively invited her in English to go wash her face. Courageously, Chateaugué let the towel drop to the floor, blushed, lowered her eyes, and didn't go wash her face. The boss pretended to ignore her for the rest of the day, and everything went on more or less smoothly. But tonight as we were getting ready to leave the establishment, our eight-hour shift over, he was back on the attack. He was in no mood to laugh.

"If you come back to me tomorrow with lipstick that garish, I'll throw you out."

Those were not his exact words. I would have found it funny, if that was what he'd said. Be that as it may, that's what he meant and what he would have said if he'd had the slightest bit of a sense of humour. In fact, we didn't get a word of what he said. English is the only language still in existence that this nimbus of massive meat speaks, and he mumbles it, that miserable tongue. In any case, he flung an ultimatum of 2,500 pounds at the head of the slim Chateaugué, and all she has to do is get herself off the horns of this dilemma. I like sentences that limp. I'm sadistic—I watch them limp, and I find that funny. So Chateaugué will either have to wash her face or renounce being useful to society. Now, she does want to keep working. She's glad not to be a useless member (an arm, a leg) of society. But we promised each other to live with black mouths until we hurly-burly ourselves. Despite my betrayal, she would rather keep having a black mouth until we hurly-burly ourselves. *She* wouldn't betray Tate. I didn't know how to settle it. I tried some diplomacy.

"You don't have to put it on all the way down to your neck," I told her. "A little, a tad at the corners of your lips, for example—wouldn't that be more subtle and just as effective? You look like a dog who put its muzzle in a jar of blackberry jam! A little discretion!"

We quarrelled for hours to the same tune and the same words. She accused me of cowardice and treachery; she called me a Judas, a Maccabean, a skeleton, a larva, a two-faced liar. She reminded me that I had said that I agreed, that I had said that our black mouths would be our coat of arms, our banners, our flags. I repeated to her that I fully agreed with her on the content, but not at all on the form. Finally, we came to a kind of intermediate, mediated understanding. I'd paint one lip, and she'd paint the other; the application of the black was plain, precise, and neat, like that of lipstick. To escape unscathed from the tantrum the boss would throw, seeing us each arrive with a dirty lip, we'd tell him that it was because our religion required it, that we were conscientious subjectors, that we were knights of the Order of the Spoon. If he insisted on throwing us out, we'd say goodbye and be off to look for another boss, for other remunerative servitude. Armed with this agreement consecrated by oaths, we went to bed. The Annes left their capes here, and their mother left her shoes. Every time Questa comes here, she leaves something behind. It's as if she were doing it on purpose. We went to bed. In the middle of the night, Chateaugué shook me by the shoulder and woke me up.

"Tate, Tate, Tate, Tate ..." she was repeating, bringing her face nearer, lowering her face, moving her face toward mine.

Her face was slowly falling onto mine. Her hair was gliding across my face, her hare (hair irresistibly makes me think of hare) was running over my face.

"What do you want now?"

"I can't sleep."

"Go to sleep!"

"You've forgotten, Tate. You're forgetting, forgetting, forgetting. You're forgetting a little bit every day. The first night, or the second, you told me not to sleep, to keep watch, to be scared, to force myself to be scared, to beware, to take you to task if you should happen to lack vigilance. You're sleeping, Tate."

"You go to sleep, too, my little munchkin, okay?"

"You call me 'my little munchkin,' like that woman. Stay with me, Tate, stay, stay. Stay with your little sister. You've closed your eyes; you're gone. There's no more Tate. There's no more Chateaugué. There's only me."

Her breath was lurking about my face like a little animal. Her silky hair was walking on my face like insects. And because of that, I felt like being cruel to her.

"Go to sleep! For the love of Christ, go to sleep! And another thing, stop calling me Tate—I'm not a whale. You're ridiculous. It's ridiculous to become attached to words that don't mean anything anymore. If you want to know, Tate irritates me, Tate makes me grind my teeth, Tate sickens me. We're not children anymore. You can stop playing the little girl; it's over, really over. And another thing, get your hair out of my face; it makes me feel like sneezing, it makes me feel sick, it gives me ideas. What I said the first night doesn't count anymore, doesn't make sense anymore. What I said that night corresponded to the reality of that night. Since that night, the reality has been transformed, has evolved. The words of that night's reality aren't those of now. Look at yourself—nothing of what you see is the same as what you saw that night. That night is elsewhere, and we're here. It's ridiculous to try to force the reality of today to be like that of yesterday. To give one night the names of another night is sheer lunacy. We can't do anything about it. We've got to let the night give us its own name, designate itself by itself. In a word, everything has changed, from the ceiling to your eyes. That ceiling is another ceiling, and you see that ceiling with other eyes. If it's not to your liking, all you have to do is take the bus."

Chateaugué was holding back her hair with one hand, I mean her hare with one hand, and wiping her tears with the other. She wasn't moving anymore. She remained leaning over me. She wasn't moving at all anymore, as if she didn't know what to do next, what to do with herself—as if she had ceased to function. I was there, under her. It was from me alone that her salvation could come and, cynically, I kept my hands in my pockets. She remained leaning over me, waiting. Poor idiot! Weakling! If only she had been a woman, a real one, a serious one. I was torturing her without really wanting to, effortlessly, without even cheating, without taking the slightest pleasure in it. I didn't even feel sorry for you, idiot! Idiot! She was faltering. She was trying to say just the right thing to me in order to move me.

"You mean that we aren't going to hurly-burly ourselves ... You mean that everything ... that we ...?"

"Why would we commit suicide? I don't feel like it anymore, and you don't feel like it anymore. We mustn't let ourselves be led by words, especially when they're dated, like the ones you're thinking about."

She started to gesticulate as if she had been overcome with severe pain. She started to utter deathly cries, pulling out big fistfuls of her hair. She had lost control of herself. She couldn't see me anymore. She was flinging her arms and legs every which way. She was shouting. I was talking to her; I was shouting as loudly as she was. She couldn't hear a thing. I was slapping her with all my might. She couldn't feel a thing. "Good Lord, what have I done now?" I was wondering, clenching my fists and squeezing my eyelids shut. She was so sweet, so gay, lighter than air. What had gotten into her? I took my head in my hands so that the agitation that held sway there wouldn't make it explode. I let myself fall back on the bed, and I waited for her to finish. All she had was me. All she'd ever had was me. I had always been nice to her. I hadn't been too nice to her, admittedly. I had been just nice enough to her not to be disloyal, not to give her cruel illusions. I had nothing to reproach myself for. I didn't deserve these theatrics. She, too, took herself seriously. I never should have brought her here. All the nonsense that I'd said! What had I been thinking? If only Questa had left me her telephone number. She was shrieking, shrieking. She took herself so seriously that she was going to shriek herself to death. Oh! This awful mannequin in a wedding dress! Oh! This bitter mannequin! Oh! The hideous room, the bitter room! This awful Nelligan! These acid chairs! Everything that furnished this dream of being nothing but children, the dream of disturbing nothing, all of a sudden took a tragic, martyred, and hellish turn. She kept on shrieking louder and louder. She shrieked with so much force that blood started to come out of her mouth and her nose. I was no man. I was nothing but a dishrag. I had never known how to face up to manly situations. Cold water! Cold water! That's what was needed. Run and fill a jar of cold water and throw it in her face! There was no jar! There wasn't even a glass! Nothing had happened; I hadn't said anything; there was no reason to shriek like that; there was no reason to suffer like that. Suddenly, she collapsed. Huddled up, her eyes open and rolled upward, she wasn't gesticulating anymore, wasn't shrieking anymore. She fainted. She's still breathing. She's twitchy and stiff like a dog that just died. Finally! It's all over. Everything will be fine now that she's not shrieking anymore. It was only a tantrum. Everything's fine. I've got a job. I'm useful to society. I don't have to await Questa's indulgence in order to eat. Goddamn comedian!

33

We went back to dishwashing and serving as though nothing had happened, or almost. Before leaving, I didn't paint my lip at all, and Chateaugué carefully scrubbed her mouth. Without saying a word, we said farewell to the mouths adorned in black gold, and we went off to work. The boss looked at Chateaugué's clean, bare lips. He slapped his belly and told her bravo. The restaurant is always packed. The waitresses never stop running. I always have more dishes to wash than I can. I'm snowed under, from one end of the day to the other. At the lunch hour, I'm inundated. I'm paid by the hour, but I work at set times. I am therefore paid by the week, more or less. My gross salary is thirty-three dollars. But from those thirty-three dollars, contributions are made in my name to various federal and provincial agencies. The federal and provincial officials eat right out of my thirty-three dollars. Without me, the mail carriers and the customs officers would die of hunger. That's something to be proud of. After six months of toil, if I've met their expectations, I'll get a raise. That's something to feel encouraged about. I'm not ashamed to work as a dishwasher. I'm sixteen years old. I have plenty of time to become a millionaire. Chateaugué will only get twenty dollars a week from the boss, but that doesn't mean anything. At the Penguin, a really pretty and really servile waitress can count on at least seven or eight dollars in tips per day. That's well known. Chateaugué was congratulated tonight, and she deserved it. She was assigned to the two worst booths in the restaurant, and she emerged with more than five dollars in tips. Many customers make a point of coming back to eat at the booth where they've been served to their liking. So the future looks just as rosy for Chateaugué as it does for me. Chateaugué reports that she has to say that she hopes the customer enjoys his meal, and to ask him if it was good when he's done. "Was that good, customer?" In the kitchen, the waitresses have to shout what they're ordering and shout it in English. The Italians and the Greeks are hard of hearing and don't understand French. Now, Chateaugué—and they find this unfortunate—is too shy to shout and speak in English. Therefore, she says, you've got to be quick. But Chateaugué isn't as self-conscious about being quick as she is about shouting and speaking in English; that's where she makes up for it. The only French verb that the boss knows is step on it, and he only knows how to conjugate it in the second person singular of the present imperative. Apparently a new girl doesn't get told twice to step on it. There is not, as far as I know, any past imperative. At the Penguin, the service must be pluperfect ... Oh! Oh! Oh! Questa came to see us do our thing, and she got what she came for. Oh! Oh! Oh! She watched Chateaugué zip back and forth for a while, and she showed herself to be proud of her.

"Our little munchkin really gets a move on, huh!"

Strapped up tight in her sky-blue uniform, standing on the heels of her white shoes, her hair up, her ears in the air, Chateaugué almost looked like a young girl. Questa asked me her age.

"How old is she?"

"Forty-three years old."

"Very funny."

"I'm polite. Anyone would take you for forty-five."

She reminded me that it wasn't her age that was in question, but Chateaugué's.

"How can I think of another when you're here before me, when your enormous beauty overwhelms my gaze?"

It suddenly occurred to me that if we crouched down under the sink behind which we were standing, no one could see us. I was sure that she wouldn't cry for help. I was remembering the circumstances of our first meeting, and that titillated me. She had taken me for a ride. She had insulted my vague impulses of tenderness with vulgar words and gestures of boredom. She'll

182

see just what I'm made of! But how would I induce her to crouch down under the sink? I asked her to let go of her purse.

"What?"

"Let go of your bag, ma'am. I rolled up my sleeve when you asked me to. I obey. You obey, too. Go head, drop it."

She dropped her handbag in the puddles of detergent that were lying on the floor.

"There you go," she said.

"Now who's going to pick up the bag?" I said to her. "Guess! Guess!"

She made a friendly face, then she crouched down, slowly and delicately, taking care to fold up her narrow skirt. I didn't lose a second. I sat down in a single movement in the puddles of detergent, and I welcomed her onto my knees. I imprisoned her in my arms, and with my lips, I ran all over her neck and her face. Her mouth was soft, sweet, warm, and sort of good, despite her passivity and her total indifference.

"Satisfied, rascal?" she said, in no way surprised by my sudden boldness. "You didn't need to make such a fuss. I'll be only too pleased; that's just what I was waiting for when we were alone on Rue Bonsecours."

I helped her up. I sort of felt sorry for her; I had taken advantage of a defenceless woman.

"I don't like to be courted, ma'am," I replied.

All of a sudden, I was someone else, born again. I had just received again, in one fell swoop, baptism, communion, confirmation, and extreme unction. Questa went to pinch Chateaugué's cheek, then she left. She left me alone with an excess of dishes on my hands and a sad flavour in my mouth, a marvellous taste of raw, warm flesh. I spent the rest of the day as though my mouth were full of ether, full of a sweet and bubbly nourishment. I spent the rest of the day making eyes at the waitresses just to vex them, just to make them give birth, just to put them in a bad mood, just to get them pregnant. Coming back from the Penguin, Chateaugué took me by the hand. I let her do it, but I avoided the gaze of the passersby. I didn't want them to think that I was proud of drawing attention to myself. How beautiful, a little brother and sister holding each other's hands. But a real little brother wouldn't kiss house-wives under sinks. But a real little sister wouldn't take that thing seriously, at least not to the point of epilepsy, not to the point of hysteria. All women love me. I really don't give a hoot about them. I really don't give two hoots about them. I'm Popeye, the sailor man. On my way by, I went to look in on our apartment manager. We settled up. She seemed glad; good rents make good neighbours. I didn't care; I was paying with Chateaugué's tips. We chatted. She told me about her cocker spaniel's rheumatism. I told her about Chateaugué's accident. There's a free room on the second floor; she whispered in my ear not to tell anyone about it, to keep it to myself. I'm Popeye, the sailor man. Exhausted, Chateaugué had thrown herself into bed when she got home. I sat down in my armchair and I read. Insured people read a little in their armchairs before putting themselves to bed, in order to know everything. When I came to bed, Chateaugué woke up, the excellent Chateaugué. She looked at me with the same gaze as before, as if nothing had happened the night before. Her mouth was full of laughter.

"Heeheehee," she said. "Say heeheehee ... Say heeheehee-heeheehee ... sweetheart."

"No! No!"

The spark that had been missing flew out, and she started to grin from ear to ear. She began to laugh.

"Say heeheehee ... sweetheart. Just do me a favour; say hee-heeheeheeheehee ... It's fun; say heeheehee ..."

"No! No! No!"

She was laughing even louder. She had stopped laughing for a second, just long enough to change gears.

"Say heeheeheeheeheehee ... please! Sweetheart! For the love of God?"

"No, Chateaugué. No! No! Leave me alone! Quit bugging me!"

She was laughing, laughing; she couldn't cope anymore. She was laughing her ass off. She was laughing like a fountain. She was laughing like a beet. I seemed more and more glum. She was laughing like Isabelle Rimbaud. She laid four or five heeheehees ... laughed until she was out of breath, suffocated, laid a few more heeheehees ... and let herself once more be strangled by hilarity. She was laughing and laughing, facing the oblique wall, her hand on her belly. Her nostrils were flaring. I could see her uvula hopping. She was laughing and grimacing as though it were hurting her.

"When I was little, I used to say heeheeheeheeheeheehee-heehee ... in my little bed until I couldn't breathe."

And Isabelle Rimbaud began to laugh again. She lay down on me and crushed my nose with the flat of her hand. She straddled me without the slightest embarrassment, with the greatest of ease, and planted her hands on the two eyes that adorn my chest.

"You have some, too. Look! ... Teeny-weeny teeny-weeny teeny-weeny, like a cat's ..."

She took her hands away in order to show me my pectorals and started to tickle me by running her ten fingers over them. Once again, it was too funny. And there she was collapsing and stretched all the way out on me, shaking me with the irresistible and telluric laugh of her whole soul, of her whole belly, of all her members and all her bones. The apartment manager's secret had given birth to a good but ferocious idea. This would seem to be an auspicious moment to lay it on the table. He who laughed last would laugh best.

"The apartment manager told me that there's a room available. You'll be glad; we're going to have separate rooms. Get ready—at the next payday, somebody's going to have a brand new room, going to move, going to ..."

She put her hand on my mouth and told me to be quiet.

"Not another word, Miles Miles. Don't talk anymore. Why did you get angry again? Don't talk anymore. Let the little munchkin be a little bit happy before she dies. Shhhhh ... Shhhhh ..."

She didn't cry, but she didn't laugh anymore.

34

I am not myself today. I am never myself. My hand is itself. Every time I find myself again, I seem different. I am different from what I was a second ago. Tonight, I have something to say, and I won't manage to say it. I am not me; that, in a few incomprehensible words, is what I mean. I am not me for the one and only reason that I don't exist. I do not seek to blind with paradoxes. Painfully, I seek to understand. I have a past, admittedly—an immutable, fixed, unchangeable past, resembling itself everywhere and in every circumstance. But this past is not me, since I no longer am. We say, "This is me!" the way we say, "This is a chair!"—that is, we like to think of ourselves as things, as something that can be defined, named, and that always corresponds, with exactitude and precision, to that definition, to that name. Now, I am not the same as I was yesterday. Now, my chair is what it was yesterday, but I am not what I was yesterday. Now, I have some surprises in store for myself, but my chair has no surprises in store for me. My chair has preserved the same colour, the same form, the same weight, the same use, the same courage, the same doubts, the same certainties, the same smile, the same grimace, the same soul. Miles Miles has preserved nothing; Miles Miles has changed everything. Yesterday I was strong; today I am weak. Yesterday I was joyful; today I am sad. Yesterday I didn't need anybody. Today I need me, the best of myself. I once was thirsty; now I am drunk. The trees were once beautiful; now they are bitter. My chair has principles, like the others; it's as if it made it a point of honour, a duty, to react in an identical way to identical forces and identical circumstances; it's as if it felt obliged to remain faithful to the properties that its definition and its name have attributed to it. It will never collapse under the weight of a needle; it will always collapse under the weight of an elephant. I often collapse under the weight of a needle; often the weight of the day doesn't even make me stumble. There are remedies for the absence of a self, of a truly faithful whole, of a soul never different, always unchanging. If you want a self truly faithful to a definition, forge one for yourself, believe that you have one, believe, believe (above all, in words). The universal remedy, the philosophical stone (sic), is believing. If you believe you're a patriot, you're a patriot. If you believe you're a communist, you are. Some people remain chemists all their lives. You're a chemist, a lawyer, or a patriot, the way you'd be a chair, a beet, or a shoe. It's useful to be something, to not be just anything at all, to not fear having some surprises in store for yourself. When you're a chemist, when you've hung your diploma on your wall, you don't need to be afraid of waking up a horticulturist or a minister one fine morning. At the beginning of this discussion, I had principles; I believed. I had formed a precise idea of myself, and I exerted myself in every way to impose it on reality. I claimed, arrogating divine powers to myself, to be able to change reality and things, to bring them by force of stubbornness to adapt themselves to a simple and rigid definition that I called me. Here is that definition: the beauty of childhood and innocence moves me to tears; the ugliness of maturity, buying, selling, customers, and the sexes moves me to the point of disgust and despair. I made it a point of honour and duty to hate in the blood everything that wasn't of the colour and sweetness of our childhood. Failing to be true to my definition was equivalent to betrayal, to high treason. Taking on bit by bit the colour and bitterness of the adult, I've come to hate myself to the point of disgust, despair, wanting my death, even projecting my death. All adults were supposed to be found ugly and hideous, not because they were ugly and hideous, but because they were buyers and sellers, streaming with sins of impurity. With all my strength, faithfully, I endeavoured to find adults ugly. The world, an invention of the adults, the buyers, the sellers, the impure, underwent the fate of the adults. With all my strength, I hated them. But, as a result of the courage to live, I suspected and discovered the sham of words. Now I no longer believe. But that is not the question. I am, at the very most, the world; not the world, but an action of the world on my senses; not an action of the world on my senses, but a violent reaction—unpredictable, incoercible, conscious, voluntarily or involuntarily voluntary (I mean that the will may or may not agree with this reaction and can do nothing but contribute to it)—of my senses to the violent, unsettled, infinitely various, and infinitely variable forces of the world. But that is not the question, and the instantaneous definition of the self says why: I suffer. If there were no world, I couldn't be. A man alone in the nothingness is an impossibility; a reaction is impossible without an action. Since things do not act, and since the world is made up only of things and men, a man cannot be without men. Therefore, man is not a reaction to the world but a reaction to man—but, alas! The preceding doesn't hold water. Men are action, men act, but they act only by reaction. Man cannot be both action and reaction. That's a tall tale! When I speak of man, I do not speak of his body, which is merely a spasm, but of his soul. And the soul (intelligence and will) acts only by reaction. Intelligence and will do not set out acts; acts are proposed to them, and they refuse them, welcome them, or judge them. What soul could have the idea of understanding a door or of closing a door, if there were no door? The virtue of chastity is a sexual virtue. If there were no sexuality, there would be no chaste and pure virgins. So prostitutes aren't the only ones leading sexual lives. Fit? ... To be tied!

35

I'm a happy playboy. I love life. I want life, and I have life. In one fell swoop, I take all of life into my arms and I laugh, throwing back my head, not to mention how the axes bristling from my head make the blood spurt out. I kiss life; you'd think that it's made for that, that it's made to make me proud of my strength. Take a chair in your arms; it will do whatever you like, it has no strength. The strength is all yours. What is sickening in me and what is sickening in this world embrace each other so well! How well they intertwine and allow themselves to be possessed! I really don't give two hoots about everything I've said, about everything that I've done to you; I kiss you, I take you along, I carry you away. The more, the better. I am not embarking. I am the bark, and I'm embarking everything. Full steam ahead, Fred! Enough of this chattering! Up 'n' Adam, Eve! The whole family to the Penguin! Let the dishes fly! Let 'em fly! Quick, Chateaugué, my excellent one! Quick! You're not ready? You're not all washed and dressed yet, you say? What does that matter? Come on! Come on! Come quick! The customers will appreciate your services much more concretely if you have one side clean and dressed and the other side undressed and dirty. Let Customer see a bit of naked, filthy skin! He'll love that. He'll give you enormous tips, vast tips. He'll fill up the plate with them. The plate won't be big enough. He'll swoop down on the cups. The cups runneth over. He'll fall back on the saucers. He'll tie tens and twenties to the handles of the knives, forks, and spoons. He'll run to empty out his bank account. You'll make more money than the fat Greek. Come on! Quick! Enough of this chattering! Long live lewdness!

"What's making you laugh so hard?" Chateaugué asks me. She's moving tomorrow—that's what she's thinking about so bitterly.

"It is," I reply, "the prospect of being rid of you! Get going, move it. Hurry up! I'm waiting on you. Snail! Tortoise! Hare today, gone tomorrow!"

She's down on the floor, in the middle of slowly tying her shoes. She's tying them with so little enthusiasm that I'm overcome with compassion, that I throw myself at her feet and tie them for her. Oh! How I tied them!

"That's how you tie your shoes, bumble-thumbs. You've got to tie your shoes while laughing, in the blink of an eye!"

Outside, as we go out, what do we see? We see automobiles. One of them is still sleeping, despite the late hour. It's shining in the sun, in front of the house. I jump up on its back and I spin like a top, I dance the flamenco. Chateaugué is rooted to the spot, sadly watching me, waiting for me joylessly. I lean over, catch her by the shoulders and, in the effort that I expend to lift her up, I slip, lose my footing, and fall. I crash down on Chateaugué, I drag her down with me in my flight, and we smash into the asphalt, I mean the assfault. What do I do about this tragic clumsiness and about Chateaugué's panic attack, about the panic attack of the dog that you mistreat after petting it? I laugh it off. A great laugh fills the street hemmed in on all sides by the houses. A big bump has sprouted on Chateaugué's head. What do I do about that mountain? I laugh it off. My laugh spreads outward in a spiral. Laugh, let's laugh, you laugh! No need to stand on ceremony. All the way to the Penguin, Chateaugué limps. I persist in walking behind her to laugh at seeing her limp. She persists in walking behind me so that I won't watch her limp. It's a never-ending race of one step forward, two steps backward.

"And what if I have something broken? And what if I have to go to the hospital? You don't laugh about things like that, it brings bad luck."

"If you have something broken, I'll cut off your ears."

"It's my birthday today; don't make fun of me."

"It's your birthday today? I thought it was yesterday."

Automobiles have killed all the dogs I've ever had. They've run over them all, with no discrimination whatsoever, whether white or black, whether frizzy-haired or long-haired, whether little or big, whether bold or cowardly. Go ask the neighbours if you don't believe me. And I had to be the one to bury them. Poor dogs! All behind the times! They thought they were still in the Middle Ages; they didn't know that you've got to look both ways before crossing the road. You'd hear the shriek of an automobile, then the shriek of a dog. It was always the dog who'd die when the combat proved to be mortal. Zero, my last dog, was tough; he was unkillable. However, he was only able to survive the first four encounters. In the end, his four paws were in tatters; he could only get around by bounds, like a toad. He'd make three hops and be tuckered out; he'd stop, stick out his tongue, and pant. He seemed to find it the most natural thing in the world to have four dead paws. I never saw him in a bad mood. I never heard him howl at night. Every time he'd catch sight of me, he'd flash me that toothy grin, wagging his tail in delight, calling to me. He was like Chateaugué—he was always grinning from ear to ear. One day, when he had chosen to make one of his characteristic stops right in the middle of the road, he got his skull ground down by a mastodon with toothed wheels. I couldn't look at a dead dog without a friend to help me; I couldn't touch it without wanting to heave. When a blackbird would bump into my window and I had to hold a funeral, I'd go get Chateaugué. If it was a little dog, I'd pick it up with a shovel; Chateaugué would hold it with her feet so that it wouldn't slide in front of the shovel. If it was a big dog, holding a funeral with anything other than our arms was out of the question, and Chateaugué had to take charge of everything. She'd drag the dog, biting her tongue; I'd follow the funeral procession, my hands in my pockets, crying. Turning her face away, Chateaugué would take a dog as big as she was by the tail and would lean, pull, sweat, and fall on her bottom. She loathed the job of funeral attendant. She would invoke every possible excuse to get out of it.

"What if his tail breaks ... What if he comes back to life and jumps on me ... I can't ..."

Before going into the Penguin, I hurl at Chateaugué these words that have come back up my throat and are as bitter as vinegar.

"My dog's been killed. Come help me bury him."

On the grave, she would stick a cross, a minuscule cross, a cross so small that she had to get down on her knees to plant it. Chateaugué's world is minuscule, so small that a breath of air can dissipate it, so fragile that it could be carried off by a gust of wind, like the top of a dandelion. On the grave, she would stick a cross no bigger than a finger. However, despite the bitterness of these memories, I think of them with a growing joy that expands and deepens as I welcome it, that I find good. But the prospect of getting paid has no small share in facilitating this joy for me. It's Friday, payday. What's honking outside? Automobiles. Automobiles as useful to my joy as the dogs whose blood they have drunk. Nice automobiles. Automobiles a bit stupid, a bit brutal, a bit carried away, a bit vampirish, but meaning no harm. Good old automobiles from the province of Quebec. Morons! Anything can nourish my joy; anything, from despair to ridicule; anything except those moronic United States automobiles. Even as I wash dishes, I think joyfully of my dogs. For an eight-hour shift, I wash dishes. For an eight-hour shift, she serves. Finally, we get paid. We're going to go celebrate that.

"Let's go stuff ourselves!"

Chateaugué takes me by the hand, perhaps without realizing it, perhaps even out of habit, and we're off, we go for it. I never stop talking and laughing. Everything is a pretext for me to poke fun, to be ironic, especially with Saint Pay up ahead on the sidewalks paving the way. The awareness, the pride, and the novelty of my taking possession of my life give me wings. A few bad jokes that make Chateaugué totter with laughter elate me, and this elation is expressed in a loquaciousness of such vivacity, such brilliance, that I myself am dazed by it, dazzled by it. I am another sun. I've got to initiate Chateaugué quickly, introduce her to the splendours of the New World, wise her up, and put her back in the world. Wake up, Chateaugué! Don't you feel like being another sun? We're walking behind a woman of the New World. Her head is laden with gold earrings whose deafening melodies punctuate her stroll and whose gold evokes the gold of the bugles of the brass bands. Chateaugué gives me a dig in the ribs and, anticipating a fight, puffs out her cheeks with laughter and prepares to die laughing. I pretend to scowl and, talking too loudly to not be overheard by the gold-clad woman, talking in the voice of a political orator, I apostrophize Chateaugué.

"Those aren't earrings. Those are anchors. It's because women's heads are as light as Christmas-tree ornaments, and the breeze would carry them off. There's a lake called Pend Oreille (which is French for *earring*) in Idaho, in northern Idaho. The lighter a woman's head, the more she piles them on her ears. It is written in the Gospels that, in the olden days, men had to put a millstone around their necks to stay at the bottom of the water. Those were their anchors. You're a woman, Chateaugué. Your head is light. You've got to wear earrings. The absence of earrings is a sign of a head as hard and heavy as a rock. Wear earrings, Chateaugué, if you don't want to look like you have a head as heavy and hard as a rock. Men like to fear breaking the woman's head that they take in their hands."

A bit cynical, the intended target of this harangue turns around and thanks me. Chateaugué thinks that's funny. I'm really discouraged; despite my scintillating verve, she didn't understand a thing about earrings. But I carry on undaunted. You mustn't let yourself get discouraged. The educator's task is a thankless one. The pupils are unruly; they're constantly throwing hammers and anvils at the educator's head. He whose task is teaching risks his own hide; he lives dangerously. I've known more than one teacher who, when retirement came along, didn't have a single hair left on his head. Their pupils had torn them out, one by one, with forceps. Some pupils tear the leaves out of their books, make little spitballs that they throw, and then read the leaves of their trees. Some come to class dressed as generals, just to thumb their noses. Some have lice that promenade stark naked on their arms and are proud of it. Some spend their time brushing their teeth. Some brush their teeth with such force that the educator can't even hear the trains go by. Some sleep, and others always come in late. We pass four Chinese people, who are speaking Chinese and who are speaking all at the same time. We watch them talk. We don't understand what they're talking about. We watch them move away and get swallowed up by the crowd. After thinking that over, it occurs to me that it's possible to pronounce four consonants all at once.

"Are you capable," I say to her, "of pronouncing four consonants in one shot, of bringing together four consonants in a single utterance? You can't? I can. Look—Khrushchev, Schneiderman, Schnitzler."

Chateaugué is astonished. Flabbergasted, she does not reply. You're astonished, my dear? You ain't seen nothin' yet—soon you'll be astounded. I continue.

"The Polish city of Stettin has changed its name, you know ... Do you know what its name is now?"

As a sign of negation and of ignorance, she shakes her head excessively from left to right and from right to left.

"You don't know? I know it. It's Szczecin. But it's pronounced shche-tseen."

This display of toponymic science staggers her. She is astounded. She can hardly swallow her saliva. She begs me, beseeches me, entreats me to teach her. She humbly requests that I introduce her to the spelling of the pronunciation of *Szczecin*. I cede to this request.

"*Szczecin* is pronounced *shche-tseen*: s, h, as in *shoofly*; c, h, e, as in *chevalier*; t, s, as in *tsetse*; e, e, n, as in *teem*. There! If you want to remember it for the rest of your life, all you have to do is remember this baralipton for the rest of your life: The SHoofly tripped up the CHEvalier as the TSetses tEEMed over him. A baralipton, for your guidance, is a mnemonic device. Are you capable of repeating my baralipton without making mistakes and without hesitating?"

"Yes," she says. "Look—The shoofly tripped up the chevalier as the tsetses teemed over him. It's easy to remember; there are lots of animals."

"I protest. There are only two: the fly and the tsetses."

"Three! Three! The horse, the fly, and the tsetses."

"What horse?"

"The chevalier's horse from Ticondéroga."

We argue. We expand on the topic until, having jumped from one subject to another several times, we agree on the real pronunciation of *Szczecin*. She shows herself to be proud of knowing how to pronounce *Szczecin* properly. There she goes, showering our poor sidewalk companions, male and female, with *Chetseen*, *Chesteen*, *Shtettseen*, and even *Shchetseen*. She hurls *Chetseens*, *Chesteens*, *Shtettseens*, and *Shchetseens* at them while looking at them right in the eye, in an aggressive way, as though she were hurling *Go to bed*s and *Quit bugging me*s at them. I'm ashamed of being the escort of this harpy, but there is joy in everything, even in shame; the main thing is daring to take it. It's not forbidden to be bold while blushing. Chateaugué knows nothing yet of all these subtleties about joy. I pity her. I can't let her wallow in ignorance. I'm already starting to choose words and to perfect allegories that will facilitate her task and mine. Suddenly, before us, the heel on an old lady's high-heeled shoe gets chewed off by a manhole cover. Realizing what has happened, the old lady stops dead in her tracks, freezes, and is rooted to the spot, as if her entire ability to walk had just been chewed off. Chateaugué gives me a dig in the ribs and is ready to burst out laughing. She is confident that, by some clever remark, I'll make her burst out laughing. What to do? I try to be funny, valiantly.

"All she's got to do now is start rowing, poor Lady Bountiful."

Chateaugué relieves herself of the greater part of her fit of laughter while nodding in agreement.

"Yes! Yes! She really does look shipwrecked, indeed! Look at her limping. It's funny. She's limping like it was her real heel that was gone from under her foot."

I pull together all my earnestness. I have something to say to Chateaugué about high heels. Joy grants certainty. Certainty incites one to teach.

"Listen!" I tell her. "Listen carefully, really carefully. I insist that you understand what I have to say to you. For you, high-heeled shoes are like the mask that you've got to put on in order to go to a masked ball. Without a mask, would you take any delight in a masked ball? You'll take no delight in the world, and you'll feel alone and abandoned there if you don't wear high-heeled shoes like all other women."

Straining and impatient like a know-it-all, she can't wait to serve up to me the objections that she believes are fatal to my lesson.

"With you, I'll never feel alone and abandoned. I don't need anybody. I don't like pleasure. I think pleasure's sad."

After that long, merry, and edifying walk along Rue Sainte-Catherine, we enter the chic restaurant whose façade adjoins the shop window where we stole the bride. We like to eat in the restaurants whose façades adjoin the shop window where we've stolen mannequins. They take hours to serve us. You'd think they weren't particularly keen on seeing their business prosper.

"The service stinks here," cracks Chateaugué, an expert on the subject, which, in these circumstances, is serious.

We observe the diners. In the neighbouring booth, two lovebirds, leaning on their elbows, nose-to-nose over the table, are playing with their hands. The boy of the two has longer hair than the other. He looks gay, and she looks like a lesbian. Masculine and feminine mix in however they can, meet up however they can. But those are not suitable thoughts to be transmitted to Chateaugué. She seems to find the topsy-turvy idyll they form touching. I take advantage of it to resume my lesson.

"Do you know what it's like to be an adult? Listen to me, really carefully. A little while ago, you were holding my hand ... What effect did that have on you? None, right? You didn't even notice it. Look at those two who are holding hands. They seem to like it, right? You may not believe me, but their hearts are pounding. The first time they gave their hands to each other, their courage failed them. What will happen to you, do you think, when you're kissed on the lips by your boyfriend? It'll be as if all of a sudden, all the air were leaving the earth, as if you were swallowing all of the earth's air at once."

I draw a deep breath to illustrate what I'm saying. I continue.

"That's what it's like to be an adult. Everything that was flat starts to excavate abysses under your steps. Everything that was light starts to crush you. From the age of laughter and sorrow, you switch to the age of delirium and despair. You become as vast as all of life. That's all. That's it."

Her wide eyes, increased in size by the tension and the attention, seem to fill up her whole face.

"Are you an adult, Miles Miles?"

"Yes, Chateaugué," I say without blushing. "I am a man."

"And me?"

"You're not a man, my little munchkin. You're nothing but a little girl, because you don't want to understand anything!"

No one likes to be treated like a negligible quantity. She rebels.

"Oh, mister! You're only a year older than I am, after all. I'm fifteen now. A man! You should take a good look at yourself! Oh! It's my birthday. You haven't yet wished me happy birthday. Wish me happy birthday if you're a man."

We each eat a pizza, a real one, an enormous one, one as big as the sun going down—a pizza with red peppers and green peppers, with mushrooms, anchovies, pears, vinegar, tomatoes, peas, lettuce, cucumbers, pepper, salt, multicoloured cheeses, and even fruitcakes (the restaurant is full of them). It's so hot that we sweat. We want some wine to extinguish our tongues. They don't want to serve us any. We insist. They call their manager to the rescue.

"It's her birthday," I tell the manager. "Do you think we're going to drink water?"

The manager replies that there's nothing to be done, that the laws are strict. Chateaugué says that she's a drinking woman, that no bottle of wine will scandalize her. There's nothing to be done; the manager remains inexorable. He says that if he serves us wine, he'll be put in jail. We're much too young; there's really nothing to be done. We'll have to extinguish our tongues with water or Coca-Cola. The waitress, an old gal, winks at us while serving us our bottles of Coca-Cola. We taste. Victory! It's not Coca-Cola, it's wine. My tongue is on fire; I down the bottle in a single gulp. Chateaugué is determined to ape me. Overcoming great difficulties, she manages to swallow her fake bottle of Coca-Cola in one gulp. I reprimand her.

"With manners like those, you'll never find yourself a husband."

"I'm not looking for one."

The wine makes us sweat twice as much as before. Chateaugué wants to leave a two-dollar tip for the waitress.

"She'll be so happy!"

First, I chew her out. Does she think she's a billionaire? Afterward, discouraged by her firm purpose, I give up the fight.

"It's my birthday. It's my money. It's my tip. She'll be so happy! You wash dishes; you don't understand these things."

Outside, it is bone-chillingly cold. It's a bit windy; we can feel the sweat drying on our foreheads. We're off in search of fifteen candles. We cover at least ten miles in all directions without finding a thing. In spurts, to warm ourselves up, we run. Nobody has any candles for sale. Nobody wants to sell us fifteen candles.

"Do you sell candles?" Chateaugué asks the boss of a strange grocery store.

This grocery store boss is deadpan, a Molière, a smartass; in a very witty way, he turns the question back on Chateaugué.

"Do I sell candles? I sell nothing but edibles. Do I sell candles?"

In the back of the store, we see Chinese lanterns swaying, we see toys shining. Chateaugué can't make up her mind; she ponders with all her might. Molière comes to her aid. He seems good-natured. He doesn't seem to be making fun of her, not at all.

"Are candles edible, Miss?"

If Chinese lanterns are edible, thinks Chateaugué ... She replies that yes, that candles might be edible.

"Therefore, I sell candles," concludes Molière brilliantly. "Now, I don't sell any candles. I don't even know what a candle is, Miss. I know nothing about candles, Miss. I've got a doctorate in groceries. I don't have a doctorate in candles. I'm so ignorant of candles that, if I saw a swift kick in the pants, I'd take it for a candle and be delighted to give it to you."

Goddamn comedian! We leave. We walk, tired, discouraged, and out of breath, our heads down. We see a cathedral. Our hopes revived, we race toward it, we slip under the trusty, rusty gate. Finally armed with our fifteen candles, we go into a restaurant to drink and warm ourselves up. Chateaugué says she's so thirsty she could drink a ton of water. In honour of her fifteen years, I order fifteen Coca-Colas. Chateaugué thinks the idea is crazy but touching.

"It's a bit crazy, but it makes my heart quiver. It's true. You're nice when you want to be. I'm going to remember this evening until the end of my days. It's true. You don't know me. I hide all kinds of things from you."

"So, do you have any lovers?"

The waitress brings us our Coca-Colas with the tops on and in a case. I look at her. I see that, once again, we're dealing with a deadpan character, a Molière, a smartass. I ask her to open the bottles, to serve them to us so that we can drink them.

"Oh!" she exclaims. "It's for here."

We look at each other, Chateaugué and I, and we burst out laughing. "That's right, Miss. We're not exporters."

The waitress is a Molière fanatic. She serves us our Coca-Colas again with knives, forks, spoons, napkins, and plates. Chateaugué proposes that we drink the fifteenth bottle first.

"It's the only one that counts, since I'm fifteen years old. What's more, it's the one that we have to divide in two if we want to drink seven and a half bottles each. Drink the first half all at once. I'll drink the other half all at once, too."

I follow through. I drink, gulping it down blindly, throwing caution to the wind. Judging that I've already swallowed more than my share, she pulls on the bottle to grab it away from my mouth and hands. She strains; I resist. She braces herself. The table takes a hit from her knee, the fourteen other bottles dance up and down and oscillate dangerously while clinking together. I give up the fight. I give her the bottle. She tells me that she was carrying a lighted candle in one hand during her first communion and that the wax was running. The wax was running onto her white glove and hardening. The wax was running slowly, then stiffening.

"By the end, my whole glove was covered with it. It was like great frozen tears. It came right off, like a skin. I took off a piece, and I put it in my mouth. It was hot, it was good. I ate it. Candles are edible ..."

We do our best to drink all our Coca-Cola. The more you force yourself to drink a carbonated beverage, the more you burp. We're burping like the damned, like the unleashed. I want to talk to her about joy, and I don't know how to tackle it. What's more, her gaze is so tough, so clear, so straightforward, and so sweet, that I doubt what I have to tell her will ever be of any use to her.

"I've thought it over, Chateaugué. I think that what we're waiting for, both of us, is joy. Why wait for it, huh? Why are we waiting for joy? Why not affirm it for ourselves ...? I'm sure, Chateaugué ... Stop looking at me that way; you look like you're about to cry."

"You've never talked to me like this. I've never seen you like this. It's true that you're a man now."

"I'm sure that you'll be happy all your life if you know how to say to joy, in a unanimous surge of all your strength, that you've got it by the gills and won't let go. All your blind struggles, all those blows that you let fly in the void, all those cries, all those tears, all your strength—give them a meaning, a target, a prey; apply them to make joy—your joy—triumph. You don't wait for joy; you take it, once and for all. Now, at this very moment, take it, steal it, seize some for yourself! You secure it. You've seized it, you've taken it, you've locked it away in your heart, you've got it. You've got it, Chateaugué. Understand: you've got it. You've taken it by force; you've got it, now, at this very moment. All you've got to do now is dare to make it reign over everything, over the magnificent as well as the unclean, as if it were a distant star. You find yourself ugly in your mirror ... What do you do? You experience joy. Joy is always there, in your heart, like a flower, waiting for you, waiting for you to take it in your hands and feel it. I've been mean to you ... What do you find in your heart? What do you take there? You find and then you take a big blue flower, joy. Your joy cannot leave, since you've locked your heart up as tight as a drum. You've got nothing to be afraid of—you've put it in a cage. All you have to do is close your eyes to see it. Close your eyes and look at it; it's blue, it has big petals. Joy is your slave, but in order for it to protect you, it also has to be your master. It cannot disobey you, and you must not disobey it. Know, Chateaugué, that whenever you're unhappy, it will be because you've disobeyed joy. If a friend betrays you, what do you do? Do you cry? Maybe ... But you cry without bitterness ... On the contrary, with tears in your eyes or not, if you enter your heart, you'll find joy. A friend's betrayal is nothing more than a circumstance, another circumstance, another castle over which your joy may reign, unhesitatingly and mercilessly. If you find yourself disgusted by something, by someone, or even by everything, what do you do? You turn your back, you go away, you go take a stroll in your heart, you go see your joy. You feel disgusted, admittedly. But you don't suffer, since, behind the bars of your heart, your joy has remained intact and whole, still remains intact and whole. You're disgusted ... with the greatest joy in the world, with the only true joy, with joy."

One more time, Chateaugué interrupts me.

"You're frightening me. Stop! You'd think that you were trying to warn me of a danger, that you wanted me to beware of you."

"Chateaugué, listen! Think of the ceremony of the laying on of hands ... always. You've got your joy the way you've got your hands. All you have to do is impose it on everything ... always, on yourself ... to the degree that you find yourself otherwise. It's so easy. What is more obedient than your hands? With your hands, you can touch everything that touches you. That's all. You own your joy. Now laugh."

By way of laughter, she begs me not to abandon her, never to speak to her again like that.

"Don't abandon me. You're all I have, Miles Miles."

In order to illustrate so that she'll understand, so that she'll at least remember, I improvise for her personal use a ceremony of the laying on of hands. I tell her to close her eyes; then I make her stretch out her arms and join her hands, the way sleepwalkers do. Then, following my instructions with a touching docility, she puts her eight little combined fingers on everything whose name I tell her—on the air, the light, the wall, the table, her eyes, the bottles, the plate, the knife, the darkness, the passing time. As I tell her to do it, she repeats, for herself, alone in the depths of the darkness behind her eyelids, that she has her own joy the way she has her own hands.

"You can open your eyes again now. The rites are over. If you don't understand by now, you'll never understand."

"No!" she says, squeezing and screwing her eyelids up tighter. "I'm not done yet."

We're seated across from each other. Her right arm before her and before me, she gently explores, with her blind hands, the void that separates us. Her hands, with the utmost care, are hunting for something. Suddenly, they settle on my face and stop. They remain there for quite a while, barely touching me, as light as butterflies, alive like birds, although immobile.

"You are my castle, and I'm guarding you. You are my castle, and I'm going in, and I'm closing all the doors."

Here we are back in our room. We're beat. We're dying of fatigue and indigestion. We've lit the candles, and we've set them one by one on the floor with a drop of their honey. In silence, we watch these stars of a world all our own shine. Soon, the danger with which Chateaugué feels threatened because of my speeches fills up the room and envelops me. I'm frightened. I feel the same fear that she does. Suddenly, it's as if I were her. Goddamn lesbian!

36

Automobiles

On the way to the restrooms,
Men and women go by
Grafted to vehicles
That extinguish blood and soul.

They go by in automobiles,
These madmen, these madwomen.
And they believe themselves, alas, clever
For living on nothing but oil.

They don't speak; they honk.
And they don't walk; they run.
Since I get by on two legs,
They laugh; they call me a hen.

They're yellow, or green, or black.
Among themselves, no segregation at all;
They move between the sidewalks
Side by side and in unison.

Eleven days ago, I discovered joy. For leaven (did you see the
bread?) days, I haven't jilted joy, and joy hasn't jilted me. I won't
jilt my joy. I have a headache. A splitting headache. Women
have laughed at me. I lost face in front of the Penguin waitresses. All I had left was twenty dollars. I lost twenty dollars. I
fought with an assistant cook. An assistant cook smashed in
my face in the Penguin kitchen. I came out of all these situations, from the easiest as well as the most shameful, with my

joy intact. For eleven days, I've been playing everything (even the imbecile), and I've been taking everything (even punches on my face) with joy, with an invincible and imperishable joy, with a joy that is all the more lively because my soul is keenly shaken by the unpredictable forces of this world. Whichever one of my conceits is agitated by the blows and the terrible states, whichever one of my ideas they extol, conceits and ideas only writhe and unravel, only expend energy, in order to excite and nourish my joy. For turbines, all the colours of water are of equal merit. For generators and transformers, the green or the blue of water is irrelevant. Everything that happens is all the same to me, since my joy feeds on it all with a stomach of steel. But my joy is not a humdrum joy. The joy of losing twenty dollars is not the same as that of drinking a glass of lukewarm water. I am proud; I don't like to get my face smashed in by a Greek. With a single blow, that Greek floored me. Dazed, twirling around in the void, I saw him smiling. He was smiling; all my hatred only added to his total satisfaction with himself. He was smiling with that insolence that I encounter in all Greeks and Romans, with the same insolence that had displeased and aggravated me to the point of making me lose my cool and provoke the altercation. He was smiling; tears were coming to my eyes, out of anger, impotence, and anguish. All my might had been dead set against me, was straining to the breaking point against me, had come together to destroy me—I was in despair—I was at the limits of mental resistance and on the borderline of hysteria. In other words, my pride was struggling like a demon in holy water. What was I going to do? I remembered joy, my joy. I apprehended suddenly, all at once, all the richness of my shame, and I unleashed into that richness—so that he might devour it—the unassuageable lion of my joy. Calmly, I got back up again. Wildly, I was laughing. Wildly, I was enjoying myself. I felt a bit crazy, but I've never in all my life felt joy in such a bizarre, burning, and uplifting way. The word *unassuageable* is not in the dictionary that I have, cannot be found in the dictionary with which I am conversant. I should have bought myself a thicker one. The Greek is a smartass, one of those smartasses. They are smartasses, and they live dangerously. I know a few smartasses who are stockier than they who will end up smashing their faces in. I even know a few who won't always be sixteen years old. I haven't finished getting bigger and filling out. I'm full of my joy the way Hail Mary is full of grace. Stupid. It's all I think about. I'd like to tell everybody about it. Who is it? It's my joy. I'm keeping Chateaugué with me for a few more days, just to talk to her about my joy, just to put my joy to the test, just for her to look at my joy. Earnestness is eminently aphrodisiac. When I talk to Chateaugué about joy, I can tell she's tense and shuddering; she has difficulty breathing; her sonorous deglutitions of saliva show that her jaw is clenched and that she has a lump in her throat. Tonight, on our way home, we found Questa sitting on the threshold.

"What are you doing there?"

"I'm doing what everybody's doing, my children—I'm living."

"You were waiting for us. You were living ... while waiting. Come in quick, so we can talk to you about joy. We know all about joy, Chateaugué and I. Ask Chateaugué if you don't believe me."

Questa didn't seem very talkative. Without even removing the bird of paradise that she was using as a hat, she flung herself across the bed. She fell asleep immediately, face down on the bed. She's sleeping, since she's snoring. Sitting on the floor, our backs to the partition, we're talking about joy, very low, so as not to wake her. Not having a couch in our room, we are reduced to having to sit on the floor in order to sit next to each other. Her nose between her knees, embracing her folded legs, Chateaugué defends her happiness and attacks my joy.

"If everything's all the same to you, that means you wouldn't care about hurting my feelings. If you think everything's funny, that means you'd think it's funny to see someone cry."

"Exactly. Yes, I want you to believe that when you cry, I won't suffer, that when you cry, I will joyfully watch you cry. I'll joyfully watch you cry, just as—now listen to this—just as, if you dare (and all you have to do is dare), you will joyfully watch me cry. You mustn't torture yourself needlessly. The tears of one have no effect on the tears of the others. Plus, your joy at seeing me cry is not the desire to see me cry, it's not mean. You can be happy to see me cry while at the same time feeling sorry to see me cry. I got my face smashed in; I'm happy about it. Being happy about getting my face smashed in doesn't stop me from feeling sorry about getting my face smashed in and from swearing revenge. You don't have to feel unhappy to actually want me to feel less unhappy. Besides, there's only one good way to cry—it's to cry joyfully, to cry laughing. Don't get sad when I cry. You'd get sad for nothing; I cry laughing."

Chateaugué aims her scandalized, bewildered, and amazed face at me as if it were the mouth of a cannon. Caressing her cheek on her knees and hugging her legs with renewed passion, she ripostes.

"That means you'll never suffer? That means you'll never have real sorrows? You're heartless! You're hard-hearted. You're so hard-hearted that just by trying to understand what you're saying, I feel my heart hardening. Just thinking that I might never suffer again, that I might never feel sorrow again, hardens my heart. You must not have a heart. I can sense that you have no heart, that what you want is not to have a heart anymore, and I'm scared. You scare me."

"That's because you don't understand. You're as thick as a brick. You're doing it on purpose. Heart! Heart! Who wants a heart if a heart is only good for suffering? If you get your arms cut off, I won't feel any sorrow, I'll laugh. Tears don't make arms grow back. Tears and despair, whether friendly or not, are destructive; they kill, they harm life. Joy helps life. You don't need me, Chateaugué. Even if your arms were cut off, you wouldn't need me. What help will you need if you have joy? What do you need if you have joy?"

She hastens to reply with her voice and with her sweetest, saddest eyes.

"You, Miles Miles. I need you. You can say all you want; it doesn't change a thing. You're all I have. But that doesn't matter much to you. That makes you laugh. That makes you laugh! You can't deny it; you just killed yourself proving to me that everything can only make you laugh."

"You don't like me to laugh. That bothers you, huh? We're a lot better off when everybody's dejected, huh? Despair is much more poetic. Do you believe, sincerely, that laughter harms friendship, that my laughing is because I have no friendship for anyone?"

There's no way to talk to her. She contrives to distort everything and reduces everything to the dimensions of herself. With such an animal, a conversation would last five years, extending in all directions, getting nowhere. I'm not complaining. I like to talk about my joy. I like to listen to Chateaugué drone on and on when she drones on and on the way she's droning on and on tonight. We're sitting next to each other. In the heat of the conversation, our hands collide, our legs and our arms rub together. Our clothes touch, I feel them touch, and I like that. My face is smashed in, but that doesn't stop me from having the gift of gab. It's midnight, and I haven't stopped talking. We've forgotten about Questa.

"Do we sleep with her, or do we send her back home?"

I'm the one who lays down the law here. I'm the king of this castle; I decide where Questa sleeps.

"We sleep with her. You go in the middle. Okey-dokey?"

"Okey-dokey. I'll have to undress her. Her dress would get wrinkled."

With no excess of tenderness, Chateaugué starts to undress Questa. You can tell that the one who's doing the undressing doesn't like the one she's undressing. You can tell that if she could undress her with punches, she would. Turned back and forth, moved here, there, and everywhere, Questa finally wakes up. Before Questa brought her zoological multicoloured blankets, we had to go to bed with all our clothes on to avoid freezing. *Okey-dokey* is an abbreviation of *Okeechobee*. Some people think that *okey-dokey* is an abbreviation of *Okefenokee*. They are morons. You mustn't pay attention to what morons think. In the bed, everybody's sleeping. In the night, everybody's sleeping. In life, right now, everybody's sleeping. If you prick up your ears, you can hear the stars walking. They make no more sound than the tiniest fish in the world swimming. That's joy.

37

I told the Greeks and the Romans what I thought of free trade. I told them that my stomach gets tied in knots when I hear them speaking Greek and Latin. Really, sometimes it's intolerable, oppressive, unbelievable. They talk, argue, get wound up, laugh, cry, adore one another, and detest one another—and all that in the tongues of Caligula and Euripides. They make no bones about speaking dead tongues. They pretend I'm not there, as if I were excommunicated, as if I were despicable, as if I were a stranger in their house, as if I were nothing but a scrounger off the Greek and Roman Empires, as if I were no good at all. Without even thinking about it, with the natural arrogance of the gods of Olympus, they exclude me, they ignore me; they're certain that even if I could participate in the debates, I wouldn't be able to contribute anything worthwhile. I'm not worth it. I'm not worth wasting their breath speaking French. When they're in a good mood, they put their hand on my shoulder and tell me to learn the dead tongues. They're among citizens. Shame on the colonized, on the parasites of the Pax Romana, on the drifters of the road, on the vagabonds who dawdle on the roads of the Greek Empire. I told them so. I didn't mince my words. I suffered no intermediary.

"You make me unhappy. Take pity on a wounded heart. Allow me to be one of you. I'm not a spy. Don't leave me out of it. Is it so bad to know neither Greek nor Latin? You don't even address me. Am I not, like you, a guest? Do you take me for a dog? Am I a dog for you—that is, something that has nothing good to exchange in the commerce of friendship? Do you take me for someone who has nothing funny to say? Greeks and

Romans aren't the only ones who know how to make Greeks and Romans laugh. Miles Miles also knows how to make Greeks and Romans laugh. This is Canada. Here, when several people are seated around a table, to avoid running the risk of offending one of them, French or English must be spoken. You know me to be a stranger to your tongues, and you speak them anyway. It's as if you were exiling me in my own country. It's as if, having won some war, you had come to occupy the country. If I were in China, I wouldn't feel at home. You don't feel at home where everybody speaks Chinese. This is Canada, this is my country. And I have no intention of feeling like a stranger in my own country. The reason I was born in Canada is because I thought it wasn't China. The reason I was born here is because I thought that here everybody spoke in an intelligible way. You always try to be born in your own country, in a country where you don't run the risk of being taken for an intruder or a Gentile. Speak so that I can understand, so that I know at least if your words do or do not put me in danger. This is my country. The Chinese, the Greeks, the Romans—they are elsewhere."

I told them what I thought. I wasn't aware of anyone standing behind me. I didn't know that the boss was standing behind me. All of a sudden, something grabbed me by the shoulders and whirled me around. All of a sudden, I was facing the executive council in person and, clearly, it was not in complete agreement with me. So that I could understand, he was speaking English.

"I am Greek. I am Greek like my father, my brothers, and my uncles. This is not Canada. This is my restaurant. In this kitchen, I am the Queen of England. I am your master, your Charles de Gaulle. I pay you to wash the dishes. Wash the dishes. This is my house. I worked for it, I paid for it. I stole nothing. Wash the dishes and shut your trap. I am not a thief."

Anyway ... Let's change the subject. I had something to say to you about Bluebeard, but it has slipped my mind. I had something to say about parents who cry and children who cry. Oh, yes! Why do children cry when they see Papa and Maman crying? Do they cry for the same reasons as Papa and Maman? No, since they don't understand why Papa and Maman are crying. Do they cry because they're kind-hearted? They're not kind-hearted. Why do they cry? Why do they feel the ground giving way beneath them? Why does all their strength abandon them? Why do their arms fall by their sides? I know why. I can sense why. But I don't understand a thing. I understand nothing. To understand nothing is discouraging, exasperating, very exasperating. Nothing could be more insuperable than the confusion that reigns in my head. It's like understanding nothing at school. It's like reading a hermetic poem. It's as if someone didn't want me to understand, took pleasure in my not understanding, spent his time clouding the issue, and was bent on mixing everything up for me. There's a practical joker behind this. There's a hoaxer somewhere in all this. When I don't understand a thing at the movies, I'm furious. When I know that there's something to understand, and I can't manage to understand it, I'd rather be a hen, a beet, or a stone. When I don't understand a thing at the movies, it's because I lack the strength to understand or because the writer of the screenplay is nothing but a common hoaxer. Often, we can tell that we might understand, that we're almost there, but that the light within us isn't quite strong enough to really clarify everything. We're not quite strong enough to understand, and we feel it. Let's talk about whodunits. Oh, how many I've read! It was particularly when the plot was being resolved that I wouldn't understand anything. When Maigret would smoke, I'd under-stand—smoking makes sense. When Mike Hammer would have a few, I'd understand; me, too, sometimes I get thirsty, so I drink. When 007 would kiss a beautiful female spy, I'd understand perfectly. But when the culprit was found and was saying why he had killed, I wouldn't understand a thing; every-thing would become muddled, everything would elude me. I've never been able to understand a thing about motives, grounds, consequences, causes, effects, whys, or wherefores. There's the motive: he killed her because she had cheated on him. There's the motive of the motive: she had cheated on him because he hadn't found a way to get her to love him. There's the motive of the motive of the motive. Why did he give a hoot about her despite everything? Why do men kill women who cheat on them? What makes people start to get angry? What is the motive of the motive of the motive of the motive of the motive? How I envy Maigret! How I envy Sherlock Holmes for understanding everything, for being able to grasp, with a single glance of his intelligence, the entire scope of the problem. To understand only one thing completely, you've got to understand everything. I'm stupid; I don't understand anything. How I envied him, the author of my textbook of world history. In a paragraph of thirty lines of simple and precise French, he gave the impression of exhausting the question of the fall of the Roman Empire. But I didn't understand a thing. The teacher and all the other pupils were unanimous in their understanding. So that we could understand more quickly, the teacher summarized the thirty lines in four rhymes of four words each. Everybody got a perfect score. I understood less than nothing about the four rhymes, and I didn't understand a thing about the paragraph. I got up and declared that I didn't understand a thing. Everybody started to laugh. I was the only one not to understand the four causes of the fall of the Roman Empire.

"You don't know your four causes of the fall of the Roman Empire?"

"No, sir. Yes, sir. That's not it, sir ..."

I was stammering. Walls, inkwells, crucifix, hair—everything was laughing at me.

"That's not it, Sir. I mean that everything is too ... linked together. In my opinion, the bees, the lions, and the flies had to do with the fall of the Roman Empire. The bees, the lions, and the flies were involved in the fall of the Roman Empire, since there were bees, lions, and flies at the time of the fall of the Roman Empire. I mean, everything is linked together in life. That's not it. I just don't understand; everything is too linked together in my head."

"Linked together in his head ... That's not it ... It's in your head ... Bees, lions, and flies ... We've all understood."

Lions, bees, flies—everything was laughing at me. I had to sit back down, go back into my hole. You can watch for a bit. You can listen for a bit. You can't understand a thing. With your eyes closed, you can take your mouthful of life; that's all you can do. You can't understand. Science? Chemistry? Hens know a good deal more than scholars do about eggs. Can a scholar lay eggs? All scholars can do is watch, listen, and describe eggs. All the treatises that I've read on the topic of eggs conclude by claiming that eggs really are eggs. But I haven't read a single treatise on the topic of eggs. What could I possibly gain from such reading? Scholars give such personal and poetic versions of eggs that you'd think we'd never seen any eggs in our whole lives—you'd think that they had laid them themselves. By doing such reading, all you do is risk plunging more deeply into confusion. It's like in French composition. I didn't know how to conclude, to soar aloft (as Rimbaud would put it), to reach the sublime. "And that is why, since the beginning of time, man has had difficulty finding a needle that he loses in a haystack." From ages past, a French composition topic comes to mind: "Your flag." Flags have never said much to me. Today I can feel the blood of the soldiers beating in the flags. In those days, I was less of a sucker than today; I didn't see anything beating in the flags. The required minimum was two pages. I sat down, I opened my inkwell, I turned on the light, and I spent the night at the task. I picked my nose, I rubbed my hair to make the dandruff fly out; my sheet remained empty and implacable. In the wee hours, giving up hope of being visited by my muse, I gave my inkwell free rein, and I wrote whatever came into my head. The day after we turned in our papers, the teacher had written on the blackboard, so that everyone could get an eyeful, a few of the marvels of my masterpiece. "My flag is like my sister's kerchief. It is rectangular, of many colours, and was cut from a fabric whose name I am unacquainted with." Last night, Chateaugué and I went to the movies. I had something to say about Bluebeard, but I can't remember it anymore. We went to the Canadian. Before going to sit down in the dark, we stopped at the refreshment counter to buy some junk food. Chateaugué is wild about potato chips; she bought herself a bag. I bought myself some cough lozenges, the ones that taste of cinnamon, the ones that taste like the cinnamon goldfish from the old days. On the screen, we saw an immense Pope; it was the week in review, the news. They said that the Pope had just crossed the

Atlantic in a plane and that everyone had seemed surprised. Ever since *The Spirit of St. Louis* and Santos-Dumont, everyone ought to be accustomed. What would have surprised us, Chateaugué and me, would be if the Pope had fallen into the Atlantic and had drowned. When the Pope died, in the days of our youth, we were surprised. Every time the Pope dies, we'll be surprised, as in the days of our youth. O past! It's like the queen. We'll be surprised when she dies. When she crosses the Atlantic, we find that quite natural. We saw, on the immense screen, the Pope speak of love to the nations at the United Nations, like a schoolgirl. Chateaugué opened her bag of chips, I shoved a good dozen lozenges into my mouth, and movingly, the movie began. In the time it took to say *Jack Robinson*, we found ourselves in Hochfelden. The action took place in that charming village of Saxony, in the days of the victories of Daun over the Imperials. We perched our feet on the backs of the folding seats in front of us. We were comfortable. We were in a fantastic black train, and we were enjoying the ride. Chateaugué was stuffing her face with fistfuls of chips that she was crunching with innocence, love, delight, and organs. Organs, because every crunch of her innocent jaws reverberated in the meditative room like the banging of organ pedals in a cathedral. The smartass who was sitting next to her didn't like that. Molière started tapping his foot, sighing like a locomotive that's going to explode, gritting his teeth, and fidgeting on his folding seat. Chateaugué didn't notice the smartass's nervousness; she was too busy being in 1758. I glanced at her from time to time. Her eyes were straining like arcs toward the giant notebook that was turning its coloured pages in the darkness.

"Look! Listen!" she kept saying, digging me in the ribs.

Our four eyes and ears were not enough to take in all the fun that she would have liked to. However, Molière, the smartass, had worn out his bit by chomping at it.

"If you don't stop annoying me, I'll strangle you!" he cried out. "This is not a picnic. Go picnic somewhere else. Go picnic in Parc Lafontaine."

He had spoken with such vehemence, he looked so mean, that she just couldn't catch her breath. She was staring at him in spite of herself, as though fascinated by a monstrosity, while exhaling under his nose with the enormous gasps of someone who's run too far. After thinking it over, after understanding her crime and recognizing her guilt, Chateaugué choked back her tears and resigned herself to sacrificing the best of her chips—their crispness. She was a sorry sight. She'd open her mouth, delicately deposit the golden, corrugated chip, and would wait for it—as though it were a Eucharistic wafer—to dissolve in her saliva before swallowing it. Every time her bag crackled a bit, while she was fishing for a chip at the bottom of her bag, she would remain paralyzed for hours on end. The film was bad; it had stopped interesting me a long time ago. I was watching Chateaugué and her smartass. She who is always afraid of getting in the way, who feels unworthy and clumsy in public ... I was thinking of the smartass of the fifteen candles. There have been others. There is always, wherever she may be, a smartass to prove to her that she is right, that it's true that she gets in the way, that it's true that she's unworthy and clumsy. But she feels much less ill at ease with the smartasses than with those who show her the slightest respect or friendship. Once, her coffee was served to her in a cup whose rim was plastered with lipstick. The waitress realized it, blushed, and fell all over herself apologizing. Chateaugué blushed even more and, in an almost imploring voice, tried to persuade the waitress that everything was fine as it was, not to go get another cup of coffee, not to apologize, not to go to such trouble over so little. It was ridiculous.

"What do you mean, 'so little'? There was at least two dollars' worth of lipstick on your cup!"

"But I'm only me, Miles Miles. She mistakes me for somebody else. If she knew me the way you know me, she wouldn't get so upset. She'd be quite right. It's only me, after all. She was apologizing as if she were my maid. She was mistaken. She is mistaken. I'm not a marquise, not anything ..."

Chateaugué ended up concluding the eating of her chips; she ended up bringing the Eucharist of her chips to a close. She took my hand with her salty and greasy hand. Since her smartass kept watching her and hating her (he was a real Molière, he was a second Molière), in order to make him feel our solidarity, I took in both of my hands the hand with which Chateaugué had taken my hand. On the screen, the hero was running. He was running bare-chested. He wasn't running because he was pursued, but because he was pursuing. He was no ordinary man. He was so muscular, so well made, of such a virile appearance, that you'd have thought he had breasts. His pectorals were so well developed that he really did have breasts. In his frantic race, they jump, they jiggle, they gesticulate. Chateaugué asked me if he wore a bra when he was fully dressed. The smartass was still on the lookout; he jumped at the occasion. He told Chateaugué that he was no longer accountable for his actions, that he was going to wring her neck if she didn't stop talking.

"Go talk somewhere else. Shut the hell up. Go talk in Parc Lafontaine."

At the same time, the strong and resonant voice of a decent man scandalized by the fop's Homeric physique arose from the back of the crowd.

"Don't run too fast, your milk will go sour."

Everybody laughed. We were all laughing. I felt proud to laugh at art, with them, like them. But it was a sad and mortified Chateaugué that I brought back to the room.

I remember now. We were walking, and we were holding hands. We were walking straight ahead on the sidewalk, and we were stopping in front of the shop windows. We were taking a tour of the shop windows, in a straight line, on Rue Sainte-Catherine. In the shop window of a children's bookstore, there was a big, flat, beautiful book called *Bluebeard*. It was illustrated, on a canary-yellow background, with a portrait of Bluebeard. This Bluebeard resembled Dostoevsky (Fyodor). But—and this is what affected me like a bolt out of the blue—this Bluebeard had a blue beard, a sky-blue beard, a beard all blue, a blue bluebeard. Unconvinced, I asked Chateaugué point-blank what colour she would make the beard if she had a portrait of Bluebeard to do."Blue," she replied.

"That's too simple. That's far too simple. You've got to use your head. You've got to use your imagination. Come up with something original! Think of something brutal, extravagant, mischievous, surprising!"

This Bluebeard with a blue beard was too intelligible, too direct, too perceptible, too clear. Accustomed to understanding nothing, I found myself almost encumbered with understanding. I made a scene about Chateaugué's manners in bed, not about her manners at the dinner table, a scene that consummated our little breakup, a scene that ratified the decision to have separate rooms. Before relating that scene, I'd like to note the fruit of some thoughts that have been running through my head since this morning. My thoughts are non-thoughts; sometimes they come from my head, sometimes from my feet; sometimes from my heart, sometimes from my belly; sometimes from the past, sometimes from the future; sometimes from joy, sometimes from despair; they are from a human being—they cannot be strung together like those of a logical being. I want to talk about literature and the desert. I'll teach you to beware of sentences, of those ideas of men whose faces you cannot see. Often, what we call grandeur in literature is nothing more than the appearance of the discomfort that the intellect experiences when confronted with absurd, incoherent, incomplete, or meaningless sustenance. Those who, for example, persist in imposing Rimbaud as sustenance for their intellect will always find more grandeur there, for the intellect will feel more and more uncomfortable with it. Here are a few sentences, a few ideas that are profound, thrilling, inspiring, eligible for learned treatises, stupid. "Mice pee in my cup, leaving an aftertaste." "After shooting a bullet into his body, a Hungarian who has dirty feet but has principles uses up his last ounce of energy washing his feet." "Can man be, or does he merely exist?" "Instead of surrendering them, the captain burned his flags; but he had surrendered everything apart from those flags." That concludes the examples. When the intellect sighs, it's not because it finds that what it was served is good; it's because it has indigestion. Words are mirages. You say *tiger*, and you think you see a tiger. But how beautiful the word is when you know that it's not a tiger but a mirage! A mirage is so beautiful when you know that it is one. Do you know what the

Mona Lisa is? The *Mona Lisa* is an image. The *Mona Lisa* is not the Mona Lisa, is not a woman with an enigmatic smile. Look in your mirror. What do you see? Do you see yourself? Imbecile! You say that you see your eyes, your hair, and your shoulders? Imbecile! You see a mirror that reflects your image and the image of what surrounds you. Mona Lisa's smile! Oh! Oh! Some people forget that Mona Lisa is on a canvas and that smiles on canvases aren't smiles. I'm doing my little iconoclast act. Mona Lisa has never appealed to me any more than a post-card churned out by the millions. Michelangelo, Toulouse-Lautrec, Pascal, and Manet have never appealed to me. And I want everyone to know it. That's all. I prefer a truly tremendous cigar deep down in my green armchair to *The Absinthe Drinker* by Ludwig von Mozart. I have no taste, if having no taste is what I have. I am not ashamed of having no taste; I don't even think about it. I don't understand why the plowmen and the plumbers don't have any museums. Is it because they don't sign their works? The differences between a false pearl, a real pearl, and a cultured pearl escape me. I'm too busy. I'm too tired to expend the effort necessary to see the differences that people say exist among them. To take seriously such little things (the big pearls are much smaller than some stones that I'm familiar with) to the point of taking up a microscope is stupidity, avarice of the spirit. Chateaugué is like me in this respect. The gentleness of plaster has for her a gentleness that the gentleness of marble doesn't have. If swine love pearls, let them eat pearls. I wouldn't be displeased to see swine eating pearls. I'd be delighted. *Margaritas ante porcos!* Pearls before swine! Swine have beady eyes; the pearls are a good match for them. What I mean is, that for me, multicoloured birds printed on wallpaper are as beautiful as the *Mona Lisa*, and that the utter madness surrounding the *Mona Lisa* sickens me and makes me feel fear and contempt for the world. I've always wondered why thieves lose their tempers when they realize that the diamonds they thought they were stealing are just for show. I'd give pewter a chance—an alloy that flakes off the faces of Catholic statues, a weak alloy, an alloy susceptible to corrosion. Solid gold is nothing but a pale imitation of pewter. In the future, I won't talk about my joy so much anymore. It's good, it will always come in handy, but it's not as insuperable as I had thought at first. My joy is based on force, on violence. I've said it before, but I only understood it yesterday. Yesterday, I was so tired of enjoying myself for a week that I had to let go, that I had to let myself be sad and suffer. There was no shortage of reasons for me to enjoy myself; every reason is a reason to enjoy myself. I lacked the force, the violence to enjoy myself. It therefore is not a total victory. But I've made progress. I've learned something good for myself. Now I'm better toward myself and for myself. Now the world is better. Now despair is no longer possible. Washing dishes eight hours a day just isn't as funny as it was before.

Yesterday was, for Chateaugué and for me, our last day of living together. The room is now free, rid of her, rid of everything that made me feel uncomfortable when it was a question of friendship somewhere inside me. Now Chateaugué can sleep with nothing but her panties on without disturbing anyone, without stopping anyone from sleeping. Ring out the innocent obscenities! Ring in the guilty obscenities!

"You're not even wearing a bra!"

There was no way of getting her to listen to reason. I'd have had to give her a biology course. She had all the winning arguments on her side.

"You sleep with nothing on but underwear, too. You don't know anymore what to say to get rid of me. You don't know anymore what you're saying."

How could I have replied to her when, rightly, she has claimed that, with Questa's blankets, no one needed to keep their bra on to avoid catching cold? With what words could I have told her that often, in the radiance of her fresh and burning skin, my hands and my mouth would start itching? When, for the last time, she held out her back to me so that I'd unfasten her bra, I complied with good grace. Let her make the most of it while there's still time, I told myself. She got up on the bed and started making waves.

"Chateaugué, I can't put up with you anymore. Tomorrow you'll set up shop on the second floor. That's where you'll practise your nudism. You'll be free to practise everything on the second floor, even vegetarianism. I know that taking off your bra soothes you, and that it doesn't disturb anyone since we're all alone, but I don't care. I'm narrow-minded. You'll go off to the second floor, with all your belongings. But nothing has changed between us. We are friends. We have always been friends. We may well be friends for the rest of our lives. We are brother and sister, the way we have been so far. If you think that something will change because you're leaving, you're wrong. If you feel like it, you could come get me to go to work. Do you remember? You used to come get me to go to school."

Without a word, Chateaugué had stopped making waves, taken a shower, covered herself properly, and turned her back on me.

"Chateaugué ..."

"Leave me alone!" she murmured, burying her face in the feathers of her pillow.

"We're like brother and sister, Chateaugué. There are some things that we won't be able to do together, things that aren't done between brother and sister, that each of us will have to do with someone else. Do you think that, when you're married, your husband will let me live in your house, eat at your table, brush my teeth with your toothbrush, and sleep in your bed? My wife won't put up with you for long in our house; I'm sure of that. The days of hare-brained schemes are over, and each of us has his life to make, his children and his house to have. So that each may make his life, so that each may have his children and his house, we've got to split up. Isn't it reasonable for us to begin to split up right away? Answer. Don't you think that's reasonable?"

To avoid hearing anything, Chateaugué was pressing each side of her pillow against her ears. Even so, she had heard everything.

"I don't want a husband. No one loves me. No one has ever wanted anything to do with me. You don't know what to dream up next to get rid of me. Come right out and say it, if you want to get rid of me. Do you think your lies hurt me any less? Plus,

219

it's only since you've known that woman that you've been trying to get rid of me. Plus, I don't care anymore."

She fell silent, and her back started to shake. She was crying again. All of a sudden, she did an about-face and flung herself against me. She was pressing herself against me while clutching her belly in her arms, the way a boxer would who's been punched there.

"I'm in pain ... I'm in pain ... It hurts ... It hurts ... Miles Miles! Miles Miles! I'm suffering ... I'm suffering ... I have so much sorrow that I've got a stomach ache. I'm trying not to scream. Help me not to scream. Say something sweet to me. I feel like screaming. I have screams in my throat that are swelling, shoving, and straining. I'm in such pain! How can you? ... Miles Miles ... Miles Miles ... Keep me. Keep me. Keep me. Let's stay together. Don't leave me all alone. When you want to be alone with her, all you have to do is say so—I'll leave. I'll be your gofer. Many people have gofers. Why couldn't I be your gofer? Why don't you want to take care of me anymore? I'll do whatever you want. I won't disturb you anymore. I'll obey you like a slave. Keep me. Don't you like it that someone loves you? I love you, and it won't stop. You love me a little bit, too. But you'd think that you're trying not to love me at all. What do you get out of that? Don't hold back. Keep loving your little sister, even if it's only a little bit. I wouldn't know what to do without you. I've already forgotten everything mean that you've said to me. You've already forgotten everything, too. I'm no longer in pain. I'm no longer in pain. Let me put my head on your shoulder. I'm cozy. Say no more, no more no more no more ..."

I am an inexpugnable fortress. Nothing sways me. Nothing disturbs me. I let her talk as long as she liked. I let her say as much as she wanted to. Talk is cheap, fickle one. As you like it, fickle one. As you like it, Chit-Chat Gabby-Gabby. I was moved to the tips of my toes. I almost peed in my pants. She was so unhappy that she was squirming like a worm. Maybe she was in heat? How could I find out? Who is familiar with all the secrets of zoology? Take a glass of beer, pussycat. She could always stand on her head if she wanted to. I had made up my mind not to give in. Never would I tell her to stay. I told her no, three timcs, roughly, in a virile way. She started to scream like some-one possessed by the devil. I didn't pay much attention. Even through the mist that was filling my eyes, I continued to be excited by the spectacle of her wide eyes in distress, by the spectacle of the fresh face that her tears were inflaming. She was grappling with despair and disgust; I was watching, my eyes were full of water, but my heart was elsewhere. Against my soul, my body was desiring the almost nude, almost anony-mous body that was rebelling against who knows what. In my heart of hearts, I didn't give two hoots about friendship. I was watching Chateaugué, and I was watching myself. The more I watched us, the more I thought that everything was in peril, that it couldn't go on any longer. If I told her to stay, the treas-ures that we had been were going to be swallowed up, the wonders that we had been were going to sink into filth, ridicule, remorse, and hatred. She saw that my eyes had gotten misty.

"You're crying, Miles Miles? Is it yes? Is it yes? You've changed your mind?"

"It's no, no, and no. I'm crying, I adore you, and it's no. Sleep. Sleep. Trust me. Know that I'll do everything not to give up on us. Believe me when I tell you that it's to save us that we're separating. It's no. Tomorrow, you're moving."

For the first time in our lives, I gave her a kiss. I did it on her forehead, and I felt a great deal of turmoil about it. She stopped protesting. She poured out the rest of her tears and fell asleep. At present, she's in her room on the second floor. She brought the bride, her last will and testament, Émile Nelligan, and two of the postcards portraying Marilyn Monroe. All women love me. I'm Popeye, the sailor man.

38

Two Soon to Pass Away

Soon, darling, our time will be up.
It will be our last hurrah.
It's your move. Play your trump card!
Fill up this beer glass! Let the beer flow!

Arthur! It's your turn to shuffle.
Ernestine, that's not true!
Do you remember the days gone by?
I think I would relive them.

We haven't seen Jean this month.
I wonder what he's up to.
Maybe he's at the sawmill
Still working reluctantly.

Jean has never had any luck.
Jean is yours. That's all, old gal.
Jean-boy is nothing but a big lazybones.
Watch the crow go by
Under the black telephone wires.

I borrowed two dollars from Chateaugué. She makes twice as much money as I do, the little bitch. It's been ages since I've seen Questa. She went by Chateaugué's a couple of times since the last time I saw her, but she didn't go to the trouble of coming up here. I'm a little bored. Since she moved, I only see Chateaugué here in the morning. She's the one who wakes me up. She makes the bed. She thinks it's dirty. She says that she'll come sweep up one of these evenings. She doesn't say much. In the evening, she doesn't stir from her room. I was expecting her to come knocking on my door twenty times a day. I was kidding myself. She comes to wake me up in the morning. In the evening, she conscientiously occupies her room. I've never known her to have such pride. When I'm bored, I go down. She gives me a cool reception without any red carpet. She doesn't welcome me; she lets me in. She's in the middle of reading, of resting, of doing her laundry; I'm bothering her. She has to do her laundry often; she only has one uniform. When she has a couple of dollars to spare, she'll buy herself another uniform. She doesn't say much. She tells me to sit down. She asks me if I have any dirty laundry. She asks me if I've swept my room. I have the impression that before we were always in the middle of debating vital questions when we were together, that we were rushing from one drama to the next. Now we have nothing left to say to each other.

"Everything okay upstairs?"

"Are you cold at night? Come get a couple of blankets if you're cold. What are you reading?"

"A novel."

"Who by and what about?"

"I don't know. It takes place during the war. He's a paratrooper. His girlfriend cheats on him. He writes to her. He gets no reply. Did Questa go up to see you yesterday?"

"No."

"She came by here for a while. I thought she had gone to see you. She brought her oldest daughter. She's such a sweetheart, that little girl!"

"Was she drunk?"

"She'd been drinking a little."

"What did she say to you?"

"Nothing."

"She didn't say anything to you?"

"She didn't say much."

"What did she say to you?"

"She talked about her husband. She doesn't like him very much."

I whortensturbate while I wait; I try to delight in my own company. I lower my head, I fix my eyes on myself, and I stare. I won't add—without a certain irony and a certain disgust—that it's often the idea of a scantily clad Chateaugué that makes me feel like whortensturbating. I loathe whortensturbating and talking about it. I write these lines the way one mounts the scaffold. But, as I told Chateaugué, you've got to be disgusted joyfully. With the waitresses, I'm wasting my time. To them, I'm nothing but a young pup, a fake, a negligible quantity. With them, you've got to go out, go dancing somewhere, go to friends' houses, and, above all, have wheels. For them, art for art's sake, kissing for kissing's sake—it makes no sense, it's not relevant. Even with the waitresses my age (sixteen or seventeen years old), I'm wasting my time. They talk and act as if they were as old as their lovers (thirty-five or thirty-six years old). I often have the impression of being ridiculous, of being born ridiculous, and of having to remain that way for the rest of my life. I'm nothing but an inoffensive and ridiculous kid for those ladies, those vulvas, those powder puffs, those insured people, those champagne-sickened women. I find them vulgar and moronic, but my reaction is not to despise them. My reaction is to admire them, to feel inferior, to wish to be as vulgar and moronic as they are. To be honest, at the Penguin, I'm no match for them. I get my face smashed in by the Italians and the Greeks; I'm laughed at by the waitresses. Becoming an intimate stranger is not as easy as you think when you're sixteen years old and a dishwasher. The women who could help you become moronic, vulgar, and sick of copulating don't want to cooperate, don't want to play their little game with a young snot like you. I can't wait to be twenty years old. They'll get a taste of me, those sluts. The other day, Ginette was in a bad mood, the kind of bad mood that adults get into. Adults get into really stubborn, dogged, aggressive, absolute, absolutely mean, and insuperable bad moods. A mere nothing can provoke a bad mood in children; nothing can make it last longer than five minutes; and a mere nothing can dispel it, turn it into the desire to laugh. So, Ginette was in a bad mood. I tried to make her laugh.

"When are we going out together, pussycat?"

She zinged me with a stinging glance. It darn near killed me.

"Maybe you'd better go (whortensturbate), baby," she retorted. "Maybe you'd better not count on me."

Lisa is a beauty. Lisa was in a bad mood that morning. Foolishly, I smiled at her. Foolishly, thinking perhaps that she found me handsome, I asked her to smile at me.

"Lisa, change your tune. Smile at me, Lisa."

"Not today," she replied, somewhat curtly.

I insisted. Perhaps I thought myself irresistible. I sang to her of wonders. I told her that she had no reason to be in a bad mood, that she was pretending to be in a bad mood to stand out in the crowd, that she had all the reason in the world to be in a good mood.

"I'm not in a bad mood, huh? What will it take? Proof? Do you want to see the proof? Do you want to smell it? Do you want me to put it under your nose?"

All the others burst out laughing. One of them started playing the comedian.

"Don't do that, Lisa. He might lose consciousness. Maybe he can't stand the sight of blood, the poor dear."

At the time, I didn't understand what it was all about. I had to think it over before understanding. When I understood, I blushed to the ends of my hair, and I wished I were six feet under. Lisa! So beautiful, so gracious. Lisa with a face full of flowers and eyes full of sunshine. So the mindlessness has spared no one? Dear Ginette and dear Lisa, you're right a hundred times over. I don't measure up. Maybe I'd better shut up, go away, go back into my hole once and for all. The smiles of others, one's own joy and boldness of spirit are child's play compared to this year's Chrysler, periods, cocktail parties, and Saturday-night adventures. What are you when you don't move in the world of the Plymouth, of periods, of cocktail parties, and Saturday-night adventures? You're nothing; you're out of luck; you're not taken seriously. All you have left to do is whortensturbate. All you have left to do is fall back on your childhood friend. All you have left to do is deprive yourself of dignity and pride forever.

39

I wash a hell of a lot of dishes. I don't really care to talk about it. In life, you've got to wash dishes, die of hunger, or be supported by an old biddy. I'd be more than happy to be supported by an old biddy, but none of the old biddies I know want to support me. I'd be glad to, but they don't want to. God proposes, and Biddy disposes. I'm sick of washing dishes eight hours a day. I'm thinking about a career move. I've talked with the corner grocer. He needs a delivery boy, and I fit the bill. As a delivery boy, at least I'd have peace. As a delivery boy, I wouldn't have any Greeks and Romans. As a delivery boy, I'd have a bike. As a delivery boy, I'd be alone, alone on my bike, alone in the street, alone in the world. I could resume the struggle against the automobiles, a struggle in which Chateaugué's bike perished. Above all, I'd have peace. Around me would be silence, the absence of Greek, Latin, and the swearing of women. I'd be alone on my bike. On my bike, there would be neither Greeks nor Romans; there would only be me. On my bike, I'd be alone, alone like Cavelier de La Salle in his canoe, like Joan of Arc on her horse. Yesterday, Sunday, we didn't work. On Sundays, the Penguin is closed. Never on Sundays. We work Mondays, Tuesdays, Wednesdays, Thursdays, Fridays, and Saturdays. Sundays, we live our lives. The other days of the week, we live the life of the Penguin, the life of the fat Greek. The boss's belly has extended its empire to other countries of his anatomy; it has conquered his neck and threatened his head; it has enlisted his legs and has reduced his arms to impotence. The boss has nothing but a paunch and a head, like a penguin. The day before yesterday, Saturday, at the Penguin, at the busy time,

Chateaugué pulled one of her pranks. Laden with soup and veal cutlets, she was rolling along at full speed between two rows of booths crammed full of customers at the end of their patience. All of a sudden, she took a nosedive. She crashed down head first; soup and cutlets went flying. Thinking that she had tripped, the smartasses couldn't resist laughing. But she didn't get back up again. She didn't budge. She remained sprawled out in the garbage until someone deigned to intervene. She had fainted. When they raced over to see what was wrong, I followed the procession. They moved her into the boss's office and stretched her out on the table. When the boss spied my face at the door, he was enraged, he started to shout.

"The dishes! The dishes! Go! Go! Step on it!"

I was frightened, and I returned to my post. Don't abandon ship. They called Questa. They asked her to come take care of her protegé. They all seemed furious. The boss was roaring. The waitresses were swearing. The cooks were hitting the customers with pots and pans. The customers were threatening to take the kitchen by storm. It was anarchy. Everything was going badly. Questa arrived and took her out of the office. She was as white as a sheet. Her eyes were dead. Her legs gave way with each step, refusing to carry her. Questa had taken her by the waist in order to support her. They went right by me. Questa saw me but said nothing; she didn't even smile at me. Chateaugué didn't even look at me. What had gotten into them? Why were they all putting on cothurni? Nothing aggravates me more than tragedy. I find nothing more false, more ridiculous, more useless, or more mediocre than tragedy. On my way back from the Penguin, I went to knock at Chateaugué's door. I got no answer. This is it, I told myself, she's getting away from me, I'm losing her. When I woke up yesterday morning, I went down to the second floor. They were shouting, laughing, and creating an uproar behind her door; you'd have thought that the jolly troubadours were gathered there. She opened the door. With the three Annes on her back, she looked like a mother possum. When she saw me, her cheerful expression disappeared; her face hardened.

"What are you doing here?"

Trying to outsmart her, I told her that I had come to kiss the bride. She tried to smile and told me to come in.

"Come in. The bride is all yours."

The smallest of the three Annes was pulling me by the sleeve and dragging me toward the bride. She threw me into its arms and forced me to kiss it.

"The bride? The bride? Come! Come! I know where she is. Come on! She's over there. Look, there she is. I've seen you somewhere before. You won't kiss her? You were saying you wanted to kiss her? Go ahead and kiss her!"

I kissed her. Proud of how she pulled it off, my go-between was hopping around like a toad, laughing and clapping her hands.

"Questa gave them to me," Chateaugué said, pointing to the little ones. "You know how she is. She told me, 'Keep them! Keep them!' She told me, 'I don't want them anymore; I'm giving them to you.' I thought it was her when I opened the door."

"That's why you changed your tune ..."

Once again she changed her tune. A kind of ferocity came over her face, which new shadows under her eyes were already darkening.

"I didn't change my tune. Yes, I changed my tune. But I didn't really change my tune. All I did was go back to the tune that I sing when I think of you these days. You made me suffer too much, Miles Miles. You pulled the wool over my eyes one time too many. I think that I'm starting to hate you. Yesterday, everybody was there when I came to. There were about thirty of them looking at me like I was some kind of alien. But there was no Miles Miles. When I came back here, I waited for you. I waited for you all evening, all night. At four o'clock this morning, I still wasn't sleeping, I was still waiting for you. I was crying and hating you. I almost died, and you didn't even go to the trouble of coming to see if I was doing any better. I hated you so much that I started to cry. The little ones were all frightened, and they started to cry, too. You should have come, you who so love to see others suffer because of you. You wouldn't have been sorry, you wouldn't have missed your chance; you'd have gotten your money's worth."

The littlest of the three Annes had grabbed hold of my sleeve again. She nodded in agreement.

"Yes. It's true. Everybody was crying. Me, too. Auntie Chateaugué, too. Her, too. And her, too."

"I don't want your pity. Don't be deceived. I only want to tell you that I know now who you are. You're a coward and a heartless beast."

I had good excuses, but they all ended up turning against me.

"The boss wouldn't let me come into the office."

"I swear to you, Miles Miles, that if I had seen you lose consciousness, I would have been so afraid of losing you that I wouldn't have been scared of anyone, that no one would have been able to stop me."

"I came by last night, but you weren't here. I knocked and knocked, and there was no answer. I wanted to come back later, but I was so tired that I fell asleep as I was getting into bed."

"Getting into bed! Getting into bed! You weren't too worried. Worry wasn't eating away at you. Worry doesn't keep you from sleeping!"

To close the discussion, I proposed that we all go out for some fresh air.

"I don't feel like it. Who knows what one might risk, out for some fresh air with a heartless beast like you."

"You feel like it, but you're too embarrassed to say so."

I grabbed one of her arms, and I twisted it a bit, buddy-buddy, to force her to admit that "it" tempted her.

"You're hurting me!" she cried.

The Annes got scared, burst into tears, and came to the rescue of the victim. One of them was biting me. The other two were kicking and punching me.

"No, Miles Miles. No joking. It's too cold outside. The little ones haven't a thing to wear."

"Does that really matter?"

"Plus, I'm expecting Questa any time now."

"So what?"

"You think you're joking, Miles Miles, but you're wrong—you're very serious. You think only of yourself. What do you care if the little ones catch cold? What do you care if Questa worries herself sick when she finds the room empty? You're ... You're ... I detest you. I'm as scared of you as I am of the devil."

"Don't look at me like I'm some kind of alien!"

"Let go of me. Let go of my arm. You're hurting me."

"Cry uncle."

"Uncle! Uncle!" she cried. "Nothing is serious, right, Miles Miles? Nothing, huh? Absolutely nothing, huh? Everything is funny. Everything is sugar-coated! Everything tastes of joy!"

She really had a heavy heart that morning, my poor friend. I was walking ahead. I was clearing the way. I was escorting the littlest of the three Annes. I had put my hands in my pockets, so that she wouldn't take me by the hand. Little girls have the odd habit of taking others by the hand. She couldn't go two steps without bending down to pick something up. Before rejecting the wonder that she had picked up—a shard, a splinter, or a rusted spigot—she gave it a long lecture. She didn't pay much attention to me, but she loved me. She loved me since she herself had chosen to walk with me rather than with Chateaugué and the others.

"Let's go take a walk with Uncle Miles Miles," Chateaugué had said.

For them, I'm an uncle and Chateaugué is an auntie. Chateaugué, in our younger days, used to call my father "Uncle" and my mother "Auntie." Now I've become as old and senile as my parents. It was cold. The sky was as white as snow. There was no sun. The sun was behind the white. The white was fog that was breaking up. The fog was full of light. The air was calm; it wasn't moving. We were going by the College of Fine Arts. We saw an old man in the little Fine Arts park. The old man was dressed in rags, and there were a thousand pigeons massed at his feet; he was crumbling bread for them, his gaze elsewhere. My Anne dashed off; she was running, charging at the pigeons, sowing terror among the pigeons, stretching out her tiny arms in vain toward the sky to catch hold of the pigeons so that they'd come back. My Anne came back to me, quite discouraged. We went by the Saint-Sulpice Library. We saw an automobile; it was sleeping under a maple; many multicoloured leaves had fallen onto it; it looked like a tapestry. We went by a newsstand. The picture of a factory chimney was splashed across the front page of all the morning newspapers. The night before, while I was sleeping and while Chateaugué was moping, a man had killed himself by falling from the top of a chimney 425 feet high. Billions of men have died since the beginning of humanity. Humanity is starting to get used to it. Natural deaths, accidental deaths, and the majority of other deaths leave me cold. The only ones that matter to me are murders and suicides.

"Who do you love most? Uncle or Auntie?"

"My maman. I love her as big as a house."

And my Anne opened her arms as far as she could, as if she were hugging a house. I realized all of a sudden that I hadn't yet asked Chateaugué why she had fainted, in honour of what she had suddenly fallen into the soup and the veal cutlets. I took advantage of the fact that I was thinking about it to acquit myself immediately of that social obligation. She turned all red. With me, up until then, nothing had made her blush. She was so red all of a sudden that I blushed. After a minute of embarrassment, she shook herself, she walked all over her new modesty, and she became once more my good old Chateaugué. She didn't spare herself the slightest detail. With an audacity as great as the truth called for, and with a halting voice that revealed that she hadn't yet gotten over her horror and astonishment, she told me everything.

"My thighs were full of blood. It was alarming how bad it stunk. They were talking about calling an ambulance. They thought it was a hemorrhage. Questa said that it should have occurred long before, and that's the reason it was so serious. It's going to happen to me every month now. It's only for women. I can have children now. Questa explained everything to me. I was so surprised. We have to use a cloth so it won't drip and stain our underwear. I was so scared, I almost died. I've never had such a stomach ache in all my life. Did you know that, that women ..."

We spent the rest of the day together. When I went up to go to bed, Questa hadn't yet come back. When Chateaugué came to wake me up a little while ago, she still hadn't shown up. Chateaugué, who won't be able to go to work, is starting to believe that Questa really did give her her children.

"I never should have accepted."

40

I have nothing to say. I am empty, body and soul. Nothing has happened to me. Nothing ever happens. I am ugly, body and soul. I'm repugnant. I aggravate myself. Already, before my eyes, wrinkles are coming on. I'm losing my hair already. I whortensturbate every day to the point of bleeding, and that still doesn't avenge me. The skin under my eyes is darkening. My face is covered with fetid pimples. My back is full of pimples. My butt is full of pimples. I have elephant ears. I have a big nose. My nose resembles a potato. I have thick lips. My lips resemble sausages. I have greasy skin; it's as if I had just come out of a grease bath. My hair is full of dandruff; when I comb it, it snows. I'm as dirty as a pig. I stink like a skunk. I can't bear to put up with myself anymore. My legs are crooked. My fingernails are bitten and in mourning. My clothes are as dirty as pigs and stink like skunks. I'm half-dead, and nothing has happened yet. My teeth are as yellow as pimples. I have a toothache. As for my soul, as for my mind and my heart, there's nothing much to say about them—I'm a whortensturbator. Those who want the truth about me need only help themselves. I'm an undesirable. I'm as undesirable to myself as to the world. Those who don't believe me need only come see me, need only come watch me. Everything I eat is transformed into pimples and gall. Everything I do is turned into pus and bitterness. Everything that happens to me is ugly, awful, hideous, and pimply, like me. I wasn't like this before. I've only been like this since I've no longer been a child. A famished cannibal would vomit upon seeing me on his plate. I have nothing. I have nothing to say. Everything that comes to me, I vomit along the way. Everything that comes to me is vomited along the way. Why don't I kill myself? Do I have the right to live? Is a dishrag like me allowed to live? Does someone who knows himself to be irremediably unclean have the right to let himself live? You sicken me, Miles Miles. As a child, I found myself ugly. If I had seen myself as I am today, I'd have blown my stack, I'd have shouted till the blood came, like Chateaugué the other time. Someone's getting a big kick out of torturing me, someone who occasionally gives me his hand only to drag me down deeper into the darkness and the cold. Every time the dazzling hope is gone, the world that I cross is colder and blacker.

41

My friends the men, if they can hear me, must have found disgusting what I said to them the last time I talked to them. But I'm not talking to them in order to be understood. I'm talking to them, but I don't need to be truly understood. I'm talking while pretending to be understood, and pretending to be understood is good enough for me. As for the poets, they pretend to talk in order to be understood. To think that I have friends among the men is also pretending. Besides, what I said the other day doesn't count any more, isn't true any more. Everything is back to normal again. Now, once more, order reigns supreme. But what are order and disorder in all this? Is joy disorder? Is despair order? Either there's too much darkness or too much light. The picture that you see is always false, I believe. A lot of things have happened in the past week. Drunkenness has thwarted torpor, and the taciturn one has turned into a chatterbox. I haven't yet talked about bugles and trumpets. I hear them every night. They're not bugles and trumpets that children get out of breath from, but it's as if in all four corners of the city, children were getting out of breath from bugles and trumpets. I can hear them right now. Nothing could be more out of tune. Here, the flourish of a trumpet, belting out its note until exhaustion. There, a bugle cries and calls. In fits and starts and in disorder, from all over, a thousand other trumpets and a thousand other bugles follow suit all of a sudden. I have no way of knowing exactly where all this comes from. It's somewhere, outside, across the city. Who do these lost voices in the night belong to? Are they the voices of some skyscraper builders and their steel monsters? Are they the voices of a few demolishers of cathedrals and their cranes? Since the cry of a lone trumpet or bugle provokes the cries of entire jungles of bugles and trumpets, the cacophony will continue all night. I don't dream. I hear bugles and trumpets. I even listen for them. And I have heard them since I've lived in these valleys of asphalt. Chateaugué also hears them. Bugles and trumpets aren't all she hears. She also hears horns, trombones, trains, circular saws, and even angry tigers and elephants.

"It's like the shrieking of the rails when the train wheels hurt them."

Last night, I was at Chateaugué's. We opened the window, we leaned on our elbows, and in the way that you watch a brass band go by, we spent part of the night listening to the music hidden in the white darkness of the streets. But I'm playing a bit fast and loose here with the chronological order of events. I must note that we no longer live on Rue Bonsecours, but on Rue Saint-Denis. I must note that three days ago, we had to find another refuge in a hurry. We suspected nothing. It was cold. After an honest day's work, hastening our steps, we made our way toward our hearth and home. When we got there, it was already too late. We hadn't been thinking of moving, but we were unable to do otherwise. They were there with their cranes, and things were in full swing; they were in the middle of demolishing everything. We just had time to roll up our few possessions in Questa's blankets, grab the bride by one arm, and hurtle down the stairs. Cranes have no ears.

"There'd be no point in telling the cranes to stop," the engineers in charge of the cranes told us. "Cranes are like walls, they have no ears. If you don't get out of this house before they demolish you, you'll both end up demolished."

We were quick, it goes without saying. We were strolling down Saint-Denis, without any roof over our heads, and it was cold. With my undone bundle under my arm, the bride on my shoulders, and Chateaugué behind me, I looked like a madman, a gypsy, a beet, a hen from Cochin-China. Leaving the bride on the steps, we rushed into the first hotel we found. We didn't even take the time to see whether the hotel was seedy; we rushed into it and rented the two least expensive rooms for the night. I chanced upon a funny room. It enchanted me from the outset. Crossing the threshold, something singular, magical, and mysterious took hold of me. I flung myself on the bed, and I wondered what it was. The ceiling was high, so high that my gaze only attained it with difficulty and only maintained itself there with dizziness. What's more, as a result of studying the ceiling, I realized, to my great stupefaction, that it was in the form of a trapeze. This was not the end of my surprises. My gaze jumped from one wall to the next, without flagging. Something was missing on these four walls unequal among themselves. There was something that ought to be there that I didn't see. What was it? I didn't see any windows. There were no windows! I was in a room without windows! The bride was waiting on the steps. I went to get her. As is right and proper, I took the bride in my arms, and I went back up the stairs whistling a wedding march. The landlady and her husband watched me go up, looking to all the world as if they had swallowed their cigarettes. I shot them an insolent glance and held my head high. Chateaugué welcomed the bride and me with her sweetest wide eyes. Chateaugué clasped the bride and spread her out on the bed. Chateaugué called me a hero; without me, perhaps the bride would not have been rescued from the demolition. We went off to explore the floor. The hallway was covered with a thick carpet that gave us wings, that gave us angel feet. The shower stall was as big as a basilica. Chateaugué couldn't get over it.

"When you think that back there there wasn't even hot water!"

I was taking it all in, dreaming of white feet, white fingernails, and the scent of soap. Without saying another word, by common accord, we went back down to the ground floor, and we expressed the wish to take up a permanent home in this palace.

"We have student prices. Are you students?"

"Of course."

"What do you study?"

"We study ... everything," Chateaugué replied.

"That will be twelve dollars per week, each."

"What? ... Twelve dollars? Per week? Each?"

"There isn't even a window in my room," I mentioned, like a coward.

"It's twelve dollars per week."

But our sudden reserve didn't last long. All the landlady had to do was enumerate for us the priceless and numerous advantages of hotel life. The administration takes care of us as if we were oil tycoons (tycoons of oil?). Our beds are made every morning. The rooms are cleaned every morning. The sheets are provided free of charge and changed free of charge every week. So for three days, like American tourists, we've been living in a hotel. Chateaugué still works at the Penguin. That's not the case for me. I'm in the grocery business now. I'm in charge of shipping. Some people are doctors of medicine. I'm a delivery boy of groceries. I'm a railroad man, a truck driver, a traveller, a globetrotter. I scare the automobiles. I sow terror among the sidewalks. When they see me coming, the automobiles honk like lunatics, smash into each other, pounce on the pedestrians, climb up the façades of buildings, fly to take refuge on the roofs of buildings, and wait patiently on the roofs for me to ride away. I deliver veal and pork cutlets, intact, to affectionate widows in dressing gowns, to overwhelmed mothers whose half-open bathrobes exude lukewarm aromas, to scorned wives whose dressing gowns, like half-peeled bananas, give off sweet and appetizing warmth. They smile at me, as if it were nothing. They give me thanks, without ulterior motives, like cats and dogs who love you. They make me feel that I belong to a superior sex, in spite of my young age and my clumsiness. They do me good, and I praise them. Long live widows! Long live mothers! Long live wives! Long live women! They give me tips, when they manage, with gracious fussing, to extract some change from one of the hundred bags full of handkerchiefs, jewellery boxes, and perfume that they open before my eyes.

"As young as you are, you should stay in school," they say.

"You must have quit school! What a shame!"

As for the Annes, Chateaugué was stuck with them for four days and four nights. For four days and four nights, she had to feed them, quench their thirst, put them to bed, wash their faces, wipe away their tears, and assure them that Maman would come to get them. Monday, I arrived alone at the Penguin, and the shit hit the fan. The fat Greek accosted me: what had happened to Chateaugué? I pulled the wool over his eyes, saying she was sick and bedridden. He replied, in the language of Macbeth, that she didn't have the right to be sick, that he had relied on her and she had let him down, that if she didn't come back the next day she would lose her bread and butter. I lost my temper. I had just left a Chateaugué racked with worry, extremely ashamed, and full of regret because of this bundle of rancid meat. I got angry, and in a fit of rage, I tendered my resignation. As I was about to slam the door on my way out, Questa was coming in, dressed in the sky-blue uniform of the glorious Penguin waitress team. From afar, she seemed sober to me. Talking to her, I had the impression that she was so drunk, you could touch her with your fingertip and she'd fall over.

"Why are you coming here?"

"To work."

"And your children? Chateaugué is going out of her mind with worry. The responsibilities that you've put on her shoulders are crushing her."

"Poor thing! But she loves them; I know it. She loves children. She loves children, and I'm giving her mine. She'll get used to the worry. She loves them, and I give them to her gladly. She deserves them, and she's the one they need. I'm not much of a mother. Just look at me. Do I look like a mother? I was going to cause them nothing but unhappiness and disgust. I'd lean over their little beds, and I'd try to feel like I was their mother. But most of the time, when I'd lean over their little beds, I had drunk so much that all I'd feel was an irresistible urge to vomit."

Questa clung to the collar of my windbreaker, to secure a more stable equilibrium, and as if to make me better feel the weight of what she was telling me by making me feel her own weight.

"I didn't even have time to drag myself to the sink. I'd lean over their little beds with tender intentions, but I'd feel like heaving, my head would spin, and I'd just about vomit on them. I don't love them enough, my dear Scin Tillating. Do you understand? They love me too much; I want no more of it. They'll be too disappointed when they begin to realize it. I don't want to see them anymore. I drink too much. I've aged too quickly; it's made me go bonkers. Chateaugué is not only the mother of my daughters, she's my own mother. She's kind-hearted. They risk nothing with Chateaugué. There's no more danger."

Then, without awaiting a reply, Questa pulled herself together, found her bearings, aligned herself, and, without straying from the straight and narrow, sailed toward the kitchen. She replaced Chateaugué at the Penguin that day and the following day. On Tuesday night, the father, a man that Chateaugué found to be tall, handsome, and polite, came to take back the Annes.

42

O my friend man, how is it that I have yet to address you on the subject of the symphonic delights of hearing you hear me? For I hear you hearing me. You hear me, and it's as if you were talking to me. You don't hear me in a hushed voice, you hear me out loud. Every word that I say to you reverberates within you as it does in a golden grotto or a golden well. My murmurs strum you the way the fingers of the guitarist strum the guitar, O golden grotto! You are a deep and sonorous well, and a well has no strings, but you are a guitar, you are my guitar. I play the golden well the way others play the organ. I hear you say that I'm exaggerating ... however, I hear nothing; however, there's no one in this room. My mouth is all full of ether; I've just kissed Chateaugué. My mouth is full of her blood, and hot blood is intoxicating. I only kissed her for laughs. I really kissed her; my mouth has no sense of humour. Chateaugué grazed her knee, falling on the asphalt. So as not to ruin her first pair of nylons, she applied two Band-Aids to it in the form of a cross, like in the comics. Today at noon, like all the noontimes since we stopped working together, she was waiting, in the little Fine Arts park, for me to pick her up for lunch. She insists that we have lunch together. She hoists herself onto the frame of my two-wheeled delivery tricycle, and I take her out to lunch. She crouches in the basket of my three-legged dandy horse, and I take her out to eat hotdogs on Boulevard Saint-Laurent. There's nothing reprehensible in all that. Today at noon, Chateaugué was waiting for me in the little Fine Arts park. It was cold, and waves of grey pigeons were coming to die at her feet. It was cold; she had pressed her legs together and crossed her arms so that she would shiver better, so that her teeth would chatter better. I swept in like a whirlwind. Intending merely to just miss her, dangerously, I blew it and ran over her toes. Intending to brake brilliantly, I blew it; my tires skidded on the wet asphalt, and I collided with a maple that lost consciousness due to the force of the impact. I moored my two-wheeled delivery tricycle, and I pretended that nothing had happened. I went to sit on a green bench, across from her, and I made eyes at her. She understood right away that I wanted to play, and with no further warning, we played at not knowing each other, at being two total strangers. I made eyes as sweet as butterfly wings at her, as sweet as pigeon necks. She turned up her nose. She looked elsewhere. She pretended to find my audacity vulgar and uncalled for. She pretended to be waiting for someone else. She pretended to check the time on her arm, and her arm had no wristwatch. She pretended to be used to having people make overtures to her. She had difficulty refraining from laughing. The white lace of her petticoat was showing; it encircled her skinny knees with an ocean fringe, with a crown of snow crystals. Her knees were sticking out under the lace and, bizarrely fascinated, I had fixed my gaze on the little cross of adhesive strips under which a wound was healing. I was watching her knees ochered by the nylon of her stockings, coiffed with bonnets by the lace of her petticoat. I was watching the knee that had bled. My gaze was seeking to plunge between the clenched knees of a woman, tasting her tender skin, going beyond, reaching the fresh pulp. I thought of the potatoes and the legs of the worn-out women. When a potato comes out of the earth, all you have to do is rub the transparent skin with your thumb for it to peel off, for the pulp, firm and glistening with sap, to appear. When a potato has spent the winter in a cellar, its skin is rough, hard, thick, and opaque like a rock; it has lost all its tenderness, it has suited itself with armour, like a deep-sea diver, like an oyster, like a rhinoceros. All kinds of things went through my head. I deserted my green bench. I took my heart in my hands. I told her I was hopelessly in love with her. I picked up a fistful of leaves in tatters on the asphalt, a fistful of leaves oozing with rain, and I sprinkled them on her head, from far above, the way you sprinkle salt on a roast.

"Beautiful stranger!" I exclaimed, falling at her feet and flinging my head on her knees as round as fruit. "Open up! Give me shelter! Welcome me to your mysteries!"

I was kneeling in a puddle. A little old lady passed by close to us. Her black coat brushed against us; she barely touched us with her black wings. My head was cozy on the knees as round as oranges; it was almost asleep; its nerves had let go, and all its weight had left it. All of a sudden, in my hair, fingers were searching.

"You handsome insolent thing, you have lice. Your hair is full of little animals. I notice, as well, a significant number of large animals. All these deer and these snakes! You'd think it was a forest!"

"Wander there, ma'am. Stroll around! What do I see? Your knee! What have you done to your knee? What has struck your knee? Have you been stabbed? You were desperate, and you stabbed yourself at the hinge of your poor leg ... That's it, isn't it?"

That's when I kissed her. Brutally, so as to make her lose her balance, so that it would be taken for antics like the rest, I clasped Chateaugué's legs, and, my mouth having taken over her frozen knee, I felt under my lips a lukewarm sap rise to the surface.

"Full steam ahead, Fred!" I cried out, to break the spell, to get away with it. I took her onto my shoulders, like she was a sack of flour, and I pitched her into the basket of my two-wheeled delivery bike. Here goes! She's not difficult; she doesn't mind being pitched into a basket.

"Step on it! Step on it!" she shouted, laughing, imitating the stentorian tones of her boss.

I was laughing with her, but I didn't feel like laughing. My mouth was too numb. My mouth was inhabited, full, full of fire. She was being taken for a ride ... Afterward, at the restaurant, in an unaffected, maternal voice, she made a revealing slip-up.

"Your head is still full of dandruff, Miles Miles. Come to my room tonight; I'll brush your hair properly."

I'd like to hear voices, voices like the ones Joan of Arc used to hear. I'd like to have a horse like hers and weapons like hers. I'd like to have Englishmen like hers. I'd like to find her joy. The only voices I hear are cries of steel. All I have is a two-wheeled delivery tricycle. We stole daggers, and we'll never have to use them. The Englishmen that I do have are desperately kind and peaceable. I have whoops of glee sometimes, but I've never seen joy. Saint Marguerite had better come back and take a stroll under the blue sky. Saint Catherine had better come tell me what to do, reappear and point out to me my enemies and my wars. The truth had better strike me like a thunderbolt along one road or another from Tarsus, dissolving my confusion and my doubts. I have no task to fulfill; tell me that I have one. I possess nothing of what a man ought to possess. Joan of Arc possessed truth, and truth made her a judge. She possessed duty, and duty made her a soldier. She had God, and God gave her the right. Joan of Arc had truth, duty, and the right, and I have nothing. She was a judge, a soldier, and a saint, and I am nothing. How rich she was! How poor I am! Everything was simple for her. She knew where white was and where black was, who her friends were and who her enemies were, where good was and where bad was. She had everything; all she had to do was to charge and suffer and let herself become what she had. What is it to become a judge when you possess truth? What is it to become a soldier when you possess duty? I have nothing. I'm not even capable of enemies. I have nothing. How would I become something? I have nothing to do, no one to kill, no king to go to. There is no master here. No one knows what to do here. There's nothing but eating and drinking; the other voices are too blurred. The other voices are too obscure for you to be able to obey them without running the risk of falling into a trap, without running the risk of playing the game of the hypocrites and the paranoiacs, without running the risk of following the path of the champagne-sickened people who are more cynical and misled than you are. At the movies, I saw Goebbels deliver his last speech. In a strong voice, his arms tense with vehemence, he asserted to his brothers the Germans that a great offensive was going to sweep aside their enemies in both the

East and the West. Goebbels must have found it funny to hear himself talk in that way, he who had a sense of humour, he who knew that the Russians were at the doors of Berlin, he who knew that only a few children were still defending Germany, he who knew that all was lost, he who knew that he was going to go blow his brains out. Goebbels must have been laughing up his sleeve. He must have really laughed at those he called his brothers and who listened to him as if he were a prophet. Leaders are laughers. Shepherds of the people are practical jokers. Prime ministers are harmless hams who like to dress up like El Cid. "He helped Jeannie take off her bra and her slip. She sat down on the side of the bed to take off her garter belt and stockings. He was watching her, with hungry eyes and thirsty hands." I would have more confidence in the typewriter of the anonymous pornographer who wrote those lines than I would in the phonographs without orthographs of those who compose the speeches of national leaders. Peoples of the world, on your feet! Men have been sitting down for so many centuries that if they stood up, all of a sudden, all of them at once, all the ceilings and roofs of the world would fly to pieces. Don't vote! If you've voted, devote! If you've registered, unregister! Let them die of hunger in their Houses of Commons! Let them talk to themselves! May no one ever hear them again! What silence would reign over the world if their records, if their 45s, if their LPs stopped revolving! We're cozy together, Chateaugué and I. We don't need anybody. What's the matter with all of them, wanting to defend our democratic system? Come on, we'd defend it perfectly well ourselves if we really cared about it. Let's defend ourselves all by ourselves. I'm all she has, and she's all I have. All we have is friendship. We have so little! We'd be so glad to have to defend, occasionally, the little that we have. Leave us alone! Go do your parliaments someplace else!

43

When I'm happy, it's not halfway. A little while ago, I was out for a stroll along the façades, and I was laughing to myself, and I was laughing my head off. My laugh was making my head reel, making me stagger and zigzag. I was watching my fellow sidewalkers as if we were having a fantastic time on this earth, as if we were all at a ball, as if the world were as small as a surprise party and we had experienced pleasure all night. The prettiest among the female passersby had a sense of wild glee, of glee full of boldness, of glee full of fragility, of a glee that you can feel has the fragility of a cracked vase. The pretty female passersby responded. They pursed their lips in complicity, they smiled with their eyes as tenderly and viciously as I did. Is there anything bolder, in view of its fragility, than a yellow and black caterpillar crossing a highway? Is there anything more auda-cious than a flower that sprouts in the middle of a field, in the middle of a world where the best constituted of beings—man—has trouble subsisting? Everything in me is full of glee—my head, my body, my sky; and, despite the acute butterflies that I get in my belly, I'm not afraid. Everything that I defy without being afraid, while remaining gleeful, does nothing but flatter my pride and increase my glee. "Oh, so gleeful that I fear burst-ing into tears! ..." No, Nelligan, I'm not afraid of bursting into tears. "We only remember God when he's crushing us." I know that someday God will floor me, will have me pinned to the ground with the weight of his mountain, but I'm not afraid. The more I see what God the Evil is up to, the nearer God the Desperate and the Disgusting gets, the more gleeful I am. I am more gleeful, just to thumb my nose at him, just to make fun

of him. We went to the library, Chateaugué and I. The author that we read there claims that disgust alternating with glee is the vengeful jealousy of God. It would appear that God takes offence at how we forget him during glee. Before, I had the same feelings as that author. I wouldn't dare to be happy, to devote myself to my joy, to surrender myself to my joy; I was afraid of falling into a trap. "Oh, so gleeful that I fear bursting into tears!" Nelligan, my sweet Nelligan, this is what you should have cried: "Oh, so gleeful because I know that sooner or later I'll have to cry! ..." There is no one more joyful, when he's joyful, than the man who has nothing, who understands nothing, and who is needed by no one. I look at myself in my mirror; I spend hours there. I find myself to my liking. I find myself good-looking. My hair, streaked clear and straight, shines with cleanliness. My complexion is matte and dry; the shower water just dried on my face. My fingernails are impeccable, the fingernails of a bishop, of an archbishop, of a conservative, of an archconservative. I'm coming; I could eat myself. My eyes are burning, brilliant, of a clear blue; the wrinkle under each one is astonishing and surprising. It's an old man's wrinkle under the eyes of a child. I'm as good-looking as Cassius Clay. I don't need anyone to love me anymore—I love myself. I'm the male lover and the female lover. I'm jealous in advance of the unknown female who'll come to snatch me from my arms, as jealous as the God that that author was talking about ...
Questa, after a disappearance of several weeks, has come back to me. She came. Sitting on the bed, side by side, we wooed one another, we spoke in low and husky voices so as not to disturb the neighbours. Chateaugué came knocking at the door, and that all but broke the harmony of gentleness, passion, silence, and words that had developed little by little, after the bumps, the fragments, the clumsiness, and the hesitations. Chateaugué identified herself and knocked. Questa made the move to answer. I had just enough time to react. I flung myself onto Questa, grabbed hold of her mouth, and kept her gagged until Chateaugué grew tired of knocking, of calling, and of shaking the door. Questa came. Her automobile, seriously wounded during an accident, was at the hospital, so she had to take the

bus. I went to see her off at the bus terminal. The bus terminal benches were all taken. While waiting for her bus, we felt up the sexual books at the little newsstand. With her finger, she pointed out to me the undressed men on the covers of the sexual books. Vying with her in audacity, I pointed out the undressed women on the covers of the sexual books. With their fingers, the professional bus-waiters pointed us out. But we didn't care about their pointing. But we weren't afraid of them. There were two of us; we outnumbered any one of them. My sister Questa. God must be embarrassed to hear her laughing so loudly and so clearly, a woman he made grow old in order to stop her from laughing. I'm not as faithful and attentive as before to my dear journal. Ever since I reread what I had written in it, it has disgusted me. It's only out of nonchalance that I've come back to it now.

44

Chateaugué went to the movies alone. I wanted to go with her, but she didn't want me to. I don't know what's the matter with her. I was too busy to have lunch with her at noon today, and, out of presumptuousness, out of being used to her self-abnegation, I forgot to let her know. She waited for me, all for naught. She must not have liked that. She had bitter words.

"We have separate rooms, we work separate jobs, we take separate walks, we eat separate meals ... Who knows what'll be next. We don't open the door when she knocks. We handle her with kid gloves. We quietly get her used to being alone like a dog."

I have a splitting headache. Right in my head where I'm good at math. I'm getting shooting pains. Ow! Oh! Ah! Ah!

45

O men, how is it that you do not love men's vulgarity, men's avarice of the soul, men's petty cruelty, men's painstaking and malicious sensuality, men's great boredom and thankless solitude? You don't know what you're missing, O men, if you do not love men's vulgarity, men's avarice of the soul, men's petty cruelty, men's crude sensuality, men's great boredom and thankless solitude. You're missing everything if you do not love man. What is there here, apart from men? Where is the St. Lawrence, my river? It is there. You cannot hear it. It's like the horse that awaits you in the stable. You cannot see it. But I sense that it's there, that it flows by pretending not to flow by, that it kisses the city, that it carries a thousand cargos on its back as if they were nothing. It carries a thousand boats crammed full, just as easily as I wear my windbreaker. You cannot hear it. It says nothing. It never cries, never complains. It is always stronger than what happens to it. Never have I seen it angry. Never does it burst its banks, never does it cause a flood. It never pries a dock loose. It doesn't uproot any trees. It's so big. It doesn't give a hoot. If you sit down next to it, you can hear it whistle. It whistles very low, always to the same tune. But to hear it whistle, you've got to cup your hands to your ears and close your eyes. Some people say they have an automobile. They are mistaken. You don't have an automobile; you are an automobile. You can be born a dwarf. You can be born an idiot. You can be born a deaf-mute. You cannot be born an automobile—you become an automobile, all of a sudden. At school, most of my classmates couldn't wait to become automobiles. Gripping an imaginary wheel with their fists, making their mouths imitate the booming voice of the mufflers, they'd do a hundred miles an hour, they'd take the curves leaning to one side and uttering deathly screeches. Just by seeing it turn a street corner, almost all of them could say the name, nickname, and birthday of any automobile on earth.

"Look! It's a 1949 Dodge Windsor."

"Look! It's a 1962 Cadillac DeVille."

I knew one who didn't even know that he had a spinal column and who could, by lifting up the hood of an automobile, give us the volume of its engine in cubic inches and its capacity in horsepower. When a delivery boy goes into a house without ringing the doorbell, what does he find there? He finds the pregnant wife whose dress is dripping and who has cried so much that her eyes are bleeding. He finds the table upside down. He finds the cat in the pan. He finds the children shut up in the refrigerator. He finds the husband barefoot, in his underwear, and unemployed. A delivery boy goes into a house without ringing the doorbell. What does he see? He sees the record player on the floor, its cover wide open. He sees the sink full of dirty dishes. He sees empty beer bottles on the floor. He sees the young woman lying on the sofa; she has punched the sofa so many times out of boredom that it is full of lumps. The delivery boy goes into a house without ringing the doorbell. What does he see? The woman is sitting on the edge of her chair, her dress over her head, and the pedigreed hunting dog is licking her sex organs. I never ring the doorbell before going in. I go in like a thief. I'm trying my luck at seeing naked vulvas. A naked vulva is such a rare spectacle. The sight of a naked vulva takes your breath away, especially when you're neither married nor a woman. But even undressed, a vulva has nothing naked about it. A vulva is a camouflaged closure made of bad fur. It's all inside, like the soul. The fur of a woman's vulva is attached to the woman's beardless body like leftover skin to a skeleton's chin. Vulvas vex curiosity. If, instead of that disguised door, the creator had put a squawking toad, some fat white toad, curiosity would be satisfied, and the world would not have lost its dignity. But it would seem that the creator had less poetic and more pornographic views. Tonight we went to a massacre. We just got back from a massacre, Chateaugué and I, from the massacre of the ten floors of the old Boismaison

Building. A single crane was enough. It was a yellowy-orange crane. Its jib, a kind of arm, was equipped with one of those enormous weights of steel called wrecking balls. The Boismaison Building, with its grey façade decorated with foliage, rosettes, and acanthus leaves, was my favourite building. When the blow of the ball made a hole in the sculpted mask of the impassive giant, prolonged laughter, shouts, and applause arose from the platforms. When one section finally gave up the ghost, when it caved in—when, crumbling from the foundation up, it seemed to fall right through the ground like an immense elevator out of order—it was even funnier. Then, from the heart of an appalling crash, a hurricane of dust was born that we hardly had time to see spreading in billows; everything, in a single breath, became dim and was drowned within it.

"Here comes the dust!" shouted an unnerved man.

It was the signal for the galloping of the stampede. They all took to their heels. They uttered cries of delirium. They were afraid of getting dirty. We remained where we were, Chateaugué and I. We remained standing at the heart of the thick, flowing powder. As solid as Rocks of Gibraltar, we were not knocked over by the deserters as they passed. Once the cloud dispersed, we had changed colour, we were a pale yellow from head to toe. It was as though we were painted. Our shoes were of the same blond as our heads. Only our eyes had escaped the roughcasting. They were gleaming like lakes at the summits of the standing deserts that we had become. We looked into each other's eyes and laughed. Those who had run faster than the dust were pointing at us and laughing. The crowd was involved in the action; they were encouraging the crane, they were booing the crane when it missed its mark, they were giving it advice, they were clapping their hands, they were stamping their feet, they were clicking their tongues. Each time the ball hit, they let out a groan of exhaustion. One by one, I surveyed the faces of that mass of unfeeling people. They were tense, edgy, avid, attentive faces, turned toward the scene. They were all the same, whether women's or men's.

"Look at that girl over there," Chateaugué said to me, calling my attention to a group of rowdy adolescents.

Standing somewhat apart from their circle, her back to the carnage, her arms hanging listless at her sides, her head on her chest, a girl was crying. As I watched her, she glanced in my direction, and I saw her face; she was pretty. She seemed so sweet and so vanquished next to those fanatical sadists that we couldn't take our eyes off her. She was crying without a sound and without tears, the way you do out of great sorrow. Her companions, the jolly troubadours, were unaware of her pain and were letting this party-pooper go her own way. She was rooted to the spot near them, with those very people, no doubt, who had caused her ordeal and who, by their coldness, were helping to sustain it. They were the ones she loved, the ones she had been given at the allocation of friends. Despite the spiritual crudeness of her own people, she preferred to stay close to them rather than venture into the unknown, into the cold of the outside world. There were other girls among the group, but they didn't take any more notice of her than the boys did. The jolly prince consorts started to get annoyed and impatient. Soon, they'd had enough of the weeping one. One of them brutally grabbed hold of her shoulders and shook her, the way you shake an old coat to get the rats and mice out of it. An effeminate, pot-bellied man with a cowardly voice intervened next. It must have been her brother. He lambasted her in the most clerical, most academic, most pontifical way possible. She was a disgrace to them; she was trying his patience; she was compromising the reputation of the family; she had to stop bawling, immediately. Her head down, she let herself lean over; she let herself be dragged down by the weight of her pain until her head rested against the tie on his fat chest. And she stayed like that, continuing to cry. You'd have thought that, for her, the importance of the person she was leaning against was negligible compared to the importance of leaning against someone. We vacated the premises of the hecatomb around three o'clock in the morning. We were barely on our way back when it started to salt. It was salting full time. Grains of salt as big as a fist were falling. It was as though the good Lord, judging that the earth had cooked long enough, was salting it before taking his first bite. When we were kids, Chateaugué and I, we used to eat our apples with salt.

Apples seemed too sweet for us. It was salting so heavily that there was no room left in the night sky for any darkness. But it wasn't the good Lord who was making it salt, it was the English-speaking money-grubbers. We suspected something when we heard the humming of bombers, but we were far from suspecting the truth. We ran. We arrived at the hotel, as salty as the apples that we used to eat in the olden days. At the hotel, they knew all about what was happening, and they had a good laugh over my sister Chateaugué's terror. The money-hungry Canadians, wanting to take pictures of a snowy Montreal for the filthy rich American tourists, in order to make their mouths water, had chartered thousands of bombardiers and told them to drop millions of bushels of salt on Montreal. I'm not making this up; that's what they told us. Going back into her room, Chateaugué was startled—there was a prime minister of Latvia on her bed. When the prime minister of Latvia caught sight of Chateaugué, he flung himself to the foot of the bed, dashed toward a corner of the room, and there, at the risk of strangling himself, crept between the quarter-round and the floor. I'm not exaggerating. It's true. It happened just like that. A prime minister of Latvia, for Chateaugué and me, is a rat. For example, the Boismaison Building was infested with prime ministers of Latvia. Through each breach that the wrecking ball made, hundreds of them came pouring out. They went right between our feet. They ran to the sewer grates in the gutter and, there, they flung themselves under the street, under the city, under the ground. Anyway! The fact remains that Chateaugué was armed with a good pretext to come sleep in my room, and she didn't miss her chance. I can still see her straightening her panties. I can still see her finding a place for herself in my bed, with her panties with the stretched-out elastic. My bed is so small that my feet stick out. It's so small that two prime ministers of Latvia couldn't sleep together in it comfortably. What is a prime minister of Latvia, my little student? It's a mouse, sir. I'm giving you a zero! I'm giving you a fucking zero, you damned little pontificating bastard! That's how they talk in France. Damned Grandgousier! Damned pawn-tag-rue-hell! What's a pawn tag, sir? I've already talked about the woes of the teaching profession. I've already done the

palinode of the professors and the apologia of the pupils ...
What's done is done. You shouldn't wash your hands twice;
that's repetition. After washing them once at the beginning of
your life, you shouldn't go back over that territory again. Repetition engenders habit. Habit engenders insipidity. Repetition is
the philosopher's stone that transforms everything into boredom. Damned pawn-tag-rue-hell! This is plagiarism, copying,
lack of imagination, rehashing! There! I haven't yet talked about
Chateaugué's nose. It's small, very small. There, that's done. I
have nothing left to say to the demolishers of cathedrals, to the
dollars whose pawn tags rue hell, to the saints of the dollar, to the
virgins and the martyrs of the dollar, to the builders of bank
accounts. One of them, in Burlington, Tennessee, has built for
himself a bank account of 4,500,000,767,890,000 floors. The
yellowy-orange crane should have gone through there before
demolishing the Boismaison Building.

The One with Ten Storeys

You were crying. You were pretty.
The crane was destroying the building.
You were crying as if in your bed,
Just trying to get through the pain.

You couldn't have cared less about the crowd
Assembled in the street to see the floors
Cave in. One would have thought
They weren't even your age.

You were alone with cowards
Wearied by your helplessness.
"Stop whimpering, or I'll lose my temper!"
I would have built you a palace.

Your straight hair and your pale skin,
I would have taken them to sleep on.
You wouldn't need a shawl.
You would sleep like a fakir
Naked on his nails, naked in my arms.
The ten storeys were full of rats.

46

As a general rule, words ending in *x* take *es* in the plural (*hex, flex, vortex, rolex, sex*). Tex, an exception to the rule, takes *as*. There are many people of colour in this hotel. They talk loudly. They talk about love more often than not. They laugh loudly, they cry loudly. The women arrive in tears and leave in tears. I've heard one of them talking and crying for a good hour. She talks in a warm and husky voice, like all people of colour. She talks while sucking up her sobs. She breathes heavily more than she cries, which is the in thing among adults. He told her again and again to clear out. She doesn't want to clear out. She won't go away. She won't budge.

"Scram!" he barks. "Go away! Make yourself scarce!"

"I won't go away!" she barks. "I won't make myself scarce. Why did you lie to me? Why did you lie to me?"

The black man gets up on his high horse. He shrieks, he shouts himself hoarse. But the black girl won't hear another word. She shrieks, she shouts herself hoarse.

"Do you want to make love to me? Do you want to sleep with me?"

"No, I don't want to make love to you! No, I don't want to sleep with you!"

"Well then, go away! Beat it! What the heck are you doing here if you don't want to sleep with me?"

One good shriek deserves another. One good yap deserves another. They seem to know all about love. He doesn't say to her, "Do you love me?" He says to her, "Do you want to make love to me?" He doesn't say to her, "If you don't love me, cruel beauty, I'm going to start sulking, I'm going to start getting desperate." He says to her, "Beat it, if you don't want to copulate." He hasn't read Malherbe's sonnets. He didn't learn his Middle Ages and Renaissance lessons very well at school. He doesn't know that the knights of the Middle Ages dropped to their knees when they saw a woman go by. He thinks that to love is an action verb; he doesn't know that it's a stative verb. He's not polite; he doesn't know that you've got to take off your hat in the presence of a woman. He is ignorant. How ignorant he is! How ill-bred! To think that all he'd have had to do was be born somewhere in Europe, instead of being born somewhere in Africa! If he'd been born somewhere in Europe, he would have a civilization of twenty centuries behind him, and he would know how to conduct himself with a woman. He would know that the woman is a queen, and that he's got to give her roses. He would know that, when you love a woman, you give her your heart, and you wait patiently for her to accept or reject it before starting to talk about the temperature with her. He would know that you've got to sip with a straw the holy water in which the woman you love in vain has dipped her fingertips. He certainly didn't frequent the Sorbonne. But he does seem to know what he wants. He is ignorant, but he doesn't seem to be ignorant about what he wants. "Go away, if you don't want to copulate!" He doesn't seem to suffer from kiss-assism and unavailable sex. If all men of colour are like him, I understand why the United States is afraid of them. It's dangerous, someone who didn't learn a thing, someone who didn't learn everything that a man ought to have learned in order to be easy to handle. It's dangerous, someone who didn't learn to genuflect and dance the rondo gracefully. Pity the poor human races without civilization in their past, without a Map of Tenderness in their past, without a Renaissance in their past! Pity those who don't know how to conduct themselves like fops! They read so little! They buy so few books! They contribute so little to heightening the prestige of literature! "If you don't want to sleep with me anymore, I don't want to see you anymore!" He didn't even go to the trouble of telling her that her cheeks are like rose petals that the evening dew has just quenched. He didn't even tell her that his heart was beating only for her. He knows nothing. Really, he didn't learn a thing at school. Really, he hasn't read anything. He shouts at her what he has to shout at her. He doesn't know that you've got to think about what you shout. When he shouts, he shouts. He doesn't know how to do two things at once. French nouns ending in *al* change the *al* to *aux* in the plural. *Bal, cal, carnaval, chacal, festival, régal, aval, bancal, caracal, cérémonial, choral, narval, nopal, pal, récital*, and *gavial* simply take *s* in the plural; they are the exceptions. French nouns ending in *ail* take an *s* in the plural. One *éventail*, two *éventails*. Nine French nouns are exceptions to the rule; they are *bail, corail, émail, fermail, soupirail, travail, vantail, ventail*, and *vitrail*. As for *bijou, caillou, chou, genou, hibou, joujou*, and *pou*, we all know where we stand with them. I was on fire inside, from the top of my head to the soles of my feet. I was waiting. I was waiting for her. Questa, through the intervention of the telephone (the telephone is an invention), had promised me she would come. It was nine o'clock, and she had not yet arrived. She wasn't exactly late, since she hadn't specified when she would come. At ten o'clock, I went to buy some hot blanched almonds for a dollar at the shop across the street. An hour later, my blanched almonds were cold, and there was no sign of Questa. I brushed my teeth to kill time. After killing time for three hours, I had to stop; I didn't have any teeth left. Waiting! Waiting sets me on fire inside. When I wait, I'm like an intercontinental missile that lacks holes for the flames to shoot out of—I feel like I'm about to explode; I can't keep still. The fire and smoke add up and multiply inside of my shell. I'm as swollen and taut as a vortex. *Vortex* takes *es* in the plural. Had she said that she'd come in the evening or that she'd come tonight? She might not come, the bitch! I did the shuttle between my room and Chateaugué's room to kill time. I rolled myself cigarettes by the hundreds to assassinate the hours. All of a sudden, the time started going by too fast. I had promised myself that I'd give up waiting for her if she hadn't arrived by midnight, and it was a quarter past midnight. It was twenty past midnight; the hands of my alarm clock were racing, galloping. As best I could, I kept waiting until 2:30. Suddenly, more resounding and more surprising than an artillery shot, the buzz of the doorbell exploded, struck me like a thunderbolt, seized me, drowned me, and tore me away from the bitter contemplation of my alarm clock. I knocked the door down, I charged down the stairs. The woman who was standing at the foot of the stairs was not the woman I had portrayed in my mind. The woman who had buzzed was not Questa; she was pitch-black. It wasn't Questa, it was a Negress. I was so surprised that I was frightened.

"I must have the wrong room number, sir. Sorry ... 6B?"

"6A."

I went back to number 6A on all fours. I got undressed, I got into bed, and I fell asleep. I had a bad dream. A woman was hitting me on my forehead with a hammer, and my head was reverberating like a cymbal. It became unbearable, and I woke up. It was Questa. She was on top of me. Her eyes were opposite mine. She was smiling. She smelled of alcohol. She was hitting me on the forehead with her forehead. She had been a long time coming! I was sick to my stomach; I thought of all those blanched almonds that I had crunched on, one after another, while waiting for her. I pretended not to be surprised. I asked her how she had been able to get in.

"You don't have the key. How were you able to get in?"

"I went under the door, my little creep. You seem surprised, my dear."

"You're still drunk."

"Don't talk so loudly, my dear. You'll wake up all the tourists, blockhead. You'll wake up everybody."

"I talk however I want to! I'm a free man!"

"Don't lose your temper, big-nose. Maman's gonna give you a big fat peck."

Questa gave my cheek a smack with her mouth. I got dressed again, and we went out for some fresh air. A man in the prime of life was walking in front of us on the sidewalk. His black apron spoke volumes about his occupation: he was an innkeeper. Questa started to lambaste him, just for kicks.

"What good are you, man in front of us? What good are you, man in a black apron and black pants? You're good for a drink, you say? How ridiculous! What good are glasses? What good are cups?"

We walked for hours. We had nothing to say to each other. She taught me all kinds of games.

"Let's play at counting."

"At counting what?"

"Anything at all. One bread. Two breads. Three breads. Four breads. Five breads. Six breads. Seven breads. Eight breads. Nine breads. Ten breads. Leaven breads. Your turn. Count casts."

"One cast. Two casts. Three casts. Forecasts."

"That's it! I have one ant. I have two ants. I have three ants. I have four ants. I have five ants. I have six ants. I have seven ants. I have eight ants. I have nine ants. I have tenants."

"One cloud. Two clouds. Three clouds. Four clouds. Five clouds. Six clouds. Seven clouds. Eight clouds. Nine clouds. Ten clouds. Eleven clouds. Twelve clouds. Thirteen clouds. Fourteen clouds. Fifteen clouds. Sixteen clouds. Seventeen clouds. Eighteen clouds. Nineteen clouds. Twenty clouds. Twenty-one clouds. Twenty-two clouds. Twenty-three clouds. Twenty-four clouds. Twenty-five clouds. Twenty-six clouds. Twenty-seven clouds. Twenty-eight clouds. Twenty-nine clouds. Thirty clouds. Thirty-one clouds. Thirty-two clouds. Thirty-three clouds. It's gonna rain."

We played at counting. We played other games. We played until we were sick of them all. We walked until we were despondent. Our legs were no longer able to carry us, so we sat on the sidewalk. It was starting to get light. She put her hand on my shoulder. She took off her shoes and threw them into the middle of the street. No automobiles were going by in this street. Nothing was going by, and nothing was going on. On the other side of the street, there was a rail yard. We got up and went over there. We put our hands on the railcars. We couldn't stop ourselves from putting our hands on the cars whenever we went close by one. We lay down between two rails, just for kicks. But we were so tired that we fell asleep.

47

Chateaugué is dead. She killed herself, the poor idiot, the poor fool! If she killed herself in order to soften my heart, she killed herself for nothing, she blew it. I don't give a hoot! I almost fainted when I opened the door, but now I don't feel anything anymore. I feel like laughing. She was wearing the wedding dress. There was a lake of blood on the tiles. The wedding dress was way too big for her. She looked like a lunatic. She killed herself with the two daggers that we had stolen, that we had stolen to play a trick on the pharmacist, that we had stolen just for kicks. She stuck them into her neck, where it's soft, where there are no bones. She was ugly. She looked stupid and mediocre in her dress three times too big, in the unmade bed, in the messy room. The acrid smell of the blood seized me by the throat, the way it does when you go by a slaughterhouse. I feel like laughing. I'm as tired as a goddamn comedian.

Réjean Ducharme

Novelist and playwright Réjean Ducharme was born in Saint-Félix-de-Valois, Quebec, in 1941. His first novel, *L'Avalée des avalés* (*The Swallower Swallowed*, 1966), won the Governor General's Award for French Fiction in 1967 and the CBC Canada Reads francophone competition in 2005. This work also garnered him a nomination for France's prestigious Prix Goncourt. His second novel, *Le Nez qui voque* (*Miss Take*, 1967), was awarded the Prix littéraire de la province de Québec. These two, plus a third novel, *L'Océantume* (1968), published during the years of the Quiet Revolution, contributed to the recasting of the literary canon of Quebec. In 2011, he was honoured with the Révolution Tranquille medal, given by the Ministry of Culture of Quebec, awarded to artists, creators, and artisans who began their careers between 1960 and 1970 and who still have an influence in their field of practice.

Will Browning

Will Browning holds a Doctorate of Modern Languages in French and Spanish from Middlebury College in Vermont. In 2011, he retired from fifteen years of teaching Spanish and French at Boise State University in Idaho. Browning publishes French-language reviews and articles, in addition to his translation work. The other two novels by Réjean Ducharme that he has translated are the *The Daughter of Christopher Columbus* (Guernica Editions, 2000) and *Go Figure* (Talonbooks, 2003). Browning lives in Boise, Idaho.